A
KILLING
SMILE

Also by Christopher G. Moore

Fiction

His Lordship's Arsenal
Tokyo Joe
A Killing Smile
A Bewitching Smile
Spirit House
Asia Hand
A Haunting Smile
Cut Out
Saint Anne
Comfort Zone
The Big Weird
God of Darkness
Cold Hit
Chairs
Minor Wife
Waiting For The Lady
Pattaya 24/7

Non-Fiction

Heart Talk

A
KILLING
SMILE

A NOVEL BY
CHRISTOPHER G. MOORE

Heaven Lake Press

Distributed in Thailand by:
Asia Document Bureau Ltd.
P.O. Box 1209
Bangkok 10110, Thailand
Fax: (662) 665-2587
Web site: www.heavenlakepress.com
E-mail: editorial@heavenlakepress.com

First edition 1991 by White Lotus
Second edition 1992 by White Lotus
Third edition 1996 by bookSiam
Fourth edition 2000 by Heaven Lake Press
Trade paperback edition: copyright © 2004 Christopher G. Moore
Printed in Thailand

Jacket design: Jae Song
Author's photo: copyright © 2004 Pamela Hongskul

Author's web site: www.cgmoore.com
Author's e-mail: chris@cgmoore.com

ISBN 974-92335-7-3

For Julie and Anne,
and Smik

INTRODUCTION

I had moved from a Soho loft between Canal and Grand in New York City to a Bangkok slum dwelling within ghetto blast distance—if one really cranked it up—from Soi Cowboy. The apartment was in a Plan B mode. If no one rented the units, the owner was ready to convert the building into a toothbrush factory. Owen Wrigley posted a notice on the bulletin board at the Foreign Correspondents' Club of Thailand that cheap apartments could be rented. He lived in the house in front of the apartments and had a horror of toothbrush factories.

I took a bus from Silom (I had rented a room along Covenant Road in a building which has long ago been knocked down and replaced with a swank office building) and walked the soi, stopping at the doorway of a small business with a sign advertising *Siam Canadian*. I read the sign as an invitation to provide advice and assistance to any wayward Canadian walking down the soi. I found a young Canadian named Jim sitting at an empty desk with a silent phone, a notepad, and pen. He was playing chess. Against himself and losing. I asked Jim if he knew anything about the toothbrush factory building farther down the soi. He nodded. Everyone in the neighborhood apparently knew about this place. He agreed to escort me to negotiate with the owner. It turned out to be the maid of the owner. Jim, the owner of Siam Canadian negotiated a repainting the premises, a rent of $150 a month. From his negotiation skills I knew one day he would be successful. I was set. I had a place within walking distance of the old Thermae.

Old Thermae meaning the establishment called the Thermae Coffee Shop and Massage Parlor that opened in 1965 (plus/minus two years) and closed for demolition in 1996. Call it a thirty-year run. Agatha Christie's play "The Mouse Trap" had much longer run. But the Thermae, in its unique way, was a vintage mousetrap and the mice (granted more than a fair number were rats) that were trapped were, eyes bulging, kicking and squealing *farangs*. If you had even a slight imagination, you could imagine hearing dozens of traps snapping, a virtual chorus of necks wretched, as you walked down the dark alleyway into the back entrance. The toilets were next to the kitchen (a Thermae tradition that continues at the new Thermae). Above the sink was a cracked mirror thick with a yellowish nicotine glaze where the girls took turns puffing on their cigarettes, putting on lipstick and makeup.

This was early 1989 and the jukebox was in the center of the basement of this dive. After midnight the front door was locked and you could only get in by walking through the alley. There was a sign in Thai at the back entrance that said Private Members Only. There were about a dozen tables and the walls were lined with booths. Around the top of the booths were mirrors and the clever people knew how to use the mirrors with more skill than a driver of a ten-wheeler, changing lanes on the expressway.

When you are young you never know that the territory you've staked out will turn out to be the crossroads of a thousand stories. The Thermae was for a writer what an open vein of gold in California must have been like in the 1840s. Characters spilled out of the alley diplomats, journalists, brokers, businessmen, schoolteachers, ex-military, pimps, grifters, and oil field men. The women came from *Isan* and Bangkok, the South, and the North. There wasn't a point on the human desire compass that wasn't represented. Hill tribes. Burmese. Chinese. They all had a story, a dream, and a nightmare. Some came every night. Others came when they were short of money. *A Killing Smile* is about being cut adrift into a world of the night, looking for redemption, seeking out a new life, a chance to make a deal that might lead somewhere other than a one-night stand in a short-time hotel.

Over the years many people have come up and said that they recognized themselves in the novel. For a novelist, this is a compliment. Readers want to feel it is their story. They are vested in what happens next. They were there. I have no problem including them all, one after another, until *A Killing Smile* is a book a hundred miles wide. All books should aspire to such a goal.

A Killing Smile has been called the expat bible. That assumes there is an expat religion. If religion is based on belief and faith in some higher being looking down and answering prayers, then *A Killing Smile* isn't a bible. But as road map to the state of mind of *farangs* and the women they met in the old Thermae, it offers a glimpse, a small insight into the human condition. If that is religion, then *A Killing Smile*, can give some material background to blurry line between commercial sex, love, hatred, and desire. In the world of the Thermae, men and women from different cultures and backgrounds converge in a market exchange, speaking different languages, wanting different things, expecting what is often impossible, yet, in some strange way making themselves understood for a night that can end the next morning or last a life time.

The place that once was destined for conversion into a toothbrush factory still stands as an apartment house. The place that was the Thermae is no more; though a new Thermae opened twenty meters down the road from the old site. Arguments over whether the new place is as good as the old one are as pointless as whether you were as good a dozen years as you are now. The Thermae has changed. So has Bangkok. So have I. Buddhism teaches that change is natural; and inevitable. Clinging to the past guarantees suffering in the present. But not everyone agrees. People from all walks of life passed through the doors of the old Thermae. That show has closed. *A Killing Smile* is a testament to the old mousetrap and to those who were caught, and those who broke away.

Christopher G. Moore
Bangkok
August 2004

1

Sex became a serious, violent chase through the cupboards of Sarah's memory. For Lawrence sex remained—as it had been in his youth—hall surface light, sound, and fury, and the next morning as memorable as a late-night talk show the night before. There was no middle ground in which husband and wife touched. At least, Sarah no longer fought for one. She was happy enough to be left alone as Lawrence penetrated her, and her chase through the shadows of memory could begin. Sex was the fuel for her speed chase. The place of action was the mind. The thought of speeding down the old gullies and narrow passages made her passionate, all claws and teeth. Lawrence was convinced of his skill as a lover. He told himself that he had satisfied his wife like no other man had ever done before, or could ever do again after him. He told himself that he was indispensable for Sarah's sexual happiness. He was partially right. Without gas in the tank the car didn't start. And he was partially deluded: there were thousands of service stations all selling the same product at roughly the same price.

His thrusting gathered a steady push-pull action. Enough to launch Sarah and exclude Lawrence; shut him out, and leave him behind where he was unable to track her through those old cupboards filled with old songs, old faces, places and smells.

He was left outside a pinpoint of darkness as small as a needle mark: the place which had pulled Sarah inside. "Yes," she moaned, rocking on him. "I want you to fuck me hard," she said. What she was saying inside her head was different: "I'm hungry for it." As she lifted up with a raging moan that caught in her throat, her body shook and then she slowly moved down on Lawrence. "Yes, baby, come. Come hard," he whispered. She did not hear him. It had nothing to do with him, this rush of sound from her throat. She felt herself screaming through that point of darkness swallowed whole as if some larger hunger had been waiting. On her lips a word formed. A man's name that came only as movement and never as sound. The name "Bobby" roiled over her lips like emotional lava blown out from deep within. He was waiting inside for her and she went straight to him and he took her standing against the wall. Lawrence moaned and pulled her hips, moving her back and forth, his face turned to the side, and his eyes squeezed close. "I'm coming," said Lawrence, his death rattle sounds in his throat. And when he went limp and she stood above him, she was filled with enormous sadness. The cupboard door had been slammed and she was back in the dark bedroom more alone than she could possibly believe was possible.

"Was it good for you?" Lawrence asked, patting her ass.

"Wonderful, darling," she said.

She could not look at his face. She could not open her eyes. Not yet, not for a moment. And when she did the void was the larger darkness of the bedroom. But even if the bathroom light had been left on, the door left ajar, they would not have looked at one another. Sex games had run the course during their marriage: the role-playing, porno films, wife swapping, and the occasional solo infidelity. All that had happened a long time ago, another lifetime, when there was a sharing of imagination, images, and the light offered each a glimpse of bodies locked in motion.

Sometimes she wanted to tell him the places she flew to. But that was too dangerous. She always returned to the same place, night after night, year after year.

"Do you ever think of anyone else when we make love," he asked her, not able to see the laughter around her eyes in the dark.

"Never," she replied.

"Only you, Lawrence."

"Some women do," he said.

"Not if their husband is a great lover " she replied.

Lawrence leaned over a timesheet and ran the numbers on the keyboard of a solar-powered hand calculator. Sitting silently opposite, her legs crossed, Kelly Swan, a fifth year associate, brushed back a loose strand of blonde hair from her thin, angular face, her eyes watching Lawrence's fingers dance over the keyboard. The billable hours for Pegasus House Press file read eighteen twice in a row. He double checked her time record. Slowly he looked up and found her smiling, her head cocked.

"I'm throwing out a couple of these lunches, Kelly."

"But we discussed the publisher's pension plan, and the one for Harris, the new editor, both times, Larry."

"And a lot of other things the client shouldn't foot the bill for. Harris is an old colleague of Sarah's. Last year she helped him land the job. He was grateful enough to give me the pension business, which, by the way, should have gone to a New York law firm. So we cut the bill, okay?"

"It will make me look bad. I'm short on hours this month. It's partnership this year. Or out. You do want me to make partner, Larry?"

The only other person who called him Larry was Sarah, his wife of twenty-two years—and then, only when they were alone in private. Kelly had taken the liberty, and he had not stopped her the first or second time. It had been a small forced intimacy he had allowed to happen; he had liked the bridge of that private word in his office. He was a man who loved control: the hours he billed, the names people used to call him, the clients he accepted, the clubs he joined, Sarah's orgasms. In each case his hand was on the throttle. In the last year, as Kelly's partnership became an issue she had taken extra pains to show her attention, devotion, and loyalty to Lawrence as if he were a feudal lord and she was a serf worthy of promotion.

She called it "their" partnership; a kind of professional marriage. Sarah was his official, at-home wife; and Kelly was his official, work relationship wife. Both were essential for his well-being, and provided a kind of balance of affection and admiration. The unwritten rule between them had been no sex. Once or twice he had brushed his hand against her arm, and quickly withdrawn it. He had wanted to tell her what sexual bliss he could bestow on her; he wished Sarah could be his witness, provide a testimony.

He sometimes wondered if having sex with Kelly might tame Kelly. Such thoughts never lingered. In his mind, he had achieved that balance of pain and pleasure that most people label as happiness. The private and public spheres rotated in a perfect harmonious orbit. Conflict arrived as a brief, sudden, narrow detail and quickly disappeared without a scar. For instance, a disagreement over a decision to pad a client's bill. It was his call to make. Whatever he decided would be accepted.

During the billing conference, Lawrence ordered his secretary to hold his calls. He liked most of all this control over the access other people sought for their claims, pleas, wishes, and requests. Important people denied access. Important people were accessible by appointment only. Kelly had asked for over a week for a meeting on her partnership. He kept her waiting for a time slot in his schedule. When she came to his office, she was already half-defeated, beaten down. She had come for hand-holding. Even though she was thirty-one, she had the temperament of a college student greedy for recognition. She was his submissive child and he offered her sanctuary from those who made her fearful. It was a role Lawrence enjoyed. Though forty-five years old, he occupied the position of father figure. Once she had stung him with a remark about another woman lawyer her own age who had moved in with a really old guy, a businessman who was forty-six. This candid, innocent observation caused Lawrence an extra ten minutes before the mirror the following morning examining his face for wrinkles.

"A really old guy," he had repeated to himself, tracing the grooves the size of hairline fractures that fanned out from the corners of both eyes.

"What do you think? Am I going to make it?" Kelly asked.

Lawrence didn't blink. "Make it?" There was irony in his tone. "By which you mean, 'what are my partnership prospects?'"

Before Kelly answered, his phone rang. He grimaced, dropped his hand, with a look of mild irritation. His secretary informed him there was an emergency call from the hospital.

"Will you take it, Mr. Baring?"

He looked over at Kelly Swan, noticing her perfect makeup. The eyeliner, lipstick, the makeup softening the lines of her jaw. He wondered how many billable hours it had taken her every morning to apply the potions and paints.

"Your wife has been in a serious accident," said a police officer. "She's been seriously injured. You'd better come right away."

"What is it, Larry?"

He stood for a minute with the phone receiver held away from his ear.

"Sarah's been in an accident." His voice sounded small and frightened; the sense of authority drained away.

On the way to the hospital his lawyer's mind raced through the possible meanings of "seriously injured"; alarming words that suggested hope, however slender and feeble. He rehearsed how he would tease her about a cast running from her toe to her hip. He missed the traffic lights on the way. Lawrence prayed. Make it two casts. That's serious. That's injury. He wanted to control the words; fill them with his content; decide what was their fair measure.

He swung his BMW into the driveway in front of the emergency ward entrance and ran inside. The waiting room was filled with a couple of stabbing victims, a boy with a broken arm, and a couple of women watching the news on television.

"My name's Lawrence Baring. My wife . . ."

The orderly looked up at Lawrence and said nothing. Then he nodded for Lawrence to pass down the corridor where two uniformed policemen, who looked suddenly very young, stood drinking coffee. A young doctor with a blood-flecked white coat appeared from between curtains pulled around a cubicle. Lawrence caught his eye, and he knew from that second that Sarah was dead. He couldn't move forward or back. The older of the cops caught sight of him. Experience had taught him to spot a relative half a corridor away; that face blurred with apprehension was a billboard waiting to record a message of grief.

"Mr. Baring?"

Lawrence nodded. The doctor walked up to him. Lawrence noticed the funny way the doctor's Adam's apple moved. It registered an emotional pulse; a pulse fluttering between frustration and resignation.

"I'm afraid I have bad news for you, Mr. Baring. Your wife's been in an auto accident. She's dead."

The banality of death was an eventuality no one ever expected. There was nothing special, clever, or original in the lines. Something from the typical fare of prime time television. Sarah was a professor of English. She goddamn deserved a better message; an older, more distinguished messenger. The doctor and cops were just kids. They were pretending to be officials in control of the situation.

Lawrence pushed past the doctor and two cops and into the cubicle. No one tried to stop him. A nurse was cleaning up the sink; she had blood-stained patches on her uniform. Tubes hung down from the bed. Hospital machinery had been silenced and pulled to the side.

Lawrence folded back the white sheet soaked with Sarah's blood. He didn't recognize the woman underneath as remotely resembling his wife. The flesh on the face had been partially stripped away; peeled, twisted, and sliced; nose and mouth and eyes had collapsed into a wreckage that might have been anyone. He glanced down at the wedding ring on her left hand. It was Sarah's ring; the only way he knew the body had some connection to him. Lawrence sobbed; he bit the corner of his lower lip and slowly shook his head. "Seriously injured," he repeated to himself. She had been dead the moment he had received the call from the hospital. His hands began shaking. He couldn't stop crying and he began slamming a fist into the wall. The numbness seemed to swallow him; and he wanted the pain.

The nurse quickly covered the body, turned and reached for Lawrence's hand. One of the cops moved in and pulled Lawrence back. The cop explained the circumstances of the accident, in soft, measured tones. There was a tenderness and caring in that young man's voice. He didn't hurry the details; he didn't make it sound like a standard accident report. He hovered near Lawrence and stared into Lawrence's eyes. The pupils were dilated and there was little response. Lawrence clenched his fists and smashed them down on the trolley. He collapsed onto the floor, pulling the sheet down with him.

A few moments later, Lawrence remembered the doctor had given him an injection. He thought the doctor's Adam's apple had frozen still the moment the needle slid into the vein on his right arm. As he slipped into unconsciousness he thought of Sarah inside the supermarket, looking at the expiry date on the muffin package. He ran towards her, but she kept several steps ahead; he yelled for her to stop, to look around, to wait for him. He saw her climb into the red midget MG with the top down and pull out of the parking lot. He heard the crash. Lawrence saw a face beneath a sheet that he didn't recognize. When he awoke it was morning and a nurse was standing over him taking his pulse. Behind her was Kelly Swan and three of his law partners. His room bloomed with baskets of flowers; floral arrangements stacked back to back.

The ordinariness of Sarah's last day, a day filled with minor errands, paperwork, routine matters, were inappropriate to her death. A series of insignificant events ending in shattered glass and broken, smashed metal. His eyes closed, arms folded across his forehead, Lawrence shifted through the miscellaneous details of Sarah's final journey. Sarah had gone home early from the university to do some shopping. She had felt the wind in her face as she drove her little red MG. The tape deck had been locked onto a Beatles' golden oldie album—'*Hey Jude*' blasted out of the duo speakers. In the back seat she had two bags of groceries. A dozen bran muffins, skim milk, diet coke, and two large sausage pizzas. Sarah's special health-kick diets never omitted the pizza. She had pulled out of the supermarket parking lot and had caught the right sequence of traffic lights. Sixty feet beyond one green light the road sloped off to the left and down. Two cars were stopped. The lead car was turning into a 7/11 Store. The driver, an overweight computer science graduate student, who occupied the first car, told the police he was making a left-hand turn across traffic. He had seen a sign advertising a 46-ounce giant Slurpy for 79 cents and on an impulse decided that sign was talking directly to him. He had a sudden urge for junk food.

The car Sarah rear-ended was a 1988 Olds. One of the cops said that she must have, for a split second, lost her concentration; she'd been distracted, by a memory, a thought, an idea. Some image had flooded into her mind twenty seconds after the graduate student decided on the giant Slurpy. She hadn't left a skid mark. The driver of the Olds climbed out unhurt and vomited in the street as he looked at Sarah's head smashed through the windscreen. *'Hey Jude'* still blared from the wreckage.

They had been married twenty-two years last October. By the time of the funeral, the impact of Lawrence's nightmare had grown dim for most people. Sarah had become another Christmas holiday traffic accident victim. After New Year's, Lawrence had become that unfortunate man who had lost his wife; the man who had grieved through all the major holidays. Kelly had found him sitting alone inside his office at two in the morning weeping. Papers were scattered in messy stacks on his desk; open boxes stuffed with more papers had been pushed next to the desk. One box contained stories and articles from Southeast Asia.

When he observed people, Lawrence discovered their concentration had moved into reaches far beyond loss and sorrow; as life moved on, only Lawrence seemed to stand still at the moment of Sarah's death. In a short time, idle gossip replaced sympathy. People made strange remarks; and not knowing Lawrence was in earshot, compounded his loss in a thousand painful ways.

"At least they didn't have children," someone whispered behind him. "She didn't feel a thing," a voice said from a cloak room. "Her face was reconstructed from wax. I know for a fact. It wasn't really her. That's why the casket was closed."

A girl in the typing pool said to another as he was in the firm library, "She had a cool million dollars of life insurance. People have killed their wives for a lot less."

In the dining room of his club, where he had sat with his back turned, "Did you see that young woman at the funeral? She was all over Lawrence. As if people couldn't see through her little act. Christ, she could have waited until Sarah was in the ground."

His law firm insisted that he take six weeks' leave. A leave was the last thing he wanted or needed. His office was the surviving continuity in his life—the place where he could stake out and enforce his claim for control and deny access. He had no idea how he survived those first days and nights alone in the house. He had been exposed to the telephone calls, the flowers, the telegrams, and faxes. There had been no refuge, no shelter for him to hide.

8

At ten one evening Kelly came into his office and shut the door hard. "Why are you so curt with me? Have I done something wrong? I know this thing has been horrible for you. But does it have to affect our relationship?"

"Sarah had a relationship with a friend of mine before we were married. His name was Robert Tuttle. You were about five years old at the time."

"Don't play that game, Larry."

"And guess who I heard from? Bob Tuttle. He's in Bangkok."

"What's he doing in China?"

"Thailand."

"China, Thailand, Hong Kong. The point is, Larry, what the hell is going on inside your head. Did you just use me the other night? Didn't it mean anything to you? Are you ashamed? Is it me? Did I say something wrong? Tell me what's going on, for godsake."

"I'm going to Bangkok."

"How long?" Tears had welled in Kelly's eyes, breaking through a ridge of black eyeliner.

"I don't know. I can't put a cap on it. Not now."

"It's a place to run to if you can't handle women. The sex capital of the world. Just the place you need, I guess."

Lawrence stared at her for a moment, shrugged, and returned his attention to a stack of papers. His eyes were black-rimmed and puffy; his face a sallow yellow. Shaving, he had missed a small patch below his right ear. Slowly his appearance was evolving to match the collapse that had happened inside.

"And here you're the guy who couldn't fudge an extra two hours on a client's bill," she said. "I believed in you, Larry. I thought you had integrity. I looked up to you. I know you lost your wife. I'm sorry. Everyone in the firm is sorry. But you can't drag on like this forever."

He had an answer of sorts; but it was not one he was able at that instant to provide her. One telegram had come from Bangkok. "I was distressed to learn of Sarah's death. It' s been many years since we have spoken. When the time is right for you, please come for at least one week. Stay as my guest. There are some matters we ought to settle."

Robert Tuttle was a name that had surfaced no more than two or three times in the quarter of a century he had lived with Sarah.

What possible things could they talk about? Had Tuttle gone mad? Sarah was dead, and he invited him to Bangkok to put matters to rest. Christ, what matters? He knew nothing of his life; and hadn't given him a second thought.

Tuttle's telegram was stuffed away and forgotten with hundreds of other people he had once known and had come out of the woodwork at the time of Sarah's death. But Tuttle's reappearance came with the discovery of personal effects in Sarah's office. Tuttle catapulted into his life by Sarah's own hand. The second week after her death, Lawrence found Sarah's diaries going through papers in her filing cabinet inside her office in the English department at the University. There had been twenty-two. One for each year of their marriage. He read two diaries, sometimes three, sleeping little, eating even less until he lost track of the days of the week and the date of the month.

She had not forgotten Robert. He appeared in every one; from year one to the date of her death, Tuttle's presence had evolved into something large, immediate, and significant. Tuttle had been conscripted into her fantasy world; a secret conspiracy with the past that she had taken to her grave. Lawrence's grief congealed into anger, and the anger cooled into bitterness. She had deceived him all these years. They had never kept secrets from each other. Lawrence felt utterly betrayed; a fool, and the following night he slept with Kelly Swan in the bed he and Sarah had occupied. After that night, Lawrence began ignoring Kelly, and putting some distance between her and himself.

He stayed home studying Sarah's diary as if new meanings would gush from the bedrock of each text. He stopped answering his phone or the door. For ten days, he didn't shave or shower; he wore jeans and a T-shirt. He had opened a data base on his computer named "Tuttle." He had counted the number of times his name had been entered; and the number of times Sarah had mentioned Lawrence's name. Then he listed all adjectives she had used to describe Tuttle; and all the ones she attached to him. He ran the figures three or four different ways. He made charts and graphs. In the end, Lawrence had spent more time poring over the diaries than Sarah ever had.

On the day of her death, Tuttle's name had cropped up. He reread a cryptic line in Sarah's perfect handwriting: "Tuttle had this smile the day of our wedding. A killing smile. He had stood in the back of the church as my father brought me out for the walk down to the altar. Tuttle mouthed the words, 'Goodbye, Sarah. Be happy inside your safety net. I hope it holds and you never tumble; that you never take the hard fall.'

"Less than half an hour later, when Lawrence and I turned to walk out of the church as man and wife, Tuttle and his smile had vanished in the warm October sun. What did Tuttle always say in the dark room after we had made love? There are four thresholds of life; deserts to cross, and they were fear, doubt, loneliness, and the last one he always said with a grin was the largest and the most difficult to cross. He called this spirituality. Everything in the '60s was spiritual this, spiritual that. It is possible he was a creature of his time. That he no longer remembers himself what he once said. That you throw yourself deep in the web of narrow distractions and pretend the treadmill you're riding is crossing the vast deserts of life and that you'll never disappear. And what does Lawrence say after we make love? We are keepers of the perfect life. We have earned our place; we are in control for an indefinitely long period. He stares at his appointment book and sees order. Tuttle, can you hear me? Our lives are in perfect harmony—as if we were in a contest and were judged to have won the competition. My rough guess from your stuff that I've read in the last year is that you're wandering, lost and stranded, inside one of those unscheduled deserts. Sometimes I long to meet you and ask you what I can ask no one else: When does the net become an anchor? When does the appointment diary become sea floor where you can no longer breathe? Answer me that, Tuttle. Leave a message for me in the cupboard."

Lawrence looked up from her last diary with a grim expression each time he finished that passage. Was she saying that he had become an anchor? Or their marriage was this heavy weight in her life, bolting her down? That she was suffocating in their relationship? Perhaps Sarah had been thinking of Tuttle at the crucial moment her MG had collided. When she departed this life, she had been thinking of questions she wanted to ask Robert Tuttle. An old boyfriend she hadn't seen or talked to in twenty-two years. Or had she? It was possible. Lawrence wasn't in the habit of checking up on his wife. Sometimes she had attended a conference on her own. Tuttle might have been waiting for her. He was angry. Why hadn't she said something? Why had she written about Tuttle in her diary after all these years?

Back inside his house, Lawrence frantically searched through the stacks of messages. He found Tuttle's telegram. Lawrence read the words again and for the first time understood that Tuttle had extended an invitation of sorts. "When the time is right for you, please come for at least one week. Stay as my guest."

Why had Tuttle invited him? They were strangers after so many years; their lives had gone in opposite directions. What could they possibly have to say to one another after such a length of time? He had remembered one characteristic of Tuttle from their college days: his love of the dramatic, the theatrical—a turning of a situation into a staged event for a specific purpose. He had slipped over the Canadian border at night and camped out near the church in Seattle; he had waited for Sarah to appear on her father's arm inside the church; he had come in dirty jeans and unshaved face to make his final farewell. This was a standard Tuttle gesture, thought Lawrence.

Lawrence could only guess what drama awaited him in Bangkok. It could have been as simple as Tuttle's wanting free legal advice. It would not have surprised Lawrence to discover that Tuttle had hit the sharp blades of the law. He liked the idea that Tuttle might need him, and for once Lawrence would have the upper hand in dealing with him.

Lawrence had gone on to graduate first in his law school class and become an editor of the Law Review. He had achieved success while Tuttle had dropped out of UCLA in their third year. The draft board sent Tuttle a notice to report. Tuttle burnt it in a small ceremony in the student union cafe to a round of applause. That same night, Tuttle asked Sarah to go with him to Canada—he had decided to leave on a Greyhound bus heading to Vancouver on Monday morning. Sarah had agreed to meet him at the station. She never arrived. Tuttle left Los Angeles alone, and a week later Sarah had become engaged to Lawrence Baring.

Robert and Lawrence had roomed together for six months. Lawrence had fallen in love with Sarah the first time Tuttle introduced her as his old lady. She had long braided brown hair, wore no makeup, faded blue jeans, and a thin white blouse without a bra. Sarah's father was a federal court judge in Seattle, and Tuttle was her rebel act of defiance. She stood in the doorway of their apartment with an arm wrapped around Tuttle's waist.

"Larry wants to be a lawyer," said Tuttle, giving Sarah a little poke in the ribs.

"To help the poor?" Sarah had asked. This was 1968, the day before the Fourth of July.

"Civil rights law," Lawrence had answered with firm conviction.

The phone line to Bangkok was surprisingly clear as if the connection was next door in Arizona; as if Tuttle had never really been very far away. "Robert, I thought about taking a trip to your part of the world," Lawrence said. There had been a long pause.

"I hoped you might phone."

"Just one question, Robert. Did you and Sarah write during the last few years? Or maybe run into each other at a conference or something?"

Tuttle laughed. "The last time I saw Sarah was in Seattle on the day of your wedding. She was walking next to her federal judge father to marry you."

Lawrence booked a suite at the Bangkok Regent Hotel. A palace of fountains, gardens, white marble floor, servants, and staff who glided gracefully through the lobby. The courtyard cafe filled with lunching generals, politicians, and businessmen. High-society Chinese ladies in Paris fashion drifted through the exclusive shops. He had taken a suite of rooms and everyone called him Khun Lawrence, bowing from the waist, slender fingers and hands together to form a *wai*. Kelly phoned him three times from Los Angeles. She wanted reassurance; and, in his own way, so did Lawrence.

The newspapers were filled with stories about four minor wives fighting to control the estate of a deceased land developer who had been shot dead. Under the photograph of the women seated outside the courtroom was another photo—a death mask of the deceased slumped over the wheel of his car. Lawrence thought he was going to be sick; but forced himself to look at the picture. The face was falsified by death; all the features had been frozen, exaggerated, and twisted by the departure. It was like a lifeless husk and Lawrence found himself crying alone in his hotel room. Male, female, young, or old, the face of death had never evolved beyond the picture in the newspaper or Sarah's face in the hospital. Later he tore off the death photograph and flushed it down the toilet. He wanted to destroy the entire paper but found himself going back to it. He studied the photos of the young women seated side by side. Each one looked ten years younger than Kelly. They were half his age; and the deceased had been more than thirty years older than his wives. They each had one child by the deceased. Another wife claimed the four minor wives had no claim. He couldn't imagine four wives. Each day he bought both English newspapers and read the details. The access to power in relationships was rearranged in strange patterns, weaving multiple families, disconnected children into an emotional overlay he tried, but could not, understand.

He kept coming back to one of Sarah's journal entries. "It is a wise man who knows that the woman who sleeps beside him is a sharp knife he keeps at his throat. The man who doesn't see the knife is betrayed by his innocence and deserves death. The man who throws the knife away is only half alive. It is the man who respects this knife at his throat who has mastered the instinct for survival and makes no appointments for his destiny. A man like Robert Tuttle."

One of the minor wives was rumored to have engaged the services of a professional killer. Each of the women looked innocent. He studied their faces, looking for signs of sadness, despair, and gloom to match what he saw in his own face. Instead he found smiles and blank expressions; formal, polite, and businesslike faces. His mind flashed to Kelly "Will I make it?" she had asked about her partnership prospects. He saw her face in the minor wives staring out from the newspaper. The land developer had not survived. He had had a butcher's drawer full of knives at his throat.

On the third day, he phoned Robert Tuttle and asked him about the photos of the women which kept running in the newspaper. "It's called estate planning in the land of smiles," said Tuttle. Lawrence had insisted that he not be met at the airport and that he have several days' rest before they saw one another.

"I would like an appointment," said Lawrence.

"I don't make appointments. What if we just hang out?" asked Tuttle.

As he put down the phone, Lawrence regretted coming to Bangkok. He read about the minor wives. He worried about his law practice. His income tax return was not prepared. The insurance money from Sarah's death had been placed in stocks and bonds. He worried about the market falling while he was halfway around the world. He read the newspaper accounts about the litigation and the minor wives. He had over a million from life insurance proceeds invested in Disney, McDonald's, Boeing, and AT&T. Bedrock American stocks that captured the bookends of American culture in the 1990s—Ronald McDonald and Mickey Mouse, along with the means of communication of the audiences trapped between them. If Sarah had been one of four or five wives, would he have felt the same? He hated himself for even thinking that way. What was in the newspapers in Bangkok had nothing to do with him, Sarah, or their marriage.

Tuttle had suggested that they meet at a coffee shop on Sukhumvit Road; a place that was a kind of expat club, and they could spend the evening catching up. "Plan to relax and spend the evening. The place doesn't close until six or seven in the morning. That should catch us up on a few of the missing years."

"Is it in a safe area?"

"Is anywhere in the world safe, Larry?"

"One more thing. Why aren't the widows weeping and clawing out each other's eyes?" asked Lawrence.

Tuttle paused before he answered. "You need lessons on how to read a smile, Larry."

❖

Lawrence recognized Tuttle immediately—the man Sarah's father had referred to at their wedding reception as "the felon." The same broad, athletic shoulders, high cheekbones, and dimpled chin. His brown hair was cropped shorter than twenty-two years earlier, but the moustache remained the same, covering the edge of his upper lip. Lawrence had dressed much like he did every day: in a dark gray suit, a navy blue tie, and a pair of two-hundred-dollar shoes. He nervously played with his Rolex as he crossed the room to where Tuttle sat alone in a booth. The laugh lines crinkled around Tuttle's eyes as a slim waiter with a patchy black moustache and wearing a light tan traditional Thai shirt brought him another drink. The standard dress attire for men was informal; the most overdressed man wore cotton pants and a short-sleeve shirt open at the neck. This was not the Bangkok Regent Hotel crowd.

"Didn't you say we had an appointment at your club?" asked Lawrence, as Tuttle stood up and offered his hand.

"I said hang out. That means informal. You'll be okay. It takes a week of living in the future to adjust." Tuttle waved to the waiter to bring another drink as Lawrence sat down, removing his jacket and undoing his tie.

"Future?"

"It's Tuesday in Bangkok and Monday in LA—the Crips and Bloods hometown teams," said Tuttle, smiling.

"For a guy who's not been to the States since LBJ you've formed many opinions."

The waiter brought a whiskey and soda for Lawrence.

"Come to think of it—and it didn't seem like it at the time—those were probably the good ole days."

Lawrence sipped his drink.

"Whiskey and soda. You remembered."

"Some things never change." Tuttle raised his glass and touched Lawrence's. "Welcome to Headquarters. Maybe you're not ready for HQ. We can head out someplace else."

Tuttle sounded genuine; there was no hint of irony in his voice. But to have gone would have been a kind of defeat, thought Lawrence. The man had asked him to a place where he felt comfortable, and already Lawrence had managed to insult him.

"I came because of Sarah. And I think we should stay put."

16

"I thought you might have come because of you."

Lawrence looked embarrassed. "I wanted to clear my memory on a few things. That's all. Sort out some old stuff that's been clogging up my nights and days since Sarah died."

Lawrence was sincere in what appeared an absurd proposition. One of Sarah's diaries contained a passage that haunted him through a month of sleepless nights.

"We are marked by what we forget as much as what we choose to remember. What things, events, and people shape that memory define us as a person. It may be our only definition. Why and how and what we forget is our reality machine in forward motion. We forget individually and collectively. Forgetting shapes our destiny. That's why Robert left. He was afraid of what everyone around him was forgetting. Including me. He watched our memories going down the drain. He left to remember. I only wish there was some way Lawrence or I could reel him back and reclaim from him what he preserved over all these years; and restore the things we've forgotten and thrown out over all these years."

Lawrence wondered what kind of club had accepted Tuttle for membership. A place he now referred to for the first time as Head-quarters, HQ for short; a coffee shop in the basement of a massage parlor, the Bangkok gate into the night. Tuttle had become a legend at HQ, and over the years had become the collective memory of HQ. Two decades earlier, Tuttle had first strolled down the long back alley and entered the backdoor of HQ, passing the common toilets and kitchen. The unreality of the night quickly struck Lawrence as he saw Tuttle had grown middle-aged just like himself. He looked for some piece of memory from their old friendship in this strange man; all he could recover, was the odd way Tuttle sometimes cocked his head to the side when he talked. He still had that habit. Tuttle was alive, sitting next to him, and actually lived in this place. He listened to Tuttle speak Thai to a waiter; hearing him speak in an alien language, one which excluded him, feeling the damage of being left out.

Tuttle saw a middle-aged American, conservative, off balance, anxious, a ridge of sweat covering his forehead, trying to make small talk about their old apartment. Lawrence, the old college roommate from the States; the man who had married his college sweetheart drinking a whiskey soda, bending his elbow at what had to be the end of the earth for him. Lawrence, the widower, the lonely figure who had avoided the invitations of the few early-bird ladies of the night. Tuttle had been living in Bangkok so long that he had begun to sleep with the second generation of HQ girls. The new generation of eighteen to twenty-three-year-olds would creep into HQ throughout the night; freelance girls, moving like cats, eyes circling the room for their prey, tongues licking the night air.

Lawrence Baring had stolen Sarah from him. Throughout those years, Tuttle wondered what price would be sufficient repayment for that betrayal. The morning he sat inside the Greyhound bus, nose to the window as it pulled away from the station, Tuttle knew one day he would meet Lawrence again. Only Sarah's death had changed his plans. This time Tuttle had the right woman for Lawrence; the woman who would even the score and settle the outstanding account. Before the moment Lawrence would pay in full on that debt there was the sticky business of the past, and psychological disturbance of the present moment to overcome. Tuttle delighted in the drama he had planned for his old roommate.

"The girls sleep with customers for money. Three reds for short-time," said Tuttle, stopping as a look of confusion filled Lawrence's face.

"Three what?"

"Three hundred baht. About twelve bucks. A purple or five hundred baht buys the whole night. Twenty dollars."

"Twenty bucks? Do you have any idea how much I bill out my associates?" Lawrence suddenly thought of Kelly. Tuttle shrugged. "Two hundred an hour."

"As a rule of thumb it should never cost more to get divorced than to get laid," said Tuttle, nodding at one of the passing girls who was a regular from the old days. "Exactly what kind of lawyer are you, Larry?"

"I specialize in pension law. Federal pension law."

"Civil rights for old people. Wasn't it civil rights law that you were once interested in? Going to devote your life to? Why do I remember civil rights?"

One of the girls had leaned over the table, resting forward on her fingertips, her face a couple of inches away from Lawrence's face, as he sat erect against the back of the booth. "Friendly, aren't they?"

"Noi, meet Larry. My lawyer from America."

Noi stretched out her hand and shook hands with Lawrence. "You want lady?"

Tuttle spoke to her in Thai. "He has a lady. Thai wife who is very dangerous with a knife. You want him, it's up to you. But I think she come after you; find you and cut your throat."

Noi rose up from the table, turned, and quickly retreated to her friends.

"What did you say to her?"

Tuttle smiled. "I told her your hourly rate."

Tuttle's presence at HQ provided the girls with some sense of continuity; the *farang* who spoke their language; the body-builder using exercise and drugs to carve a body that wouldn't be destroyed by time; the businessman who had been a writer for newspapers and had published stories about hill tribe shamans, life among the exiles, whores, and crazies in Asia.

Stories that Sarah had discovered reprinted in various odd places and had admired, stories that Lawrence had found after her death in a folder in the back of her filing cabinet.

"After Sarah's death I found a collection of your stories in her office," said Lawrence. He hadn't decided whether to tell Tuttle about the number of times he had been mentioned by Sarah in her diaries. He hadn't told anyone else; he struggled to find some way to pull out this secret harpoon Sarah had thrown from her grave. Lawrence kept the secret from Kelly. It was humiliating, a strike against the memorial of his marriage with Sarah, and worst of all, the diaries created the perception of huge amounts of energetic emotional activities that had gone unnoticed by him for over two decades. His marriage had begun to fall apart in his mind; the realization of his exclusion in volume after volume of Sarah's most private thoughts was beyond his ability to understand.

"Funny you asked on the phone. If I had seen Sarah after '68. I never took you for the suspicious type."

Neither had Lawrence. He moved uneasily in his seat, rocking forward on his elbows. He looked at Tuttle's hands and thought about them having once been wrapped around Sarah's naked body.

"Sarah thought your stories were a kind of message," he cleared his throat. "From the desert to her." The phrase sounded awkward coming from Lawrence's lips.

Tuttle fingered his glass. "She said that?"

Lawrence nodded, carefully watching the smile fade from Tuttle's face. Sarah hadn't as far as he knew ever said that; at least to him; but it had been in a diary entry she had written one night when Lawrence had been in New York City working on a corporate take-over. Lawrence reached into the inside pocket of his suit jacket and pulled out one of Tuttle's stories. He laid it out on the table. In the margin were notes in Sarah's handwriting, and passages underlined with a yellow Magic Marker. He shoved it across the table to Tuttle, who looked down at the page. The story had been inside one of Sarah's folders. The story had been published two years before in Hong Kong.

"You came halfway around the world because of a piece I wrote?"

Lawrence rolled up the sleeves of his tailored white shirt.

"Because Sarah harbored this illusion you had something to say. I don't see it from this. But I'm just a lawyer. So I'm curious. Was she taken in by a bullshit artist? Or is there some outside chance you have something to say. I'm here to find out. To see if the case can be made. I need to put this thing to rest if I'm to get on with my life."

2

A CHANGE OF HEART

A Short Story
by
Robert Tuttle

The hilltribe shaman wears a set of ordinary clothes to the ceremony reclaiming the spirit of an ill villager. "Where are his robes?" a tourist asked, disappointed his vision had not found a counterpart in reality.

"He wears sacred robes inside his heart," answered the guide. "And if you believe, you can see him go into this room locked in his chest. If you believe."

EVERYONE goes North on the same search, looking for the same shaman spitting in the dirt by a dead dog and reciting homespun chants. And everyone thinks the same at first. Here's a framework—a point of reference, a map I can follow once back in Bangkok. A way to restore myself when I start to drift. And I always wish them luck. Like I wish you luck. And I'll tell you my lesson of twenty-one years of living in Bangkok. That the ringside seat is at the Zeno after midnight.

Zeno, Headquarters, HQ, the Star Wars Bar on Sukhumvit. You can't miss it. Fake Greek columns in front of a sign that reads Turkish Bath, Barber, Massage, Espresso Coffee Shop. Fritters frying in big pots of palm oil outside the entrance. Beggars, bar girls, diplomats, spies, writers, bums, ex-Nazis, merchants, gangsters, tourists drifting in and out, eating at makeshift sidewalk cafes beside food carts and stalls. Cuttlefish and lottery vendors working the crowds. Like you, they're all looking for shamans and ghosts.

You get a flash that you've seen this room somewhere else. After a couple of years, one night, an ordinary night, you've ordered the usual, and it hits you, that memory of the very first room like HQ that you entered. You were a kid, and the room was downstairs in your house. HQ was an elaborate replica of that basement; the handyman job performed by your father and a couple of neighbors back in the '50s. Tongue-and-groove panelling. Your dad got so carried away that he even panelled the support columns with the same shit as he nailed to the walls. He got cute and hid the fluorescent lights between a gap in the acoustic tiles and the panelling.

Now, close your eyes and throw in a wet bar, stools, tables and chairs, and curved booths with black plastic-covered benches and a television set on a shelf at the far end, a hundred girls, and you're back in time but no matter how hard you try, you can never truly get back to the starting blocks. But what if there was a way back? Where everyone's thirteen again, but this time they are flush with money for tits and ass. You don't care what you saw when you looked in the mirror, or the '68 photo album the morning before; and you think about the eggs inside that girl's body last night. One night, someday in the next century, another Noi will walk past the jukebox at the Zeno, and now even though its all compact disks and lasers, you'll hear golden oldies like '*What a Wonderful Life*' playing over the loudspeakers, and you'll eye her. And you go into that trance of yours. Haven't I seen her somewhere before? Didn't I take her back one night? Last month, the year before? Your mind is like a dripping faucet, each thought breaking the skin of the surface with a tiny splash. Before you can say Jack Spratt, there is hysterical shouting from the toilets, and a cop tells you another girl took a razor blade to her wrists. All that comes out of her mouth are the words, "*Chai, ka. Chai, ka.*—Yes, sir. Yes, sir." Time after night, night after night, an echo of sound from this life into the next.

YOU know when you've gone *hard-core*. One night you're sitting at a back booth in Zeno's sucking back a Mekong and soda, and she comes up to your table in a tight-fitting dress and extends her hand, and you're asking yourself that same question you asked before, that question born of two-in-the-morning doubt. Have I had her before? And you're deciding to take her back for the night, and she's sitting on your lap. You close your eyes and touch her cheek, the nape of her neck, her breasts, and work on down to her thighs; nothing registers for certain as familiar.

In the back of your mind you hear her voice from some indefinite horizon in the past, or is it an illusion of the early morning, and the jukebox, and the buzz of conversations from the tables and booths? The acoustical ceiling tiles gray with age have soaked up a million conversations since '68, including your own. But you're not certain what you can retrieve, and agonize in two languages. She sees this hint of a frown around the corner of your mouth and eyes. And if you ask her straight out: she might not tell the truth, because she needs the money for another dress or her mother is leaning on her, a brother is in school and the fees are due, or someone is sick—someone is always sick in the family—and doctor bills and bills for medicine and shots and hospital beds mount on her shoulders and float above her head. Even though you speak fluent Thai she sees you're one of those with a purple to burn tonight. That is her target, and several times now she's asked where you work, thinking about how many purples you spent each week at Zeno, Headquarters, HQ, the public commodity exchange where purples change hands on the runway of memory. You're one of those who has a good heart—there won't be too much pain or discomfort in your bed where the transaction takes place. And for a very long time you look inside the arms for needle marks, and when you look up in her face, you see eyes grown old with worry. Eyed masked by a finely tuned smile. For a second you look away, distracted by another face, on another girl who has walked over from the jukebox and talk about how the air conditioner in Soi 15 used to break down in the middle of the night, and you feel good. She has punched the memory card from your past.

And the girl on your lap spits out an English word that is in half of the poems that have ever been penned; but she makes it sound as if it were a curse word—she calls you a butterfly. She crosses her arms together at the forearm and flaps her fingers as if they were wings. Moving from girl to girl like a butterfly dusting flowers. And of course that is the truth, and you are disgusted with yourself. And you've been warned about the early signs of going *hard-core*, and you've ignored them because you think you're different from the rest. That you play by a different set of rules; that your memory is iron-tight; and that no matter what, you have a will to control your own destiny with a true vision of your own past. But everyone felt that. Then you look up at her again in the reflected light from the bar and jukebox, and her face blends in with so many other faces, so many other smiles, and so many other shining black eyes, that you can't be certain whether you are focusing on the moment, the past, or this is some horror of the future come to warn you. And you decide to take her back, because you—convince yourself that once back into the apartment, your context, with your things, and your music, she will reveal herself in your memory. One way or another. That the confusion is that of a large, busy bar where the true *hard-core* no longer recognize themselves in the mirrors above the booths. And when you have her home at last, and you watch her undress and that knot swells in the back of your throat. You can't be certain still. You tell yourself it doesn't matter. She's of a type. Wide mouth, flat nose, high-pitched voice. An upcountry girl from a village between *Ubon Ratchathani* and the Laos border, and you know in the morning her footprints will be on the toilet seat, and you'll stare at them like a shaman reading the entrails of a dead chicken trying to understand whether this spirit is for good or evil.

Before she leaves, she comes into the bathroom and watches you looking at her wet footprints. She wants to show you something. She opens her bag and takes out a small photo album from inside and hands it to you. Leaning against the wall, you flip through the photos, pretending to pay attention. Then she says with incredible feeling and pride and love, "Mother . . . me." And you take a double look at the photo, then take it out of the plastic cover in the album and hold it up to the sunlight. She can't imagine what you are doing as the light slopes down through the window on her photograph and your hand. You look at the girl, and for a moment freeze as that hydraulic hammer strikes deep into your memory. Twenty-one years ago you had taken her mother. The two small brown moles on the left jaw had gradually grown darker, and the face was older—much older, and you look in the bathroom mirror at yourself. That guillotine of sharp first morning light behind you and you see what generation you fit into; and you refuse to believe it. You tear out of the bathroom and into the locked closet with the photograph albums you've kept of the girls. You take out the '68 volume, squatting on the floor, and her mother's picture is there. Two brown moles.

And when you glance up, the girl is looking down at the nude picture of her own mother, not recognizing her. Thinking she's a ringer from HQ. And she calls you a butterfly. But the truth is always more difficult to explain in Thai. You've passed that magnetic field where few have ever trod: you're second generation *hard-core*, and at best you have one generation left ahead of you before your knees buckle, the food won't stay down in your stomach, and you can't get it up. Reality sinks home: you've begun to pollinate your last spring of flowers at HQ. Down the road, you dread the inevitable end zone. You've become a geriatric, planted in an old folks' home where young nurses treat you like a dirty old soi dog. Second generation, you repeat to yourself, and give the girl back the picture of her mother. You had been inside her mother when this girl was still an unfertalized egg, and you thought one generation lasted forever.

And two years down the road, not even the news has really changed—peace talks somewhere are snagged, a plane crashes in a mountain, a madman kills children with an automatic weapon halfway around the world, someone has misappropriated funds, a river floods, a drought causes starvation, disease, and suffering—and you're back at the same table in Zeno, and this beautiful girl comes up to your table and smiles, and you're trying to remember if this is the same girl who you thought that night was the same girl as before. Then there is no pulling back, you look up into the mirror at yourself and you repeat by moving your lips but without making a sound. 'I am *hard-core*. I will always be *hard-core*. I've gone over that edge. And I can never go back. Not tonight. Not tomorrow.' And you take the girl back without even asking this time whether she has been inside your apartment before. Because it no longer matters. And in the morning when you stare down at the toilet seat with her tiny footprints on either side, you laugh and piss into the plastic hole and pretend the prints belong to one of Santa's elves who got lost many Christmases ago.

You can never really remember again. That part of your life is lost. Bangkok has trapped your memory like it has done with thousands of men, leaving you to wander through the heat, dust, traffic, looking for what has been lost and not knowing what you are exactly looking for. This mental fogging machine that blows that fine mist of forgetting through your mind, tangling every limb and happy face that ever looked up from your bed. And all that is left when you walk out of the Zeno with her on your arm this time is the thought that the *tuk-tuk* drivers remember you. They call out your address and quote a price like commodity brokers, and you choose one. She slides over the plastic seat and you slip an arm around her waist. Two cars drag-race down Sukhumvit Road. A red Italian sports car and a tan BMW. And you remember every single detail of a car crash in that same spot last year. The dead, blood-soaked Thai faces and hair as black as midnight. The shattered glass and crumpled metal. And you wished life had been tailor-built another way. That our memory of pain, hurt, and violence went numb and vague from one day to the next, and our memory of pleasure was as vivid and real forever. In such a world there would be no *hard-core.*

You arrived at HQ tonight because you were pulled along by the same forces waiting to meet you in the North. Forces you can't even give a name to now. HQ is the cargo hold and you have just run up the gangway. And you're still not certain exactly where you are, who runs this place, how to get out in case a fire breaks out. HQ is like an exit wound from a bullet. You can never find where it entered, how, or the exact course it took before blowing out that hole you're looking through. So you'll travel to the North like I did. Like every *farang* who passes through Bangkok thinking you know what you're looking for, and you'll recognize it when you see it. You think that you've got some theory, some belief, or piece of poetry that means something, or serves some purpose. I've eaten off that same menu. The one where you order the mystical special expecting a blinding flash of insight or faith. And you'll think the *hard-core farang* at HQ are lost souls and you're saved because you've found the entry hole for their wound. That you've stumbled into a black hole that's sucked out their memory and made everyone and everything they reached out for break apart, crumble, and disappear.

Block out the laughing and joking around the jukebox that is playing too loud. Think about last night, or the night before, until you hear the sound of a shower running in the bathroom next door. There is a nagging voice running in the back of your head when she's washing, cleaning herself in cold water because you don't have any hot and a candle is burning on the dresser. If your life depended on picking her out of a police line-up, could you do it? At that moment? Without running in and looking at her face? That's the litmus test. Chances are that you can't remember who you've sent into the shower other than her name is Noi, and you've known hundreds of Nois. Generations of Nois. And with each new crop of Nois from a shithole village in the north, your memory becomes more and more foggy until it seems to belong to someone else you once knew but no longer remember where or for how long.

What frightens you—terrorizes you—is not one *chai ka* girl, not even one who had some spark of personality, but the one who has left more than an insignificant trace of nitrogen and oxygen smeared across a wall of your own prison of time and space. All those other walls out there that you've brushed against with your desires and your heart and your reason—you've got it. It's in the expression on your face as you seek some trace of yourself among the girls working the floor at Zeno's. You come here to look at the great wall of your life. Those emotional posters you bought and put up deep inside the bulletin board of your night. The Great Wall of China is snaking through a thousand half-lidded eyes against a pillow on which you rest your head; then you are on the wall, you become the wall.

That's why I come here night after night—all those years running—because I have no other place. All those heartbeats around the tables, the jukebox, and the bar, each alone with an overnight kit, waiting to be your choice. Anointed for the night in your bed. They climb the outer wall of your memory looking for a trail, afraid of falling to the bottom, and more than anything, they come here to find someone to hold onto. Someone who remembers them; someone they remember. A small spore of remembrance in a cracked mirror, an old lyric of a song, a smile. I can't find a trace of myself so far tonight. But I'm hopeful, the night's young. And I know you because we had lunch only yesterday and you asked me about *Lahu* shamans, burial rituals, marriages, healings, chants, and old beliefs in black magic. We only scratched the surface. The burning of paper money and appeasing the ghost of the dead. I know every waiter in this room, the bartenders, and the cops at the table in the corner smoking cigarettes and talking to those three girls. And they think they know me. But they're not sure. *Farangs* are like wallpaper: the Thais see the pattern but the images are open to a thousand interpretations. The girls see *farangs* not as wallpaper but bearded ones, the ones with hair over the arms and the rest of the body, ready to spring on a human buffet. Now you've got me started. Started right where we left off at lunch. You can sleep in tomorrow. The train to *Chiang Mai* doesn't leave Bangkok until later.

Another drink? Pace yourself. It's gonna be a long night. Have a look . . . over there. The one who just came in the yellow silk blouse and tight black skirt. You know what she used to dream—this going back five, six years? She dreamed of running her own import/export company. She never had any idea exactly what she'd import from abroad—or where abroad was—England, the States, Italy, Middle East, she couldn't locate them on a map—or what in Thailand she'd export. It didn't matter. That was her dream. About eighteen months ago, she tried to kill herself. Look at her wrists. She walked into one of the toilet stalls in the back, took out a razor and cut her own wrists. Not very deep. But there was a lot of blood. Another guy and I stopped the bleeding and took her over to Soi 49 to the hospital. The next morning I went back to see her. She looked long and hard as if she didn't recognize me which she probably didn't, and I sat on the chair beside her bed, grabbed her right hand, forced her wrist up, and looked at the bandages. Tears welled in her eyes and I couldn't look her directly in the face. I knew she had her head turned into her pillow, looking away, and that she wanted to die all over again because I had caught her crying. She had lost face and I sat next to her killing off that part of her that she couldn't let fall away. I kept my eyes on her hand, touching her fingers, and I asked her why she did it. Tears rolled down her cheeks and splashed on the back of my hand. And I watched her tears. Each a perfect droplet caught in the black hair on the edge of my hand. And she said, "The only import/export company I'm ever gonna have is here."

She moved my hand between her legs. "Make love with *farang*. That's all I can do. Maybe I have another four years and then no one take me. Then what I do, Tuttle? Who gonna look after me then? Who's gonna remember me?"

She'd taken a vertical plunge into her own remembrance and had an insight about laws of life inside HQ. That glimpse of revealed truth that made a girl take the knife and turn inward for pleasure of spilling their own blood.

She had gone *hard-core*. All those faces and all those names of *farangs* and girls she had once known were a secret buried inside herself and she had lost the ability to recall them, bring the images forth inside herself. When she comes into HQ tonight, you'll look for scar tissue but there are only unhealed wounds on her wrists. A few months later, what remains are the small, raised white lines on her wrists—as if someone had tattooed cocaine lines as a bad joke—and you will wonder about her despair until you reach a stage of nervous exhaustion; and you will try and decode those lines for their pure and full public statement.

Whatever you decide about them, symbol, allusion, spectacle, you will convince yourself that here is one girl I can never forget. The heat of those old wounds fires off a flare in your mind. That hard, metallic light burns an image deep in the core of memory. Glory is explored inside that space. Because it is the moment you've been waiting for so far tonight. That small opening in the wall; the first hint that going *hard-core* isn't absolute; some biographical data survives the night, the year, a lifetime. That's your import/export company dream, otherwise you wouldn't be going up North to write about shamans and things that go bump in the night.

Dreams are precious. All that matters in life are your dreams, your intellect, and your health. The rest scatters, folds, dissolves, renews, and is replaceable. Before you put too much faith in those razor marks as memory tracks that will last, ask yourself why they seduce you like the seduction of a prize-fight. You see too many razor marks on the arms of working girls, too many cut left eyes in the ring, and you are back to the solitude of your forgetting; surrounded by blank walls, and the next time you understand the threshold of euphoria is going to demand something more violent, magical, and mad.

And you come back here and slide into the booth next to me, and together we'll keep watch through the night. Because what we are looking for might come through the door at any moment, order a drink, push the buttons on the jukebox, someone to crawl into our bed, and show us the way out.

3

Tuttle had planned every detail of the evening; each act of the night had been artfully constructed to reveal as much about Lawrence Baring as Bangkok. The beginning, thought Tuttle, was the hardest with someone you hadn't seen in years; one specific element about Lawrence snapped back into place a few minutes after he had sat down. Lawrence was a formula man. Toothbrush always hung in the same place inside the medicine chest; cap always on the toothpaste; always studied between the hours of eight and eleven every night. Lawrence was a man who had developed a rule for every eventual encounter life might bring to his table, office, car, or bedroom.

Lawrence naturally walked through the world with the burning desire to engineer handholds for each step along the way, for systematized patterns, for a method of design and organization. Lawrence's personality, ironically thought Tuttle, was ruled by a fundamental need that was also a basic characteristic of Thai culture. Coming to Bangkok after Sarah's death may have been the first time in Lawrence's entire life that he had risked breaking out of his formula. He wouldn't have come without a reason; without a mission or expectation, thought Tuttle. He came to Bangkok to bury Sarah and, the past they had shared. And Tuttle suspected that he might be, in Lawrence's mind, the only person on earth who could perform that ceremony.

"Have you gone to bed with anyone since Sarah died?" asked Tuttle. Lawrence was slightly startled. It had been a lifetime since he had seen Sarah's name come from Tuttle's mouth. The strange feeling that it had been all a dream flooded Lawrence's mind; they could still be in college, and the year 1968; and Tuttle had created an elaborate opera, a network of strange images and exotic ideas.

"Have you?" repeated Tuttle.

"Have I what?"

"Had a girl?"

Lawrence looked away through the gray cloud of smoke that hung over a row of old tables with scuffed metal legs. A slender man in a straw hat leaned forward kissing an eighteen-year-old hilltribe girl who sat with her friends in the opposite booth.

"A young lawyer. She's an associate in my office. I've seen Kelly a few times," said Lawrence, watching for some reaction from Tuttle. Kelly's name had an alien warp inside HQ; and using her name with Tuttle seemed like an infringement of her privacy.

Tuttle sat with his arms stretched out batlike on the upholstered booth. He smiled. "How old is she?"

"Thirty, thirty-one."

"That's what you call a young lawyer?" asked Tuttle, increasing his grin until his moustache was a straight line across his face.

"Is that supposed to be a joke?"

"It depends on your sense of humor."

Lawrence's hands closed into fists; his jaw set tight, and the slight nodding of the head began that signalled anger. "This is getting highly personal, Robert."

"It's a highly personal kind of world. Or have you forgotten?" Tuttle's smile vanished. A second later, as if he had caught himself, pulled himself away from an edge, he recovered, bounced on his seat, moved his head to the music.

"Thirty years of erosion on a woman's body can be bad. That's why I asked. Maybe your girlfriend's an exception to the rule."

"She's not my girlfriend," said Lawrence.

Lawrence made a gesture to the waiter to bring him another drink. "She's Stanford Law Review," he said in a matter-of-fact way. The kind of remark he might drop inside his own club.

"You gotta be the first *farang* in HQ to brag that he scored with a woman who made Stanford Law Review. She's an institution. She's a label, old buddy. I had forgotten how much labels impress you. Now it comes back to me. Sarah's father was a federal judge. Her mother lived from Dupont trust funds. And what was my label? Draft dodger."

Lawrence's drink arrived and he took a long time counting out the money for the waiter. "This was a mistake," said Lawrence and he began to push out from the booth. Tuttle grabbed his arm.

"Do you want my help or not?" asked Tuttle.

A long silence swept between them. A long sigh came from Lawrence; he laid back his head touching the upholstered bench and laughed. Bangkok had suddenly become the place where he was knee-deep in the past; together, they had shoved up enough dirt for one night. But neither one seemed able to stop digging, ripping up the pavement of the present with the wild jackhammering of old memories. Tuttle knew the truth. Lawrence needed him. He believed that Tuttle could help him. Why was it that the one person on earth he wished to avoid was the only person he trusted to point him in the right direction? He had been sending metaphysical roadmaps to Sarah through his stories for years. What he loathed the most was that Tuttle had the upper hand. Tuttle had always had the advantage. He was like a man who had tapped into inside information at every stage in his life. Only this time there was a difference; one that had registered on Lawrence from the moment he had received Tuttle's wire. Tuttle had wanted something from him. He had desire to confront him, to confess to him, to destroy him—the desire continued to shift until desire shifted to obsession.

Lawrence decided to stay; to continue the game, to let Tuttle play out his hand through the balance of the evening.

"She has a good body," said Lawrence.

Tuttle broke into a grin and tapped Lawrence's arm. "She has planted the hook. Next she starts reeling you in, Larry. You're vulnerable. She can see that. After twenty-two years with Sarah you're not exactly cut out for dating or whoring. So pretend you're shopping for a luxury item. This is my BMW, my Rolex, and my Stanford Law Review girlfriend."

"And you've found truth, right, and wisdom living in Bangkok flesh palaces? Spare me, Bobby. In your own way, you're just as *hard-core*—to use your own word—fucked up as anyone. Look down on the rest of us. Remember as you sit up there, you're no different—you only thought you were different. Pretended to be;

put on a great act. And where is this place you're looking down from? HQ? You're forty-six years old and you spend your nights in a broken down whorehouse."

Lawrence surprised himself with his outburst of emotion. The feeling had been running wild through his mind ever since he had discovered Sarah's diaries. He had promised himself to remain in control; that any loss of temper would simply play into Tuttle's hands. Tuttle's reaction wasn't anger or hurt; he smiled, and let out a long sigh.

"Sorry, Bobby," Lawrence said.

"Sorry for what? For some genuine honesty? Before you put a deposit down on your Stanford Law Review, just hear what I'm saying tonight. Keep an open mind. There might be a woman in this coffee shop; in this city waiting for you."

"A woman who sells herself?" asked Lawrence, the words rolling off his tongue with a sense of disgust. "A whore?"

"Interesting word, whore. A cruel, mean word. A western word that distorts who these girls are. When all we really want to talk about is cost. Miss Stanford Law Review has her cost. And she has you paying one way or another. Emotional funds or dollars, whatever currency works on your psycho balance sheet. Does that make her a whore? And when Sarah and I were together in '68 before you came along."

Lawrence raised his hand, making a fist. "I don't want to talk about Sarah now. Not in this way. Okay?"

"Forget about dividing good girls from bad girls; rich ones from poor ones. Whether she loves you or fucks your brains out."

Tuttle had Lawrence's full attention like a prize-fighter who had landed a series of punches to the face. Lawrence shifted uneasily. He nodded slowly as Tuttle waited for a second. "It's a question of her sense of obligation to you. That's the only virtue that matters; the only virtue worth acquiring in another. That separates a lot of Thai women from most *farang* women. The Thai woman's perspective doesn't stop at—what do I want from you? What can you give me? There's another part to the equation—what do I owe you, and how can I repay my debt to you?"

Lawrence thought for a second, then turned to Tuttle.

"What is it I owe you, Bobby?"

"What did you owe Sarah?"

From across the room, the young hilltribe girl had begun scream-ing at the middle-aged man in the straw hat. Suddenly she picked up a green Kloster beer bottle by the neck and broke off the end. Two girlfriends restrained her as the man backed away, edged up the stairs and disappeared.

"She would have killed that guy," said Lawrence, looking back at Tuttle who raised an eyebrow and smiled.

"She lost face." The drama with the broken bottle ended as quickly as it had begun. A flash of violent anger, the shattering of glass, the retreat of the offending party, and the restoration of passive, smiling faces around the floor.

"I can understand something about Bangkok." There was a smug tone creeping into his voice. "The constant drama appeals to you," said Lawrence.

"You've figured out Bangkok after three days, Larry."

"I've seen barroom fights before. Tempers flare. Bottles get broken. So you call it face in Bangkok. In LA we call it hurt feelings. It all amounts to the same thing."

Lawrence protected himself like most Americans freshly arrived in the city; his emotional reflex translated every experience into an American counterpart. The American and the Thai version were simply different expressions of the same hidden stream bub-bling under the surface. The problem was breaking through those automatic defence layers. Tuttle fell silent for several minutes, lost in thought as more women continued to enter the room. Lawrence was forcing him to refine his own thoughts; rewrite the script for the evening as they were in actual progress.

Weren't there degrees by which face could be lost, Tuttle thought. Once a Thai woman lost face with a man she really liked, the emotional reconstructive surgery was expensive, painful, and a long-draw-out ordeal. *farangs* wandered in twos and threes into Headquarters, and most of them didn't have any idea that, over there, that beautiful girl in the corner walked a tightrope, and at any moment her face could fall from her head and land on the floor before the only people who mattered in her world: her friends.

Tuttle explained as the waiter swept up the glass the man in the straw hat was paying the price for causing her to lose face. That made the *farang* dangerous, wild, unpredictable creatures; barbarians who woke up in the morning and realized that they had gone *hard-core*. They were like the Emperor wearing no clothes. The *farang* looked in the mirror and didn't see what every Thai girl who knew him saw clearly: his face had gone, vanished, and along with his face, his personal sense of dignity, respect, and honor. All had disappeared, dooming him to spend his life haunting Headquarters, one among all the other faceless souls, whose lives had been washed away in a flood of purples.

"Purple?" asked Lawrence.

Tuttle pulled a five-hundred-baht note from his wallet and laid it on the table. "The color of what it costs to take a girl for the entire night. A purple. One of these."

Of course I don't understand, thought Lawrence. He's right, after three days in Bangkok, I still haven't figured out Thai money. What do I know about Thailand? Or about any place in Southeast Asia? Two months ago I would have had trouble finding it on the map. So maybe I'm not ready for all of this. I still think a girl with a college education who works in a bar is an aspiring actress. What if Kelly were a secretary with a high school education, would I still feel the same about her? Maybe Tuttle's right, about this Stanford Law Review thing.

If only I could reach this guy, thought Tuttle. He's no different now than he was twenty-odd years ago; press him and he dives inside his opinions as if they were an underground bunker. Most nights for twenty-one years I've seen the Americans, Canadian, Swiss, Germans, French . . . with their tightly wrapped *farang* egos, fashioned out of paper mache, looking at these girls as if they were Western women with brown skin and slanted eyes. Lawrence proved to be no different. These women lost their public faces when they became service workers of the night.

They shared the gift of illusion with each other. No people were more difficult to separate from their new reality. What they had lost was far beyond the walls of HQ, they needed to believe that their new face would survive; that this new face had replaced the old one; that this new face would last even though they saw face destroyed every day of their lives.

"Face has a spiritual dimension," said Tuttle. "The one perspective every working girl, tuk-tuk driver, merchant, and prince understands, believes, and would die or kill for. A couple of times a month the newspaper reports a traffic accident. A bus, a truck, a tuk-tuk crashes head-on with a ten-wheeler or smashes against a bridge, pole, or drives into a ditch. Four, eight, ten people are killed. Fill in the blank. A grainy photograph of the burnt-out bus dipped on one side is printed on page one. The last line of the story has two possible endings. Bus driver was among the dead—a rare occurrence; or the driver fled the scene of the accident.

"The sentence, 'The driver fled the scene' is standard boiler plate. It's a computer macro; hit F1 and it automatically puts the sentence at the end of the story. You'll see it more often than any by-line. The driver's gone because he's made a mistake, he has failed. The Thai can't tolerate that he's failed. There is no stand-and-deliver attitude; there is a take-off and run and never show your face. Bury it far away. It comes out of China. There is no shame in running away, only in getting caught and shown in public."

Lawrence watched as two waiters began laying down plates of rice, noodles, and soup on the table. "Is that why you ran in '68, Bobby? Is that why you never came back. Because Sarah let you go. You didn't believe that was possible; that she wouldn't run with you. Bobby, if you want to come home, I can find you a job. If that's what you want, all you have to do is say. It's no loss of face to say you need help."

"Come to think of it, there may be something you can do for me," said Tuttle, turning his spoon into a plate of beef with oyster sauce.

"I thought there might be," said Lawrence, feeling back in control of the situation again.

AN almond-eyed ex-bar-girl named Lek squeezed into the booth between Lawrence and Tuttle. She helped herself to a plate of shrimp, chilli, hot peppers, and rice. Lek explained why Toom had broken the green Kloster beer bottle and tried to kill the *farang* in the straw hat. The guy who had bought her two nights in a row had negotiated to take out another girl. Toom had shouted at the top of her lungs the ultimate insult: butterfly. With rage and anger, the word—butterfly—echoed across the room. Her little fists clenched. She threatened murder. After the *farang* left, Toom threatened to kill herself in true Thai style: slitting each wrist. This was a drama for her friends at the table; an acting out of pain.

Not that she particularly cared about the *farang*—she probably didn't—but his rejection of her for another girl, a stranger, a younger girl, in such a public way, had caused her to lose face in front of all friends. The only people in the world she cared about had looked on as the *farang* rejected her. He had treated her with contempt; as an interchangeable commodity that mattered no more than a bottle of beer. Her face had been lost. If a person lived and died on account of face, the first thing she did was to adopt proven formulas for self-protection. Thais were obsessed by formula; everywhere one looked—at hairstyles, clothes, gold jewels, go-go bars, business, commerce, education, the military, the formula defined, shaped, and controlled the surface: within each sphere was a cage of unwritten rules to measure every action.

There was a formula for selling daughters to brothels. Another formula for being a night worker. Even the names followed a formula. There were about a dozen common names for girls—*Cheu len*—or nickname. The men all had nicknames, too. When you met the girls in a go-go bar at first you had the idea they were mixing up the names. Being coy, or playing social games, or trying to hide their true identity. Nothing could be further from the case. All the Nois, Leks, and Guys, were using their real Thai formula names. Names tagged on them at birth. Usually the name came from a physical attribute or a feeling the mother has about the baby.

"Bun." Tuttle sighed as a twenty-year-old in tight jeans slowly passed their table, surveying the food. "How do you like that for a girl's nickname. *Bun* means merit. Her arrival into this world was merit-making for her mom. Except now Bun makes her merit working at HQ."

"Will you think about coming back to LA? " said Lawrence, sipping his soup. "I'm serious."

"I've lost the template for doing business in America. Or maybe I never had it. In Thailand I know the framework. What you look for at Headquarters is what you look for anywhere else in Thailand: the template of business. Every shop in the country that sells gold is painted red on the outside. Every restaurant that serves non-Thai kinds of soup always delivers it to the table with a cover over the top; but never with a Thai soup."

"This place is like a K-Mart restroom in East LA. Look at that smudged, cracked mirror." Lawrence said, running his finger over a small mirrored panel directly behind his head. "God, it's patched with electrician's tape. Fingerprints. Smeared lipstick."

"That's their secret!" Tuttle was waving his hands and talking in Thai to Lek about the black electrician's tape. "The Thais are an extremely practical people. The world is to be patched not recreated."

The mirrors, though, had a purpose; they were like rear-view mirrors on a cross-country ten-wheel rig, where the entire traffic pattern of the night was captured; a half-step there, a relay of signals between one group of girls and another, a dramatic gesture; Tuttle used the rim of mirrors that circled each booth. He knew they were more than a system of mirrors, they were the communal lens that reflected the tone, image, and mood of everyone who passed, stood, or raced down the narrow ramp of the long, lonely night.

It had taken Tuttle nearly five years of hitting his head against the wall before he understood the Thais' mistrust of anyone who suggested a technique or plan that hadn't been tested. There was almost no curiosity about being the first to try something new just to see if it might work. Something new existed only as a concept and far outside the horizon of a known formula, and the center might not hold. This became "bus driver flees the scene" territory.

If everyone knew precisely the rules, what was expected, what was forbidden, and how things worked, how people reacted, then the chance of losing face was reduced to nearly zero. If you wanted to make an HQ girl happy, you let her know you were aware of the formula, believed in the formula, would honor the formula, and because you had given her a solid guarantee, she could relax and know that her face was safe with you.

There was a formula for handling newly arrived *farang*. Tuttle understood that in Thai there was even a formula for revenge—one that he had taught himself over the years. The first rule was patience; the second rule was gaining the other person's confidence. And the last—the most important came last—create an event that challenges the victim to defeat himself. Tuttle had waited many years for his chance. As he watched Lawrence trying to politely and quietly eat the noodles, Tuttle knew his old roommate didn't stand a chance. He had lived inside the tube of America; and now he had tumbled out and couldn't find his feet. And what were among the first words off Lawrence's lips?

"Do you want a job? I can help you find something. I have connections. I have people who owe me."

All the while Tuttle was laughing inside at these words rolling off Lawrence, the lawyer, and into the smoke-filled air of HQ. Tuttle had his own debt to collect and his own way of collection. But the night was young, and there were many hours before Lawrence understood the scale of things that Tuttle had organized; understood the strategy that had gone into his own defeat.

A couple of tables away from their booth, at one of the center tables four deaf and dumb women—the silent ones some residents called "Tommys"—sat around waiting for their regular customers. The Tommys signed each other over warm Cokes, moving their hands with feeling. They made sex jokes and traded gossip about sexual encounters solely in sign language. The Tommys had a large vocabulary of hand gestures for every sexual act: straight sex, oral sex, anal sex, bondage, S&M, and countless positions and locations for sexual organs and the execution of the sexual act. If it had ever happened in a bedroom or the back of a car, they had a sign for it. Their hands went a hundred miles an hour like major league baseball catchers. Giving a signal. The pitcher waving off that one. Then giving another, followed by a nod as the Tommy and the customer left the premises holding hands.

"What are they doing?" asked Lawrence, pushing back his plate. By now Lek was stroking the inside of his leg with her hand, and nestling her head against his shoulder.

"Two Tommys are discussing the merits of oral sex in parked cars," said Tuttle, giving Lek a pat on her thigh to send her scurrying off.

"Hey, where you going?" asked Lawrence, as Lek slid over his lap.

"She's looking for work, old buddy. You're not buying her out, so you are wasting her time. Or in lawyer's terms, there are other files." Tuttle kissed her hand. A moment later, she turned and disappeared among a group of girls who huddled around a table where the *Maw doo*—fortune teller—was turning over cards and making predictions.

The old woman seated at the crowded table had a wrinkled face caked with makeup; each night she read a Tommy's palm, or some other group of girls, she was an expert reading cards and tea leaves for nineteen baht.

"What's she doing?" asked Lawrence.

"Chances are she's telling the girl that a *farang* with a good heart will appear in the next couple of weeks. He will give her a lot of money, marry her, take her back to America. Buy her a jeep, microwave, and split-level house in a burb outside Houston. The usual list of prizes sought after by girls who grew up working in rice fields and who know a reasonable number of oil riggers."

"She looks ancient," said Lawrence.

"She's two years younger than you, Larry. It's been about two, three years since anyone bought her out. But she never misses a night. Her name, you ask? You'll like this. Her name's Bun. She was here the very first night I walked in twenty-one years ago."

"You actually slept with her?" asked Lawrence, shaking his head, and smiling to himself.

"She told me she was Harvard Law Review."

Lawrence laughed and nodded to himself. "I deserved that."

"Back then she was my neighbor on Soi 22. After three or four years of seeing her almost every day, talking to her, just passing the time, she stopped me and pulled out a chain with a Buddha in a small case. She wore it around her neck as a locket. Most Thais wear one. Another formula. Bun wore a small Buddha image. One night in bed she asked me if I had any idea where she got this tiny Buddha. I shook my head. She smiled with those perfect teeth of hers, and said it was an amulet made from a tooth—a tooth from her deceased father. A tooth pulled out of her dead father's mouth and turned into the perfect formula: a Buddha image."

Another girl with a shy smile sat in the chair in front of the fortune-teller. She laid down two ten-baht notes and shuffled the deck of cards while her friends, standing behind her, looked on. Lawrence moved a chair over from the next table and joined the girls. The fortune teller loved that she had an audience; a *farang* in a Western suit showing interest in her talent brought out the performer in her. She looked up at Lawrence and smiled, keeping her lips closed as she remembered at the last moment that she hadn't put in her teeth. Perhaps her own fortune was changing. The girl leaned forward, all eyes, as she cut the deck into three piles, Tuttle pulled alongside, and began whispering to Lawrence.

"One night I took a friend from Las Vegas to the strip in *Patpong*. I tried to explain the idea of formulas in Thailand to him. I thought he understood. But you can never be certain when people nod their heads, if their brains have registered anything remotely similar to what you said. So we sat in Superladies, watching the girl bathe in a large plastic champagne glass, bubbles lathered over her body, pouring water over her shoulder from a champagne bottle. The red Harley-Davidson motorcycle descending to the stage with a Thai girl and man screwing. The girl straddled the skinny Thai who wore a biker's hat and heavy, black leather jacket with big metal studs stitched on the lapels and chains draped over the shoulders.

"In the best biker tradition, he pumped away, holding her hips as he kept tune to the music: *Jingle Bells*. They shifted position, and the man stood on his knees on the black leather seat as the girl slowly sucked his erect cock, working her mouth to the beat of *Jingle Bells*. My friend gives me a nudge, and leans over and says, 'How could anyone ever celebrate a family Christmas around the piano with Mum and Dad, cousins, uncles, aunts and grandmother again?'

"Everyone singing *Jingle Bells*. You see in Bangkok, there was a motorcycle on stage, and a couple of . . . well performers in mid-March. Yeah, Grandma, it was kind of a religious act. No, they weren't carollers.

"Next, two naked girls on the stage started eating each other. One strapped on a large black plastic dildo, ran a thick strip of K-Y jell down the shaft, rubbed it around until the dildo glistened in the overhead light. The girl wearing the dildo mounted the other girl in the strict missionary position, and had pumped no more than three or four times when the lights flashed off and on. That means a cop has come up looking for a paycheck. The girls bounded from the stage. The dildo bouncing up and down as they ran away. Bus driver fled the scene of the accident. Twenty dancers jumped on stage, their slips pulled to cover their breasts and began dancing in a slow, shy fashion; as if they were standing along the dance floor of a high school prom, moving to the music, innocently looking for a dance partner.

"After the cops left, the fuck show started up again. The glistening dildo reinserted into the pussy of the one girl who lay back with her legs spread high into the air. Her face filled with pleasure as she moaned to the music. Twenty minutes later, my friend paid the bar fine and bought out the girl from the floor show. He took her back to his hotel room. The dildo business had turned his crank; he travelled with a couple of dildos in his suitcase. Put them through airport security x-ray machines, custom inspections, I mean this was a fairly determined guy.

"I heard all of this later from the girl, from a doctor friend, as well as the guy. He's got her stripped down on the bed. He has her distracted with a lot of tongue action. Meanwhile with a free hand, he's grabbed one of his travelling dildos from under the mattress and begins to insert it in the girl's pussy. Her eyes spring wide open, her body stiffens, her hand travels down to between her legs and she feels the plastic dildo, no different in color, texture, or shape from the one that she had taken with such pleasure on stage, and she uncoils like a tiger.

"She's all fist and nails and teeth. He's got scratches all over his face, neck, back, shoulders. He looks like he's been mauled by a wild animal. All because he violated the formula. He robbed the girl of her face. What had happened on stage was a "performance" with another Thai girl; this was a business arrangement with a *farang*. What she did on stage was not an attitude about sexuality; the prescribed template only existed in the context of the show and on the stage. It had little to do with her. This wasn't a tease factor. These weren't Western girls who would try anything once. These were teenagers who walked from one spotlight into the next and never stopped long enough to draw a connection that some *farang* might confuse the public performance with the private one."

The fortune-teller turned over the jack of hearts and smiled. The girl applauded as the fortune-teller explained that a man would propose to her within three months, and that he would have much money, and that she would have a great deal of good luck. Tuttle had begun to translate the fortune-teller's predictions for Lawrence's benefit. Though Lawrence's lawyer mind was still digesting the images of the scratched face, limbs, and back of Tuttle's friend and the enraged face of the bar girl turned lunatic.

Finally Lawrence leaned over and whispered to Tuttle. "They really believe this fortune-telling stuff?"

"And in ghosts and in multiple lives. Along with quantum physics and cancer research. And they see no contradiction."

Tuttle had learned that in Thailand people believed that they were born with a karma. Life was not a process of bettering oneself; but accepting one's lot with serenity, a smile, and a *Mai bpen rai*— "no problem" attitude towards adversity. Whatever happened in this life was destined from a prior life. And there was no way to alter one's fate. Happiness was accepting one's position. Happiness was being with people who understood and respected that position. People who always smiled and laughed; people who were lighter than air. The unhappy or angry were avoided; no one who complained was liked. They danced to one simple tune—and the beat went on, and on. Accept your fate, gain merit, respect those above you for they have earned this life and if you're an HQ working girl, then you've earned that from your last life. That's your rain-making dance; looking for the heavens to open and the money to pour down.

"What did that girl just say? The one who was pointing at us?" asked Lawrence, looking over a short Thai girl in a miniskirt, who was smoking a cigarette and smiling at them.

"She said, 'You can fly only as high as your wings will take you.' It's an old Thai saying. Don't ever expect your wings to take you higher. Or you will crash and burn, and the ashes that fall into the next life will be remoulded into a creature that you don't even want to give a name."

"What a curious thing to say."

Tuttle waived for Meow to come over. She bounded over and sat on Tuttle's knee.

"This is my friend, Larry. He's from America."

Meow raised her hand to shake with Lawrence. As Lawrence reached out to shake, she pulled the old bar trick of quickly withdrawing her hand, leaving his hand foolishly isolated in midair.

"How far have your wings taken you?" Tuttle asked, spinning Meow around on his lap. He asked the question again, this time in Thai, and Meow leaned forward and kissed him on the nose.

Meow's friend began massaging Lawrence's shoulders.

"How far will your wings take you, Bobby?"

Tuttle smiled and nuzzled his nose into Meow's neck. "As far as the moon." Sarah's death had suddenly sprung open the cage door and Tuttle was perched ready to take flight, and Lawrence was the runway.

YOU stayed inside the established formula. Don't risk breaking new ground—if you value your face. Avoid people who spring surprises on you; the *farang* might throw you off balance. Outside the formula you were lost. You can fail; make mistakes. Failure accumulates bad karma in this life. The loss of Sarah had been Tuttle's first major failure. The first emotional bruise that had never healed. If there was a next life, Sarah was in it at that moment. And she'd be in the next one after that. She was locked inside a hall of mirrors.

Tuttle had spent years searching for the elusive spiritual dimension. The shaman's trance, the monk's begging bowl, the temple Buddhas, the amulet from a dead man's tooth, the nineteen-baht fortune-teller, came to him as fragments of that same dimension. If a person could make enough merit, she might be reborn in the center of the universe, Bangkok, to a higher position than the one she had left. It had been Lawrence who had thrown her off-track; stopped her from going away with him; the man who had phoned Sarah's mother and father, who flew down to prevent their daughter from leaving.

He knew, however, that he needed to counsel patience. Lawrence had to be handled carefully; he couldn't be rushed or the entire plan would collapse. Why had his friend left Bangkok with twenty-eight stitches in his body? He had pulled a rabbit out of his hat at the last moment. The girl hadn't been prepared.

Suddenly she turned all claws and teeth against this force that threatened to load her down with a mountain of bad karma; she slashed, ripped, and cut the devil who came to secure her rebirth at a lower position in the next life. He had pushed her over a spiritual edge that in her eyes had condemned her face and her soul. And there was a bill to pay. A bill she collected by burying her nails in his flesh. Tuttle was convinced he would have the pleasure of presenting his own outstanding bill to Lawrence. With the accumulated interest, there was a large outstanding debt, Tuttle told himself; a debt that he would have the satisfaction of collecting.

4

By the third drink Lawrence had relaxed, his clipped speech slowed, his tense posture loosened. The aloof exterior had begun to crack, concealing a keen interest in the whirl of girls washed in by the early tide of the evening. He had taken off his tie and rolled up his shirt sleeves. He had paid the fortune-teller to read his cards. Tuttle sat next to him, leaning forward looking at the card, listening to the old woman, and translating her prediction. "You will meet the woman of your life in Bangkok," said Tuttle.

"Get away," said Lawrence.

"She will bring an emotional disturbance. But you win her."

"I like that," said Lawrence.

Later, Tuttle led the retreat to his booth as the crowd of young women in bright, painted faces, their red fingernails clawing the air, swelled; here and there, a girl discreetly scooped up her handbag, nodded towards a *farang* and disappeared through the narrow passageway leading to the alley, the *farang* walking two feet ahead, turning, motioning, waiting, and joking. Reappearing a couple of hours later, she might buy a round of drinks for her friends.

"Erotic encounters all night long," said Lawrence. "I could use a few associates with this work ethic."

"You might want to take one back," replied Tuttle in a serious tone.

"For what?"

"You're the pension lawyer. Think of her as an annuity." Lawrence laughed. "Think of me introducing a Thai service girl at the firm Christmas party."

"You could tell them it was in the cards," said Tuttle, looking over at the fortune-teller, who met his glance with a stiff nod of recognition.

"They would think I had gone off the deep end."

"The deep end is more interesting than the shallow end, Larry."

Lawrence produced a note pad and a pen from his suit jacket and began writing. He looked up for a moment, and then resumed. Then he folded the paper in two and handed it to Tuttle, who opened and read it.

"Sixty-thousand dollars," said Tuttle, refolding the paper.

"That's what I would start you at the firm. Office Manager," said Lawrence. "Computer systems analyst. You tell me what title you want. It can be in the cards for you."

Tuttle slid the paper back to Lawrence. "Sixty thou and I can create my own title? Thanks, Larry. But I figure I wouldn't fit in too well back there."

Lawrence shook his head. "I don't get it. What's the attraction. Bangkok's polluted. Gridlocked with cars, criminals, and crazies. No one speaks English. It's hotter than hell. The army calls the shots. Rabid dogs on the streets."

"All true. But you're missing the carnival."

"What carnival?" Lawrence blinked looking at Tuttle, then down at his own handwriting.

"The carnival all around us. The one we are part of. This is what I belong to. I can't pull out. This is what I am, always have been. Sarah's parents' worst fear come true."

From the way Lawrence looked down at the table, Tuttle was certain he hadn't made the connection. Tuttle thought of him as someone who had stepped out of the new Dark Age, someone who harboured the illusion that he lived in the Golden Age of Man, a place where titles and dollars were in the hands of the Gods of that place. Lawrence's world mirrored the same commercial values which had taken root in Southeast Asia. In America and Asia, there were no longer any ceremonies performed to rescue the fallen man, the fallen woman; they had fallen because they lacked merit in this life, and this life was the only one that mattered. There could be no resurrection from failure in such a world. Economic progress was the gravity that warped the system of thought, values, and activity, not so much replacing morality as making it just another market force.

Tuttle wasn't clear where to begin; or if he should even bother explaining. It had taken him years before he understood the attraction of HQ—nearly a generation of back-to-back nights of spending time at HQ before the realization hit home. The attraction that made him get out of bed in the morning, and put one foot in front of the other all through the day, so that when midnight came, he had cleared away the debris and obstructions of the day. He knew what to expect; inside were two generations of exiles, Thai and *farang* fragments of the same whole, resting against one another, finding themselves in each other and with no other place left.

In all of Southeast Asia, this was the one place that drew him back, forced him to return; and in that space between choice and no choice he found himself sweeping the room. He had long ago stopped expecting to find a surprise inside HQ. What he found was a time chamber in the heart of Bangkok where on a given night the clocks and calendars appeared to have stopped in 1968. On another night-time locked into 1975, and yet another in the misty future of 2050. HQ was a spiritual transport system that travelled in excess of the emotional speed of light. Inside that time lock Tuttle searched for something he had missed before; something hidden away from sight, in his own past, in one of the girls . . . and then, he had spotted her.

A girl who fell outside any formula. Although Thai society did everything in its power to seal off all avenues of surprise; they were possible to find. Because such women—ones like Sarah—were so rare, they possessed great personal value for those tired to death with the formula. They possessed great power in a world of sameness, of patterns that repeated, of words that said nothing. Tuttle knew the *hard-core* mind ultimately drifted away from the whole to the individual part; those were the small details that kept the memory from turning into a vast still gray ocean; the girls a large pod of silver marine mammals turning as one large shiny wave deep below the surface.

He nodded toward the jukebox. "Larry, see the girl in the red running shoes dancing between the jukebox and the bar? I'm particularly interested in the region two inches to the right of her belly button. To the right heading toward her crotch. What does that look like to you?"

Lawrence strained his eyes in the bad light. He shrugged his shoulders. "Some kind of scar." He guessed, twisting his mouth at the hard moment of decision.

"Looks like a shadow hole that an old bullet wound leaves. A .38 police special slug makes a punctuation mark like that."

Lawrence looked closer. "Christ, you are joking?" From Tuttle's expression, though, it was evident that he was serious. Lawrence recovered, shaking his head. "Who would shoot a girl like that?"

"You never forget the look of bullet holes in a body. Every coup and bush war throws out bodies like hers. Maybe her secondary navel was created by a freak accident or by a bullet. Every old hand in Asia has their own story of strange scars on the bodies on the girls."

Sarah's shattered face loomed before Lawrence. His hands began trembling, and the color drained from his face. A freak accident, Lawrence thought. The fat slob of a graduate student had stopped. The result was no different than if he had shot Sarah through the head.

"You okay?" asked Tuttle.

"Bullets. Bullets. Bobby, you ever take a girl who'd been shot?" Lawrence tried to smile, keeping his trembling hands beneath the table, out of sight from those who would judge him.

"Only on one live girl. Bullets in the dead don't count. Because those holes never heal up. Only bullet holes rich with scar tissue are ever discussed in polite company at HQ. We have our standards; our traditions and values to uphold. My bullet hole victim was an HQ girl nicknamed Nop. About seven years ago I booked her for a home appointment after the usual five-minute interview. A power center interview near the jukebox. Nop came into HQ alone. First rule of the night is to find out what *peu-un pod* the girl belongs to. The girls run in packs of three to five in number. *peu-un pods.* Thai-English which translates roughly as friendship groups. The *hard-core girls* travelled inside a *peu-un pod* with the navigational skill of dolphins. But Nop was a straggler. She was smart; she knew strategic location straight off. She came in like she owned the place. No one intimidated her. She stood her ground near the best location in the place—beside the jukebox. The regular girls huddled in their *peu-un pod* grumbling about Nop; she was an invader in their territory, someone pretty enough to snatch a purple from their clutched hand. All those eyes watched as I ran her through the regulation interview.

"Nop was not just another strikingly beautiful girl. The kind you forget six months down the road as if she had never entered your life. Was she ever in my bed? Immediately there was something different about her. She had come from Jakarta, and was no more than twenty, though she tried to pass herself off as seventeen."

❖

IN the bedroom, Nop faced Tuttle as she undressed by candlelight. Thai girls were reasonably shy about removing their clothes in front of a stranger. They hated men staring at their nakedness. But this girl seemed to invite Tuttle's eyes on her breasts. She had been born in Jakarta and she spoke some English. Tuttle put her boldness down to her background. Just as he had made up his mind, she made a half turn to hang up her blouse. Tuttle saw her scar. Halfway between her shoulder blades was a depression large enough to insert a tongue tip. The depression of flesh in her back looked like an empty eye socket in the shadows crisscrossing the room.

The surprise caused Tuttle to shift his mental gears. One minute earlier, he had been stripped naked, arms stretched out, and ready to pull her onto the bed. Instead, Tuttle found himself sitting on his knees, his erection gone, inspecting this weird hole in her back. She looked like she'd stepped in front of a rocket launcher sometime in the not too-distant past.

Tuttle asked her, "When were you wounded?" Perhaps one of the most strange questions ever to be asked in the realm of sexual foreplay.

The question didn't seem the slightest bit odd to her; he obviously had not been the first to ask. If she had wanted to hide the scar, that would have been possible with an artful combination of darkness and dressing gowns. Nop had displayed the scar because she had wanted it to be noticed; because she wanted to talk about it.

The scar had come from a spear. Nop had been in the army.

"The army? No way," Tuttle had said. What was she, a time traveller? Out of some *Blade Runner* territory? "Spear? No one has been speared for five hundred years." A statement he knew was not literally true; but he couldn't bring himself to believe that this tender, young, beautiful girl had been speared. Raped, yes.

She had heard that tone of disbelief before. Nop disappeared out of the bedroom and into the living room where she had left her hand bag. A couple of minutes earlier, Tuttle had slipped into a pair of red jogging shorts. And Nop had climbed into a matching pair. They sat next to each other on Tuttle's queen-sized bed. Half a dozen candles continued to burn though every available light had been switched on. Together they looked through an incredible series of photographs. There was Nop in picture after picture. She was dressed in a camouflage army uniform and holding a rifle. Her black eyes stared straight into the camera. In another she was on a shooting range; another in a bar. The last photos were of Nop in the hospital bed, turned on her side, the bandages pulled back and the large, red hole stitched with a reel of thread. Beside the bed was a spear. A long wood spear with a metal tip. Tuttle glanced over at Nop who lay on her stomach, legs raised, ankles hooked behind and then back at the photograph.

"You got speared?" Tuttle pressed his thumb against the spear in the photo.

"Ambushed by a bullshit tribe," she replied.

"A hellava lot more interesting than a bullet hole," Tuttle said, turning her around and inspecting the spear hole again. Bullet holes are a dime a dozen compared with spear wounds. You've got it documented. You got speared in the army. Must have hurt like hell."

"Got out of the army. No so bad," she said.

"You're a veteran. In America they'd have given you a Purple Heart and a pension. Here all you get is a purple." Tuttle fell back on the bed and wrapped a pillow over his face. From beneath he asked her in a muffled voice to leave. He rose up and gave her a thousand baht.

During the rainy season, Nop was one of the women he thought about when flood waters turned his soi into a river filled with snakes and shit and garbage; and soi dogs and fruit bats disappeared for days at a time. And he would say to himself, things aren't so fucked up. It could be worse. He could have been speared. He found himself using her explanation whenever something bad had happened: Ambushed by a bullshit tribe.

It had crossed his mind that she was smart enough to pay a doctor to engrave the scar; like the beggars who had limbs amputated to increase sympathy. He had given her a thousand baht; she had left without doing anything more than show her wound, tell her story, and flip through a book of old photographs. Whenever those doubts filled his mind, he remembered the photograph of the spear near her hospital bed. She had deserved a Purple Heart. Like all combat veterans, Nop was a true survivor; and that was the lesson she had brought to the bedroom. Wear your scars out in the open, carry your past into the light, and never forget your feeling at the moment the tip of the spear enters your flesh.

TUTTLE pointed out the arrival of a regular customer named Pablo. He was a pale, thin Spaniard, with a pockmarked, narrow face, sallow except around the eyes where the folds of skin had turned a lumpy grayish color. Pablo fondled a girl sitting on his right; he had brought her into Zeno's. His nickname was the Ratman of Bangkok. For more than ten years he had owned bars in Soi Cowboy. Each time, though, the Ratman became too visible in his success; he was always around the bar, bragging about his profits and how many girls he took back to his apartment each night.

The Ratman couldn't keep his hands off his talents. They had no respect for him; they gossiped behind his back that he was a lousy lover. Tensions built up. The girls stopped listening to him. Around the same time some influential person would learn of the Ratman's success and his personnel problems. The Ratman never paid attention. Not until someone would come to the bar one night and inform him that he was selling.

"But I don't want to sell." And the progression was always the same.

"You stay Thailand long time. You know it wise to sell if right man make you offer. I that right man, Khun Pablo." The speech was not difficult for the Ratman to decode. He had been in Thailand long enough to understand how threats were made. But the Ratman had never learned from his mistake; and he repeated the same one over and over. His next question was always the same. Standing on one foot, leaning over the bar as the Chinese businessmen in the tailored suit reached into his jacket pocket.

"How much am I selling for?"

And the buyer would hand him a cheque.

"This amount." And the transaction was done.

"THAT'S duress," said Lawrence. "He could have the transaction set aside. Don't people use lawyers here?"

"They have found that a gunman is cheaper and more efficient." Tuttle waved at Pablo, who bent over and whispered something to the girl at his side. He began making his way through the crowd to their booth. "He's coming over. Maybe you can give him some legal advice."

The first thing out of Pablo's mouth was his usual story that he had forever abandoned go-go bar ownership. This time he had found the right business. He had become an exporter, selling expensive clothes to wealthy Latinos in Miami, New York, and LA. He shook Lawrence's hand, his eyes falling on Lawrence's Rolex and moving over to the label on the suit jacket draped over the booth.

"Noi was getting her fortune told," the Ratman said, glancing over at Tuttle. "All bullshit. Didn't you once know her?"

Noi slid into the booth and pressed her thigh against Tuttle.

"We've met," said Tuttle, putting his hand on Noi's knee.

"I warn you about Tuttle, sir. Do not ever let him around any woman of yours. He can't be trusted. I know from bitter experience. Ever since the days of the three sisters of Sukhumvit, he's always been first. He's the only man in Bangkok who had all three sisters." Pablo's rodent eyes, watery and bloodshot, blinked several times, as he slowly shook his head.

"That was a long time ago, Pablo."

"I never forget," the Ratman said.

Tuttle had turned his attention to Noi. "Where you working now?" Tuttle asked Noi in English.

"*Tilac Bar. Soi Cowboy.*"

"Long time since I see you," Tuttle said.

"Your friend buy me out."

"Quality goes early," said Pablo. "And she's new. Less than a month on the game."

This was the first time in almost a year since Tuttle had seen her. He had first met Noi several years earlier in *Nana Plaza* in another go-go bar. At that time she was a dancer only; she refused to go out with the *farang*. Tuttle had been her first man ever. In twenty-one years, his second virgin. He hired her as his maid so she could quit the bar. Noi had fallen deeply in love with him. She owed him obligation; for taking her out of the bar; for taking her into his house; for giving her money, clothes, and affection. Yet something about her had frightened Tuttle. Her passion, or intensity, or basic decency. She was a rare commodity: a nice kid who had been no more than eighteen when he took her virginity.

There had been a trial separation. She had gone to the Philippines to stay with her sister for almost four months. When she returned, Tuttle shipped her off to *Chiang Mai*; she stayed with her family. Then less than a month ago she had drifted back to Bangkok. Taking a go-go dancer's job at Tilac. The one in the low-cut bikini with the sad eyes and big breasts. She had been bought out every other night.

In HQ as she laid her head against Tuttle's shoulder, she began to cry. Lawrence took a white handkerchief from his jacket and offered it to Noi. The Ratman rolled his eyes and lit a cigarette. He had bought her. There was his purchase crying her eyes out against the one man who had always been first around the corner.

"I love your friend too, too much," she said, turning to Lawrence, blowing her nose in his handkerchief. "But he no love me. I cannot forget him. Try and try but cannot. Maybe you talk your friend you for me."

Tuttle, with a frozen smile on his face, clutched his hand in a fist and pretended to pull on his heart and throw it on the floor. Emotions clouded Lawrence's face as he looked between Noi and Tuttle. If only Sarah could be alive this moment, he thought. She had put this man on some kind of pedestal, and he had almost fallen for Tuttle's myth as well, offering him a job. Lawrence felt like a fool; his face flushed, and then he felt angry.

55

Noi fought that wave of desolation as it rolled over her, knocking the wind from her; she had trouble holding her head up, looking at Tuttle's eyes. Pablo reached out with his tiny, bony hands and pulled Noi's wrist tight in a vise grip. She clutched onto Tuttle's leg and rested her head against his shoulder as if to say, "Please help me, don't let this feeling suck me down—rob me of my smile—rob me of my dignity." She was hurting so much.

"Ambushed by bullshit tribe," said Tuttle softly to Lawrence as Noi and the Ratman had a tug-of-war inside the booth. Tuttle had left a wide, deep scar. Did she deserve this? Did anyone ever deserve to be ambushed in life? But it happened every day and night in every bar, city, and bullshit country. Noi's wound would heal and she would toughen up on her way down the *hard-core* path. Down a road where the sad, lonely, and abandoned pressed forward with lives that no longer dreamed. Pablo finally levered Noi out of the booth as Tuttle simply stared straight ahead pretending not to notice. He wouldn't meet her eyes. Perhaps he couldn't.

"How can you do that to another human being?" Lawrence asked, losing his sense of speech; he started another sentence but couldn't find the words to complete it.

"You mean I didn't offer her a title and sixty thousand a year?" Tuttle was addled by the confrontation. He leaned back, legs stretched out. "Instead, I speared her, right, Larry? You look for the still point, and that's where the dance is. And when you find it, out of time and out of space, that's non-space where you choose your weapons. Where you find and discard your partners. It is the non-time and non-space where you have the chance to find and discard the self. Her self. Your self."

"That's just bullshit. You fucked her over. Dress it up any way you want. Bangkok hasn't improved your character, Bobby." Lawrence followed Noi's backward-looking eyes as she left through the back entrance. The Ratman dragged her along like a child.

"Another F in my report card," Tuttle said, glancing at Noi one last time before she disappeared. Tears streaked down her face. It all depends who sets the questions, marks the answers, and the standard of what is passing; and beyond, the meaning of conduct that passes and that which fails, thought Tuttle. He decided to leave Lawrence with that warm feeling of vindication.

Every safari-shirted waiter who passed the table paid Tuttle respect, and addressed him by name. The same waiters who wouldn't know the names of more than a dozen people, including their own family called him Khun Tut, his nickname. They automatically brought him his beef in oyster sauce and white rice and Mekong and tonic. This was his club, his life, the place where a million dreams had passed through the still point, and became part of the dance that never moved but never stopped. Why was it that he felt so strongly Sarah's spirit that evening? Lawrence's physical presence, of course, was the obvious answer; the conservative lawyer who held up the mirror to his past and he no longer recognized his own face in that old glass.

Twenty-one years was a long time in a place like Bangkok for a *farang*; sufficient time for his life to wrap endlessly around the coiled lives and hearts of people to whom he would always remain an outsider.

"That one in the far booth. Nice girl. I've known her since about '75. Sometimes I help her out with a letter. And that one over there with the ponytail. She's inside the booth with the black guy. I've got photos of her ten years ago. She has a nearly perfect body. And the one in the yellow dress. I never had her, but an old roommate of mine did. He said she was very sweet. You can see it in her face."

"I see a lot of sadness," said Lawrence. "In her face. Forget the cute girl smile; it doesn't fool me. Not for a minute."

"Count yourself a lucky man. You've never been fooled by a smile or a frown. I haven't been so lucky. Not even with Sarah. Sarah used to hide letters from her mother. She said her parents were out of her life. That she was standing on her own two feet. That there were just the two of us. Of course, it was a lie. The whole time she was plugged into this secret channel open to her past. Right under my nose. I told her how brave she was. That it took real guts to put me above her own family. To cut herself off from them and their guilt."

Lawrence said nothing, turned and ordered another drink. He had decided to order doubles from that point on. Another plate of food arrived: hamburgers and French fries. Lawrence's eyes lit up; at last, here was some food he could recognize. A secret channel, thought Lawrence. If only Tuttle knew the underground passage

Sarah had built beneath their married life a few letters would seem trivial. He wished he had implied Tuttle was a fool; he wished Tuttle hadn't admitted it so quickly.

"The burgers are from that guy at the bar," said Tuttle, motioning over at Crosby who was deep in conversation with a girl, no more that sixteen, in an old ballroom gown. "He thinks Americans only like hamburgers. It's one of his little jokes."

THERE were strange connections between the circles of Bangkok *farang*. Wisdom was allocated in scattered pockets of memory. Tuttle often acted as the memory exchange; at times, he appeared to know more than the individual parts that had been stored in his mind over the years. Sooner or later, all their paths crossed in Zeno's, their common hunting ground. The old hands knew the good places to spot fresh game. They talked like hunters, stalked like hunters, bragged and lied and drank like hunters. Some of the expats were smarter on the hunt than any other compartment of their lives; others excelled at their job but never developed the instinct for the hunt.

The key was learning how to track, how to patiently wait out the prey, and how to aim and fire at the target from the hip. With unlimited game and an open season, it didn't take an enormous amount of natural talent to have success. A generation below was a new breed of younger male hunters. A male *peu-un pods* of *farangs*. And Andrew Crosby acted as their unofficial leader. A young Englishman born in Bangkok. His father ran a successful trading company. Crosby had been born into wealth, the large house, servants, and fast cars.

His pod members, like Crosby, were in their mid-twenties but more cynical than any forty-five-years-old. *Farangs* didn't come any more *hard-core* than Crosby; at twenty-six, he had slept with over one thousand women. An impressive number until compared with a popular fifteen-year-old brothel girl who worked behind a plate glass window in the back streets of *Isan* towns like *Udon Thani* or *Nakhon Ratchasima*. She might run up Crosby's lifetime number in six months of work. In Crosby's case, the exercise of the night was less like hunting than it was shooting fish in a barrel. He could find a whorehouse blindfolded.

Crosby timed his move to the booth carefully. A couple of minutes after Lawrence had finished one of the hamburgers, he strolled over to the booth. He had a fleshy round face, receding hair where blue veins were visible just below the skin as if his head was one of those wristwatches that allowed the wearer to look at the moving clockwork inside. Crosby stood on one foot, smoking a Lucky Strike cigarette, his nicotine-stained hands dug into his trouser pockets. His small double chin gave him an elflike quality, giving the appearance of a world-weary choir boy with eyes as bright as polished chrome. Crosby's narrow, rounded shoulders and the makings of a potbelly were physical characteristics most responsible for his premature middle aged look. His smoky, pale complexion suggested too much time had been spent inside closed rooms. He nodded back at the sixteen year-old in the ballgown.

"You had that one?" asked Crosby.

Tuttle shook his head and glanced over at the youngster who stood with her back leaning against the bar as Crosby carried out his intelligence mission.

"She admits only to three days on the game," he said.

Tuttle stepped in to the girl's defence. "It's possible. New girls show up every week, Andrew."

"But she could have splayed toes?" asked Crosby. "I hate that. Or even worse, is she a floor-pisser? I hate floor-pissers because the maid raises hell in the morning. And I can't blame her."

Lawrence had stopped chewing a French fry and stared up at Crosby.

"A friend of mine from the States. Lawrence Baring."

"What is a floor-pisser?" asked Lawrence, swallowing the half chewed fries.

Crosby's eyes lit up; he loved explaining the more bizarre habits and customs of the girls who came on the overnight bus from a remote village in the far North.

"What's a floor-pisser, you ask? Upcountry they live in shacks on poles. When they have to take a piss they go and squat in the corner of the house. Everything drops through the cracks into the dirt below. When little Noi comes to Bangkok, and you take her home, and she has to take a piss, she goes over to a corner, hikes up her skirt, and before you know it, there is a large puddle on your floor."

"A cultural difference," added Tuttle, trying to shift off the subject. But Crosby had merely warmed up as Lawrence sat spellbound.

"It happened to me," said Crosby, smiling at Tuttle.

"You urinated on your own floor?" asked Lawrence.

Crosby nodded casually. "I was pissed. A girl was sound asleep next to me. She had piled her clothes on the floor. I dreamt that I was standing over a toilet. I ended up pissing on her clothes. Next morning she was very nice about it. Never mind, she said. I gave her one of my shirts; her shirt wasn't exactly fit to wear. Mind you, she did take it away. Gave it a good wash and she had it on when she hit the street the next night. The girls tend not to get overly stressed. Not like your average American women who have been known to maul a man who forgets to put down the toilet seat."

Crosby was in a class of his own. He roamed through that broad expanse of bars, politicians' statements, and understood the sensitive chord in what drove that overheated sex itch seven days a week in thousands of locations through the city. It was not a push for him, or for anyone. He knew one of the secrets—there was no competition for women, every man crossed the finish line a winner night after night. On the flip side was the boredom of knowing one could always possess what one desired sexually any time of the day or night. Such knowledge could take a toll. But Bangkok was the only home he had known. He carried no emotional luggage from another place. This was a normal way of living as far as he knew.

Crosby had so much contact with that reality during the crucial, painful growing-up period of his life. He had no delusions about the meaning of pleasure in Bangkok. About what the girls wanted, what they thought, or dreamed. Crosby had taken that small boat of dreams out from the shore many times with countless girls over the years. Nothing ever happened. The earth didn't move. The sky didn't dissolve into an immense choir of singing angels. Crosby's truth glistened in the neon-lit eyes of bar girls, their bodies streaked with perspiration, and their narrow hips pounding to a ritual dance.

The truth was a vision of a world that was small, stagnant, insipid, timeless, and savage. A colossal observation tank with thousands of tiny compartments, serving up girls with exceptional and gifted bodies. The Crosby peu-un pod had lost their memories altogether; all their women having merged into the night, faces they could never reclaim. All they remembered was the act of collecting; what had been collected was simply forgotten, shed like a snake's skin down the road of the past.

After Crosby had gone away, Lawrence shoved the plate of half eaten French fries out of reach. "He pissed on her clothes," said Lawrence, shaking his head.

"It was a mistake," said Tuttle, reaching for a French fry. "Everyone makes mistakes. Even lawyers, Larry."

"But he doesn't know me. How can you tell someone you just met that you were so drunk you urinated on a woman's clothes? Doesn't anyone screen their private acts?"

"Maybe Crosby doesn't care one way or the other whether you like him," said Tuttle, leaning on his elbows and watching as Crosby waved off the ball-gowned teenager. She had failed the standard interview; the screening process where the *hard-core* ask if the ceremony of innocence is drowned in her. Because it has long been drowned in him; and he still clutches to the belief that innocence can be reclaimed.

"It's not a question of liking him."

"What's the question then?"

Lawrence paused, drummed his fingers on the table. "I don't know." He cracked a smile and shook his head, as he was unable to escape from the intellectual corner he had parked himself. Tuttle had been throwing his shock troops at him. His personal life was filled with men sheared off from a normal life; men whose lives were not embroidered with the same pattern of obstacles, interests, or loyalties. They shared a dark struggle but Lawrence couldn't locate the alley where they hung out their fears and doubts to dry. That's what troubled him about both Crosby and Pablo; these men of ice who lived at an emotional altitude where everything was rock and dirt; a place where nothing of life grew, let alone flourished.

"I simply don't know," repeated Lawrence, looking back at Crosby.

For the first time Tuttle remembered why he had liked Lawrence in their college days. Lawrence was honest; pushed in the corner, he had never lied to get out. What Tuttle also remembered, the dark side, where Lawrence wasn't above letting someone else lie for him.

5

George Snow danced over to the booth, his weathered face stretched tightly over his skull the shape of a light bulb. Snow was stoned and grinding his teeth in a twisted smile at a couple of HQ regulars blocking his path. A few sweating matted strands of chest hair sticking out of his Hawaiian shirt. Snow always wore the same uniform: an untucked Hawaiian shirt, jeans, and white tennis shoes. His thick glasses made his eyes appear two times larger than life. Snow's short-cropped hair thinned at the temples, and the ragged edge of a cheap haircut curved around the base of the neck. He always looked in need of a shave. Sweat dripped from his chin and nose, and he was constantly wiping his face with tissues that he balled up and tossed on the floor. He loved Bangkok, the Beach Boys, and California. And he hated lawyers.

"Tuttle, hey, man. I gave one of our old-time favorites, good ole Lek, two-baht for a golden oldie. Jukebox number? . . . number 215 . . . Man, you won't believe what this guy knows! He's the only man in the universe who remembers the number of every song on the HQ jukebox."

"I'm impressed," said Lawrence, smiling at Tuttle.

"He's not wasted twenty years." He turned to Tuttle, reaching over and scooping up a hand of French fries. "When you die they're gonna put a bronze plaque with your name on it over the jukebox. It's gonna say Tuttle knew every song and face by heart. Number 215. 'Like a Virgin'. That ought to be the theme song on Friday nights at HQ. They should use some imagination. Come up with themes. A little inspiration. Something that draws in a better kind of crowd. And most of all, it gives you something to look forward to. If you can't be a virgin, be like a virgin. There's the theme for the '90s. There's always another way, man. There's always another way in Thailand."

"I've been in Bangkok three days. And the advice I'm getting is all over the place," said Lawrence. Tuttle's eyes narrowed slightly, a grin appeared on his face, Lawrence was learning faster than he thought possible.

"Forget everything Tuttle's told you. Just listen to this plan; you follow it, and your life will be filled with women and the good life. Scout out a remote, a to-hell-and-gone *Lahu* village. Man, you gotta travel light. Tuttle here is the expert on packing the small bag and finding a girl to carry it. Put everything in a light shoulder bag. Staging is important. The most important thing in any fucking production. That and light and costume. What do you put inside the bag? All you pack are half a dozen magic tricks. You phone a speciality magic shop in Manhattan. It'd cost you fifteen bucks for ten minutes. Give them your American Express number and just fucking order and order. Make certain they courier the stuff or you'll be waiting around HQ for years like Tuttle here trying to get your shit together and break away."

Tuttle raised his head and Snow stopped talking for a second. "Ask him what goes on the shopping list," said Tuttle, giving Lawrence a wink as a nineteen-year-old who spoke no more than a dozen words of English climbed on his lap and kissed him on each eyebrow.

"The shopping list? Okay, first buy that illusion of fire that leaps from the palm of the hand. It blows people away. They can't explain it; they can't fucking believe it. Fire jets. A crowd forms in seconds. Next go for the illusion called "Hot Lava"; mutant lava spits straight from your fingertips. And to keep your act in high gear, throw in a few multicolored scarves, some ropes that you cut into pieces and then with a move of your hand the rope is one piece again. And the clincher act is great, man. You swallow a handful of needles and about three feet of white thread. Then you slowly pull the thread out. Each needle is lined up like clothes pegs on the thread. Five minutes later you're crowned as Lahu Godman. Your audience becomes your subjects. They only want to please you. There's no future in pissing off a god.

"You won't be the first Lahu Godman to come down the pike. The Lahu got a fucked-up history of Messianic movements. Like clockwork every twenty-five years some wando stumbles into one of their villages, claims the title, leads them to revolt, and gets a large number of them massacred. The Lahu are overdue. It's been more than twenty-five years, man. Show one or two of the illusions—magicians never call them tricks—to the headman of the village, and you're in business as Lahu Godman XIV."

Droplets of sweat rolled off Snow's upper lip as he spoke. He drank two Klosters, and ordered a third as he laid out the Lahu Godman plan for Lawrence. Tuttle had heard Snow's struggle with reality before. He was content to let Snow carry on uninterrupted. Lawrence had showed some interest in Snow's planned compact with the devil. That intrigued Tuttle; this spore of interest in a mechanical device used for deceit. He tried to imagine Lawrence dressed up in hilltribe shaman clothing, and the troubled, awe-struck faces of the villagers as he pulled threaded needles out of his throat.

"Why haven't you applied for the job?" Lawrence asked. "Why hasn't Tuttle?"

It was one of those questions that carried the merchandise of their mutual past. At college Tuttle had led an exclusive group of students. He had the kind of power that people would have gladly relinquished their possessions or money to join his band, if he had asked that of them. Even after he had gone, his ghostly influence had remained; an underground voice that could never be ignored or dismissed. Tuttle had become a *hard-core*, another two-bit high-density Lahu Godman, Lawrence thought. Tuttle had forfeited his claim to the myth of a man who had fled civilization to find spiritual communion deep into the jungles of Southeast Asia. But when fully understood, Lawrence was convinced, Tuttle had not become some primordial explorer but another of countless *farangs* who had been stranded on the slime mould of Zeno's.

"Every night Tuttle auditions for the Lahu Godman role. Does he get a call back? No way, Jose. He pays his purple COD like the rest of us. He's not a student of the visuals. Tuttle would only get hurt. The Lahu would take him apart like an edible berry."

"Why not stay here? There's no shortage of women," said Lawrence.

Snow glanced at Tuttle and smiled. "You ain't told him, man?" asked Snow. Tuttle shook his head as the girl on his lap massaged his neck.

"Told me what?" asked Lawrence, looking back and forth between Snow and Tuttle.

"You share this ant colony with every anteater in the world, man. We're talking about well-used girls who have been fondled, fingered, licked, and sucked by legions of the unwashed rejects from New York to Berlin. Get real lucky and you might find a ringer. And you know what? Every resident shows up looking for the same invisible, supernatural girl who descends from the heavens above the jukebox. She walks over to your booth, hooks her finger, and says follow me. But she ain't never coming; she don't exist, and that's why we have to invent her. Pray for her coming one night. Meanwhile, you end up with another girl who Gunter or Wolfgang has pawed and gnawed the night before."

"Magic," said Tuttle, brushing the hair away from the girl's face on his lap. "That's what you were saying, Snow."

"That's it. Magic. Take the bus north of *Chiang Mai*. Stop at any shithole village. Climb off in the middle of nowhere and hike up a mountain. Find a hill tribe with a tradition of Godmen. Then audition for the role. You show them a lava flow, and straightaway you get a long term contract. Next, you settle into the village. Close it off to those fucking trekkers. Man, no fucking trekkers, yuppie lawyers and accountants ever get in. To make your point, leak a little lava; throw a jet of fire out of the palm of your hand. You got their attention now. So you roll with it. Second order of the day—and this is why you've called New York City at great expense, paid for a courier to get the illusions delivered—is the numero uno. You call the headmen of the village, sit them down in a circle. Smoke a few pipes of opium to mellow them out. Then you lay the trip on them."

Snow paused, licking his thin, dry lips; his eyes looking blurred beneath the thick glasses. He unwrapped a piece of hard-rock candy and popped it into his mouth and made loud sucking sounds.

"And lay what on them?" asked Lawrence.

"Lahu Godman wants virgins," said Snow with a sense of satisfaction. He crinkled his nose as he continued to suck the candy.

He unwrapped a second piece of candy and dropped it into the open mouth of the young girl sitting on Tuttle's lap. "That's the first phrase you learn in Lahu. It's the first phrase out of the mouth of any self-respecting Lahu Godman. Round up all the virgins, man. You make one of the head guys your major domo. His job is to deliver virgins. You let him know this is a full-time job. He's on call twenty-four hours a day. And if he fucks up, man, there's a massive price to pay. Lahu Godman's got no fucking sense of humor about virgins. Every night and every morning, like clockwork, you get a virgin in a white silk gown carried on a chair and put down in your room. Sooner or later, you have to face the reality of life. Your major domo's gonna crawl on his hands and knees across your floor, looking as grim as death, and holding his balls—because, man, you've threatened to have lava leaking out of his balls if he ever doubled-crossed you—and he lays on the bad news. The village has gone virgin dry. There ain't a single virgin you haven't fucked before breakfast or after dinner.

"The first crisis of your reign. You can't let them think for one minute that any Lahu Godman is gonna put up with this shit about no more virgins. You throw a jet of fire and graze the right earlobe of your major domo. That does the trick. He's pissing in his pants and thinking that it is lava leaking down his leg. He's freaking out. Word spreads quickly through the village just how much the godman is disappointed in this no virgin news.

"More virgins, you roar. Lahu Godman say, go to next village and steal their virgins. This is, of course, an act of war. But the villagers have no choice. You got them entertained and scared out of their gourds, man, I'm telling you, they'll raid every fucking village between Chiang Mai and *Mae Sai*. You'll get their relatives Federal Expressing virgins from Burma and Laos.

"No more goddamn condoms, worry about clap, AIDS, virulent herpes, killer crabs. Just give the line, Lahu Godman want official visit with morel virgins. Or shoot a spike of flames up the ass."

Tuttle stretched his legs out as girl left to join her friends at a table near the television set. They watched a Thai kick-boxing match with a couple of waiters.

"You've left out the down side, George," said Tuttle.

"Which is?" asked Lawrence.

Snow held the melted down piece of red rock candy between his teeth and pointed at his mouth. Then spit the piece of candy into an empty Kloster beer bottle.

"You need self-will, man. You've got to know when to stop. Tuttle and I've gone over my Lahu Godman trip. You see, he's got a point. All these Lahu Godmen ruin it for everyone else. Each one gets a little taste of power, and before you know it, fucking virgins isn't enough fun for a day. He's getting his rocks off at breakfast, lunch, and dinner. Then he gets a real funny idea. He forgets about making the call to New York, his couriered tricks, his American Express bill—and he convinces himself the illusions are magic. He thinks he is a real Lahu Godman. People filter in from other villages to bow down at his feet. He's an event. What began as sex ends as politics. He becomes a politician with a mission. With an agenda. With an ideology, man, and that's the worst of all. He thinks he's figured out some great system for how time passes through the world. It's not that hard. The villagers believe him; after all, he's fucked every virgin in a hundred-mile radius. But this is a different scale. Every Lahu Godman ends up not only fucking all the virgins, but everyone else. So the villagers do the right thing. They get their revenge. They get rid of him. Shoot him, man. Spear him, bury him alive, cut off his fucking head, his dick, and his balls and bury them all in different ratholes. No Lahu Godman dies a natural death in his bed with his grandchildren around him.

"So I stick to the safe ground. Just the standard bullshit, no tricks, no virgins, one night at a time, purples handed out COD. Maybe you could handle it. Ask yourself if your contentment factor is two virgins a day. Or three. You've gotta be brutally honest with your answer. If you want to go for it, my old man works in Hollywood, and I might get some development money for a script. But I need a real life character who's done the trip, man. Think about it. You'd get a story created by credit, and some back-end money. Lahu Godman and a cast of virgins is the kind of stuff people want to see. Man up against himself and the hill tribes of Thailand. Special-effects heaven. People would go nuts over the story.

"Or you can hang out at HQ like the rest of us, listen to the music on the jukebox, knock back Mekhong and Coke, and ask yourself if you've ever taken Noi back to your apartment. I'd go upcountry and take on the Lahu, but I know my own limitations. I wouldn't stop with the virgins. Man, the American State Department would have to send in a team of forensic experts to dig up a mountainside just to find where they had buried my ass. And I'll be perfectly frank with you. The Lahu are exporting most of their virgins to Bangkok. The Chinese characters in that business aren't impressed with my cutting into their supply of virgins.

"But while the power lasted, think of the possibilities. Each morning, the first words out of your mouth, 'More virgins. Lahu Godman wants more virgins.'

"The best you can hope for in Southeast Asia is a war. During the war, Vietnam was a well-ordered society. All the women in the bars; all the men in uniform getting their asses shot off in the jungle. Peace sucks. You get desperate thoughts. And before you know, you've had two too many drinks, and you're on the telephone, and the guy answers the phone over a crackling line. You tell him—this is Bangkok, listen carefully. I'm an apprentice Lahu Godman, can you give me a quote on a few illusions. Does all your shit come with clear instructions. And when you're packing the order, put in an extra couple kilos of lava dust."

"Lawrence practices law in Los Angeles," said Tuttle, a couple of moments in Snow's thoughtful silence. The revelation darkened Snow's face; his features twisted into a look of scorn. He slowly unwrapped another piece of hardrock candy, staring down at the tabletop.

"What kinda law, man?"

"Pension law."

"A Lahu Godman for the ancients in America," said Snow, shaking his head. His tone had changed as well as his expression. A crude bomb had exploded his dream.

"We were at UCLA together in the '60s," said Tuttle to fill the awkward silence. "We shared an apartment together. It's been a long time since we've seen each other. He's a good guy, George. Not every lawyer's a complete asshole."

"Thanks," said Lawrence, who had grown uncomfortable as if it had been announced he was the carrier of a fatal virus.

"I guess it could be a comedy. Lahu Godman racks up a thousand billable hours with hilltribe virgins," said Snow, with a slanting

A Killing Smile

glance at Tuttle. "Lahu Godman sues major domo for failure to deliver. Lahu Godman pleads insanity."

After Snow had gone, Lawrence slumped in his booth, a confused, perplexed expression on his face. Snow's unscheduled arrival and departure had left skid marks on his ego. His livelihood had always been a source of pride; of course, he knew of the anti-lawyer jokes, but knew underneath that his position provided a powerful identity and monetary significance. His name and the name of his law firm opened any door in Los Angeles. But in Zeno's he was a displaced person; Snow had treated him as if he were a representative of evil, someone devoted to the force of decline, greed, and intolerance.

"It's an irrational thing with Snow. His hatred of lawyers," said Tuttle, rubbing his jaw. "Don't take it personally."

"I didn't," said Lawrence, lying. "He lives in Bangkok?"

"He has a room at the Highland Hotel on Sathorn Road. Your basic box that comes with no windows or carpets. The girls love it, he says. It reminds them of their own rooms. They can't afford windows. Outside his hotel on Sathorn Road is a traffic nightmare. Ten lanes of tuk-tuk hardbraking all night. Sirens wailing. Paint thinner heads going one-hundred-ten-plus on motorcycles. The sounds of madness pounding in his head. He uses the place to refine his Lahu Godman act. He picks up girls from Silom Road and takes them back. They are like Valley girls. That Silom Road Valley girl and her deflowered friend know people who gossip to rangers, cops, Thai males with guns, bikers who eat bags of *yah mah*—speed. One day Snow's going to be an item in the *Bangkok Post*: Thai male with paint thinner on his breath flees the scene. That's after he's wrapped three blocks of piano wire around Snow's neck for screwing his sister."

TUTTLE had logged enough time in Thailand to know that magic wasn't for the cities. Not in peace time. Bangkok was a one-shot, try-out location for certain drifters like Snow who sooner or later found enough courage to take their show to a hilltribe audience. Tuttle didn't tell Lawrence the real reason for Snow's disappointment about the lawyer business. Snow had been looking for some years among the newcomers to Zeno's for a sponsor. Someone to finance his trip. His father had nothing to do with Hollywood. But life had dealt Snow the hand as a major domo to watch, in his mind's eye, some other *farang's* ass busily pumping away on a virgin that by rights, he believed, belonged to him.

'Like a Virgin' played on the jukebox. Several girls sang along to the lyrics, dancing in an open circle, bumping hips, laughing, and ignoring the kick-boxing on the television at the other end of the room. The song got played several times each night that Tuttle came into Zeno's. Snow got a little tearful each time it played. "I'm fucking serious," he'd say, "I'm buying the rights to the music for my film." No one ever believed that Snow was serious about the song, the Lahu Godman movie, or his own life.

Snow had gone for a smoke in the alley. Before he left, he warned Lawrence to keep his plan confidential. "And don't tell anyone about the Lahu Godman idea. You're a lawyer. You understand that original ideas can't be used. Anyway, I don't want it getting around."

The more Snow had thought about it, the more he convinced himself that he should go upcountry and apply for the Lahu Godman job. After a few months at the Highland Hotel he had begun to miss not having a window. Besides, as he once confided to Tuttle, once Zeno's started filling up with American lawyers, Bangkok was over; it would be time to head to the hills and take one's chances with the villagers. Tuttle hadn't forgotten that conversation months earlier when he dropped Lawrence s occupation into the conversation. He knew, however, that Snow would be back; Tuttle's plans called for his reappearance.

6

Old Bill arrived at eleven-thirty dressed in a freshly ironed safari suit. Bill, who was in his sixties, had a wardrobe of hand-tailored suits made to fit his six-foot-two frame. Lanky, with perfectly erect posture, combined with sparkling gray-blue eyes, and straight white hair combed back with the hint of a part on the left side, Old Bill had a patrician appearance. Someone who had estates abroad; servants and staff running his local manor, and Royal Polo Club obligations as a former president. In truth, Old Bill lived on a small pension in a simple apartment.

In the long, wide dimly lit alley behind Zeno's, Old Bill on any given night was known to stop and run his eyes over one or two parked red Lotus or Porsches parked near the rear entrance. He had an attraction for fast foreign sports cars and was rumored to have been a professional race driver before the war.

"Where do they find the money to buy these cars?" A question Old Bill sometimes asked Tuttle, his hands calmly folded.

"Business deals, Bill," Tuttle would answer with a wide, open-faced smile.

"What kind of business deals, Robert?"

"Shipping, gold, cement, oil, or whatever."

"I once worked in a lighthouse in Cornwall," Old Bill would say. "The entire structure, foundation and all, was cement. Could that cement have come from Thailand? Made the fortune for one of those boy's grandfathers?"

"Maybe, Bill. But it would have been cheaper to have used Cornwall cement," Tuttle would say, as Old Bill passed. "Think of the shipping cost."

"A point well made, Robert. Personally, I think the money from the cars comes from the whatever.'

"The whatever gets my vote as well, Bill."

Neither Old Bill nor Tuttle believed the cars were bought from legitimate business transactions in shipping, gold, cement. But it never stopped Old Bill from asking the question and talking about his stint at the lighthouse in Cornwall. They talked in the coded language of expats; the "whatever" categories of human activity that went without specific names. The expensive sports cars attracted hungry eyes. As the overcrowded two-baht buses belched thick black fumes up and down Sukhumvit Road, crammed with Thais squeezed and dazed in the exhausting heat, sweating, standing silently, some hanging out of the open doors or leaning out of a window with a white handkerchief held over their nose, a new red Lotus was looked at with amusement or indifference; a transitory reflection of chrome and light from another cycle, another world.

The fact such an expensive car would always be unavailable, beyond reach in this life, was not a cause for resentment. Tuttle discovered early on that one of the first things *a farang* new to Thailand was to relearn the limits of his world, his language, his capacity to acquire; he learned to describe a hurricane as a wind storm; and he understood for the first time that there were ways he was unable to help others.

Old Bill who always paused in the alley of Bangkok's most famous *farang,* gathering spot was a master of indirect language. He was also a master of the royal "we"; and the girls who employed his services came from a great distance to seek his assistance and advice.

One of the girls powdered her nose in the large wall mirrors above the dirty sink outside the bank of open toilets. She caught sight of Old Bill passing behind; a smile ignited on her face, and she turned away from the mirror, proudly holding an airmail letter with cancelled American stamps in the right corner. Old Bill stopped, hearing his name called, glanced in the mirror, smoothed back his white hair with his hands and lifted the envelope flap. He nodded as he read as if the truth of the man's letter was being recovered bit by bit, considered and examined, and then Old Bill looked up with a studied expression in his flashing gray-blue eyes.

"I think we can write a pleasant reply," Old Bill said.

At the far end of the HQ where the television was suspended from the ceiling in a small metal framed cage, an old woman, her bare feet crossed, wriggling her toes painted fire-engine red, sat deep into a bench and smoked a cigarette. Sitting directly opposite her, slouched in a chair behind a table, an old Thai man propped his dirty feet on a smudged chrome chair where he watched the kick-boxing match on television.

Five hard, long rounds. Feet flew at the thighs, shins, ankles of the opponent. The barefoot kick struck out of nowhere. A foot aimed at the midsection, neck, or face blocked by a gloved hand. Another punch, another series of blows exchanged. A foot struck out but missed the face. The fighters circled each other, light on their feet, looking for an opening. Suddenly, there was a flurry of quick kicks followed by a couple of punches to the chest and stomach. A kick landed hard on the jaw of a fighter no more than seventeen years old. He blinked, shook his head, and stepped back to land a kick of his own. Round after round of punishing, brutal blows, but there was rarely any sign of cuts or blood; as if prolonged violence that everyone had witnessed could never be proved. It had been inflicted; but where was the evidence?

The sport was a national practice in not showing pain or anger no matter how brutal the punishment had been. Kidney punches landed in quick succession but the boxer didn't lose his balance; he didn't fall. The expression on his face was the same pitch. He fought back. A hard right to the head. The boxers had reached a level beyond pain or hurt. Body hurled at body as if the skin, muscle, and bone could endure forever. The red Lotus was a punch delivered to the kidney; the idea was always to conquer the pain by transcending the experience. The same idea that had attracted Tuttle to the Far East; that search for the healthy way to regard himself after he had been injured. From the Thais, he had learned an invaluable lesson—how to look expressionless after an opponent's foot slammed into his face.

"Bill, this is an old friend of mine from the States," said Tuttle.

Old Bill stood erect, holding out his hand. Lawrence felt the strong, firm grasp of his hand. "You didn't happen to notice that new Lotus out back?" asked Old Bill, staring directly at Lawrence.

"I have the same one in Los Angeles," said Lawrence. "Mine is blue."

For the first time in years, Tuttle saw Old Bill raise an eyebrow. The cars had always been ownerless; the drivers faceless. The mystery people had abandoned their luxury cars for a couple of hours, leaving street people with instructions to guard it with their lives. Never had Old Bill actually witnessed anyone getting in or out of one of these cars.

"You're a businessman?" asked Old Bill, as several other girls with letters inside foreign envelopes began gathering near him.

"I'm a lawyer," said Lawrence. After the reaction he had received from George Snow, Lawrence feared another setback with Old Bill.

Old Bill glanced over at Tuttle and smiled. "Robert, perhaps that's the "whatever" we've been looking for over the years." Indeed, Lawrence was the "whatever" Tuttle had been waiting for.

The huddled girls surged forth and claimed Old Bill, taking him by the arm to his place at a back booth. "Whatever, what?" asked Lawrence, feeling excluded by this private code.

"Cement in Cornwall had been an early theory," said Old Bill. "But Robert pointed out the obvious. Transportation cost would have been excessive."

They watched Old Bill half carried away by half a dozen girls. "It's a kind of word game," said Tuttle. Lawrence was temporarily reassured.

"What does he do?"

Tuttle looked in the booth mirror and saw Old Bill bending down to slide into the back booth. "He helps the girls write letters to the *farangs* who have gone home."

"And he makes his living that way?"

"He never charges them."

Lawrence shook his head. "Doesn't anyone have a normal job here? Get up and go to an office in the morning, work, go to lunch, come back to work until six then go home to a house with a wife and kids? They must have some damn structure and pattern in their day? This guy looks like Prince Philip's double and he does nothing but write free letters for prostitutes?"

"That about sums up Old Bill." Tuttle watched Lawrence's nostrils flare. As a student, Lawrence had this behavioral tic whenever he became annoyed or frustrated. He wondered how many times Sarah had witnessed the flare billow into the nostrils as Lawrence looked for a rational, logical explanation. Every trauma of life could be soothed with logic; either it was solved or ignored. Of course there was always a gram of white crystalline powder as a passport out of the disorder; needle marks on the arms were evidence of the formula broken apart and life reconstituted in a drug rush. Tuttle wondered if Sarah had ever told her husband about her thrill at the sight of a loaded syringe slowly down-loading heroin into the back of her leg? Had he ever found microscopic traces of powder on her dressing room mirror?

"What does he put in the letters?" asked Lawrence. "Let me guess. Get me a greencard. I want to come to America."

Tuttle snapped back from his first apartment near UCLA when Sarah was shaking, withdrawing from drugs, crying, doubled up naked in the center of the floor.

"Think of them as business letters," said Tuttle.

"What kind of business?"

"During the tourist high season a good looking girl collects three or four boyfriends. They come through Bangkok for a weeks or two. The guy becomes attached. Feels sorry for her; falls in love. Who knows what emotional atoms fly around inside anyone's brain? Once back in Bonn or Brisbane or Boston, nostalgia kicks in. Time and space curve and little Noi's shape shoots like a rocket through his thoughts. He writes her a letter. The guy's so miserable now he gets a nosebleed just thinking about her body next to him in bed. He sends a cheque for a hundred-dollars. In Noi's mailbox are three or four letters from three or four different guys every month. The money sees her through the low season. Old Bill helps keep the fires of their passions alive over that long stretch between May and October. Or the cheques stop coming. Old Bill isn't much different than a lawyer. He helps his clients communicate with their suppliers. He just doesn't bill them."

"Have you ever read one of these letters?" asked Lawrence, glancing back at Old Bill who had unfolded a pair of silver wire-framed glasses and slipped them over his nose.

"Many letters over the years. I've written a few myself."

Old Bill had around eight to ten standard replies that he wrote in longhand; the girls recopied them in their own hand or signed their name at the end of the original. Sometimes the girl penned a flourish all her own, a personal touch, that the *farang* in a cold land would recognize as a shared intimacy. "Monkey you buy me. We name Nick. He die. Monkey dead. Want new monkey. Send money, please. Miss you. Miss monkey. Think of you every day, every night."

The minor detail created intimacy, or as close to that edge as a Zeno girl was willing to go. That was the high end of the market, Tuttle explained. Most of the girls were content to let Bill do the thinking, organizing, and writing for them.

"Old Bill's probably written about a thousand letters," said Tuttle. "He's the man for your sixty-thou-a-year job." He caught a glimpse of Old Bill from his booth mirror: unscrewing the cap of an expensive fountain pen a group of girls had chipped in and bought him three years ago. Old Bill had a formula for the girls; one that worked, kept the cheques coming in, and they showed him pictures of their children, mothers, fathers, sisters, and shared the simple landscape of their dreams.

"Funny we never wrote all these years," said Lawrence, stretching out his legs under the booth. "Not even a Christmas card. And now we're in Bangkok talking about letter-writing for prostitutes."

"Who knows. If you were to hook up with a girl, she might end up sending you a letter that I drafted."

"Like what?" Lawrence moved closer to the rim of where Tuttle had been waiting for him all those years.

Tuttle smiled, for years he had been writing a letter in his head for the girls. A new formula that incorporated all of the formulas in one.

"You want to hear it now? Before you've even met the girl?"

"Now, what are you going to have her tell me?"

"Okay, Larry. Remember it's from a bar girl. A working girl. And not from—" he broke off before mentioning Asanee's name.

"The girl you want me to meet," said Lawrence, as their eyes locked for a moment of recognition.

One of the girls dropped a couple of two-baht coins in the juke-box, and punched #168—*'One Night in Bangkok'* and the paragraphs of Tuttle's standard form letter registered inside his mind. Some of the thoughts belonged to her while others came from him. The letters became a combination of multiple voices and tones. Where did the sex worker leave off and the expat letter-writer fill in his own perception, language, and voice? He looked around the room, kick-boxers on TV, sleeping HQ girls, waiters smoking cigarettes, and a couple of old-timers at the bar, and he knew this was the one place a letter-writer could never get writer's block.

Dear Larry,

Bill, who normally writes, is out of action so I asked an old friend, his name's Tuttle, to help write this letter to you. Perhaps you might like a quick update on HQ and the scene since you left in March. What are Tuttle's credentials, you ask? Old Bill is a reliable war-horse, I hear you saying. Is this Tuttle a lover or what? Don't be jealous, my darling. I met Tuttle five years ago when I worked in a massage parlor. It was around the corner from the New Fuji Hotel on *Surawong Road*, up three flights of red-carpeted stairs. All of us girls wore small red plastic badges pinned to our white uniforms. We sat inside an enclosure of glass waiting to be picked. The manager, a very attractive Chinese woman collected the 100-baht fee from customers at the front desk. She asked Tuttle to write a sign in English to put in every cubicle. He wrote: Please check that you have taken your valuables with you. We are not responsible for any loss. Thank you.

My mind floats around inside the cubicle. A *farang* groaning and moaning under the touch of my fingers on his calves, thighs, shoulders. My eyes would look up at Tuttle's sign. And I thought to myself. I remember Tuttle. I remember the night he wrote out those words for our manager. And I remembered him from before. On the strip. In Patpong and Cowboy. Our paths always seemed to cross. Listening to some English broadcast on Radio Bangkok in a *farang's* hotel room, I'd hear an English voice reading the news, and I'd think, maybe that's Tuttle.

Since you've gone back, all that is left are *farang* with bad hearts. Cheap Charlies who not buy you drink. They bargain girl. I no like. Some hunt in wolf packs. Some are like boys collecting and trading baseball cards. They cross-index us according to our badge numbers from our dancing days. All of us have done the go-go bar gig. One resident *farang* named Richard went through a six-month period taking only girls with the numbers 22 and 46. He said it was the quest for the perfect 22 or 46 that was his goal. After nearly a year, he find her in Patpong. She a perfect 22. Those days gone now. At a clinic on Sukhumvit Road, one little clinic out of thousands, I hear doctor say 200 girls have AIDS. I have friend who die of AIDS.

At Malaysia Hotel—I been on the second and third floor so many times that I have memorized every room by heart—someone else said the needle users have AIDS much, much. My friend she work in the local pharmacy tell me she sell gallons of saline solution to the junkies. They make heroin with needle in arm. Dirty people. Not like. Larry, if you can send your little Noi an extra two thousand baht, I won't have to go out at night. I'm afraid of these *farangs* who no have a good heart like you.

Some girls no work bar. They go to Zeno every night and to find a man. Go to hotel. These girls no wear number. They have good body. Go with man two, three times each night. Not good so many men. *Farang* call them HQ girls. Man from Toronto call them "Termites." My friend explained that this was a term of affection, but I don't know whether he is joking. He says like termites we bore straight through all the wooden hearts that come here. He also say HQ girl like termite, once you get one they very hard to get rid of. Think he bullshit me. All I care about is your heart isn't wood. Because you are going to send me that extra two thousand baht so my father can have the operation on his throat. He has trouble breathing since his accident in the tuk-tuk. But I not worry you, so I won't say anything more about Papa.

I worry much about my thighs. *Farang* don't like stretch marks on a girl's body. They have these red spectrum flashlight eyes that see the smallest ripple, any slight hint of a line on our thighs, upper legs, or bellies. Always asks us, do you have baby? They think girl have baby, then bad for stretch marks. I no have stretch marks. My baby now three years old and is very smart. He need some new clothes. I hope you can send extra two thousand baht so my baby has some clothes. I lose my face if my baby wear old clothes like rags. Everyone say, Noi is a bad mother. Cheap. No put good clothes on her baby. Let her Papa stay home with no operation on his throat. Maybe Papa die. Maybe baby die.

Be glad you no live in Bangkok. *Farang* sit around talking about bar girl's wearing pasties. Call them tiny fluorescent hearts that glow a bright orange in the overhead lights. They all worry now that maybe HQ gonna change. Now HQ a good bar. It's in between the old man's bar and the young man's bar. Maybe HQ become an old man bar. No more young. Talk about the past. Old men talking about why someone lost one war and won another.

These old men on the down escalator with only one more stop to the basement floor. Maybe that's why Tiger fled to the Philippines to start over. He couldn't stand running the major old man's hangout in Patpong. It started to get to him after awhile. No *farang* ever moved on from the Tiger bar, they merely died. You come back soon, okay. You young man. HQ need you here. I need you in my arms every night. Maybe extra two thousand baht I get doctor to fix little, little stretch mark on my tummy.

Last night, my friend me go Silom Road shopping. Street food vendors sell us pineapple, mango, and grapes. We pick fruit laid out on blocks of ice. It keep real *yen, yen*—cool—inside a glass case. Little fluorescent light inside make me sad. Think of your hotel room. No like you gone. Why you no take Noi with you? Maybe you send me airplane ticket.

Thai man move old cart on old bicycle wheels in street. His tires all worn down. Noodle stands in the alleyways. A few tables and stools. The pavement full Thai people and some *farang*. Go-go dancer from Patpong going to cheap hotel for short-time business (but me like you all night. I true! True!), beggars with rented children. One baby missing hand; one have chewed-up face. See gangsters in expensive suits, cops in military uniform with black-handled pistols in leather holsters, tuk-tuk and taxi drivers showing *farang* picture of girls for sale in massage parlors and whorehouses. See many *farang* women with white skin (I wish my skin not so black) and I think they sexy girls. I feel very sad, and jealous for you. I think now you go home, maybe you like *farang* woman and no like your little Noi. You forget about me in Bangkok. Maybe you no care about your little Noi now. Not think about me.

In Bangkok, *farang* women come up to me in street or HQ and say, why you a whore? Why you go with old man for money? We only fuck men we like, and they fuck us good, make us happy or get new man. She say Bangkok no good for lady. Man just take, take, not give. She say she not go for money. That a bad thing. I think she bullshit me. I ask her, who want to fuck you here? In Bangkok? You got man here? *Farang* take you to dinner, movie, hotel? She first get hot heart, very angry with me, then she cry.

She say to me, I don't understand. And I say she no understand Noi. I frightened here. Noi all alone. No one take care of me or baby. I stay in Bangkok. Why *mem* no understand Thai lady? Girl sell T-shirts, maybe give body massages, blowjobs, handjobs, stuffed PingPong balls, bananas, and Coke bottles up her pussy. She no like but she do. Must have money. No money cannot eat.

Mem says over and over, what it all mean? This Bangkok, I tell her. Merchants of sex coming out of every alley and lane. You no escape tuk-tuk driver who got his fold-out glossy brochure with pretty smiling Thai girl in a bubble bath. He shove it in every *farang* male face dozens of times. Until it became a subliminal message. Always sexy Thai girls perched like songbirds in a glass cage with the numbers on their chest smiling into the camera. Pick me. I need the 500 baht. I will make you feel good. Promise. Come fast. I need the purple very much. Come quickly. You have good heart. My child wake me up at nine this morning. I get no sleep. I so tired. But I make love with you. Make you feel good. You have a good life. You get lots of sleep. You get money. I make you feel good. You like me?

I explain her what we must do. She no like to hear me speak. Girl at twenty-four, she old. She no good anymore. *Farang* want young girl. Sixteen, seventeen, maybe twenty. I tell her, Noi now twenty-three. Young one more year. I know you no care because you got good heart. Cool heart. But *farang* in Bangkok they only want young girl. *Farang* woman she get red in face. Say she twenty-eight, and she say she very young girl. Says she's still a baby. No good with man forty, fifty. No good. Too old. I say, never mind. You not understand how we think in Bangkok. But never mind. It okay. It's up to you. You think whatever you want. Not up to me to tell you. No one stop you thinking bullshit

Farang woman run away down Silom Road crying and beating her fist on tuk-tuk driver's head. He duck around vendors stretched out behind their wooden tables on beach chairs, sleeping, curled up like cats. Dirty soles of their feet pointed at traffic jam in street. Above them the swallows of Silom Road motionless in trees. I last see her chasing tuk-tuk driver down Convent Road. Then my friend and me go back shopping for jeans.

She not feel so good. Have abortion three days ago. Go with man last night. He not know she no feel good. He give her five hundred baht. She happy now. She buy me shirt. A nice vendor sits on a small stool and leans into his drink. A pink liquid in a plastic straw. He sucks hard and smiles. A man carry underwear in a wicker basket on his head through the crowd. *Tuk-tuks* and taxis double-parked in street. Vendors read comic books, do crossword puzzles, read horoscopes, slap bugs, drink and eat, talk so much about money. I'm feeling good, and happy. This is my world. My City of Angels. I know you say Los Angeles City of the Angels, too. But no think it same as Bangkok.

I like sidewalk fashion; it very good and it very cheap. T-shirt trendy fashion. Blue jeans. Shirts with silver sequins. Tight skirts and low-cut blouses. Buy me I'm sexy, I make you feel good, this is what I hear drifting up from the clothes on the wooden tables. The clothes talk to me. You need me, they say. I help you make money. Thick leather belts made of gator or snake or eel. Small leather pouches to strap on the belt. I have no money to go shopping with friend. She still bleed from abortion on Monday. Maybe she go back to doctor Friday. Maybe go with other man tonight.

I stay home and wait for your letter to come with your sweet kisses at the bottom. I no need clothes, just your letter. I liked your last p.s. where you say this cheque is for my beautiful Noi. It make me feel good you say that.

I forget tell you. I quit massage parlor. Boring. Not like. I go to Zeno Coffee Shop. Watch television and talk with friends. Listen to music. Your little Noi worries about ringers on Saturday and Sunday nights. They no have peu-un. Just come alone. Shove handbags on top of Jukebox. Knock off my friend me's handbag on the floor. They no care. Girl just say, 'Never mind.'

Ringer a circus word, says Tuttle. Girl like professional axe thrower who goes on tour with a carnival out in the sticks. But as a performer she very good. Number one. No sleep with many men. Weekends, *farang*, come Zeno and look for the ringer.

Farang journalists write bad thing about us. Maybe you read it. Journalist say HQ girls same as cat. Same, same almond-shaped eyes look room as girl perched in your lap. Cats purring and nudging against you. Cats wanting to be fed. Cats ready to jump. One cat eye on clock, other eye on man's lap where she sit and purrs. Third eye hunting for a meal elsewhere just in case the bowl empties out and doesn't get refilled. Thai girl better than cat. No can teach cat to play cards in hotel room. Who can write such bullshit about your little Noi. I know you throw newspaper in the fire. Burn that bullshit. I think of you every day I live. No cat think about anything. My Papa had five cats. Two got killed by truck. He say they no care about him. I say Papa I care about you and your operation. My sweetheart Larry gonna send you money for your operation. I know it. Larry good man. He not ever forget his little Noi. And Noi no ever forget his handsome face. (I still think you only twenty-seven; no believe you can be forty-five.)

Last night I go with Englishman from London to same place you stay in Bangkok. He hold my hand as walk down the soi, and I thinking of you every minute. I pretend he same, same you. Then I hear Thai man shouting in the night. I very scared, think maybe he crazy, got a knife. Ghost fighting him. I see him through old tumble-down fence all overgrown with banana tree and bamboo. Old Thai man in sandals, shorts and a T-shirt, wave fist at the door of shack. He screaming to woman inside, I no like you any more. You got chicken pussy. I no care if you die. He says all these bad words. Chicken pussy, monkey piss, shit mouth. I no tell *farang* what he say. Just say, "He not care about her."

My English friend, he makes me laugh. He afraid of fruit bats flying over the soi. He say they like a computer game. Maybe they run into tall *farang*. Maybe they got rabies. And I tell him the soi with the canopy of trees reminds me of Chiang Mai. As we turned left along the soi, I pointed at a huge tree, "My family live up there," I said, smiling because I am making a joke.

He looked up and then over at me "You a monkey?" I give him a playful punch. "No, monkey. Just poor. My father work for 40 baht a day, my mother 30 baht. Not good money." I smile but I hurting much inside. No like him call me monkey. Him not understand Thai people.

His bathroom different from yours. I always clean myself good. Like a cat (make little joke for you). I wash behind my ears, neck, breasts, and tummy with special attention to what this Englishman calls my combat zone. I take a shower head and put between my legs. Then Englishman comes into the bathroom and I'm very shy. He tells me to use the bidet. You ever see a bidet before? I not ever see. Think maybe toilet. Dirty. Or little sink. I get very scared. He pull me over to bidet. With his other hand, he turned on the water. A tiny jet of clear warm water cascaded up, making a miniature fountain.

I craned my neck forward, "Toilet?" I asked. I no floor pisser but I no see this bidet before.

"No," he said. "It's for cleaning the combat zone," he said. He picked me up and sat me on the bidet. "I'm certain you didn't have a bidet in your treehouse in Chiang Mai."

Water pumps against my pussy. It's cold. This Englishman's still holding me down. I think maybe he pervert. Make girl do dirty thing. Shame her. Only he keeps telling me it make girl feel good. And I think about *farang* woman chasing *tuk-tuk* driver across Silom Road, her crying, and tearing at him with his massage parlor brochure. Maybe she pissed off she cannot find bidet in Bangkok. Or I think, maybe *farang* woman have different sex with *farang* men. They sit each other on stream of water. No get VD. No get AIDS. So I think maybe it a good thing. And relax a little bit, only thinking when the Englishman's gonna let me get off.

After he let me finish, I raid his fridge. I opened every drawer and plastic container. I look in a large one full of pineapple. No good cut up. He not have a maid, I think. Maybe he poor. Maybe he not pay me. So I'm gonna at least get food. I take a box of cream-filled cookies. Rolling back foil, I stick two cookies in my mouth. I pulled off the Tupperware lid and examined his pineapple.

"This not good. Look at this." I pointed at the large brown inverted nipple-like growths that he hadn't cut off with knife. "You like a baby." I giggled, pointing at the cookies and pineapple.

We make love and I think of you all the time. After finish and roll off me, I turned on his radio to a Thai radio station. I not like his jazz cassette music. The Englishman he ask me what the Thai song say. So I explain him the lyrics. It's a soft love song. "She say her mother and father very poor. That she love man. That his woman come from abroad. She take her man away. That make her heart break." I turn over on my side. I crying now. Englishman sees my tears on my cheek. He have a good heart, and give Noi one thousand baht. I get a little smile on my face. I think you understand I no like sleep with Englishman. Not butterfly. Love only you. But no have any money. How can Noi live without money? Noi's Papa get operation? Noi's baby get clothes?

Englishman, he say to me, Thailand a strange, exotic land of smiles and sad love songs. And I say to myself, American man name Larry, he my true lover for all time and number one friend, and I just know you send me at least two thousand baht so I keep smiling during sad love songs. You no forget now. Love you like monkey loves banana. You come back Thailand soon. I wait you. Noi.

LAWRENCE slowly looked away as Tuttle finished. From the beginning of his journey he had tried to figure out what Tuttle had wanted from him. The offer of a job was a pre-emption. As he had listened to Tuttle recite the letter, he had begun to wonder what kind of halfway house his old roommate occupied. After all these years, Tuttle had not married. He had not mentioned the name of a single woman in his life. What bothered him the most was the almost perfect execution of the evening. The appearances of the Ratman, Snow, Crosby, and Old Bill; each a hinge on a door that Tuttle had refused to open more than a crack. Lawrence recognized the loose knit grouping of people who zeroed in on Tuttle through the night. What had Tuttle said earlier about obligation, Lawrence asked himself. That was it. Each acted as if he had made a solemn oath with Tuttle: had traversed some dangerous waters together, and Tuttle—like Snow's Lahu Godman—had created an oasis of serenity amidst the chaos of Zeno's.

Lawrence's lawyer's mind examined the shades of meaning in their coded language. Sarah had given a paper on language codes some years earlier at a London conference. She believed that coded language hid one of three things: the sacred, the blasphemous, or the desirable. According to Sarah, the supreme power, the power that held up the political order, was a power rooted in true desires, desires only half-spoken, desires shrouded in fear, and desires which were treacherous to practice. As far as Lawrence was aware, he might have been the only man to have taken what Tuttle had desired. Sarah had been Tuttle's property at UCLA; he had owned her, no matter how contradictory their relationship, the miscalculations, or the optical illusion they had parted, Sarah had never stopped belonging to Tuttle. Her breaking away had been the only true defeat he had ever suffered. At that precise moment, Lawrence knew that he should slide out of the booth, go back to his hotel, check out, and take a taxi to the airport. But he lingered over his drink.

"Who do you have in mind for me?" asked Lawrence.

The energy and force of the question caught Tuttle off guard. "You look puzzled. Certainly the thought must have occurred to you. An old friend, perhaps? Someone who might even up things between us. That must have crossed your mind as well. Respectable Los Angeles lawyer busted in whorehouse scandal. That would make for interesting reading in my law firm back home. That's too obvious. You could have already arranged that during my first three days in Bangkok. Or maybe you wanted to see me face-to-face first."

Tuttle looked up at the ceiling as if he were reading a message in the dusty tiles. He began to chuckle, then laugh. He sloped his head to one side, and stared straight through Lawrence. "You think I'm still angry. Like I'd lost a prize-fight. And this is some kind of weird rematch between two old guys twenty years down the road. And what is Larry's great fear? That I'm going to ruin his social status and professional reputation?"

"Then what do you want, Bobby? And don't tell me it's to talk about old times. What in the hell is it you want from me?"

Tuttle paused, inhaled deeply, held his breath and slowly exhaled. "I may need you to help a friend of mine. A girl who works in a school with me. Her name's Asanee. She's twenty. And I'd like to break her out of the spiral. Tomorrow I've arranged for you to meet her."

"That's it! You want me to help one of your girlfriends?"

One of the young girls dressed in a Japanese kimono came shuffling up to the booth babbling in Thai to Tuttle. The distress registered in her voice.

"She's not a girlfriend. Gotta get out," said Tuttle, sliding across the bench. He stood up and gave Lawrence a backward glance. Girls were flying past as the word spread. The boisterous merrymaking vanished at the jukebox end of the room." One of the regulars has sliced her wrists in the john." Then he was gone.

Lawrence watched him disappear ahead of the crowd of girls and waiters. At UCLA Tuttle had a reputation for earning trust. Whatever the loss or disappointment, Tuttle had an ability to restore order; to stand square in the face of dread and draw the person back to safety. Wasn't that the true reason Lawrence had gone to Bangkok? He had come to Tuttle for rescue. He avoided his own purpose of walking back into Tuttle's life until that moment. Lawrence had marvelled at university how strangers had sought Tuttle out and asked him to retrieve either themselves or someone who had fallen behind; it had been something about his solitude, his quiet contemplation as if he had a secret up his sleeve, like the Lahu Godman; and his small circle always knew he would return. He had only to be asked.

The beauty of the moment was the realization that Tuttle needed him.

7

After Tuttle stopped the bleeding, two of the girl's friends took her to a hospital for stitches. She had given a pale smile of thanks as Tuttle helped her into the taxi. The cuts in the wrists hadn't been deep; enough to draw blood—to draw attention to a crowd—but she had never intended to kill herself. In a couple of hours with fresh white bandages on her wrists she would be back in front of the jukebox, joking like a high school student with her friends, talking about grades given out in baht by customers who did not vaguely resemble teachers.

Lawrence saw fresh bloodstains on Tuttle's right shirtsleeve. The image of the nurse washing up in the sink with Sarah's body under a white, bloodied sheet caused tears to swell up in his eyes. He hated that flare of strong emotion; the way it made him feel weak, small, unprotected.

"She's gonna be okay," said Tuttle. "Four or five stitches and she's back in business."

The words burned in Lawrence's mind; the words he expected to hear at the hospital emergency room from the doctors and nurses and policemen. Instead Sarah was gone. It was a working girl in Bangkok who had survived. The sight of her blood on Tuttle's clothes had shaken Lawrence, caught him off guard. He reeled back in the booth as if he had been attacked. Her car had left no skid marks on the pavement. She had plowed straight into the back of the other car with her mind somewhere else; some image of the mind had distracted her for two or three seconds; some trimming of imagination had blocked her from reacting, slamming on the brakes. There had been no final good-bye, phrase, or fragment of a word. All that had been left was her blood everywhere. Blood the emergency room nurse washed from her hands down the sink. Perhaps Tuttle could have rescued her; found a way to pull her back from the moment of impact. Tuttle was talking about the Thai girl's problems. But all that Lawrence could see was Sarah's body beneath the sheet. A Lahu Godman like Tuttle might have pulled the sheet back and Sarah would have broken into a smile. "Just playing a little joke, Larry," she would have said.

Lawrence caught a tear with the back of his hand. Tuttle had never seen him cry before; not that he had ever given that possibility much attention. Lawrence had successfully hid his suffering behind a wall of irony, ridicule, or logic; it had caught Tuttle off guard, that tears had been so close to the surface. He reached over and lightly clutched Lawrence's shoulder. He didn't say anything. The massive distance of all those years hardly mattered. This is all I need, Lawrence thought. Tuttle motioned for a waiter and spent a long time ordering drinks; this provided time for Lawrence to compose himself and to crawl back into his lawyer's self-contained space suit.

"Have you looked at the jukebox up close?" asked Lawrence, his brow furrowed, as he nodded across the room. "It belongs in a museum. I can't remember seeing a jukebox since the '60s. There was one in that bar where you used to work. I can't remember the name."

"The Angel Lady Bar," said Tuttle. "Hamburgers, French fries, draft beer, and flies that looked like they had been bred by the CIA on Mars."

"That's right. Remember the jukebox. One Friday after a history exam, we played 'Hey, Jude' for a solid six hours one night. Remember that? Sarah had a bag of quarters and every time the song finished, she'd run over and put in another quarter. And the owner, God, what was his name?"

"Jerry Lubsack. An ex-cop, who was 'retired' for beating up a couple of black kids."

"He told you to unplug the jukebox. You refused. He said, if he heard 'Hey, Jude' one more time that 'Your ass is outta here.' And you nudged Sarah and said, 'One more time for old times' sake,' in a bad Bogart accent. Lubsack came out from behind the bar, his fists clenched, his jaw set. I thought he was going to punch you in the face. And you said, 'What's the matter, Jerry, you don't like black people. You don't like the Beatles. Who the fuck do you like?'"

Tuttle nodded. "'Don't ever let me catch your ass in here again, friend,' Jerry shouted. He was pissed off. The students organized a protest. That was Sarah's idea. Pickets were up for two weeks."

"And he phoned you, begging you to call off the boycott. He offered you the bartending job back." Tuttle issued the terms of pulling off the pickets; it was an offer the owner didn't like. Jerry Lubsack had slammed the phone down in Tuttle's ear. Hire a black student as bartender was Tuttle's idea. Four days later, a black accounting major was tending the Angel Lady Bar, and Sarah was playing *'Hey, Jude'* on the jukebox.

The jukebox in Zeno's was light years away from the one at the Angel Lady Bar in Los Angeles. Lawrence hadn't thought about the Angel Lady Bar for years. If there was a game of chance where one could have gone back to Angel Lady, Lawrence would have made the bet. Tuttle sipped his fresh drink, rolled his sleeve up to cover the blood stain and stared out through the smoke at the jukebox. Lawrence had located the center of the HQ universe, he thought.

The center of the entire universe; Einstein's universe with black holes, bending light, relativity, and the big bang. The spot where people mingled looking for the elusive emotional peyote button that would allow them to experience happiness and pleasure at the same moment, and for a moment that would extend through time and space.

Everyone was pulled to the jukebox. Over the years HQ management moved it at least four times, trying out other parts of the room. Like diviners they had used the jukebox to discover a hidden mother lode—where money rained in with the force of a monsoon gale—and instead they found the seam between the past and future, the location to transport every HQ girl, customer, waiter, and cop backwards and forwards in time. The jukebox had migrated back where it had first appeared in 1968.

Sometimes Tuttle caught a young woman following, with her finger and eyes, the curve of the colored balls painted on the plastic casing. Underneath was a small light bulb. Her eyes wide open, fired with the colors below, as she counted the red balls, then the purple, lavender, and blue circles. One night Tuttle watched as one of the girls stood still, the rest of the world cut off from her, as she calculated the movement of a cockroach imprisoned inside the Jukebox; the slow-moving black form trapped on the backside of the colored balls. She put her finger against the plastic, the roach moved from the shadow, and she traced his path round and round, making a kind of children's game of hide and seek.

Tuttle doubted the jukebox would be moved again. The stone platform underneath looked semi-permanent. Close to the bar, two steps away from where the girls could get change. The music didn't interfere with the TV at the other end of the room. Customers rotated around the jukebox, looking at the girls, playing a game of hide and seek, knowing the girls could never get away, and would be back night after night.

"During the Vietnam war, GIs came here with half dollars, quarters, and dimes, and fed them into the jukebox, or gave them to the girls," said Tuttle. "Have you read the writing on the jukebox?"

"Use nickels, dimes and quarters," said Lawrence, smiling. He hadn't read the sign; but every jukebox had the same formula.

"Six songs for $1.00, three songs for 50 cents, and one song for 25 cents," said Tuttle. An abandoned, foreign currency of the past. Now the machine took large one-baht coins; two Thai coins to play a song. "Everyone has their favorite."

"It has 'Hey, Jude,'" said Lawrence.

"Number 27." Tuttle had a generous, bemused look, as if something unearned had fallen into his lap.

"That's right!" Lawrence was more impressed than he should have been. The changeless quality of the music, of the place, of the people created a region where most of the elementary particles were known.

"You remember the Angel Lady in LA? Back then the music taught us things. Same-same here, as the Thais say. It's a marker. About who owns the place, who comes, who stays. What they dream. How they hurt. The usual suspects you line up against the wall of hard living."

The original tunes were written on thin strips of paper and placed under the lit clear plastic panel. Oldies had turned yellow, the black ink faded, leaving a phantom image of a word, and old age, dust, and heat had curled up the paper edges into a small cradle. You had to memorize the number of the songs. Because you couldn't read the words. A *hard-core farang* was liable to forget a girl, but he never forgot the number of his favorite jukebox songs at HQ.

Lek stood on tiptoes beside the jukebox and dropped in two coins. She studied the numerical keypad. She punched the bright blue number two, then a one, and lastly seven. Number 217 flashed in lights, machinery inside spun around, retrieving her record. The sound of 'He's So Shy' filtered across the room. Most of the time, the girls picked a Thai rock 'n roll or torch song. When the choice was theirs; when the money pumped into the belly of the musical beast had come from their own pocket. When a girl punched in the number of a western song, that was the tell: she had the attention of a *farang*; he'd given her two baht for a song.

"Pick a nice American song, honey," he probably said. "One that gets you in the mood. Because I'm already in the mood. But I want to hear some nice music first."

As the music blared out of the twin speakers, and Lek danced over to the middle-aged *farang* drinking a beer, Tuttle leaned back slowly as if he remembered something.

"You know what I like about the jukebox? The price of a song is immutable. It costs the same as a Bangkok bus. Everyone knows the fixed price of musical pleasure is two baht. No bartering, borrowing, or begging allowed. The jukebox only understands two baht. Nothing else works."

Crosby and Snow, having finished an extended tour of the premises, had drifted back to the booth. "What do you mean, nothing else works?" asked Crosby, sliding back over the bench.

"Everyone wants pleasure and no one wants to remember the price," said Tuttle.

Crosby squinted. "Getting philosophical, are we? You must tell your friend the truth. Everyone knows the price of an HQ girl. One purple delivered COD preferably with some discretion the following morning, when it is discretely slipped into her handbag, blouse, or skirt pocket. And everyone knows the financial cost can be adjusted on the second or third time you bed her."

"But you play *'He's So Shy'* a hundred times on the jukebox and it's always two baht," said Tuttle.

"But take a girl for the third time and you get tempted," said Crosby with authority, tipping back his beer.

Snow, owl-like behind his thick glasses, laughed. His laugh had a long, loose quality; as if his laugh tank had been filled with high octane fuel. He had gone for "a walk" and smoked a joint with Crosby. His talk about the Lahu Godman idea had got him worked up. He had come close to making that phone call to the Magic Shop in New York; City—or as close as Snow ever came—which was asking Crosby for a loan to make the call. And Crosby told him what he always told Snow, "You'd only make a fuckup of it, mate."

"Tempted to knock down the price from a purple to three reds," said Snow, finishing Crosby's sentence. "And there's the beginning of all misery; because the missing two reds get made up somehow, some way," said Snow.

Crosby chimed in. "Exactly. Now you're outside the formula and anything can happen. These girls can become very unstable. Something has to fill that vacuum. And since it's not money, you are guaranteed a serious melodramatic scene where you play the heavy."

Snow cut back into the conversation. "He means they grab for a knife—and turn from a sweet, smiling little girl into guerrilla fighter with a pressing desire to cut off your balls."

Lawrence looked at Snow and then over at Crosby. He hadn't expected them to return. It was a mild surprise. With their return, they had captured the conversational high ground. Tuttle, he could see, was drifting off somewhere in his mind beyond the jukebox. Crosby lit a Lucky Strike cigarette, exhaled the smoke away from the table.

"There's one more thing," Crosby said, picking a piece of tobacco off his tongue. He looked at it for a second. "Most HQ girls don't speak English, but I have never met one who couldn't count in a hundred languages. And I never met one who wouldn't play by the rules if you explained the rules to her in advance and once she agreed, she would follow them."

❖

CRAZY thoughts swung on a jungle gym of grotesque images from one side of Snow's mind to the other. He sat back with a smirking smile, arms folded over his chest, and nodding at every slender young girl who patrolled past the table. Since the girls knew Snow as well as Tuttle and Crosby, they swapped greetings and smiles like people who had been at the same party together for a dozen years. The half-hearted attempt at suicide became the focal point. One girl's failure to redeem herself; to cut herself off from the worthlessness and hopelessness of her world; to offer herself as a sacrificial lamb to the others, who huddled near the jukebox.

"More than one guy's turned to ratshit in six months because they fucked up on the price," said Snow, who was clearly on a roll. "You gotta pay as you go in life. There ain't no free lunch. See Ted over in the corner with Bun?"

Everyone at the booth looked over at a bearded *farang* in jeans and T-shirt, with each arm wrapped around a girl.

"You're looking at a doomed man," Snow continued. "He thinks you can find a respectable Thai girl, sleep with her for nothing, and there's no bill at the end. Sometimes I see him around the Foreign Correspondents' Club on Friday nights. He comes in HQ once in a blue moon, looks at the girls, then goes home for a freebie.

"Why doomed? You might ask yourself, Larry, because you're green."

"It's obvious. You're a lawyer. You know about balloon payments. Ted's in for a huge balloon payment at the end. That's gonna take him, by surprise. Rock his boots, man. Instead of a free lunch he's gonna end up owing more, paying more than if he had simply played it straight. You gotta think of Headquarters as a tax system. It's pay as you go. Each night you know the bill. You pay up and start the day clean. No residual shit about you said this. You promised this. Why didn't you tell me that? He's fucking doomed. It comes from all those years in the '60s living on food stamps in California. It turned him into this great human sponge. Sucking up shelter, food, clothes, and there never seems to be a bill. Paradise, you think. Man, the whole world must be organized like California. Big fucking mistake.

"You get the wrong attitude about things. You get the idea that the government provides everything for free. You want a girl? Sure, just take one, fuck her, she won't mind. Pay? Why pay when you can get it free. Anyone who thinks like that is a doomed man. That balloon payment is getting bigger and bigger each day over his head, and when it busts, forget about his clothes. You ever see one of these chicks in action with a knife or razor blade? Fucking Green Berets turn and run in terror. Any one of these girls with a razor can polish off a man's wardrobe in ten seconds. Then she turns the blade and points at his cock. You can run but you can't hide, as Ali used to say. The Thais have pioneered precious little on this planet. But they are number one in surgically reconnecting cocks. America might be able to put a man on the moon. But when that razor takes off your cock, this is the one country in the world you want to be. The doctors know exactly how to operate with the skill of an open-heart surgeon in the States.

"You gotta learn to read Thai. The Thai newspapers report some Thai woman flipping out and cutting off the dick of her husband, lover, or customer. The stuff never gets into the English press. It creates a bad image. Gunter sitting over in Munich might book his two-week holiday to the Philippines where he can get laid with peace of mind.

"The native women go savage here. But California Ted won't listen. He thinks he can perch up on a high stool and just watch; nothing bad is gonna happen to him. Doomed. Read my lips. Doomed for eternity.

"Here are the rules. You're not paying for a date, or for love, for romance, or for a relationship. You try to pay your way into any of those and all you've bought is fucking chaos that will eat you ass first and spit out your eyeballs. At HQ, you're paying to use a female body for a few hours or for the night. A young, beautiful, horny, well-dressed, big breasted, long-legged girl, who is clean, and loves oral sex. You pay her to have sex with her. You pay her COD. This is her job. She goes with you on an employer employee relationship. In that collective agreement, which every regular knows by heart, there are terms and conditions that apply.

"She fucks you once at night and once in the morning. She sleeps in your bed. She never eats breakfast on the premises of her employer, and employers never pay carfare. And you never tell her that you love her. You never tell the jukebox you love it because the music has made you happy. Never tell an employee whose body you've hired for the night that you love her. Because you don't know her. You don't want to know her. Her family, her life, her fucked-up past, or doomed future. You've gotta divide your instincts from your sentimentality.

"Think of her as a temporary typist in your law firm who's come to perform a job. You're not gonna make her a partner. She has one function. The only difference is the HQ girl is gonna touch-type on your balls. She knows the collective agreement. Man, she's been through it a thousand times. So don't try and strike a new deal. Ask her to take less than a purple for a good night's work, she's gonna expect this is something more than an employer-employee relationship. She'll have visions of advancing from the typing pool to mistress of the house. And you've put that fucked-up vision in her head simply to save a couple hundred baht. In the end you have bought yourself pure chaos. Because you have to explain you don't love her, you ain't gonna marry her, take care of her, her sick parents, and sixty dirt-poor relatives. That you sweet-talked her into believing you loved her, man. Not just her sexy little body that you fucked into the ground for several months, but *her soul.*

"Now the balloon breaks. You're outside the collective agreement. All bets are off. She knows people with guns who work cheap. She's good with a razor. And you stumble into HQ looking for advice when it's too late and you're all but dead meat. And you fish a couple of one baht coins from your pocket and you walk over to the jukebox and you scatter the English songs, and finally punch in number 104, *'We Are the World'* thinking it might be the very last song you ever select on this earth. And you wish like hell that you weren't doomed. You wish like hell you could have resisted discounting her body. You wish like hell there were second chances."

THE con man and the whore had both advanced beyond hope or redemption in their lives, and it was just a matter of time before enough fraud sluiced through the gates of the night and exposed the mechanics of how the other would maneuver. The entire night the magnetic needle of the conversation came back around to fraud.

Lawrence was vaguely aware of the frolicking about on the steep pitched roof of probabilities. The hunt was for higher stakes than one of the girls drifting around the floor. It was more like an event where bets had been put down, odds measured, a grand strategy devised. Lawrence sensed that Tuttle and his friends were closing the distance between themselves and their quarry; that's what had brought them to HQ, they had homed in on their target. A pension lawyer from Los Angeles who had married a girl named Sarah, a woman killed a couple of months earlier in a car accident, a gallant, troubled woman. Not long before her death, Sarah had offered to extend help. Maybe this was a way she used to prepare herself for death.

"You get scam artists here from all over the world," said Tuttle, glancing at Lawrence through a cloud of gray smoke left by Crosby's cigarette. "The Merchant of Bangkok was from the Big Apple. Ran a sweat-shop garment factory on the Lower East Side of Manhattan. Just separated from his wife, and came to Bangkok for some action. He had more money than brains. He checked into the best room at the Oriental Hotel. He shot through all the shops in the main arcade and bought a shitload of skirts, dresses, scarfs at twenty-five, thirty percent discount and had all the stuff delivered to his room.

"Next he found out where the best bargain in 'babes' could be found. He always used that word, 'babes. I wanna fuck a real babe.' Someone at the hotel told him about HQ and he started coming in every night. Of course, he didn't speak a word of Thai, so first night one of the sharks took him on. A *peu-un pod* leader who kept her purse stacked on top of the jukebox. A girl who spoke twenty-five words of English. That first night, he was told that the going rate was a purple—even then in '82. He whipped out a pocket calculator and did a number of fancy conversions. Howard was the kind of guy who had never paid retail for anything in his life and he wasn't about to start in Bangkok.

"He went over to Fawn—she'd been around for about four or five years—and she spoke half-assed English. Enough to make her employable for the kind of nightwork where conversation wasn't of the highest priority. If Howard wanted to go, she was ready to turn on the meter. Howard pulled her out into the alley. Under his coat, he had a couple of samples. A skirt and a scarf. He pitched her the deal. She laid out her ass for him, and the stuff was hers. Top retail for the skirt and scarf might have pushed a purple. Fawn took the skirt over to a taxi parked in the alley and got the driver to put on his headlights. She examined the fabric, label, and design in the light. She did the same with the silk scarf. She ran a few numbers through her head. Then Fawn turned to Howard and nodded. He had a deal. Howard must have thought this is easy. A five-hundred-baht retail piece of ass for about three hundred.

"If he had been really smart, he'd have cut and run. At least from HQ where the intelligence network among the girls is world class. The next night, Howard returned. Fawn occupied her post position in a corner booth wearing her new skirt and scarf. He gave her a little wave of the hand not knowing that at HQ a *farang* waving to a girl he had hired out the night before is an invitation for a new employment contract based on the same terms and conditions. Instead, he gave her the old cold shoulder, and Fawn slumped back to her booth without her face. Fawn had already told her friend about the deal with Howard, who told another girl, who told another, who spread it down the table, until everyone in the place knew Howard's idea of payment. You get the picture. So one of the regulars went up to Howard and flirted, grabbed his hand, made goo-goo eyes at him. Howard struck the same deal. Only this time, it was easier because the girl already knew this john's idea of compensation translated into clothes.

"By the end of the week, seven HQ girls arrived dressed wearing Howard's discounted skirts and scarfs. I'm arriving at HQ early every night along with about two dozen other resident *farangs* who are taking bets on just when Howard's bell is going to get rung. It happened to be a Sunday night. Howard walked in, ordered a whiskey sour, gave a girl a couple of baht for the jukebox, with instructions to play number 101, '*Sexy Eyes.*' You see, Howard made the mistake of many greenhorns.

"After a week, he figured that he understood all there was to know about whoring in Bangkok. He went back to Fawn—the girl he had started with—and Fawn, along with six other HQ girls, all wearing identical skirts from Howard, gathered around him. Fawn had done a little homework.

"She had gone out to *Chatuchak Market* on Saturday and found Howard's skirts for one red and the scarfs going for half a red. That's

98

several light-years away from a purple. She wasn't impressed that he had bought them at the Oriental Hotel. All she cared about was her ass being sold far below market value.

"As *'Sexy Eyes'* started up, she told Howard that she didn't like being discounted. And the other girls were pissed off for being taken advantage of, but that was okay.

"'Never mind,' she said. She walked hand in hand with Howard out the back door and into the alley, where Howard hired the same taxi with the driver who had turned his headlights on the skirt that first night for Fawn. Only this time the driver headed to *Klong Toey*—the Harlem of Bangkok. The driver had a few of his friends waiting near the *Chao Phraya River*. They pulled Howard out of the taxi. He was crying and pleading. His hands folded in prayer. Fawn sat in the back of the taxi, her sexy, tapered legs crossed beneath her new skirt, and smoked a cigarette. She watched as they beat the shit out of Howard. Stripped off his clothes and left him naked and bleeding along the side of the road.

"What hit him hard was the boutique at the Oriental Hotel had screwed him on the price of the dresses and shit. It took an HQ girl, a regular, to find the real price. He never came back to HQ. He never went to the police. He headed back to New York City with an important lesson about wholesale bargains. Certain things in life have a fixed retail price that is sacred. Bargain that price down and you are guaranteed, when things fall apart, to learn that the retail price had been a real bargain from the start."

LIKE Tuttle, neither Snow nor Crosby had ever been married. Women were a form of indoor entertainment, thought Lawrence. He had been married to the same woman for half his life; a stable partnership, with the day-to-day give-and-take, combining personal companionship, affection, and familiarity. He had married his college sweetheart—who also happened to be Tuttle's sweetheart; a piece of information Lawrence believed over the years was no more than a small footnote in a long, weighty text of their marriage. What was difficult to swallow was the second text—the one in Sarah's own hand; the one she had hidden in her office, volumes and volumes, where Lawrence had been the footnote.

Certainly both couldn't be true? Had Sarah worn a kind of mask, performed a part, all those years? Had he never taken her away from Tuttle? His head pounded with the whiskey and soda, with the unanswered questions from the smoke drifting across the room from a hundred cigarettes. He had arrived in Bangkok with a private mission: to uncover Sarah's secret life, looking for some small detail that could give him comfort. Instead he had been on a steady diet of deception, indifference, and he suspected, fabrications. They had been playing a game with him. "Let's see what kind of man you really are" kind of game. They had been examining his likes and dislikes at each stage of the night, deciding whether to promote him through the ranks.

Snow made out that he was an innocent; playing off the ancient wisdom of Crosby; and Tuttle, as always had been the case with him, seemed to orchestrate the group with an unseen hand. It had always bothered Lawrence that everyone else around Tuttle understood he was working out of place and time deep in a private sedimentary deposit of knowledge. Lawrence never believed it for a moment. The circles around him were being misled. Snow's Lahu Godman was a perfect description of Tuttle, thought Lawrence. It was the role he had played his entire life. Going up the mountain with his illusions and messages, Tuttle played the prophet. The oracle who haunted page after page of Sarah's diaries.

Lawrence turned to Snow. "Ever thought of marrying a Thai?"

Snow's dilated eyes blinked several times. A flicker of a smile crossed his thin lips. He revealed a photograph of a young Thai girl from his wallet. "Marriage, you say," said Snow. "I'm open-minded, and I almost married this one."

"But she created a bit of a row," said Crosby. "The usual misery, I'm afraid."

"What kind of trouble?" asked Lawrence, looking around the table. Obviously they all knew the story, and were looking to Tuttle to determine if they should continue.

"Nop had a BA from Thammasat University," said Tuttle, breaking the silence. "A regular job. She wasn't a bar girl. She came from a good family. But she wanted certain guarantees from Snow."

"Cash guarantees," said Snow, nodding his head. "She had commercial concerns."

"Sod that," interrupted Crosby. "That one would have disappeared with the bankbook."

"I could have ended up like one of those wandos who comes here, falls in love with an HQ hooker, marries her, and either hauls her back to a council house in Leicester or a townhouse in Houston. Those guys are fucking doomed, man. Beyond hope, beyond salvation. To marry the thing you've paid to fuck you is major league confusion. It's like trying to play basketball with a baseball bat. You strike out and foul out all at the same time."

Snow had picked up steam again. The fire returned to his voice, and his hands danced around the photograph of Nop on the table as he spoke.

"A sixty-six-year-old Australian married little Noi, aged nineteen. He buys a house for two-million baht and puts it in the mother-in-law's name. Six months later, he goes back to Aussieland for a two week holiday. A short R&R to see family. Big fucking mistake. He should have chained Noi to the bedroom door with a two-week supply of food. Of course, little Noi who had found her dream man. Man, she had the Aussie believing that he was her wet dream material. Forget that her sixty-six-year-old dreamboat came fitted with a diesel engine that chugged at half speed on a level grade. Wasn't this every girl's dream? What else could she ever want in life? She'd spent nineteen years waiting for this ancient dream lover to sail into her harbor.

"'Will I marry you? No fucking problem. Oh, darling, by the way, *farang* can't own land in Thailand," the Aussie said.

"But we need house," she said.

"How can we buy house?" he asked.

"She had the perfect solution. 'You put deed in Mama's name. We can live in that house forever. Just the two of us. I look after you every day, every night.'

"What an offer. No Aussieland chick's gonna knead his balls every night and tell him he's the best lover she's ever had, and that he doesn't look a day over forty. 'House in your mama's name? Why didn't I think of that? You really don't want to go to Sydney with me? You would love it. Oh, you want to stay and look after the house? Weed the garden, scrub the floors, and bake bread? Have everything just right for when I return? And see some of your friends and family. Why didn't I think of that? How selfish of me. Two weeks will go fast.'

"Fast? Man, there isn't a Thai woman who can't turn over a house and land anywhere in the Kingdom in less than seventy-two hours. Little Noi disappeared into the woodwork. The Aussie searched, went to the police, who laughed and shrugged their shoulders. Now a broken man, he writes a letter to the editor of the newspaper. She never turned up, and the Aussie lost every cent he had ever saved."

Lawrence leaned back and shifted his knees to the side, letting Crosby slide past him and disappear off to the toilets. He had heard the story before. Snow picked up the photograph of Nop, held it up, as he tipped back his beer. Around the border of the jukebox, activity was picking up. Girls filtering in from the discos, better dressed, some who looked like students.

"The story isn't finished, man. A year later a Brit marries a Thai and takes her to London. Six months of married bliss, and one day she says, Darling, I miss Papa and Mama, go back to Thailand for one week, okay? Oh, I love you like monkey love banana. After two weeks, he's not heard a word from her. Does an alarm bell go off in his head? Sure. But the wrong one. He's worried something might have happened to her. That was the romantic in him. The hopeful chance that just maybe she's had an accident, a mugging, held hostage. And with most romantics, the whole nine yards of horror rushed through his head. He had to act; he had to rescue his wife. So he flies into Bangkok, takes the train up to Chiang Mai, knocks on the door of the family shack.

"We no see Noi. We think she with you."

"Another week looking for her in Bangkok, hanging out in HQ telling his story to Old Bill in the back booth, tears rolling down his cheeks. Damn, how he loved that girl. He flies back to London, and discovers Noi's a very clever girl. She had waited until he had left England, then went to the bank and cleaned out the savings and checking accounts—which he had put in joint names, flew back to Thailand, and was never heard of again."

Tuttle leaned forward in his seat, the well-developed muscles in his forearms tensed as he clasped his hands together, looking at the latest girls to arrive. "Never heard of that until Snow almost married her. She had changed her name to Nop. She was a real success story. Someone who had learned the American dream. Rags to riches through accumulating other people's money. We did a little digging and found out her past. One smooth lady."

"Tuttle managed to get some money back for the Aussie and Brit. She broke down, cried, admitted everything. She said I had changed her, made a new woman out of her. An Oscar performance for a woman who was officially married to two husbands." Snow slowly slipped her photograph back into his wallet. The ends were worn, slanted with age. The image still inspired a mixture of fear, relief, and the recurring flash of terror that comes from a near miss with disaster.

SNOW slid out of the booth with his half-empty beer. A moment later he was smiling and joking with one of the HQ regulars. Gliding across the surface of melancholy with a squeeze, laughter at the outer rim far away from shame and wounded pride. That safe terrain where they both expected to sustain their dance until first light, then she would leave with her morning-gift tucked inside her wallet. And Snow, again in solitude, would pull out the photograph of Nop, marvel at the confidence of her smile, and ask himself why he had never thrown it away. Sometimes he told himself, he kept the photograph because it was a marker for the time he had become moonstruck. When Nop had been in his life, he had discovered and venerated romance, and for a brief intense time he thought it might be enough.

Lawrence slipped on his jacket, and began to thread his tie around his collar. Several girls were singing along with '*We Are the World*' playing. It was insane, thought Lawrence. The most crippled members of the species had found a place to drink, sing, and play. The mentality predated the invention of hand tools by mankind, he thought, knotting his tie. Tuttle had watched him, recording the emotions crossing his face like an electronic billboard; Lawrence had been mocked, excluded, alienated, and insulted over the course of the evening. He had arrived looking for a sanctuary to express his private grief, and instead Tuttle had blasted the religion of marriage.

Tuttle's message had been clear; Lawrence had found it in one of the short stories Sarah had collected. She had used her Magic Marker to underline several paragraphs. In the months following her death, Lawrence had read those paragraphs many times.

"You put another two baht into the jukebox at the center of the universe and pick your song. Any song. One that helps you focus on the price of things in life. How discounts work. How they can defeat you. And you keep coming back to the basic question, what am I buying? What is that I want to buy for tonight? For tomorrow night? How does anyone figure a price for anything beyond tomorrow night? And you go over the collective agreement, thinking about the fine print in that invisible document memorized by every working girl and every *hard-core* regular in the place.

"No matter how many times you go through it, you keep coming back to the same conclusion. This is about work for her. About the terms and conditions of the color purple.

"This is about an expression of pleasure for me. HQ operates an exchange system with known values for the instinctual drive. The color of sex is always purple. And the color of love? The color of gas, helium, the kind of gas you use to fill circus balloons. And there is the history of balloon payments in HQ.

"I call myself her customer—*look kah*—whenever I talk to her. She knows from that moment, I'm *hard-core*. She can relax, go to work, her mind can drift off someplace else; inside the jukebox, following the cockroach circling round and round the colored balls, locked inside, looking for an escape hatch, not knowing there isn't one, circling round and round for a lifetime, listening to music it can't understand."

8

Lawrence had little hard knowledge about Tuttle's recent past; he knew Tuttle had abandoned his journalism career. Sarah's diary had mentioned something about an English language school for slum kids that he had started. But the series of events that caused him to leave journalism and open the school had not been revealed by Sarah. Tuttle had little money, few books, and a few rooms on the third floor of an old building donated by a sympathetic landlord. Late at night, after a day teaching, he wrote the stories that Sarah saw rising like bubbles from the depths in magazines from Bangkok, Hong Kong, Singapore, and London. In 1984, he had written a story about an English school teacher in Bangkok; how he had gone full circle from sleeping with the girls to teaching them English.

The story was titled *Monsoon Language Lessons*. Lawrence had shown a copy to Kelly Swan the night before he left Los Angeles. She read the story like a legal document, tearing through the sentences as if looking for a single rule or point, and discovering everything else on the way. When she finished the last page, she had the look of someone bucked off a saddle. The desk lamp cast a warm yellow light over her confident, proud, angular face. A face that did not conceal her emotion of unvarnished contempt.

"Why does Tuttle focus on the helplessness of women? We have fought against this. Because the image is wrong."

He hadn't expected the tears that followed her condemnation. She balled up the story and flung it across the room, running from the room crying. Lawrence had gone after her. He found himself in the strange position of defending Tuttle to Kelly Swan. Or was he defending Sarah's decision to keep the story in her file? He no longer knew his own motives but found himself raising his voice in his own house. In the eight years Sarah and he had lived in the house, he couldn't ever remember when either of them had raised their voices. But there he was, shouting at Kelly who had locked herself into the bathroom.

"For God sakes, it's about communication," he shouted through the door.

"It's not. It's degrading to women."

"Where is it degrading?" asked Lawrence, unballing the story, his eyes sweeping across the page.

"That a man can do whatever he wants, and a woman's gotta stand for it, or she's a bitch," Kelly said as she unlocked the bathroom door, swinging it open fast enough to clip Lawrence on the chin. "And you're going to spend a week in Bangkok with him."

"I am spending a week in Bangkok and that's final."

Her anger about his Bangkok journey had been brewing up from nearly the time Lawrence announced his decision. Tuttle had become the battleground, a whipping boy for a load of things neither of them was prepared to face directly. History repeated itself in an odd way, Tuttle had been the battleground with Sarah years earlier. He hated the irony of his presence protruding into every relationship he had. This invisible fist slamming him hard in his emotional belly of his life.

"Why don't I go with you to Bangkok?" Kelly asked standing in the door with watery eyes. She had asked the same question a dozen or more times.

"Because of the . . ."

"The Ryan deal," she said, finishing his sentence. "Fuck the Ryan deal."

He smiled, still rubbing his chin, looking at his fingers for a hint of blood from the bang on the door. "That comes from a woman who wants to be a partner? That's not the bargain, Kelly. Either you're seriously committed to the firm or you're not. Which is it?"

"Does that mean if I don't like your friend's story I'm black-balled?"

"He's not my friend. I don't even like him."

"Then why are you going to Bangkok?"

"I don't know," he shouted. But he did know; it had been the Tuttle of Sarah's diaries he wanted to meet; the man who had communicated to his dead wife in page after page of her diaries; he was going in search of the Tuttle who had written about the breakdown of communication between men and women, the battle over words, the desire to say and hear certain phrases and not others.

The truth embarrassed Lawrence; he could never have trusted anyone enough to have explained why he was going to Bangkok. He wasn't certain he trusted himself with the uncomfortable feeling that Tuttle possessed the right combination of words to heal the wound of Sarah's death, of her secret betrayal, of the warning signal transmitted in his dreams—that there was danger ahead and he didn't know how to avoid the collision anymore than Sarah.

"That's right, Larry. You don't know. About me, yourself. And I'm beginning to wonder if you ever really knew Sarah."

The force of his slap knocked Kelly down. A trickle of blood spilled from a small cut on her lip. She looked up at him, with an injured expression and making a low whimpering sound. He dropped to his knee and rocked her in his arms, kissing her head. That night he dreamt the pattern her dried blood made on the front of his shirt had come alive as dark, brown animals, jungle animals. He woke up startled in the pitch-dark room, rolled out of bed and peeked through the curtains. He was still in Los Angeles, the jungle animals of Bangkok had not yet come for him.

LAWRENCE removed the photocopy of the story from his jacket and slid it across the table to Tuttle.

"I found this among Sarah's papers at the University," he said.

Tuttle looked down in a vacant stare. His own words with Sarah's yellow Magic Marker touching a word here, a sentence there, as if she were pointing out her own way through the passages. Were the markings an endorsement, a question mark, or a register of disappointment? A story about language enigma engraved enigmatically by the hand of a dead woman—Sarah would have liked the harmony of those tones, thought Tuttle.

"Could you read it aloud?" asked Lawrence.

Tuttle's head jerked up. "You want me to read out loud now? Here?"

"Why not here? Why not now? It's about this kind of place; the people who come into this place."

Clearing his throat, Tuttle paused a moment, his eyes circling the jukebox. "Yeah, why not?"

❖

MONSOON LANGUAGE LESSONS
A Short Story
by
Robert Tuttle

YOUR first monsoon season changes the way you see Bangkok. The bars are dead. The resident *farangs* are holed up for weeks. The jukebox is silent for hours at a stretch. None of the girls can spare two baht'for a song. The September rain falls in tidal waves, turning the *sois* into muddy rivers. A group of us sits below ground level at HQ. Every year there is fear the floods will enter and sweep away the girls. In the name of progress, the *klongs* have been paved over; high-rise offices and shopping centers cluster over the buried waters. Then the monsoon reclaims what is underneath the surface, and the hidden *klong* rises like a decomposed corpse.

You must take taxis everywhere now. You smoke a joint in the back seat, and tell the driver to take you to *Soi Cowboy*. The taxi seems to float above the surface of the brown river, spraying sheets of water window-high. You roll down the window a crack, and touch the surf with your fingertips. It's like skipping flat stones across the water as a kid. You laugh and joke with the driver.

By the time the taxi arrives, you're stoned. You get out of the cab, a little shaky on your feet and stumble, almost fall on one knee into a pool of brackish water. You are too stoned to go far, and you turn into one of the first bars in *Soi Cowboy*.

Inside you find twenty-five bored teenagers. Go-go dancers sitting around smoking, gossiping, sleeping, playing with their toes, or staring off vacantly at the empty stools as if hypnotized by the sound of falling rain and the ghosts of customers from the past.

You are the only *farang* in the bar. Your shoes, socks, and pant cuffs are wet. Your hat is matted down with rain. Rain runs off your face and drips off your earlobes. You have that stoned smile of a thoroughly soaked human being who is in a state of chemical bliss. You wander past the bar spinning the stool tops; the girls giggle and applaud. The girls reach out and touch your face and neck. A stroke here. A brush and pinch there.

You stop and try to focus on the girl with short-cropped black hair and long silver earrings. She sits cross-legged on the stool; her red high-heel shoes tipped over on the floor at your feet. You speak to her. She is eighteen, and coasted into Bangkok from *Nakhon Sawan* only days before. And because you're stoned you find yourself believing her. You can't get over the perfect, tiny, white teeth and full lips and shiny, open, passionate eyes.

She is drying you off with a towel, cleaning your ears, unbuttoning your shirt and wiping your damp chest and stomach. Before you can protest she has your shirt off, and you're wearing a bar T-shirt. You feel dry for the first time since you've entered the bar. And you ask yourself the Bangkok Monsoon Season sixty-four dollar question: Do you want to buy a girl for the rainy season? Not for two hours, not for all night, but for several months. Would you like to disappear into your own private life with a girl while the loud claps of thunder and heavy rains pound the city? Listening to the cadence of rain on your roof with a rent-a-wife? Cut your moorings from HQ for the rainy season.

Noi holds a cup of hot coffee to your lips. And as you're sipping, you can't take your eyes off her smiling face. She has a long-term face; one you feel certain will outlast a single night. But is she monsoon rent-a-wife material? You are stoned and prone to snap judgements. Those teeth and lips, her flat belly, perfect breasts, narrow hips, the graceful movement of her hands behind the towel over your face, neck, and chest. She's playing the piano, touching every key with perfect harmony; a song is bursting from your throat as you sip the hot coffee.

This one is what you have been looking for; you deserve her. She's a life raft with all the right equipment. You buy her a Cola, and she bows, hands folded like in prayer, kisses your cheek. She comes back and sits on your lap, her arms around your neck. The rain pours into *Soi Cowboy* as if it had been built underneath a waterfall. This isn't rain, you tell yourself. This is the end of the world. You have minutes to pack in your supplies and get out. The floods will carry away every business, bar, girl; everything not fastened above the waterline. You know where to go. This is maybe your last chance to choose the woman who will be at your side as you hear the sea rolling in, reclaiming lost territory; when you watch the tidewater sweep in, rise over your head, and in that moment when you can no longer breathe, she is at your side, holding you tight.

Three hours later, she is beneath you in bed. Her tiny hands clawing at your back. Flashes of lightning from outside pierce the darkness of the room every few seconds. Soi dogs howl in that scared, half-mad moan. Her eyes are closed tightly; her face twisted into a mask of pleasure. She moans, turns her head into the pillow, her lower teeth bite into her lip. The time is near. She arches her hips. Her breathing is fast and hard. As you are about to come inside her for the first time of all the many times you have already inside your head, she shouts out in the darkness.

She screams a single word. Not a Thai word. She shouts the word again. You are still stoned, but the word works deep inside your mind and you freeze on top of her.

"*Wunderbah*," she shouts. "*Wunderbah*."

Six days in Bangkok, she had said. Your erection goes limp inside her, and you think of a Wolfgang or Gunter pumping up and down and screaming at the top of his lungs in some rundown short-time hotel, "*Wunderbah. Wunderbah*," as he fucks little Noi for the second or third time in a two-hour stretch. And minutes later you are in your clothes, and she is in hers, and you are walking in knee deep water, carrying her in your arms like a small child bundled under a blanket. You walk slowly through the sludge of dead leaves, garbage, and sewage; the rain pelting against your face.

You stand on Sukhumvit Road cradling her in your arms, rocking her until she is nearly asleep in your arms; then you remember where you are, and you feel the hot rain striking your face, and soon a taxi pulls up. You bundle her into the back seat with two crisp, fresh purples. And she still doesn't understand what has gone wrong. She simply doesn't get it. How can you explain to her where you have drawn the line? How defeat is slung over one side, and victory over the other? That the factors that turn one into another can be one word. She looked so tiny and childlike in the back of the taxi, her hair matted down against her face. She looked so lovely. And you take a deep breath, shake off the drugs, the emotion that had moored you to her for a moment, the draw of the wish you had for her, and tell her that you were stoned back in Cowboy. That you never had taken a monsoon rent-a-wife. But that if you ever did, she would be top on the German language-speaking list.

You kiss her lightly on the lips and watch the taxicab pull away from the curb, spraying a mist of brown water on the sidewalk. She waves from the back of the taxi. You raise your hand and wave back; and you look again, and this time you see that she's twisted her tiny hand into a gesture. You recognize the gesture. She sticks her hand out the other side of the rear window of the cab and gives a Nazi salute. A formation of the fingers and palm from a distant war. And you feel sick in the knowledge that the war was still fought; and this time you lost, and next time down the road, with the tide coming to your ears, you have this feeling you may lose again.

SNOW and Crosby parachuted back to the table as Tuttle finished the last two paragraphs of the story. Snow towed along a young girl, a twenty-year-old, nicknamed Toom; she scooted across the fake black leather bench, holding her miniskirt with both hands, coming to a stop nestled hip to hip with Lawrence. Her large imploring eyes, brooding mouth, and tiny baby nose suggested the face of a child beggar who had moved up the career ladder put against the wall of life for the poor. She was shy, and Lawrence liked her. Snow scooted onto the bench and hiked Toom onto his lap. She laughed, covering her mouth with both hands like an embarrassed child.

"There's one lesson in teaching the girls English. Man, you gotta get there first. Kilroy was here. You've gotta to be ruthless and teach them that first phrase. That's the trace memory that makes you their first *farang*. About first years ago, I bought out a fresh face from Benny's Bar in Patpong. She had worked the strip about a week and she didn't know a word of English when I bought her out. Not a fucking word. Three in the morning, I'd smoked an entire joint and she sat in squat position on the bed next to me. I looked at her in the mirror. And I said to her, 'I like a banana like a monkey like banana.' I repeated the sentence. I broke it down one word at a time. One syllable at a time. Like fucking reverse engineering. I had the entire sentence pulled apart. And slowly showed her how to build it back up.

"Five a.m. and I was totally wrecked. I popped another diet pill. Ten minutes later, she finally had the phrase down pat, man.

"'I like a banana like a monkey like banana.' Then she's doing variations on the theme like, 'I much like banana like little monkey like big banana.'

"Like Toom here, she was bright, had natural timing. She could have been on Letterman's or Leno's. She looked at herself in the mirror as she said the words. She could have gone far. After a year or so on the circuit she picked up another two hundred words of English. 'I fuck you good, you buy me TV and motorbike, okay?' Or some such shit. 'You fuck me, go to PX and buy colored TV and case Johnny Walker Red. Good deal for you.'

"Or try this one, 'You like lady boy suck dick? Or you like suck dick lady boy?'

"And some wando comes across her two, three years down the road, buys her out, and just as he's getting off his rocks, she's whispering in his ear, 'I much like you like little monkey like big banana.'

"Years down the pike of wonderland, she uses the phrase in the letters that Old Bill will write for her. Letters to America, man. She's like a parrot handed down through hundreds of short-term owners. Each adding a new phrase along the way. One thing, though, she ain't never gonna forget her first English sentence. That's a buzz. Forget about popping a cherry. Taking virginity is finding that girl straight off the bus from Chiang Mai who doesn't know a fucking word of English. And knowing wherever she goes, no matter who she fucks, your words are gonna be in her mind. She can't ever shake loose from that message you stuffed in a bottle deep inside her head. In every hotel room in Bangkok, as she strips down before some green wando from London or New York City, she hears that phrase in her head. And she repeats it to the guy. And he says, 'Who taught you that?' She says, 'I learned with the Snow. Inside, the Snowman.'"

❖

LAWRENCE felt Toom's hand kneading his leg under the table. His head swivelled around. She was talking in Thai to Crosby, delivering a passionate argument on some point that Lawrence couldn't understand.

"Is this the girl, Tuttle?" he asked.

Tuttle grinned, shaking his head. "That's not her."

"You'll know Asanee when you see her," Crosby piped in, interrupting his conversation. "You won't need to be told."

"When does she come?"

Snow leaned across the table, with a look of intuitive insight into what Lawrence was thinking. "Asanee never comes in here."

"Why not?" asked Lawrence, thinking there must be some logical explanation.

"That's a long story," said Snow. He looked away as if the conversation was over as far as he was concerned.

Crosby used the lull to immediately change the subject. No sooner had a waiter delivered a Cola for Toom, than Crosby rushed in to fill the void of silence.

"It's bloody difficult to know who's a greater source of iniquity in this city. The Huns or the Yanks. With the possible exception of Tuttle, what *farang* at HQ speaks above second-grade level Thai? Not very many. This is beyond the realm of simple wordplay. Language is more than simple manners and style. You search for the valve that opens up the Thai's way of thinking. One word is layered in a hundred Thai expressions. One word modified countless times, day after day, from whorehouses, shops, schools, and banks. The word? It's heart. Thai is a language of heart talk. English is from the head. The clash is between two kinds of thought."

Toom jerked, picking her name out of the conversation. She elbowed Crosby and asked him in Thai why he was talking about her to the *farang*? Her beggar's eyes sweeping Crosby's face for a hint of deception. Crosby protested, in Thai, that he had not spoken badly of her. She glanced over at Tuttle, who with a nod, confirmed that Crosby was telling the truth.

"Tuttle *jai dee*, " said Toom.

"There's the word. Heart. Good heart," said Crosby. "*Jai dee* is very important to the Thai. Not good head. But good heart. That's your starting point. From there you build an entire way of talking about heart. *Jai tahm*—literally means black heart. Mean-spirited. And there is *Jai yen*—cool heart. That ability to take anything life throws at you with a smile. Patience is of the heart. You want to condemn someone, you say he is *Jai rawn*—hot heart, hot-headed, someone who loses his temper and the razor and knife flash hot with blood. *Jep! Jai*—the hurt, aching heart of the abandoned lover. The girl who tried to kill herself earlier was *Jep! Jai*; dumped by her *farang* boyfriend. *Bplack jai*!—surprise of the heart. *tuean jai*!—remind, you remind not the head but the heart. And in Thailand you don't change your mind, you change your heart. *Bplee-un jai*!"

This torrent of heart-modified Thai words came from the mouth of a man Lawrence was convinced had no heart. But Crosby with feeling, had movingly claimed to have discovered the hidden territory of the Thai language. Each time Crosby had used a Thai "heart"-modified word, Toom had giggled nervously. It was like watching television where there were snatches of your own language tangled in a vast ocean of foreign, clacking words.

"Don't forget *hen! jai!*," said Snow. "Sympathy."

"Or *Nahk! jai!*," added Tuttle, in a deliberate tone that made the word appear it had been said strictly for Lawrence's benefit.

"Which is?" Lawrence asked, as Toom leaned her head against his shoulder.

"The rough translation is heavy heart," said Tuttle.

The table went silent for a moment. Crosby dealt in the last "heart" card. "*Kreng jai*—awe-heart is the rough translation," he said. "But it can't be translated. English lacks a counterpart. *Kreng jai* is an attitude. It's about class and social order. About rank. Not something Americans like talking about. *Kreng jai* is how you honor class rank. In the better knock-shops, you see *kreng jai* everywhere. It's making yourself small; never imposing on the other person. Between the boss and girls, between girls, boss and customers, between the cops and boss. Each girl in a *peu-un pod* knows her role and place. They never ask for something; that violates the rule, but they wait to receive. Kreng jai circles around the English words like deference, consideration, diffidence.

"Thailand is the land of hearts in awe of their social betters. The girls show *kreng jai* to their father, boss, husband, and to an older girl. But there is a dark side. When a Thai is totally pissed off but she owes the *kreng jai*, then she locates a target below her on the social scale for a good kick or punch. Dogs are good. Children are okay. So a Thai guy might kick a dog to death as a message to his boss. His indirect way of saying, 'I'm really upset with you, and my heart which is filled with a witch's brew of awe and fear requires me to vent my anger on this miserable creature.' And the boss listens. That's why the girls love the *farang*. We fall even lower on the social scale than an HQ girl. They don't have to hold back, or show respect. They owe us no *kreng jai*. We are down at the bottom next to soi dogs; only we are better, we pay to get kicked."

CROSBY'S finishing tone of bitterness left a colorless, tasteless gloom in the air. Toom's head lay against Snow's shoulder, her eyes half-closed in a daze, locked into a beggar's blank expression. Whatever roof had covered Crosby's heart had collapsed long before. He had trained himself to live beyond the claims of heart, thought Lawrence. All around the room, as the girls drank, smoked, talked, flirted with potential customers, their aromatic perfume mingling with cigarette smoke, they performed the acrobatics of the heart on a vast stage; was Crosby right? Was the complexity of the culture poured into the hole of that single word? Certainly, a Thai fell in love with a *farang*, he thought. Beyond the quarters of HQ there were other fine grained truths.

"Bobby, do you believe that? It's all a question of heart?"

"Is that a loaded question?" asked Tuttle.

"Load it with whatever you want to think."

Tuttle scratched his moustache, sniffed, crinkling his nostrils. "You learn that *kreng jai* is one room in the house. But if you want to understand the foundation, what's underneath there's another Thai expression—*Mai pen rai*. Which means never mind. It's okay.

No problem. Forget about it. Don't mention it. Your husband was killed on Rama IV in a motorcycle accident? '*Mai pen rai.*' Your father was fired from his job? '*Mai pen rai.*' Your brother's been sent to prison for smuggling drugs? '*Mai pen rai.*' Your husband's abandoned you for another woman? '*Mai pen rai.*' Your school folding for lack of funds? '*Mai pen rai.*' Your daughter back on the street? '*Mai pen rai.*'

"There is no disappointment or tragedy larger than that phrase. It's a Zen state of acceptance. Whatever happens you've earned from your behavior in a past life. You never allow the bad to pull you down. You have no other choice. Whatever happens or doesn't happen, it comes from inside of you. The Thai language is structured to accept pain; tolerate suffering. Our language seeks the cure, the solution, the answer. English is the language of change. Of the future you can make your own. That's why the *farang* and Thai can't find a language to communicate with each other. Most of the HQ girls from the old days have married *farangs*. The *hard-core*, the ugly ones, the fat ones with stretch marks as wide as the Panama Canal, the Tommy's, forty year-old women, all of them had a gold ring slipped over the third finger on their left hand and are living in Moose Jaw, or L.A., or Sydney. And every so often one of the girls drifts back into the town after years and years away. She slips back for a quiet holiday on her own; for old times' sake. And the first night of the first day she's back at HQ feeding the jukebox, halfway into peu-un pod membership. It is as if she had never left.

"I know what you're thinking, 'You can take the girl out of HQ but you can't take the HQ out of the termite.' Or 'Silly bitch shows up looking to turn a trick for a purple.' A currency she's not even used for years.

"Lek who was sitting here earlier. She's been gone for six, seven years. She's married and lives in Rhode Island where she owns a microwave oven, dishwasher, built-in kitchen cupboards, and two car garage. Lek's back for a two-week vacation. That's her leaning against the jukebox at the center of the universe. She works in a cannery. She's happy. After a couple of minutes talking with her, you keep hearing a new English word. One she had never used before. One you never heard HQ girls using.

"She keeps saying, 'future.'

"'Our future look good.'

"'Future of husband's job good.'

"'Saving for future of kids now.'

"'In future come back to Thailand more.'

"For all her talk about the 'future,' she is looking to get her ass picked up by a *farang* at HQ. She doesn't need the money. There are a hundred other ways to find a sex partner. But she's standing by the jukebox, looking at the old song chart and slipping the coins into the slot. Just like in the old days. And she sees that I'm watching and she blows me a kiss just like in the old days. Then I look at the blue numbers come up on the jukebox as she selects a song. She hasn't forgotten. The song I have played many, many nights at HQ. The one that I try to save to the end of the night, and leave just as the song finishes. Number 132. The melody of *'What a Wonderful World'* blares out over the loudspeakers. She's remembered. That feeling of old times. The one that doesn't seem to be in her future back at the cannery in Rhode Island.

"I listen to the lyrics of the music. The same words I have heard for what seems like half a lifetime. And I look around HQ and see from the faces of the regulars—a number of them our students—what Thai words have formed the texture and shape of their lives. And I realize that I know all the songs—both Thai and English songs—by heart, every last lyric of every last love song. And somehow over the years the songs have become the internal private language. The bridge drops down and we cross over to find each other. At least for the night. And the HQ girls are mouthing the words to the song, and before the night is over, Lek will return to the table and will kiss me long and hard on the lips. And for a moment, we will sit at the still point of the turning world. Where the past and future are gathered, and where no words are moving in or out.

"Crosby puts it down to class. Snow puts Lek down as a Valley girl with a Thai accent. But I know why she's back. What drew her to HQ tonight. There's a library inside the jukebox, and every volume is right-side up, and every song feeds some dream, some hope, or feeling that connected her to a life before she learned the word 'future.' Before the word 'future' replaced the Thai phrase—*Mai pen rai*—never mind. Never mind the present; never mind the future. Most of all, never mind the past. Time had vanished from her life

117

and she came back to HQ looking for that thing she had lost; the thing that she had forgotten because she lived in a place where it had no name. *Mai pen rai."*

Someone behind the bar had turned up the volume of the music. Two girls danced with each other, singing to the music on the makeshift dance floor. "And you think I came to Bangkok for the same reason?" Lawrence asked, resting forward on his elbows, his head turned toward Tuttle.

"I think we are all looking for the same question," replied Tuttle, tapping his thumbnail against the half-empty Kloster bottle.

"You mean answer," insisted Lawrence.

"The same question," said Tuttle with a glint of a smile, as he raised the beer bottle to his lips.

9

Lawrence slipped on his jacket and pushed out of the booth. "I'm working tomorrow," said Tuttle, swallowing a yawn. A moment later and they would have gone. But Dan, an old hand and HQ regular, spotted Tuttle from a distance, and dragged a chair to their table.

"I've gotta talk to you, Tuttle," said Dan.

"We were just on our way out."

"Shit, this is important."

Tuttle nodded and sat down. Lawrence had the feeling that Tuttle had difficulty disengaging himself from the people who had come to HQ to seek him out. Lawrence didn't bother to remove his jacket as he climbed back into the booth opposite Tuttle.

Dan held a bottle of Singha beer in each large, meaty fist; the light brown hair on his arms was matted with sweat. His heavy jaw, short-cropped hair, and small eyes made the top half of his face seem like a distorted, abridged edition of the bottom half. His features were out of balance—like the rough sketch of a face that had been abandoned, and he had the nervous tic of rolling his head from side to side, as if the muscles in his neck ached.

"I know, I know. I was goin' back to the States for six months. And I'm back! I lasted one month, three days and six hours. I came to HQ straight from the airport. I just said to the driver, *bpy*! HQ—go to HQ—that's all the fuckin' Thai you ever need to know. America's murder. I ain't ever goin' back. I was so depressed, I just sat in my room, watched TV, and ate pizza. Shit, I was afraid to go out! Fucking murders and gangs and shoot-outs on every corner.

Bloods and Crips patrolling the streets between shopping centers. TV movies about date rape. You ever hear of such a thing? Any of the termites ever hear of date rape? Not a chance. And they ain't dumb. Most of them have graduated to Bangkok straight from Water Buffalo University. And they ain't ever heard of dating. They don't know what a goddamn date is.

"Tuttle, you wouldn't believe San Diego. I got a piece of property near the sea. They ain't making any more ocean front. That's all there is. Unless there's a goddamn earthquake. So I am offered four hundred thou. Shit, I only paid fifty thou for the place. And this guy says, wait until July. The price is still goin' up. And I'm sayin' to myself, shit, that means I gotta go back in July. And I get all depressed again. Someone finds out I'm having a hard time and they invite me to a barbecue. They think my trouble is I'm not meeting any women.

"So I'm sitting by the pool, and this guy comes up to me, and he says, 'Look at Sue's legs. She's got great legs.'

"I look over at Sue. She's got legs like rural telephone poles. And he keeps saying, 'Christ, would you look at those legs. Man, I'd love to have them wrapped around my ass.'

"I look at this guy, and I say, 'But she's got four kids. Forget about the legs, her guts are all fucked up from all those kids.'

"You can't believe these assholes. They're lining up to fuck these forty-year-old sweathogs. I'm shaking my head. I'm so depressed I want to dive into the swimming pool and drown.

"I say to this guy. 'Yeah, I see Sue. But I ain't sure you see what I'm seeing. She's old meat. You gotta be kiddin'. In Thailand, they'd toe tag her. Take her to the morgue.'

"Then I said to him. 'Have you talked to her? Sue's not sailing with a full sea bag. She's either brain-dead or stupid.' And so they say to me, 'Okay, smart guy, what kind of women have you been screwing?'

"I told him straight, man. No bullshit facts of life. 'You want to avoid screwing any woman over sixteen.'

"Now he's backing up a little, eyes all big and shit, telling me to keep my voice down. 'You can go to fucking jail for fucking kids. A congressman was convicted for bagging a sixteen-year-old. Don't you have newspapers in Thailand? You can get five years in the slammer for screwing kids.'

"And I try to tell him, 'These sixteen-years-old Thai girls ain't kids. It ain't a crime. Taking Sue on, now there's a crime against nature. Where I live something that old doesn't even expect to get fucked.'

"Then he starts going into this creepy moral shit. 'Man, how can you fuck a kid young enough to be your daughter?'

"This is coming from guys who think nothing of climbin' on one of these old sweathogs and pumping something with an ass the size of a first-class plane seat. They're judging me. So I give them my standard answer.

"'These girls gotta eat, don't they? I'm putting bread on their plate. I'm making a contribution. They'd starve to death unless they sold themselves. Not something you can say about an old sweathog like Sue. Man, a broad like that can go without gassing up for months and she'd still have an ass the size of the Hollywood Bowl.'

"I couldn't stand it, Tut. I was going nuts in California. Man, it was fucking awful. I was phoning the airlines two weeks in. Get me the fuck back to Bangkok. Can you believe they were fully booked? I was fucking stranded with sweathogs, barbecues, roaming youth gangs. Psychos on my right; psychos on my left. In front and behind me. And I didn't get laid once. I had no appetite. Just pizza and TV. See that sweet girl at my table? There, she just turned her head. She's a Cambodian. I'm taking her tonight. She's a little animal. I animalized her two months ago before she turned seventeen. Went straight down on her pie. Then went for the brown. Packed her mud. She didn't say boo.

"Tonight, I'm gonna pay her well. This is her lucky night. I'm so glad to be back, I'm paying her double purples. No short-time screw either. I'm keeping her the whole goddamn night. Until noon tomorrow. We got a contract.

"Man, I hope I sleep tonight. I'm having goddamn nightmares from a month in San Diego. These fat-assed broads ordering their husbands around. These guys don't know any better. You try to talk to them, but they're lost. They don't believe you when you talk about HQ. They can't imagine it. They think everyone in the world is fucking some battleship named Betty. They think that's normal. They can't imagine there's any choice in the matter.

"So the old bitch yells at them, and you hear them saying, 'Yes, darling? What can I do, sweetheart? Rub more suntan oil on your fat ass? Say no more.'

"And in my dream, I roll over in my bed and I'm staring eyeball-to-eyeball with an old, gnarled sweathog with the skin like tree bark. Sweat is rolling off her like boiled fat. She's got fucking stretch marks from head-to-toe, and she's got her hand on my dick.

"And she's calling out, 'Dan. Dan, you're my man.'

"And I'm frozen, I can't fuckin' move. And she's got pizza on her breath. My goddam pizza with double cheese, the bitch. And the phone rings, it's a woman on the other end. She's saying that she has a piece of bad news for me. Meanwhile this sweathog with a thick bush on her upper lip is kissing my neck. I'm ready to puke.

"And the woman on the phone says, 'Dan, the man, all flights to Bangkok have been indefinitely cancelled.'

"The line goes dead. I break down and cry, bury my face in this sweathog's gray hair. And she asks me what's wrong, Danny? So I tell her the truth. All I want is one of those little termites from HQ. She doesn't know what the fuck I'm talking about. I no longer speak English that anyone in America understands. So I translate the best I can. I describe a little hilltribe girl I had from HQ. Her eyes spring wide open, and she goes nuts. She starts hitting my head against the fucking wall. Calling me a pervert. An asshole. She's threatening to cut off my balls. She's gonna call the cops and have me locked up in the pervert wing of the state prison. She's going to having me branded as a fucking public monster. Testify at my trial. After they throw me in the slammer and she is gonna pay a big nigger with AIDS to fuck me up the ass. I'm telling you, it was the worst goddamn nightmare I ever had.

"I can't tell you how happy I am to be back. You're smart. You've never gone back. Take my advice, don't. They're crazy back there. They won't listen to reason. They're lost. The whole fucking country is just fat and ugly and mean. I'm lucky to be alive. And still sane. I got fat eating all that doughy pizza. There were times in the middle of the night when I gave up hope. I never thought I'd see another termite in this life. Next time I go outta here, I will be wearing a toe-tag and riding inside a body bag."

❖

IN the foyer of the Bangkok Regent Hotel, Lawrence and Tuttle occupied one of the dozen or so round tables covered white linen tablecloths and garlands of fresh white and mauve orchids; HQ was light-years isolated, existing in a separate universe. Lawrence waved over a tall, slender waitress, not a single hair out of place. She smiled, nodding her head gracefully and glided across the vast foyer. Within minutes of taking Lawrence's order, she returned, walking in that lush, catlike way, where no sound is made; the way servants walk around the rich; the way predators stalk their prey. She arrived with two tall, cool drinks on a silver tray.

As she turned away, an elegantly dressed *farang* couple walked past holding hands. His black dinner jacket lapels had a dull shine in the overhead light; her silver evening dress a thousand points of glittering light. He held her hand and smiled as if she were the only woman on the earth. Lawrence thought of Sarah. At the firm's last Christmas party, he had worn a dinner jacket and she had bought an expensive silver-sequined evening dress. They might have walked off the cover of a magazine devoted to the rich and famous. Did that man know how lucky he was? That his wife was alive; that they were in Bangkok together; and that their evening had been populated with people like themselves who shared and valued privilege, the sweetness of success, and the secret belief that they were the elite because they were the best and most skilled.

Tuttle sipped the high-priced drink; Lawrence had insisted on treating him, and he liked the awkward way the drink looked in Tuttle's hand. It was Lawrence's way to even the score for the cab from HQ. During the taxi ride, Lawrence sat gripping the front seat with both hands, as the Isan driver shifted in and out of traffic at high speed, running lights, racing a bus three blocks, nearly colliding with a tuk-tuk: the normal Bangkok late night journey. Tuttle had been totally relaxed, joked with the driver; and never once suggesting that he might slow down or drive more carefully.

"Talk about an asshole, Bobby. Dan-the-man doesn't have a lot of competition," said Lawrence, wiping the sweat from his neck with a hot towel brought by their waitress.

"But if they can't speak English, Dan-the-man is the guy who pays the bill. The girls working here wouldn't give him a second look. They don't have to. They wouldn't understand him. Dan talks in a new form of English language. One you won't find spoken outside of the rough bars," replied Tuttle.

"He has all the local expressions like *termites, Water Buffalo University, peu-un pods,* purple, or short-time down pat. And he knows other names, too. Thai words never spoken in public by Thais. *Garee* is one Thai word for whore. *Yeeng! so peh!-nee* is a more polite form, meaning prostitute. Words you hear some men whisper only among themselves. The language and usage of one-night stands. At four in the morning he tips one of the waiters to play number 119—*'Women in Love'* on the jukebox. The Thai waiter knows enough English to understand the joke.

"Outside of HQ there are other titles for the girls. Khun Kob calls our students' sex industry workers.' I have visions of workers in white coveralls and matching hats marching ten abreast through the factory gate at HQ where they punch a time clock and ask questions about their collective agreement to the shop steward. You want a language phantasm, look no farther than 'foreign guides.'

"Guides who work the go-go bars. Guides whose uniform is no uniform. Some of these girls know the floor plan of every second-class hotel in Bangkok. The new language floats through those rooms every night. I'm curious about Dan because I understand him too well. Like him I've become a nomad with a language only other nomads speak and understand. I think in that language. And that scares me. I understand the consequences of building thoughts with those words.

"The girls are inside a no-man's-land and can't find the words to get out. They have one chance. A way to learn English. Not Dan's English, but real English. A week later, I'm teaching English to a class of foreign guides. A few months later I have opened a school. A few years later I have run out of money and there is a wobble in my life, and I know what I've built is about to tip over.

"You want me to write a check?" asked Lawrence. "Is that what this is all about? You need the money but are too proud to ask?" The Bangkok Regent Hotel reeked of money, influence, and power. The deference that money bought was the tall, erect carriage and whispered tone of every staff member; an elite serving an elite. The luxury that money captured was visible in every place setting, the teakwood counters, the thick carpeting, and the air-conditioning that chilled the stately rooms for the comfort of those dressed in formal dinner jackets.

"You think I asked you to come 12,000 miles to hit you up for money?"

"Didn't you? Wasn't that the plan?"

Tuttle had the wan smile of someone who had the upper hand. "On the contrary, I asked you to come because Asanee has something to give you."

"Give me what?" Lawrence felt back in control; in an environment where he could breathe and think. "The sexual experience of my life?"

"I'll forget you said that," said Tuttle, a stern tone entering the conversation for the first time that night.

Lawrence had hit a nerve. "Oh, we are saying her, are we?"

"You might say that."

There was a pause as the waitress returned and stood at attention before Lawrence, and bowing from the waist, asked in perfect English, "Would you like another drink, sir?"

Lawrence waved her off, not taking his eyes from Tuttle, whose face was flushed. Was it anger? The drinks, Dan-the-man, his school going down the drain—or was it something going back a long distance in their common past? "Or are you afraid of the competition?" Lawrence finally said what was on his mind from the moment it was clear he wasn't going to meet Asanee that night; that Tuttle for unspecified reasons was putting him off. It was as if the years hadn't dimmed the original competition over Sarah. And Lawrence, his wife dead, in the lobby of a luxury hotel in Bangkok, found himself striking out.

"There never was a fair competition, Larry," said Tuttle, regaining his composure. He managed a smile.

"Wasn't the word *jai yen?*" asked Lawrence. "Keeping a cool heart."

Tuttle raised his glass in a toast. "You learn real fast, Larry. You were always first in your class. Being first was important in the old days. Sarah needed to back a winner. She got what she desired. And that should have made her happy."

"It did," said Lawrence, a little too quickly.

Tuttle nodded, guessing that even Lawrence hadn't fully believed that. Like most achievements, they masked an elaborate attempt to reconfigure life in terms of the winner's circle. In a strange way, Tuttle found himself resisting the urge to console Lawrence; the man whose life had been consecrated to pension law, isolated from a wife whom he never really knew.

"Besides, I don't think you could handle Asanee. She might break your heart. So why don't we forget her. It was a bad idea," said Tuttle.

"And Sarah used to call me a control freak," said Lawrence.

"You are."

"What are you afraid of?"

"She's waiting outside. I'll send her in."

"I'll be waiting."

"Just like before," said Tuttle. Lawrence had waited in the wings with his promise of money and career for Sarah; a combination that had been his edge—he had been defeated by the very forces that he and Sarah had stood against. This time, thought Tuttle, he couldn't lose. Money wouldn't buy Asanee.

And Lawrence's first night outside the sanctuary of the Bangkok Regent Hotel ended with an awkward silence. Neither had anything else to say. Finally, Tuttle rose and gave him a printed card with the address of the school in Thai. "Give this to your driver tomorrow. I'll see you at the school around nine. Don't keep Asanee out too late. She's one of our best teachers."

"Why not leave it up to her?" asked Lawrence.

"Why not," said Tuttle.

"She might like me." Lawrence smiled.

❖

ASANEE sat alone in the back of a taxi. Tuttle opened the rear door and climbed in beside her. The exterior lights from the fountain outside the Bangkok Regent Hotel illuminated Asanee's face as she leaned forward out of darkness and rested her arms over Tuttle's shoulders. She tried to find his eyes in that dim light. This was the moment of truth that he had been waiting for, planning for, living for, she had suspected, for a length of time that included all of her life. She loved him enough to do whatever he asked of her. He knew that she would never question him. Deep inside, though, she had wanted this chance as much as he had; but she had kept her feelings secret.

"He's waiting inside," said Tuttle.

Her arms stiffened around his neck. Even in the small light, her eyes were on fire with anticipation, that electric feeling of meeting a stranger; a feeling that she had long forgotten along with her days working a bar. She searched Tuttle's face for some hint of how he felt. Was he remembering that first night they had spent in a hotel in *Mae Sai*? But nothing in his expression betrayed his heart.

"I want to go now," said Asanee.

He squeezed her tight for a moment. "Go," he said.

He watched her walk away from the taxi. The sharp report of her high heels on the pavement were soon lost in the noise of passing traffic. She was steadfast, devoted, and loyal beyond any shadow of doubt, he thought. Her tall, elegant form in the night sent a sudden chill ripping through Tuttle's chest; it was less the panic of loss, than the terror of losing himself in the void of the dead. She was the only person he had ever loved more than Sarah. It was '68 all over again; a second chance, a rematch with the same stakes, only this time Tuttle was absolutely certain the outcome would be different.

After the doorman closed the door behind Asanee, the taxi pulled away. A moment later, the driver turned on Rama IV in front of the Dusit Thani Hotel. At the Belgian-Thai intersection, the taxi stopped for the light. Tuttle thought of Sarah on the day of her wedding. He had cornered her alone in the washroom of the church basement two hours before the ceremony. She had gone down alone for a quick fix. He watched her take the syringe out of her handbag, heat the solution, draw it into her syringe, then double up her fist as she injected the heroin into her stomach.

"A needle mark in the belly button. Clever idea," said Tuttle.

Sarah jumped, her face twisted with terror, she saw Robert standing a couple of feet away. "Jesus fucking Christ, are you trying to give me a heart attack?"

"Aren't you a little glad to see me?"

She finished her injection, pulled down her sweatshirt and dropped the syringe into her handbag. Her face glowed; she shuttered, closed her eyes, and let out a long whistle. "Bobby, Bobby what in the hell are you doing here?"

"I thought I might change your mind."

"Don't do this."

"You can't marry Lawrence Baring. He's a joke. And you know it."

"Then the joke's on me!" she said, moving toward the stairs.

He grabbed her arm. "Say that you don't love me. Go on, say it."

"Let me go." She tried to pull away from him but couldn't break free.

He shook his head. "Say the words. I don't love you."

"I can't, Bobby."

"Then let's get out of here. I've got an apartment on Point Grey Road. The bedroom looks out over English Bay. We can walk down to the beach."

She rested her forehead against his. "You just don't get it, do you, Bobby?"

"Get what?"

"Love isn't enough. Not for any woman. We're practical. We need to know where our next fix is coming from. Who's gonna pay for it. You think my mother loves my father? Forget it. But you think she's unhappy? She's got everything she ever dreamed of and more."

"Why Baring, Sarah?"

"What you're asking, Bobby, is why not you."

He let go of her arm.

"Because you don't have the appetite to go for the kill," said Sarah. "Jesus Christ, don't you know who you are? You're the most dangerous of all men. A goddamn dreamer. There's some decency that will always fuck you up; and if I stay with you, fuck me up, too.

Larry would do anything to win. He doesn't dream about anything except getting ahead. He'd step on anyone, fuck them up. He will always beat you. Because he knows in this world you gotta fight dirty to stay ahead in this life. Go back to Vancouver, Bobby. If the FBI knows you're in town, Christ, you'll end up before my old man. He'd love that."

"I'm going to cover the war. I'm leaving in two weeks."

"You make no fucking sense. You refuse to report for the draft, and then you want to go to Vietnam by yourself."

"Come with me. Great drugs, Sarah." He began humming *'Hey Jude'* at first a little off-key, and then she broke in singing the words.

"Christ, I do love you." Her hand slid down the side of his leg. Her tongue darted into his mouth. He pulled her sweatshirt over her head; as she unfastened her bra. As she guided him between her legs, Sarah moaned, her nails slowly digging into his back. On the floor of the church basement, as they made love, a rain shower began. They could see their breath in the gray, cold morning air. She wrapped her legs around his waist and they rolled over their clothes spread on the floor, laughing and singing, as if the moment would never end, as if it would always be 1968, and a single syringe lasted a lifetime.

FROM the first moment Lawrence Baring saw Asanee enter the hotel lobby, he understood Tuttle's reluctance in allowing her out of his sight. He clasped the edge of the table and squeezed down hard. He closed his eyes and opened them again. She was one of the most beautiful women he had ever seen. Her thick black hair fell straight to the small of her back; it had a sheen of red highlights. She was taller than he expected, tall and slender, and she crossed a room with a kind of animal intensity. Her eyes swept the tables, yielding a discernible distance, an aloof declaration that she belonged in the hotel alone that time of night. The outline of her thighs appeared beneath her dark skirt; revealed beneath her blouse were large, full breasts and broad shoulders, in total, the effect was to make Asanee closer to a work of art than a living, breathing human being.

Lawrence found himself rising from the table and gesturing to her. What he couldn't understand is why Tuttle had mentioned her in the first place. As she came towards the table, smiling, he remembered what Sarah had once said about Tuttle. "He's a man who will always be defeated by his decency." Asanee had needed help. The entire set-up at HQ began to make sense; all the stories about the danger of Thai woman, their greed, temper, and double-dealing had been for a specific purpose; the idea was to put maximum distance between him and this woman. And there was Tuttle sending her to exactly the right person, thought Lawrence. Tuttle deserved an A-minus for trying, he thought.

Asanee sat down across from Lawrence and they exchanged those first few brief words that Lawrence couldn't have remembered if his life had depended upon reciting them. What information he learned in the first half-hour was distorted, spoiled, lost in her every glance and gesture; he was in a state of pure absorption, making his way over the tall wall of emotions that he might have felt once a very long time ago. What had attracted him to Asanee with the G-force gravity that flattened him against his chair? He held on, hearing himself talk inside the loop of an immediate, uncontrolled flow that was part fluid, part light, and he was floating in the farthest regions he had only known with Sarah.

What combination of emotions, chemicals, dreams, and past had been fused together when Asanee greeted him? And whatever that truth was, he couldn't begin to understand the power of the catharsis he felt inside himself. She averted her eyes, her face flushed. It would have been easy enough to say two people have felt the surge of an attraction, a surge with enough force to wobble the carriages of the underground train that had travelled from childhood to that moment. She was looking out of every window as if she had always been in Lawrence's life. She had arrived, as people rarely do, full-blown into his life, as if she had distilled the essence of what he had always desired, leaving behind an empty shell of all those years of wasted, false desires. How or why he felt this way, he couldn't begin to understand; it was a case of reverse emotional engineering, of understanding the low melting temperature where feelings became alloys for action. Beyond all his feelings was an overwhelmingly powerful sense of lives about to overlap irrevocably.

Lawrence felt the sudden impulse to tell her about Sarah. It made no sense, this desire to explain to this stranger how he had cried out in his sleep for his dead wife. He shivered and looked away from Asanee as if he had dreamed her appearance. She was there already. Patiently waiting. Sarah's name had a strikingly sharp taste in his mouth. The girl Tuttle had sent for his assistance had caused the waves of that naked horror of Sarah's loss to wash over him again. Somewhere in the power of her attraction he had lost his feet. What sensation clustered wasn't sexual; but a spontaneous desire to be comforted by her.

"Tuttle said I was vulnerable," he said. "I recently lost my wife. It was a kind of violation of how life is supposed to work. Husband and wife should live a long time. The man dies first. Then the woman. That's the order of things. But it didn't work that way for me. I thought I was in pretty good shape. But I don't know."

"Maybe I should go," she said, pushing back in her chair. There was a shock in hearing him speak so openly about Sarah's death.

"No. Please stay. Sorry, I was thinking of Sarah. My wife."

She reached across the table and squeezed his hand. "It was a very bad thing. Sarah left an empty space " she said. "I wish for you she could be here now. She would like this room. This table. These flowers." Asanee bit her lip. She hadn't meant to say that. But his flood of feeling had swept over her, too; making her less cautious. She improvised quickly. "Is it too late to order?"

Lawrence made a big flurry of ordering her something to eat. Nothing pleased him more than providing what had been excluded behind an artificial wall of time. The kitchen was closed, he was informed. A couple of moments later, the waitress brought over the manager, and Lawrence pressed two purples into his hand. Plates of fruit, cheese, and bread appeared several minutes later. He watched her eat as if he had never seen another living being press a strawberry to their lips.

"Is Tuttle your boyfriend?"

She pulled the strawberry away from her lips; a wide smile crossed her face as she shook her head. "Not boyfriend."

"He might think otherwise."

"He's very protective. He only want me to be happy."

"Sarah used to say that about him."

Why was Tuttle doing this? The guy's sick in the head, thought Lawrence. I should be the last guy in the world he would ever ask to help a woman he was interested in. Unless, it was some kind of weird rematch. From the way Tuttle had spoken about Sarah, it was clear the loss had never really healed. Lawrence, in the end, couldn't resolve the problem; Tuttle had thoroughly confused him. What he didn't know was that it had been Sarah's idea to bring Lawrence to Bangkok. In a real sense, she wanted the rematch between Lawrence and Tuttle even more than Tuttle had. Certainly Tuttle didn't desire a home court advantage for Lawrence; he had been through that one before and wasn't anxious for a repeat. Lawrence was the "away" team. This was Tuttle's field of play, and the ball was in his hands.

Asanee had answered that Tuttle wasn't her boyfriend.

"Robert wants me to stay in Thailand. I'm not so sure. I think sometimes the United States is better for me. I was in Los Angeles."

"And you liked it?"

"Very much. When Robert said you were coming, I asked if I could talk to you about Los Angeles. But he's very afraid the bad thing could happen to me in America."

"Don't listen to him. He's an old draft dodger who could never make it in the States. He's a little bitter. He washed out a long time ago. Lack of ambition or drive. He's no different than he was twenty years ago. Only older. An aged hippie who spends the night talking to teenage prostitutes. So I wouldn't plan my life around what he's told you."

"I think you hate him."

Lawrence felt he had gone too far. Hate was a strong word. "I didn't say that. He's just different. Not like us."

There was surprise designation in the middle of the conversation; the use of "us" to put them on one side of the divide of life from Tuttle. It registered immediately on Asanee, who nodded in a gentle, reassuring way.

"How you know I'm not like him?"

"I can see it in everything about you. He would never go to Los Angeles. Who'd hire him? And he wouldn't want us to go either."

"Why you think that?"

"What if I invited you to Los Angeles. Would you come?" Asanee's observation was undoubtedly true; the improbable invitation always struck the Thai as a characteristic of overblown *farang* intentions; plans and promises never acted upon.

"You want me to write it out?" He reached in his pocket and began writing on a page from Tuttle's short story. "I'll write a contract. You can sue me if I'm lying."

He didn't really care how stupid that sounded. He had stopped thinking. Once in a lifetime, a woman like Asanee walked into a man's life. Someone who hits every chord: the sexual, the spiritual, the physical. She had a centered quality as if the whole universe was contained inside a stillness located deep within. In her selfless, quiet innocence was a quality of inexhaustible hope, a dialogue with the regions where people redeemed themselves.

To possess such a woman was to have everything, he thought. Most of life was a search for such a woman without ever knowing it. The rarest of women, the kind men wrote bad poetry for, gave up everything for, went to war for, killed over, made a fool of themselves, betrayed their friends, their family, their country to possess. Pure, selfless, quiet innocence. Someone untouched and unspoiled; that life hasn't soiled, torn, or damaged. This was a new threshold of life. Like the one he passed two decades earlier when he met Sarah.

What did he find himself talking about? She had reduced him into a schoolboy, all self-conscious, trying to impress. "And I was on law review. That helped get the clerkship on the Ninth Circuit. And my practice. Pension law sounds boring. But there's a lot of money involved. I'm always dealing with the cutting edge of the law."

"How old are you?" asked Asanee, not following most of his conversation about the law. Yet his childlike happiness was touching.

"Guess?"

She pretended to examine his features in detail. "Thirty-two, maybe."

"Tuttle must have told you we went to school together. So you know I couldn't be thirty-two."

"I think you look thirty-two. Never mind if you think I'm flattering you."

A year older than Kelly Swan, he thought with some satisfaction. They were now alone in the foyer dining area. Lawrence looked around and saw the manager make an obvious gesture of looking at his watch.

What's inside Asanee's head, Lawrence wondered. His thoughts drifted to Sarah. For the first time since her death he felt that he could go on. That he was over the edge of that loss. From across the table, Asanee watched him pay the check. I thought he would have a bad heart, she thought. So why is he very kind? I'm confused. Do not think. Thinking is bad. Just be. Now, here, with this man.

The attraction had become mutual. Despite herself, Asanee felt the pull as well, something she hadn't counted on. Would she be able to keep the motions of her mind away from Tuttle? She didn't know. She found herself in an absurd and difficult position. Tuttle had assumed that she shared his contempt for Lawrence, and she knew that he would ask her every detail of the evening. She had surprised herself; her impulse was to like this man whose eyes seem to swallow her whole. Though she wasn't surprised when he invited her to have a night-cap in his suite.

"You ever see a suite here?"

She shook her head. "It is not good for Thai girl to go to *farang's* room."

"Just to talk?"

"No one would believe a *farang* just wants to talk."

"That's because you've been around Tuttle and his friends too long. Some foreigners say what they mean." That lawyer's sense of authority rang through the words.

Inside the suite, Asanee sat in a chair, legs crossed, watching Lawrence pour a drink. "You want to go to UCLA?" he asked, turning toward her.

"To study English."

"My wife taught at UCLA."

What she liked most about Lawrence was his tenderness, almost a caress in the way he used the word wife. Most *farang* she had known hated the *mem,* always contemplating and devaluing them in their barroom conversations. His devotion to Sarah touched her deeply. It had been the principal reason, in the end, she had agreed to trust him and go to his room unescorted.

Lawrence had closed her doubt with Sarah's name. Asanee had stopped stalling for time. She long ago learned how to live with contradiction, thinking minute by minute that Tuttle would come, and feeling, at the same time, with the same degree of conviction, that he might not. Her sense of obligation to Tuttle was overwhelming, unquestioning, absolute. She tried to hold tightly on to her sense of responsibility, but a spark of something between Lawrence and Asanee; some kind of recognition, a connection, an attraction, pulled her away from her duty. In Lawrence's suite, two strangers thrown together by events larger than themselves, people who would have never met, suddenly sat face-to-face in the lavish sitting room cradling their drinks. Something had altered in the tone of the conversation, a shift of speed out of loneliness, and lost in that narrow passage of discovery. She made small talk about teaching at Tuttle's school. Lawrence made small talk about beauty of the campus at UCLA; and the commuting time from his house to the campus.

Did she really want rescue from Lawrence now that she had relaxed? He had been true to his word; once inside the suite, Lawrence made no move toward her. He remained, though, tender, gentle, and kind. He was totally unlike what she had expected. Where was the fault in him, she thought. This man who had hurt Tuttle before she had been born wasn't a monster. She didn't know what to believe; whom to believe.

TUTTLE walked briskly into the hotel lobby and paced in front of the bank of elevators. He pushed the button for the seventh floor. The journey seemed to take forever. He paced inside the elevator, finding his own face in the mirrored walls; a drawn face lined with worry. He clenched and unclenched his fists. He hit the wall with the edge of his fist out of frustration. His heart pounded in his throat as the elevator doors opened. He turned left, walked down the corridor, stopped and knocked on the door of Lawrence's suite. I'm too late, he said to himself. He shifted from side to side. Then he pounded harder. Lawrence opened the door, holding a drink in his hand, his tie loosened around his neck. Tuttle slammed a hard right hook punch, catching Lawrence just below the eye on the right side of his face. He reeled back, the drink flying out of his hand in a shower of mist. His legs went out from underneath his body and he landed in a heap beside the sofa.

Asanee uncrossed her legs and set her glass down on the table. As she rose, she smoothed down her skirt.

"I made a mistake. Let's go," he said to Asanee in Thai.

"Are you totally crazy?" asked Lawrence, shaking his head and trying to rise to his feet. "We were just talking."

"A girl wants to ask you about LA and you take her straight to your room," said Tuttle, shoving Lawrence back down. "Asshole."

Lawrence had never realized how strong Tuttle was; how the weight-lifting for twenty-five years had built a muscle tone easily concealed beneath a loose-fitting shirt. He decided to stay down on the floor. Tuttle was like a raging bull, pumping the muscles in his forearms into thick knots of hard flesh, looking for something to move so he could hit it again, and again. He smelled blood; he wanted to draw Lawrence into a fight, any excuse to finish the game. It wasn't going to be a draw or loss this time.

"Get up," yelled Tuttle.

"You're still in high school," said Lawrence. He sat back, resting his head on the edge of the sofa, touching his face where the swelling had already begun.

"Why don't you stand up?" asked Tuttle.

"He's had enough," said Asanee in Thai.

"Fuck him. I haven't had enough."

"Was that for Asanee or for Sarah?" asked Lawrence.

Tuttle didn't answer him, grabbing Asanee's hand, and pulling her toward the door.

"I've asked her to go back to Los Angeles."

"You shit," he reached down and pulled Lawrence up.

"She's not available. You understand what I'm saying to you?" He shoved Lawrence hard, sending him sprawling over the couch.

Lawrence reared up on his knees and slowly staggered to his feet. "Why don't you ask her if she wants to go? Or are you afraid the answer you've programmed into her might fail?"

"I already know the answer." This time the punch to Lawrence's stomach knocked the wind out of him. He doubled over onto the floor.

"See you tomorrow at nine," said Lawrence, looking up at Asanee. "Am I still invited to see the school?"

"We see you tomorrow. Don't forget," said Asanee, glancing back, her face sad.

It was the kind of answer that gave Lawrence a great deal of hope that Tuttle had not yet won the larger war.

10

Lawrence had been uncertain what to expect the next morning. It took his driver nearly thirty minutes to locate the school. The right side of his face had turned the bluish gray of spoiled meat; he wore sunglasses, and the combination gave him the appearance of someone who employed lawyers rather than that of a lawyer. He had trouble sleeping, tossing and turning, Asanee never quite leaving his thoughts. His wake-up call seemed to come moments after he had finally dozed off.

The driver circled the surrounding sois until he located Tuttle's slum school. It was tucked in a squalid soi lined with dusty, bashed up late-model Fiats and Honda Civics, fist size rust holes in the hoods, heat-curled for-sale signs in the windows, and flat tires. Against one wall, piles of old car tires tilted to one side. A large rat scuttled through. The driver rolled down the window of the air-conditioned car, and asked a street vendor barbecuing chicken for directions. The small, skinny man with crooked teeth pointed at a series of the dark shops with rusty metal grates pulled half-way down over the windows.

The car slowly moved forward past a cramped restaurant with a half-dozen tables. A fat cook with a large belly, sweat streaked face and watery eyes, his arms folded on the ledge between his chest and belly, eyed the Mercedes. He stood nervously at the entrance, watching Lawrence as he was driven past for the fourth time. Gangsters looking to make a hit drove in such a fashion. Lawrence had the kind of battered face that went with a king-sized grudge. The fat-bellied man's mind drifted to what possible insult or bad business deal had reshaped the *farang's* face, and who in the neighborhood was going to pay the price from the rough looking man in the back seat of the Mercedes.

Around the same soi, opposite a line of wrecked cars. several young men perched on a concrete stoop. Stripped to the waist, they leaned out of the shadows; their dirty toes wiggling in the dust. The driver stopped again, and asked directions from a second street vendor, who was lighting a charcoal fire; the man looked up, eyes everywhere, on the car, the driver, Lawrence in the back seat, on neighbors sitting nearby. This wasn't a *farang* street, his eyes said. Another Thai hacked a fish into bloody fragments with a large knife. That could be me laid out on that wooden table, thought Lawrence. No sign marked the school.

Lawrence, out of the corner of his eye, saw a girl carrying a schoolbook up a dusty, old back staircase. He jumped out of the Mercedes and followed a safe distance behind her. She led him down a path, between a row of houses, to the broken-down wooden staircase. The girl disappeared up the stairs, and Lawrence counted the number of steps as they echoed under her feet. It was a long way up, he thought. At the top of the entrance a red temple cloth from *Wat Po* had been nailed above the door to ward off evil spirits. He had no idea what the Thai words meant or the fierce half-human, half-demon creatures were intended to do. He was beginning to realize there was a lot he didn't know.

Lawrence climbed the first flight of stairs that led to a small landing. He caught his breath, bending over, hands on his knees, and when he looked up, the girl who he followed stood two feet away holding a knife. He recognized her face under a large fluorescent light on the wall.

"Why you follow me?" she asked.

Lawrence, caught off guard, put his hands up as if he were being robbed. "Me lost. Look for Tuttle. For Asanee."

The girl slowly lowered the knife and smiled. "You no speak good English. Maybe you come for lesson?" She laughed, turned, and ran up the balance of the stairs.

He pushed open a heavy door that led into a large room divided into a series of smaller rooms. From inside one he recognized Snow's voice; and another he heard Crosby's English accent, as he read vocabulary from a lesson book. The main room had bare walls and yellow lino floors cracked and stained, a giant rotating floor fan, and a blackboard, a few scuffed wooden chairs. Several rows of books, most with broken spines, were stacked on boxes against the far wall near a dirty window. A young girl sat, her back to Lawrence, bent over in a chair near the wall, writing in a notebook. She hadn't looked up as he entered the room. The girl he had followed appeared framed in one of the doors in the narrow corridor, Tuttle nodding as she spoke to him in Thai. As the door opened further, Lawrence saw Tuttle standing in profile, talking to a middle-aged Thai. He noticed that Tuttle's right hand was wrapped in a bandage, and that gave Lawrence some belated sense of pleasure.

"Any trouble finding the school?" asked Tuttle, coming out with the Thai man.

"I just followed the first girl carrying books."

"Khun Kob's our headmaster," said Tuttle.

"Robert say men jump you last night. I said, should go to police," said Khun Kob.

"These things happen in the big city," said Lawrence, looking at Tuttle and wondering how he had slept the previous night. From the puffy skin billowing the folds beneath his eyes, he doubted that Tuttle had slept much either.

Khun Kob, the Thai, who stood next to Tuttle, his head coming to Tuttle's shoulder, was all smiles; he made it obvious that he had been waiting to meet Lawrence. He had come out of his classroom with a big smile and his hand extended. It was clear Khun Kob needed no formal introduction. He greeted Lawrence like someone he had known for years. Someone he owed respect. What was the Thai word Crosby had used? thought Lawrence. *Kreng jai!* That was it, remembered Lawrence, glancing at Tuttle. Why hadn't Tuttle mentioned the headmaster? Was it some unconscious need to present himself as the headmaster of the school? Tuttle, as far as Lawrence could see at that moment, was another teacher like Snow and Crosby. What was the business about this being his school? Lawrence was filled with a hundred questions, but with no immediate opportunity to ask even one of them. And where was the elusive Asanee?

"My friend, so good that you come," said Khun Kob. "Robert say you might not come. We wait. But I think you come. "

As if to read Lawrence's mind, Tuttle interjected. "Asanee is finishing a class. She'll be done in twenty minutes. That will give Khun Kob and you a chance to catch up."

Catch up on what? thought Lawrence. He smiled and said nothing. He thought that Khun Kob didn't shake hands like a schoolteacher. The headmaster launched into a brief rundown on his own background. Nearby Lawrence listened, glancing over at the young girl, with her head down, writing in her notebook. Khun Kob saw the distraction and immediately led Lawrence and Tuttle into this back room which appeared to be an office. A small, battered window air-conditioner chugged along, the gauge turned up to high. In one corner, Old Bill sat marking a stack of papers. He glanced up at Khun Kob and Tuttle. He wiped his brow with a handkerchief and fiddled with the papers.

"You'll excuse me," said Old Bill, rising to his feet. "I have a class to teach."

After Old Bill disappeared, and Tuttle and Lawrence had found chairs, wiped dust off the seat and sat down, Khun Kob, without taking a breath, started explaining his political ambitions. He had run for political office many times but always failed to get elected. He confided his latest plan. He had decided to run again, if his party would have him, and if not, then he would form his own party. Lawrence figured out the language of his handshake. It had thrown him at first. Teachers didn't shake like that when Tuttle and he had been students. Khun Kob's political aspirations pinpointed his handshake in a larger context. Lawrence suspected that the headmaster had experimented with several variations in each losing election. And that he had spent countless hours, as all politicians did over a lifetime of seeking and retaining power, attempting to discover that inexpressible difference between the handshake of a winner and that of a loser.

Khun Kob wore oil in his hair and combed it forward from the crown to a fringe of bangs an inch on his forehead. As he spoke, Lawrence thought of those Saturday morning TV shows when he was a kid in the States. He always wondered if Larry's hairdo in the Three Stooges would make a comeback. It had in the back alleys of Bangkok.

Khun Kob, like Lawrence, wore a pair of dark glasses inside the dimly lit room. A month earlier he had had surgery for the removal of a cataract. Lawrence wasn't prepared for what followed. Khun Kob carried the cataract around in a contact lens bottle with a plastic stopper on top. He pulled it out, handed it to him, expecting him to examine it closely. The cataract looked like a tiny, yellow snail shell under the florescent light. Khun Kob kept it submerged in saline solution since the day the doctor had plucked it from his eye. Like a dead language, it had a blurred meaning in the world.

And Lawrence thought of guys like Dan who had gone language-blind living in Bangkok. Men unable to see with their words in America; they had slammed into a wall of their native tongue and bounced off, dazed and confused—because they were no longer natives who belonged. They were lost tribers looking to join a *peu-un pod* of their own kind.

"Foreign guides very good for Thailand. They make tourists happy and bring money to Thailand. And when they go back home, they send more money to the girls. My daughters, I call them. In the next general election, I think I will run on the platform of health clinics for foreign guides. No good these girls do not get good care. I think I have good idea. Maybe you can help me with it. Khun Tuttle tells me you a very famous lawyer in America. I'm thinking of export/import business. Maybe you have some idea. Many friends give me brief on business. Khun Tuttle pays me good. But I tell him maybe I'm no longer so strong. Not so much energy. Export/import business maybe better for me. Any idea you have, I appreciate very much."

Khun Kob played with his wide blue tie sliced with narrow orange stripes; it was loosely knotted against his white shirt that opened at the throat. He took off his glasses, squinted his eyes, then cocked his head, as a young woman entered the room. Lawrence had been lost in his own thoughts. Just as he thought he had figured Tuttle out, some new piece of evidence wrecked the basis of his previous judgement. The Thai girl waied to Khun Kob and Tuttle, then turned and stood in front of Lawrence.

"Hello, Larry," she said in nearly perfect English, extending her hand. Her oval green eyes shone bright in the morning light; her long, black hair cascaded down her backs. She stood a half-head taller than Khun Kob.

"Father thought you wouldn't come. I thought you would, though," said Asanee in American-accented English.

Lawrence had that confused look of having witnessed an optical illusion. He looked at Khun Kob and then back at Asanee.

"All my daughters come from the Northeast. They know nothing in Bangkok. They follow Asanee. She is their senior. Their role model. They can see how Asanee improved herself. Made her life better. So we are very glad of your offer to help. Thank you very much."

He flashed a toothy grin and left. Lawrence and Tuttle stood in an awkward silence. The best they could do was exchange a side glance.

Asanee looked over at Tuttle. "Did Khun Kob ask him for legal advice on setting up his export/import business?"

Lawrence sensed discord in her voice. "It's all right. Your father only asked me about any ideas. But I'm afraid I don't know much about export/import businesses."

"My father!" Asanee spun around from Tuttle, reaching out with a finger pointed at him. "This is my father."

Lawrence thought, at first, it was a joke. He looked at Tuttle and then Asanee; a matching set of green eyes. He had simply assumed she was Thai, like many *farang*, Lawrence had failed to observe the individual detail. His absorption of her had been so complete, and Tuttle so far removed from the moments they had shared, that it had never crossed his mind. Now that he looked at her closely, the features, not only the eyes, but the line of the cheekbone, her height, even something of the smile bore a clear trace of Tuttle's.

"No one ever made that mistake before," said Asanee, brushing back her hair as she laughed, nudging Tuttle.

The conversation of the previous night in the lobby of the Bangkok Regent Hotel made his cheeks flush red; he had, with little tact, explained to Asanee what a complete failure Tuttle was. And he had accused Tuttle of being afraid of the competition.

"Your daughter?" he asked, lowering his sunglasses and looking from Asanee to Robert, his eyes in unblinking shock. "Your own daughter."

"I wasn't certain you'd help her if you knew."

"You think I'm that big an asshole?" He immediately turned on his heels and apologized to Asanee for his foul language.

Lawrence had, with a great deal of assistance from Tuttle and Asanee, misled himself; he had leaped headfirst from the past to the present without considering there might be more than one reason why Tuttle had so carefully sheltered the mysterious Asanee.

Both Tuttle and his daughter shrugged it off. Lawrence was grateful when a moment later Asanee shifted the conversation away from his error. "Ever since Dad made Khun Kob headmaster of the school, he has been running around using the title in politics and business. But I think in his heart he cares about the students."

"Tuttle, I don't know what to say. About last night," began Lawrence.

"Forget it."

"I really didn't do, I mean, try anything. I wanted to help. Of course, I would, I mean I will help. You have a daughter who is a woman. My god, my god."

Asanee looked from Lawrence to Tuttle, standing erect, her hands clasped before her, head tilted toward her father. A beautiful twenty-year-old half-Thai, half-American loomed in the small, cramped room like an illusion. A trick performed by a Lahu Godman. The more Lawrence looked at the girl, the more apparent became her physical resemblance to Tuttle. She faced him with her father's half-crossed smile on her face.

"I'm not so certain it's the kind of help I had in mind," said Tuttle, exchanging a glance with Asanee.

"If only Sarah had seen you, Asanee. Known what an incredibly beautiful daughter—sorry, I didn't mean," Lawrence sputtered his words out in shock as if he had been forced to pay one of his own legal bills. "I wondered if. I thought she. Shit, I can't talk."

"Sarah was my good friend," said Asanee, her face clouded with emotion; tears swelling as she said Sarah's name.

"You knew Sarah? And you didn't say anything last night? Either of you. Why? What is going on? Could someone answer that simple question? I get set up, knocked down, set up and knocked down again. For what end?" asked Lawrence, dropping into a chair. He looked over at Tuttle whose face betrayed no emotion. How could Sarah have known, thought Lawrence. Jesus, Sarah, he said softly to himself. What had Kelly said that last night in Los Angeles? That maybe he had never known Sarah?

"I went to Los Angeles two times. I saw my father's family. My grandmother tell me about how Sarah was Father's old girlfriend. I'm curious. I go to university. I see her. We like each other very much. From first time we meet. I go to lunch with her every day for one week. She says she can give me a job at the university. I can work as her assistant. It will help my English, she says. I say yes I will work very hard. She helped me so much. I loved her so much, too. I am so sorry she die. Sarah *jai dee*. I think she was like a second mother. I cannot say anything last night because I want to know what kind of man you are."

Asanee broke down weeping, covering her face with her hands. Tuttle slipped an arm around her shoulder, pulling her head to his chest. She wept for what seemed like an eternity. Neither Lawrence nor Tuttle said anything. The more she had spoken, the more broken and fragmented her English had become until, at the end, only sobs came from her mouth. Asanee collected herself, a shudder of emotion shook through her body.

"You worked for Sarah. How long?" asked Lawrence, his eyes closed, as if the room would disappear, Tuttle, Asanee, and Bangkok, and he would wake up out of a nightmare and Sarah would be beside him asleep.

"Three months," answered Asanee, blowing her nose in a handkerchief produced by Tuttle. "She say I go back next year. And every year. Before I go home, she gave me something. She say anything happen to her, I must give to you. I very afraid. 'Why,' I ask her. She say, 'The bad thing can happen to anyone.' I don't understand. She say, 'Never mind. You like my daughter. Just keep for me, okay?' And I say, 'Okay, I keep.'"

Asanee pulled an airmail envelope from her pocket and offered it to Lawrence. He stared at it for a long moment before reaching out and taking it. His name was printed in Sarah's handwriting. On the back she had written over the sealed flap: OPEN ONLY IN THE EVENT OF MY DEATH. Beneath those words, Sarah had written, FOR LAWRENCE BARING, ESQ. EYES ONLY. Lawrence turned the envelope back over, tapped it on the side of his chair. He looked up at Tuttle; hot tears streamed down Lawrence's cheeks. He leaned forward from the chair, elbows on his knees, his cupped hands cradling his forehead.

"We'll be just outside," said Tuttle, taking Asanee by the arm as he opened the door. "If you need anything, you know, give a shout."

Lawrence waited for several minutes before he walked over to the window. Below a group of children played "war" with toy rifles inside a couple of the wrecked cars. A soi dog, balled up near a food vendor, scratched its ear with a hindleg. Looking away, Lawrence tore open the letter.

"Neither Tuttle nor Asanee are aware of the contents of this letter. Or the request contained in it. I met Asanee almost by accident. She was in LA staying with Tuttle's parents. His mother said if she wanted to see a nice campus she should go to UCLA, that her father had an old girlfriend working in the English Department. Larry, Asanee and I became very close. I told her a great deal about you.

"She became the daughter I never had. I made a difference in her life. I think I was the first professional woman she had ever known. I talked to her all summer about literature, writing, Thailand, about helping her own people at Robert's school. Tuttle doesn't know how close she had come to quitting the school. She was making no money. As you would expect, Tuttle runs the school on a shoestring. It's located in a slum, he doesn't have decent books, or classrooms, and his staff of teachers are a crew of oddballs named Snow, Crosby, and Old Bill. There is a weird Thai named Kob who Tuttle gave the title headmaster in lieu of much pay. The whole set-up sounds pretty desperate. But Tuttle is trying to do something important.

"Outside of Tuttle and my mother, no one ever knew I had been an addict at university. God, how I hate the look of that word on the page! Addict! It's so dirty, awful, filled with gloom and dead ends. The thing with an old junkie is they never really kick it. One day, one night, it might be years later, it creeps back and grabs you in the middle of the night. I had gone back on heroin before I met Asanee. Here was a young girl looking up to me as a mentor, a role model, this tower of strength. And I was shooting up. Asanee is the only person I ever rescued. I made a real difference in her life, and taught her to treasure the future. If she ever knew . . . the truth, it would undo everything.

146

"I am so tired, Larry. I can't keep up the game. I should be stronger, I know. But you don't know what an addiction can do. You have no idea. Checking out isn't such a big thing. Funny thing, that if I hadn't met Asanee, I would have done it before. She lengthened my life by three months! Three wonderful, incredible months.

"I would request that you set aside the $1 million insurance money in a trust fund and use it to establish a fund for Tuttle's school in Bangkok. It will secure the school's future, Asanee's future, and give her a chance to make a difference in other people's lives. By the time you read this letter, you will probably have the money. I know that it always bothered you that Tuttle seemed to be in control and have the power when we first met. This time your dealings with him can be different.

"He will never know about my request unless you choose to tell him. What I'm asking isn't for Tuttle. But for his daughter. You have the upper hand now. Please don't let the past between the three of us get in the way of the school or Asanee's future. I made my moral choice; now it's your turn, Larry. You choose the right thing. There is a Thai expression that Asanee taught me. *Dtam! jai!*, *koon*. It means follow your own heart; or, it's up to you. Sorry for the hurt, your pain. Sarah."

LAWRENCE looked up from the letter, his face tight, drawn. From outside he could hear Snow's voice.

"Man, there ain't any such thing as 'up-and-coming' bar girls. Wandos like Dan keep them on the down escalator.

"From the first day, from the first trick, they're doomed. There's no turning back. I think we are wasting our time trying to teach them English. No one's buying these girls to talk to."

Lawrence felt as if he were walled up in a tomb; caught in a dimension of disembodied voices, where the disfigured, entangled, and concealed past had flown apart and reconstituted itself as something not only different from what he had believed, but had displaced his central role. He glanced at the end of Sarah's letter again. Follow his heart, she had written. Her message gave him a sudden chill, making him shudder. She wasn't there to question, and it was impossible to pull her back into space and time. She was gone. His mind filled with contradictory thoughts. He paced in front of the window, rereading passages of the letter. The core of his marriage had been formed from substances he no longer knew how to name. They had had a perfect marriage. Everyone had said so. He was a senior partner in a major law firm; she was a distinguished professor at UCLA. They were the American dream. They had purpose, dreams, amused one another, lived in comfort, travelled together; they had shared the same state of mind, one of tranquillity, Lawrence had thought.

How could he have been so inattentive, then, that he didn't know his own wife was a junkie? He had been working at night. The big deals, the closing party with the client she never attended, the red-eye flights back and forth to New York or Washington on behalf of clients. If only he hadn't been so busy, maybe he would have noticed. Sarah might still be alive, sitting in her university office, preparing a lecture, talking with a student, or writing in her diaries. Everywhere he turned, some new secret hiding place of her life popped open; each one stuffed with unsettling surprises; each a deliberately created, self-contained world that provided her a vehicle for escape. And, in the end, she left Lawrence to collect the pieces and to put them end to end, forming a grand puzzle.

The police report had contained the same words the officer had used at the hospital emergency room. "She must not have seen the '88 Olds. She left no skid marks. The deceased was not wearing her seat belt at the time of impact." It had been a bright, clear day. What the report omitted was that Sarah had accelerated at the point of impact. She had made it look like an accident. His law firm's insurance company, and UCLA's carrier, had paid the double indemnity proceeds under each policy. Suicide would have voided any payment. Sarah had made a conscious choice. Accidental death, said Lawrence to himself, putting the letter back in the envelope.

What to say to Tuttle? Or his daughter, Asanee? No one spoke as he stood there, resting his forehead against the frame. He had never felt so alone, abandoned, or distracted. Sarah wanted him to distribute a million dollars to what? This miserable excuse of a school. Maybe Snow's overheard conversation summed the real truth. The entire enterprise was a horrible waste of time, money, resources.

Each time Lawrence tried to dismiss Sarah's idea as misguided, the Thai expression she had used, *Dtam! Jai! koon* echoed through his thoughts. Hadn't Crosby argued that the heart was the key to the Thai language; and then Tuttle had countered with *Mai Pen Rai*—never mind, no problem, that's life. Lawrence slipped the envelope into his jacket pocket, glanced out the window again. His driver was inside, the windows of the Mercedes rolled up, air conditioner obviously on full blast, reading a newspaper spread over the wheel.

The time had arrived for Lawrence to leave the headmaster's office. The time had come to face Tuttle and Asanee; time to decide how to deal with Sarah's ghost which had followed him to Thailand. And most importantly, it was time to start fresh; he had made so many mistakes and errors of judgement about Tuttle, distorting his words and motives by listening to them as a voice from the past; the time had come for Lawrence to plunge into the present, and discover who Tuttle had become. What kind of man uses his own daughter—was the obvious conclusion, but something else was troubling Lawrence: what advantage was Tuttle seeking to gain by using her? Perhaps the strangest realization of all was Lawrence's determination to bring Asanee to America and enrol her at UCLA; if that's what she really wanted. This informal step-daughter of Sarah's; this secret daughter of Tuttle's who had tumbled straight into his life, robbed him of his sleep, channelled his thoughts into an aggressive desire to possess.

11

When Tuttle and Asanee came back into the headmaster's office they found Lawrence sitting on the edge of the battered office desk, arms crossed, looking at them with searching eyes. His body and mind felt numb. Their Mediterranean green eyes tracking him from the moment they re-entered the room. Sarah had planned this moment perfectly. As she crashed into the 88 Olds, perhaps the last image in her mind hadn't been Tuttle; but visions of Tuttle and Asanee working together in shabby rooms deep in a Bangkok slum. Lawrence's thoughts were jumbled with regrets, sorrow, hurt, anger, and confusion. The spirit of the dead filled the room. It gave Asanee a chill. She shuddered, sat down in a chair, glancing up at her father. Tuttle rested a hand on her shoulder.

"Father and daughter," Lawrence finally said. "Who would have thought it! Bobby, the family man. I would have given anything to see Sarah's face when she found out you had played the paternal trump card. The troubadour turned father."

Tuttle's fixed, immobile gaze shot past Lawrence at some counter-point that only he could see. A long, narrow shadow spread across Lawrence. His troubled expression, the breaking voice, failed to conceal the waves of emotion that Sarah's letter had left. The tidal wave of emotion still left over from the previous night. That made Lawrence disposed to attack. Since meeting Tuttle, Lawrence had reached a footpath to some truth in Tuttle's life; and then, managed to get himself promptly lost, pounding down a side road, knocking down any roadblock in the way, always in the unquestioned belief that he knew Tuttle's map of the world. Law was based on people being predictable, and that their lives followed a common reality, Lawrence thought.

"This pain hasn't been easy for any of us," said Tuttle.

"What do you know about pain?" asked Lawrence, pounding his fist into the side of the desk. The gesture froze Asanee, white-knuckled, in her chair. "You don't know anything. How you get so sick in your guts you don't think you're gonna live. How your life collapses overnight. One day it's one thing; the next, it's totally changed. You don't know who the hell you are. And the future you've relied on . . . it's broken down. Shattered. You don't know what I'm talking about."

Tuttle turned, after a long, thoughtful glance at Asanee, reached over, and touched Lawrence on the shoulder. "Maybe you're right, Larry." His voice was emotionally charged; his face strained and bracketed with doubt. "I have no idea what Sarah wrote in her letter. That's between you and her. But I would like to correct one thing. Your life isn't the only one that's ever turned upside down. Dreams lost. I didn't tell you why I gave up journalism. Or why I started the school. Because you never asked. Maybe you're not interested in anyone else's life, or maybe you think you've figured everything out?"

"After last night, I don't think I've figured out anything," said Lawrence.

❖

"IN February '82 I went to *Mae Sai* to do a story for UPI. For years I wrote for the wires; my by-line appeared in newspapers all over America. One story appeared in the local press; it was about Khun Sa's raid on *Mae Sai*, a small Thai town on the Burma-Thai border in the north.

"Khun Sa and a raiding party had shot up the town. I had done the Khun Sa story before. I got an exclusive interview with him at his house in *Ban Hin Taek*. We sat beside his swimming pool. He wore expensive sunglasses and talked about a movie deal in Hong Kong. The phone kept ringing beside the pool. He laughed, threw me a wink, signed a document, and talked about this karate film he had financed. 'Better than Bruce Lee,' he said.

151

"You looked at him, and you thought, a movie producer with machine guns and an army behind him. You wouldn't want to be the guy who wrote the bad review. That had been five years before, in early '77. Back then, I had a good idea that he had killed people. Years later, when he hit *Mae Sai*, he left bodies in the street. There was no lingering doubt."

"I planned to take an overnight bus to the north. An air-conditioned job where the driver gulps down *Yah mah*—speed—by the bottle. It gives the drivers red-rimmed eyes that no longer blink. Cartoon eyes with black circles underneath, except they are pencilled on the face of a human being with one bare foot on the gas and the other on the brake. That last night in Bangkok, I had several hours to kill before getting on the bus. It was too early for a hit-and-run mission on HQ. So I stopped off at Bunny's Bar in one of the sois that snake off from *Soi* 23. Bunny and me had a history that went way back to the late '60s—a few months after I left Los Angeles—when she was in between husbands, we shared my first monsoon season.

"That year—'68—the claps of thunder came in mid-May and rattled the bedroom windows at four in the morning. Claps of loud, booming thunder that drove spikes straight into your soul. The thunder, like mortar fire, came in fixed patterns. Five evenly spaced booms. Then a pause. Five more sharp spikes with the night sky flashing a hot white. I knew the sound of mortar fire from covering Vietnam two months earlier, and for a moment I could pretend with Bunny, this wasn't Bangkok, this wasn't thunder; but the sound of incoming mortar rounds with their hypnotic explosion as each round marched closer toward our bed. Hostile, earth-tearing, window-shattering jolts fell from the sky that May.

"Bunny curled up like a baby against my shoulder, shaking, and hiding her face beneath her long, black hair. Going up to *Mae Sai* to cover Khun Sa's lightening pre-dawn attack, I thought of the past; those four a.m. mornings with Bunny rocking against my neck. She had the trace memories of real mortar fire in her head. She had covered her ears. Boom. Boom. Boom. Closer and closer.

Boom, and another loud boom twenty meters away. We lay in dead stillness, side by side, and then she felt my face, touching my eyes, nose, mouth, and ears. There was no blood. She can't understand why there are no wounds, no blood, with incoming shells landing on top of us. I tell her it is only thunder. She shook her head; she wouldn't believe that thunder made the mortar rocket sound. She accused me of lying to her. That the earth was on fire; an invasion had been launched; the rockets and mortars fired.

"Nostalgia was a condition I came down with in Bangkok a couple of times a year. The best cure was getting on a plane to Saigon, Singapore, or Hong Kong and staying out of the country for two weeks, covering a story or a war. I'd come back healed. I was a couple of months overdue for a trip; and deep into nostalgia at that time I had to go to *Mae Sai*. Nostalgia is always the greatest danger. I tried locking myself up inside the apartment. But I had the key.

"I decided to let myself breakout.

"I was on the run, straight into a taxi and pulling to the curb beside Bunny's Bar in time for the nine o'clock news. Bunny sat on a low stool behind the counter; her eyes barely cleared the top. As I came in, she gave me a long, hard look. That *hard-core* look, "Where in the hell have I seen you before? In the rushes of my early life?"

"Her smile and the eyes were the same. Everything else from her youth had been buried in clumps and rolls of fat. She wore the tent dress of fat women. Underneath, she carried an extra load; perhaps, as much as sixty pounds since the nights of the thunderstorms; the weight collected in her face and upper arms.

"'Tuttle, is that you?' she asked me.

"'Still afraid of thunder?' I asked her.

"She laughed, rose up from her seat, the loose-fitting fat lady's circus dress falling around her breasts and hips. I leaned forward and kissed her on each cheek. She still drank screwdrivers; a half empty glass, with lipstick on the rim, rested at her elbow.

"'I heard you got killed in *"Nam,"*' she said.

"'And I heard you killed off two husbands,' I said.

"'Not true,' she squealed. 'The second one, Norman. The one from Chicago. He died of a heart attack. Right on top of me. I had dreams of ghosts for one solid year. The third one, Gary, he got killed on a motorcycle in Pattaya.

"'One died in bed and one on the road. That's not a bad record, Bunny. A Thai wife with two dead husbands, and you never once used a hitman. Impressive!'

"'Tuttle,' she cried at me. 'You're so bad. You come in here like a ghost. I still don't believe it's you. You got some ID or something. A passport.'

"'You have a small wine-colored mole here,' I said, pushing a finger to a spot just below her right breast.

"'Shit, it is you,' she said, clapping her hands together.

"I was going up to *Mae Sai* and do a cover story on Khun Sa's raid; and found myself side-tracked in Bunny's Bar, killing time, waiting for the bus. I watched her tumble a handful of ice cubes into a glass and pour me a drink on the house. I was deep into a past regression with an old girlfriend, whose body confirmed every fear and story I had ever heard about the devastation middle-age brought to a woman's body.

"Three husbands had come into her life since that monsoon season. Two had died. One, the only Thai in her arsenal of husbands, Bunny had divorced before I ever met her. Number four, and her current companion, was an American who sat at the far end of the bar, shaking dice in a leather box and slamming the box down on the bartop. He wore cowboy boots, drank imported Budweiser beer, and listened to Grover Washington Jr. on pirated cassette tapes. What Bunny and I had to say about our past lasted the standard fifteen minutes it takes to remember that monsoon season. But it had gone cold; the sharp bite was gone, the sting and the cuts from the old emotional arc welding flares. Four months compressed into a quarter of an hour. She drank two screwdrivers as she ransacked her memory and found a few unbroken fragments that had survived from the old times. All that we had clearly remembered was the thunder and lightning. There must have been more during that time; things locked deep inside our memory, but for the life of me, I couldn't remember them, and neither could Bunny. We stood smiling at each other as her fourth husband slammed the dice down once again on the bar."

❖

"THE dice game had ended; Bunny's husband had disappeared upstairs to watch television by the time I had found a stool at the far end of the bar. Bunny worked up front near the door. Again, I had vanished from her life without a trace—though I was no more than thirty feet away. I no longer existed in her world. On the wall a TV set was turned to the local news. Two go-go dancers moved lazily on two small stages that were separated by a glass case housing an expensive collection of imported liquor.

"One of the girls had tan lines under her bikini bottom; tan lines that curved high on her ass. A sign, as every *hard-core* knows, of a go-go dancer who hung out on the beach near Pattaya. She floated me a kiss, touching her fingertips to the center of her warm, smooth smile. I nodded and looked away toward the television. She would warm my bed with hundreds of *farang* ghosts. She had that look.

"The diskjockey, one of Bunny's sons, played '*Unchain my Heart*', cranking up the volume to full blast. Another son switched off the sound on the TV; it is a government channel, and like the go-go dancer, it only told everyone what they already knew, running a script we'd heard a thousand times before. The dancer directly in front of me hardly moved to the music. She held onto the silver center pole and watched the news. The TV pictures cut between rice farmers in the field, a folk music festival, monks chanting in a temple, a beauty contest in the north, and street scenes of *Mae Sai*. The camera closed in on a crying woman on the street. There was a burnt-out car beside several street vendors. I glanced at the go-go dancer, who was nearly motionless, except for a small twinge as she turned on the automatic pilot that pumped her legs at the knees.

"By the time the weather report had finished on the bar TV, the girls had me sized up as *hard-core* and ignored my presence. Just as Bunny had already forgotten that I was drinking at the opposite end of the bar. A customer beside me paid his bill, the hostess counted the money, looked at the bill, then placed them on a silver tray and walked across the bar to Bunny. Two stools down a passed-out *farang* slumped over the bar, sleeping. No one paid him any attention. He didn't exist. He wasn't part of their job. No one had the courage to risk waking him.

"A new girl jumped onto one of the platforms. She wore tight jeans, running sneakers, and a designer jersey. Large silver earrings dangled from each ear and large bangles rattled on her wrists. I caught her eye; she locked me on her emotional radar screen. *Farang* sighted at twelve o'clock, approaching straight on. Appears to be a friendly. Squeeze trigger on target and launch a hip. Direct hit. Target cannot disengage. Shoot one leg, then the other. Target disabled, dead in the water, and unable to leave the scene of engagement. Push out the final weapon, the one held in reserve for the coup de grace, two large, firm breasts pressing hard against the T-shirt. Target surrendered.

"She jumped off the stage, and climbed onto the empty stool next to me. I ordered her the standard hostess drink; a Cola that arrived in a double-shot-sized glass. Neither of us blinked for over a minute, she hooked one leg over mine, and leaned forward with her forehead touching mine. This was the melt-down phase. Nothing I could do—or would try to do—could prevent the inevitable. Nothing broke my fall into the void of nostalgia better than the firm cushion of such a body. She told me her name, 'Bun.' That was her nickname. In Thai, Bun means merit; Buddhists belief that merit is needed to be born to a better life, she explained to me, stretching forward from the bar stool.

"'Tonight I go to *Mae Sai*,' I said to Bun.

"'I go with you,' she said.

"'It's dangerous. Khun Sa's men killed six people last week in *Mae Sai*.'

"'I'm not afraid,' Bun said.

"'How long you work the bar.' I asked her, because I had to know if she were a pro.

"'Off and on. Whenever I want. I go to school. I no have number. You see. I only go with man I like. Understand?'

"She worked the bar to earn money for school. An out-of-the-way bar, where she could selectively decide who would pay her school fees. I liked the idea of being chosen as her financial aid officer. She told me proudly that she studied political science; her bar-girl English suddenly sounded more fluent. And she said that she had finished a paper on Khun Sa last term; she had quoted my earlier interview with Khun Sa. By then that monsoon rainy season with Bunny might have happened in another life. I pulled out my wallet, just as the drunk *farang* lifted his head from the bar.

"'I dreamt the Bengals won the Super Bowl,' he says in a sleepy voice. 'And I beat the spread.' He pivoted off the stool and walked straight out of the bar, leaving a five-hundred baht note under an empty glass.

"Bun and I shared the joke as our first in-joke. She was nearly nineteen and didn't have a boyfriend; of course, that was the standard line. But somehow she was different. I believed her. I handed her the two reds to pay the bar fine and another red to cover the bar bill. Ten minutes later, she returned with her handbag hooked over her shoulder. She planted a passionate kiss on my mouth. All the time, I was thinking, 'If I have to go to *Mae Sai*, this is the way to go.' A nineteen-year-old political science major who had quoted one of my articles in her thesis on Khun Sa. And those full, red lips, and those eyes looking back like a high-powered mirror.

"And after she pulled herself off the stool, she leaned back on her heels and smiled.

"'You know Bunny?' she asked.

"'I knew her back . . .' I broke off because I had realized that giving a date, one that would sound ancient to her, might give her a better fix on my own age. I avoided the cold, impersonal number of years that had passed and said, 'I knew her a few years ago.'

"On the way out of the bar, I stopped and said good-bye to Bunny. She rose to her feet and wiped the sweat off her face with a large, white handkerchief.

"'You take good care of my daughter, Tut. She's a good girl.'

"'I always like your maternal instinct, Bunny. How many daughters you have working the bar? Ten, fifteen?' I asked, joking with her.

"She laughed, and nodded her head. 'You never listen to no one, Tut. Bun my daughter. No bullshit.'

"I slowly turned and found Bun nodding her head. I had bought out Bunny's daughter and was taking her to a war zone in *Mae Sai*. Even for a *hard-core*, buying out a bar owner's daughter was a first. Once I took a Noi back to my apartment from HQ and later discovered, from my photo album records that I had slept with her mother. But Bunny was different. Bunny and I lived together. She had been my monsoon wife. I remember holding her as the thunder pounded the ground like advancing mortar fire. Now she looked like a grandmother. This time I had skipped into the next generation with premeditation. I knew exactly what I was doing. I was no different than Khun Sa planning his raid on *Mae Sai*.

"There were going to be casualties; because there were always casualties every time two people meet in a *farang* bar in Bangkok. Overwhelmingly the casualties were the girls. Headquarters didn't get its name by accident. HQ was the command center in this war zone. There were many firefights on Soi Cowboy, that the strip of bars which ran between Soi 23 and Soi Asoke; hand-to-hand combat continued all the way to the back alley entrance to HQ. I had prided myself as being a hardened combat veteran who had defused every known kind of sexual landmine and booby trap. But sooner or later the odds catch up with anyone. I was long overdue for an ambush.

"I thought about it for a moment that seemed like an eternity. I could have walked out that door alone that very moment. Kissed off the two reds as the ticket price for a bout of nostalgia. I looked at Bun one more time, and her eyes, saying take me with you, don't leave me here. And I told myself that I had a choice. A moral choice. Bunny had sold me her daughter. The purchase price of her own daughter was only two reds. And in the back of my head I vividly recalled the sound of that thunder rattling the bedroom windows."

"AFTER we checked into the hotel at *Mae Sai*, I decided to get business out of the way first. We walked to the police station for an interview with the chief of police, who had been on duty the night of Khun Sa's raid. Bun, her hair tied in a ponytail, walked at my side; she proudly carried my Pentax 35 mm camera over her shoulder. She wore my vest containing my passport and film; it was so big that it drooped around her shoulders, making her look like a tiny little kid.

"We created this elaborate fantasy, where I pretended that she actually worked with me; that she wasn't a bar girl that I had bought out for two hundred baht. We were a working couple; two professionals in the same business. The purple per-day fee I had promised

158

her as my assistant journalist provided a face-saving way for her to accept the money. Given this advanced state of detached reality, I could have been hired to write the news for the Government TV.

"The truth, Larry, is, I wanted at least for one day to forget that she was a second-generation night shift worker. So we caught up with the police chief, a stocky-built Thai, with a bullet head and short-cropped hair. He smoked smuggled Winston cigarettes down to the filter. We strolled into his office, and Bun handed me the camera. I took several shots of him standing behind his desk. The more Police Chief Tong talked, the more evident it became that the raid had been the peak experience of his life. People who have had a peak experience can't wait to re-enact the whole sequence of events in front of the camera. So I suggested in a vague way that allowed him to say no, that maybe he'd like to show me exactly how he stood up all alone to the great opium baron, Khun Sa, armed with a regulation army-issued Colt .45.

"'I show you, sure. No problem,' he said.

"He pulled on his combat vest, lighted another Winston, removed his .45 from his holster, checked the clip, and then squatted on his haunches and assumed a firing position beside the window. I snapped a dozen shots of Police Chief Tong aiming at the image of a man who had passed through the town a week earlier.

"Khun Sa had marched into *Mae Sai* with about two hundred troops on January 26th at that most fragile time of day, just before dawn. The villagers had begun to stir in their beds. Some were already on their way with carts and bikes to the market. Some were deep inside dreams. Most were within that isolated pocket of time when the weight of the world was far away. Police Chief Tong had been asleep in his bed when the first Chinese AK47s opened up on the police compound. And how does the noise of an assault rifle enter the sleeping mind? On the wavelength of dreamland.

"'Chinese New Year's, I see in my dreams. I open an eye. It is dark in the room. I know now I'm not asleep and I still hear the crack, crack sound of firecrackers. Only now I know it is a gun. I think a robber shooting at bank,' Chief Tong told me.

"The police chief was a real find; the kind of official who made great copy for LA freeway drivers. The kind of cop who has seen *Bonny and Clyde* three or four too many times.

"A round from an AK47 had struck the grandfather clock in the police station, stopping time at 4.37 am. Khun Sa had marked the exact moment of his invasion. The truth was Police Chief Tong never stood at the window with his .45 shooting at the invaders. The truth was the Police Chief was on the floor covering his head and ass. The truth was he reacted to the AK47s the way Bunny had reacted to thunder: with fear, alarm, and childlike apprehension. What made the story was the photo of the chief of police standing half out of the window in his flak jacket, one eye squinted over the sights of the .45.

"After Khun Sa and his men left *Mae Sai*, cars were burning in the street. Dead bodies lay in the street and houses. Wounded cried out in pain. The police came out of the compound with their weapons drawn and counted the dead and wounded; counted the number of bullet holes in the Thai Farmer's Bank; counted the number of cars with red tongues of flames leaping into the early morning sky.

"There was a purpose in this madness of death and destruction at 4.37 a.m. Somewhere, maybe in Washington, probably in the White House, someone—try Nancy Reagan—was memorizing some jokes in *Reader's Digest* for the President when she came across an article about Khun Sa, the drug baron of Southeast Asia, who sold the tons of opium that ruined American schools, parks, and created a new class of business-criminals. She might have told the President about the article. He might have mentioned it to an advisor, who phoned the State Department, who sent a word to the Prime Minister's office that America would be very happy if the Thai government could do something to get Khun Sa out of *Reader's Digest*.

"The army sent a couple of OV-10 "Peacemaker" planes and eight "Huey" choppers to bomb Khun Sa's HQ at Ban Hin Taek. The army dropped 500-pound bombs on Khun Sa's hometown. The army marched into Ban Hin Taek, as if they were looking for any second-rate Lahu Godman, seized Khun Sa's house, and took photographs of each other in front of Khun Sa's color TV and swimming pool, and stacks and stacks of assault rifles, hand grenades, grenade launchers, and bazookas. A major loss for any warlord.

"The photos were shipped via diplomatic pouch to Washington, D.C., and I have a picture in my head, of the President and the First Lady sitting in bed with the *Reader's Digest* article open on her pillow, the one with the handstitched presidential seal in red thread, and all of the black-and-white photos covering the bed and floor.

"'Isn't that a Japanese TV set?' she might have asked. 'That's the real problem. Japanese imports. Japanese TV sets in the jungle. It makes you sick. The world once bought only American. Now the Japs are everywhere.'

"And so, once again, Khun Sa was left alone on his backwater reef in a remote patch of jungle.

"After the interview, we dragged ourselves back to the hotel room. I made a couple more notes in my notebook, brushed my teeth, shaved, and when I returned to the bedroom, Bun sat on the edge of the bed, undoing her ponytail. I didn't want to think about Khun Sa, or people dead in the street, or the police chief holding his .45 and smiling for the camera. I wanted her. I had wanted her since the moment I saw this exotic creature dancing on stage and she came around the bar and parked herself on my lap. On the bus I slept sitting up, her head resting against my shoulder. I reached out to touch her, to pull her back on the bed, but she scooted away, as my fingers grazed her shoulder.

"'Why did Khun Sa come here?' she asked me.

"'A little revenge is always a powerful reason,' I said to her, reaching forward and helping her take off her jersey.

"'You ever meet him?' she asks.

"'Make love,' you find yourself saying in broken bar girl English.

"'I afraid,' she whispers to you. *'Mai! dy!*—I cannot!'"

"AND she sat on the edge of bed and I sat next to her, looking at myself and her in the full-length mirror on the wall. Her body was rigid with fear. Every muscle in her body was flexed. And the look on her face said that she was on full red alert. I had seen that look before in war zones. That's the look of abject terror. The same look I remembered seeing on Bunny's face during the thunderstorms all those many years ago. Then reality slammed into me hard; I thought I knew exactly what had happened. Bunny had sold me her sexually frigid daughter. The one with the perfect body and the full lips and the large, sparkling green eyes. The half-Thai; half-*farang* daughter from one of her marriages. Bunny had found the perfect revenge. Her message was clear, 'Here you are, Tut. The beautiful young body that was once my body; the body you held in the early morning hours in the late '60s when we listened to the Beatles; a carbon-copy body from a time machine, only this time there is a flaw, a minor problem, you see, it fears sex the way I used to fear thunder in the night. Can you understand fear, Tut? Can you understand what happens when the body shakes and you can't breathe because your throat is so tight, and your mind is careening like a wild, out-of-control upcountry bus?'

"I remembered Bunny's voice, looking at her daughter in the mirror. I could hear her speaking as if she were in the room. 'Have you forgotten how I felt? How you held me? How you looked at me when you came into the bar and saw the fat middle-aged lady who now runs the bar? Those eyes of yours dropping 500-pound bombs on my memories of that summer. That was a bad thing, Tut. Never bomb the place of a woman's fondest memories. She has her ways of coming after you though she never moves from her stool behind the bar. So hold Bun in your arms, and pretend it is the summer of '68, Tut. Pretend that you are holding me again. That time has reversed. That her body is my body. That your body is young again. That those in the world who have grandchildren are old, fat, with one foot in the grave. The world is for the young. In *Mae Sai*, here is your chance to be young again. For a couple of nights in the distant past. Think hard, it will come back to you. What you were then is still somewhere inside. Something inside the girl you see in the mirror is from inside me. Are you getting what you paid for, Tut? Are you getting what you want? Have I left casualties in the streets of your mind? Made you think of all those bodies? And sitting next to you on the hotel bed is a perfect body that I made, Tut. And the perfect revenge. What have you ever made, Tut? After all the summers and all the winters, what has lasted for you? It's passing out of our hands, Tut. The world of thunder that echoed through the night. Sorry, I had to tell you this way. But I knew you of all people would understand. The man who always loved words more than people. The HQ man of Bangkok would understand that I lived many years with one dream, one hope. One day, I'll sell a frigid daughter to this man. And he'll know what a brilliant pre-dawn raid I had made. And he'll dream of Chinese firecrackers and overturned, burning cars in the street.'

"I collapsed back on the bed, looked up at the ceiling, the cracks and cobwebs creeping out from the light fixture. 'Which father was yours?' I asked Bun. 'The one who died in bed? Or the one killed on the motorcycle?'

"I heard her get up and disappear into the bathroom. When she came back into the room, I had fallen asleep. She switched on the light and knelt on the floor beside me. Slowly she opened her fist and inside her hand was a ring. A gold ring with a large "M" engraved in the center. I know that I looked puzzled. I picked the ring off her hand, and looked at it closely.

"'My father gave this ring to my mother. A long time ago. I never know him. My mother say the "M" stand for monsoon marriage. It was a kind of joke.'

"And when I rose up and put the ring under the light, examining the inside ridge, I found RT engraved inside. Bunny had never told me. Not even that night in the bar; she could have stopped me, pointed out that this girl was my daughter. The ghost of thunder roared in my ears. I had crashed into something that left me reeling inside that room. I couldn't look directly at Asanee. In a fraction of a second I had gone from someone trying to push her down on the bed to someone who was keeping her at arm's length.

"I couldn't keep my eyes off her, I just kept looking at her, staring, my mouth open. Why hadn't I seen the similarity before? Was I that drunk? That blinded or tired or fucked-up? How much else had I overlooked? What in the hell was I actually contributing to anything? A bullshit interview with a local police chief?

"She sat on the bed, her knees pressed tightly together. I slipped the ring on her finger. She held out her hand to the light, admired the ring, and as she looked up at me, I told her about the monsoon season Bunny and I had spent together. She listened, nodding as I spoke, as if I were pulling her on a sled through snow-blown canyons, guiding her through that season. When I finished, she looked at me in the mirror.

"'You know what my name means in Thai?' she asked.

"An unexpected initial question, I thought. I shook my head.

"'Asanee means lightening. Thunder and lightening,' she said. 'I never know why my mother give me my name. She always smiled if I asked her. One day, I tell you,' she said.

"Bunny had never told me about Asanee; about the girl she named lightening after heavy storms that cut across the fingerboard of fear late into the night during our short monsoon marriage.

"My own flesh and blood, my own daughter, a bar girl, was selling her body every night of the week. I had bought her out with the single-minded purpose of taking her to bed. God, I sat on the bed, squeezing a pillow against my belly, rocking back and forth; I thought I was going to be sick. Way to go, champion, I said to myself. From the time I left California, I had been engaged in the kind of deceptions I found amusing in the police chief; he had slept through Khun Sa's early morning raid but willingly re-enacted a scene of danger—but a danger where he had never been personally at risk.

"We both understood what we were doing; we were creating a pantomime—one that made for good copy, a distinguished myth. I had acted the part so well with Bunny that I believed monsoon marriage had been a real marriage; only she guessed from the rhythms of my own life that change would come, the conditions would shift, and, like the thunder, I had celebrated the passion and force of her presence, of her love from a safe distance, and all the time she was on the front line, the place where people hurled themselves into battle.

"I was an expert on taking an episode like stock footage in a film, re-cutting it, and editing it to produce the grand gesture, the pointing of the loaded gun out the window. Sarah and I had decorated our relationship with that kind of game; one that defrauded reason. That's why she had the good sense to marry you. You gave her the great comfort of someone who had no desire to explore the coastlines walked by Lahu godmen. Then something happened, I can only guess. Maybe it was drugs. Years later, she had forgotten what had been between us had never been real. She actually believed that I had stood at the window of life, holding off the hordes with a medieval sword. I knew where the membrane of truth ended.

"When you pick up the scent of your own myth, the hunting dogs of the past make straight for your throat, all snapping jaws and razor sharp teeth. I had a daughter, but never had a wife. Asanee's father hadn't been the *farang* who had died in bed or on the motorcycle; he had been the *farang* who occupied the blank space between the flash of lightning and the clap of thunder.

"You tell me that I have never known pain, Larry. Maybe the strange feelings clustered inside you when Sarah died were so great, so large, or what she wrote in that letter so cruel, that you will never stop the hemorrhage.

"But your life isn't the only one that has come to an abrupt halt. You're not the only one who was knocked down hard, or who felt that everything came out wrong. You carry the ashes of the dead. Sarah's carelessness; your own, because the right questions never came up. Asanee sat on the bed with the word father on her lips, and I felt the stress of combat. I could have dressed and run. Fled the scene, like I had done from Los Angeles. But if I stayed, this time, then the truth was what I had built my life on wouldn't carry over. The larger than life foreign correspondent had been a myth I had created for Sarah as much as for anyone else. It is an easy myth to fall for: journalism as a scared cathedral and foreign correspondents as high priests bringing the Word to the masses. With Asanee next to me, I knew I couldn't make that myth work any more. At the same time, accepting that I was Asanee's father, I knew wasn't going to be easy. Finding a new role wasn't going to be easy. I couldn't say, 'Okay, I'm a father. So what else is new in the universe.'

"I had to bang the shutters down or walk away from her. The joke is, that decision is the only true piece of art I ever created. Ever since leaving the States, I had been chasing after those once in a lifetime moments of other people's lives, ones that elevate, reveal or destroy them, and swindling myself into believing I could derive meaning alone for such an exploration, walking up and down the borders of Southeast Asia, as if I carried the burden for smuggling out the truth to the world.

"After more time passes, you'll find a way to make your own choice, Larry. You can either rebuild things and let go of the past; or you can shut the door on life and blame the world, your dead wife, your friends, your life; and keep that stain of pain fresh every day you live."

❖

LAWRENCE'S mouth felt sticky and dry. He coughed, swallowed hard, looking at Asanee first, emotions tearing at the corners of her mouth and eyes, and then up at Tuttle, whose eyes were red.

"I understand there is a Thai expression," said Lawrence, looking at Asanee. "I'm not certain if I can pronounce the words right. But it's *Dtam Jai koon*."

Asanee repeated the expression. "That was Sarah's advice to me. The day before I left Los Angeles. She loved that phrase very much."

Lawrence looked away and whispered, "I know."

12

Lawrence was hard pressed to say the horror of having your wife commit suicide was worse than waking up one day and discovering you had a daughter who moonlighted in a Bangkok go-go bar and spoke broken English. Tuttle had equalized the balance of pain; synchronized the language of hurt.

That afternoon, after lunch, Asanee returned to three hours of teaching. She caught Lawrence watching her eat, staring at the ring on the third finger of her left hand, her Morse code way of communicating with her father.

"There are thousands like Asanee," said Tuttle, calling for the waiter to bring the bill. "Amerasians working the bars and clubs. Girls who belong nowhere. Last night at HQ remember the girl who cut her wrists?"

Lawrence nodded. He had hardly touched the rice and shrimps on his plate. His mind had been working too fast, edging out his appetite. "Her name is Lek."

Tuttle was impressed that he had remembered her name.

"I'm going to run some food and medicine over to her room. Come along and have a look," said Tuttle.

Asanee threw a disapproving glance in the direction of her father. "You break her face, Father." For the Thai there were two disasters to avoid. Losing face wrecked a Thai's state of well-being, but to "break face" was a high social crime, causing an intense furnace blast of provocation. The girl lived in a slum. For Tuttle to willingly bring Lawrence into the overwhelming poverty of Lek's world had great risk; a strange *farang* would see the reality of the place she inhabited, not the illusion created in the night world, and that shattered image might rob her of her usual defences. She had few reserves, guessed Asanee. Lek had hit emotional bottom and was looking for some way to climb back. Tuttle was about to withdraw the offer when Lawrence cleared his throat, pushing his plate aside.

"I can't speak Thai. But maybe if you translate, Bobby, I can explain what suicide does to those left behind."

Tuttle watched his daughter's reaction quietly; she folded her hands on the table, her expression giving away nothing of what was inside her mind. "You would do that?" she finally asked in a tentative fashion as she emerged from her shell.

As the waiter returned with Tuttle's change, Lawrence felt the gravity of Asanee's question. She was protective like her father. If Lawrence were going to penetrate into Lek's private enclave, he had to understand the consequence of finding a disturbed girl undressed by the squalor of her confinement.

"Larry might reach her," said Tuttle.

"He might," admitted Asanee.

TUTTLE and Lawrence climbed into the Mercedes, and Tuttle made a mental note to instruct the driver to park out of sight of Lek's hotel. They would enter her soi on foot. The Mercedes and Thai driver in livery provided a brief moment of amusement for Tuttle. The notion of Lawrence arriving in a luxury car so he might explain to a girl caught in the grip of grinding poverty all the reasons why she should choose to live.

As they turned onto Sukhumvit Road, a dense black cloud rolled from the ancient exhaust system of buses and trucks, fouling the air with a texture as rich as volcanic ash. Lawrence's mind wasn't on the snarled traffic or the thick layers of dust and exhaust fumes that created an enclosed twilight dome over the road; he thought, instead, of Sarah's letter, with his thoughts shifting back and forth between Asanee and Tuttle. The voltage of emotions in the headmaster's office alternatively horrified him and invoked his sympathies. Neither Tuttle nor Asanee had questioned him about whose suicide he had in mind. He was grateful. He had made the offer spontaneously; perhaps to win Asanee over, and, of course, it was too late to retract and too soon to explain.

If there were absolute and universal moral laws, then some rational connection existed between cause and effect, Lawrence thought. But the large ganglion that made up causality had split apart. Each time Lawrence appeared to find a plausible progression toward an answer, the bottom dropped out. The more he contemplated what Tuttle had told him, and Sarah's letter, the less clear was the imaginary line separating disgrace from honor. He had begun to surprise himself. Where was his legendary self-control? As a lawyer, he picked apart his own conduct; only this time, he was having trouble knowing whether what he had done was as desirable or should be rejected as a flaw.

It was like a drafting problem, he thought. Every clause served the entire document. The meaning had to be clear, the purpose exact, each phrase with significance to a precise set of circumstances. Life, he thought, was outlined according to the same set of drafting rules; break one, and errors and discrepancies filtered in to the everlasting confusion of the whole. Sarah had killed herself. A voluntary act of self destruction, without bitterness or scorn, but for some larger purpose that she had never shared with him. And in her letter, she had appointed Lawrence as her sole instrument to execute her chief desire. Sarah had requested him to take responsibility and shape the lives of Robert Tuttle, Asanee, and their school, and the lives of strangers whose needs, from her own action, she had valued as having greater claims than any claims in her own life, or her life with Lawrence. She had assumed placing full power and authority in his hands was the minimum price for his consent.

A slum school in Bangkok didn't match up in value to Sarah's life. He couldn't see it; and he certainly didn't understand it.

Lawrence had been a supreme rationalist; and his wife's death and last request had the hallmarks of irrationality. Everywhere he looked Lawrence was seeing the shape of people and events without fully understanding how they were connected or, if he made a connection, he was at a loss as to what meaning to accord them. He had assumed Asanee was Khun Kob's daughter, ignoring the sparkling green eyes; he had not understood the context of HQ the previous night, or why Tuttle had made the point of selecting

A Killing Smile

that place; the exact location where, if he had looked carefully, he would have observed here was the intersection where Tuttle's life had shifted gears: from accumulating girls for bed, to bringing them into the classroom.

Tuttle explained Lek's background. Her father had been a black American. Charles Washington had played varsity football at Cornell. He had been posted for two years in Thailand, where he had been appointed the head of a UN relief agency. He met Lek's mother in a Patpong bar. Tuttle outlined the crushing banality and ordinariness of such a story; like thousands and thousands of other girls, Lek's mother had come down from the north and worked the go-go bars. Washington picked her mother out of other girls working the same bar; bought number 46—his old football jersey number at Cornell—seven nights in a row; she thought that meant he loved her. She moved into his apartment and they lived together for two and a half months. Washington got restless, and got her a job in a cocktail lounge, gave her a handful of baht notes. She didn't want to go and decided to keep him; she got pregnant. The guilt worked on Washington for awhile, and she moved back into his apartment. After Lek was born, Washington had acknowledged her as his child—what he thought was a noble gesture, then six weeks later he changed his mind and got the UN to post him out of Thailand. He never married Lek's mother.

His escape from the scene left Lek stateless. Under both Thai and American law she was neither Thai nor American. She fell between the seams, and there was no one waiting to break her descent. She didn't look Thai, and her dark skin wavy black hair, and thick lips made her an object of discrimination. Lek had been excluded from almost day one by the other Thai kids; she developed a king-sized chip on her shoulder. She enrolled in the school for a couple of months, but she kept losing confidence, saying she was stupid. A stupid nigger, she called herself. She had lived a lifetime of sorrow and rejection. Only Asanee seemed to be able to reach her; she trusted Asanee who knew the slights that had been carefully aimed at look kruengs the half-breed Thais.

Asanee spent a long time with her, talking to her, trying to get her to fight back. Learn English so one day she could talk with her own father. But she claimed never to want to see him; she hated

170

that "bastard"—the one English curse word she remembered and used whenever she talked about him.

If Washington had simply vanished from the scene, then the authorities would have been forced to presume that Lek was a Thai national. Asanee's mother had never told Tuttle about his daughter because of that very risk. Asanee could be a full Thai because Tuttle had never asserted his paternity, or made a public record of it. Lek was worse off than Asanee, and that drove a wedge between them. Lek had entered the gray world where she was nothing, a world where she could not find her own identity. And there was Asanee with the best of both worlds: her actual father at her side, and her Thai passport and nationality secure.

Half of the students who came to the school had a background similar to Lek's; *farang* fathers who never married their mothers, and left them in a no-man's-land where everything was stacked against them.

THE Mercedes let them out on New Phetchaburi Road. Tuttle grabbed a large plastic bag of food he had bought earlier in the morning at Foodland. The driver deposited them at the entrance to Soi 43, and they walked under the baking mid-afternoon sun down the soi past rows of small rundown rooming houses and hotels. Tuttle turned and entered one of the buildings. An overweight Thai woman in her early forties stood at an old-fashioned telephone switchboard, a bowl of steaming noodles at her elbow, as she pulled out a plug and stuck it into a new slot below a flashing red light. Down a short corridor, all the doors of the rooms were wide open on their hinges; the still, humid air made Lawrence's shirt cling to his damp body. Music blared across the corridor from one of the rooms. Garbage had been collected in the narrow hallway. A low, hacking cough muffled by the thin walls and heat echoed behind their footsteps.

Tuttle halted, searched for a room number, then finding it, knocked on the open door of room 104. A teenage Thai, in rumpled white hot pants with her string top unhooked on one side, appeared in the doorway. Her puffy eyes surveyed Lawrence, and then Tuttle. She wore no makeup; a money belt was tied around her waist. She smoked a cigarette with one hand, and cleaned her ear with a Q-tip with the other. Each movement jangled a dozen arm bracelets that fell like sand in an hourglass from her wrist to her elbow. She sucked hard on her cigarette, and let the smoke curl out her nose, looking bored and hot, as Tuttle and Lawrence stepped inside the narrow room.

Constructed of concrete blocks painted yellow, the room housed four Thai bar girls. Three lay in a tight row, side by side like sleeping children, jammed together in on a queen-sized bed. At one end a wooden rod ran the length of the room holding four separate, yet interchangeable wardrobes. Lawrence recognized two of the girls from Headquarters the previous night. The girl in the white hot pants jiggled Lek's arm, stopping only to inspect the content of ear on the end of the Q-tip.

Lek, her eyes swollen, her face pale and drawn, raised her head, and managed a smile as Tuttle placed the bag in the empty space at the foot of the bed. Her arm bandages were soiled, and had slipped down to reveal stitches and clogged blood. Lek was eighteen years old, and had travelled to Bangkok from *Surin*, a town in the Northeast, where her mother had gone after Charles Washington fled the scene. The pain of her injury showed on her face. She balanced herself on one arm, one arm tucked below her rib cage, she shifted from side to side, grinding from her hips, as if she were dancing in a bar, and all the while keeping her head in a half-bowed position. Her expression darkened as she glanced up at Lawrence, an unknown *farang*, who stood behind Tuttle.

"Food and medicine are inside," said Tuttle. "Stay in bed a couple of days and rest. Don't forget to eat. And Lek, don't do this anymore. It's bad luck."

"Cannot sleep. Head no good. Stomach hurt. Have period," she said.

Tuttle removed a small plastic bag of pills. "Take these. Four times a day. Before you eat. Okay? You understand?"

"Why you bring your friend?" asked Lek. A look suggesting betrayal darkened her face. One of the other two girls moaned, rolled over on her side in her sleep. The roommate in hot pants passed her cigarette to Lek, who slowly inhaled, looking Lawrence up and down.

"He saw you cut yourself last night. He feel very bad. He feel sad young girl, pretty girl, want to die," replied Tuttle, sensing Lawrence's discomfort.

"Me no pretty," said Lek. "Thai girl *soo-ay*—beautiful."

"Bobby, tell her I know she hurts inside. My wife hurt inside, too. And she killed herself," said Lawrence, his voice breaking. He tried to swallow back the storm of feeling that burned in the back of his throat as Tuttle translated to Lek.

Her expression immediately softened and she crawled forward on the bed. She stretched out and took Lawrence's hand and cradled it against her face. Lawrence tried to say something else but he couldn't; he broke down, sat on the edge of Lek's bed and wept.

"Tell her I'm sorry," he finally said.

"She understands," said Tuttle, watching the girl in white hot pants take out another Q-tip and begin cleaning the space between her toes.

"The person who I was the closest to in my life killed herself," said Lawrence, wiping his face with the back of his hand. "And that's something I can't undo. I can't change. I have to live with it. And that's unfair. There's always another day, another way around a problem. All you have to do is ask. Ask the people who care about you." He gently placed his hands around Lek's face. "All you have to do is ask. Do you understand?"

Her face clouded as she found Tuttle's face. He translated Lawrence's words in Thai, and at each pause, she nodded, looking back at Lawrence, tears rolling down his face.

AT Headquarters, Lek and her friends became the grammar for the abstract words "sexy," "good," "beautiful" giving those words faces and flesh and emotions. They floated around the floor like dreams auctioned off to the first *farang* who gave that discreet nod, wave of the hand, or any of the other signals that meant the same thing. "I know your price. And I'm buying. Buying something for myself this night. Something I can't point out but I find outlined in the way you dress, walk, and smile." And they created the illusion that each *farang* was part of their dream and the promise in each gesture and glance that their world of smiles lacked nightmares.

The posters in Lek's room illustrated the field of dreams for any teenage girl. Middle aged men, the *farang*, were absent in every poster, picture, and object on the walls, headboard of the bed, and table. The *farang* was the ghost who did not appear. Except in an hallucination, where the girls were unable to do anything to stop him from roaming the dark roads of their dreams. Then Tuttle and Lawrence arrived at their bedside; how frighteningly dangerous they looked at close quarters standing in the midday sun, straddling the equator of their own world. The *farang* who came to weep with the girl who had tried to kill herself. Everyone's world had spun upside down in a reverse orbit.

Before Lawrence and Tuttle departed, Lek nodded her approval for one of her friends to pull out a package of noodles; another of fish under cellophane wrap, laid out side by side like the girls in the room. The other two girls rubbed the sleep from their eyes, then sat back like hungry children on their elbows waiting to be fed. One girl slipped a cassette, a Thai rock song, into a new sleek black Sony. Stuck in the headboard of the bed was a toy teddy with a pair of sunglasses pulled forward on the bridge of his furry nose. Lek sat on the edge of the crowded bed staring at her feet. Her friends had clawed the wrapping off a box of cookies that Tuttle had stuffed in the plastic bag. Packets of tomatoes, chicken, and soup were scattered over the bedding.

"Phone me tomorrow. Tell me how you feel. I take you to the doctor, if you're not better," said Tuttle.

Lek stared at Tuttle, wiggling her painted toenails, one ankle hooked behind the other, nodded, and quickly looked away from Tuttle's eyes. He touched his palm against her forehead. Then he felt her neck, and pulled his hand away.

"*Bpen Ky!*—you've got a temperature."

"*Mai bpen!*—No, I okay."

"Tomorrow. I take you to doctor. He make you better."

"Your friend *Ky! jai*—sick in his heart," she said. "Maybe you take him to doctor."

Lek nodded, the edges of her mouth fighting some bitter sorrow breaking through from inside. *Farangs* had a formula to follow.

They arrived inside Headquarters and bought the girls; the girls never wanted them to see how they were forced to live. In the silence between Lek and Tuttle, the language of face—face lost, face saved—had been in every thought and gesture.

"My friend is *Jai dee*—good heart. My friend broke his face," said Tuttle, switching between English and Thai. "Because he cares about you. Anyone ever do that for you before?"

She shook her head slowly; her friends passing cookies back and forth over the bed. Tuttle turned and walked out of the room without looking back. He continued past where the telephone operator stood eating her noodles and answering the phone, and found Lawrence waiting in the lobby.

"Nothing I said could have affected her so much, Larry," Tuttle said, as they began walking toward the door. "She won't forget you. What you said came from the heart."

"Where can we get a drink?" asked Lawrence.

"I'm sorry I hit you last night."

"You call that a punch? I've been kissed harder than that."

There was that half-crooked smile, that endearing smile as Sarah had called it, passing over Tuttle's face as they walked down the sub-soi beneath the searing sun. "I have the perfect place. There's another girl who has strayed from the fold. Before you say anything, just listen to this. She's studying law. Okay? That's her day world. And at night . . . Fawn dances in a go-go bar. Asanee says Fawn's in over her head."

Lawrence felt exhausted, his neck and shoulders stiff and aching. He was drained, used up, and patched together by sheer will-power. From some memory loop, he heard a whisper, telling him to call it a day. He had turned himself inside out in Lek's cramped room. For a brief second, it hit him what Tuttle must have experienced that moment he realized that Asanee might have been alone with him inside his hotel suite. That accelerated force of such emotion flattened every decoy rolled out to deceive another; and to realize that all along one had been ultimately fooling oneself. The realization followed with that strong sense of conflicted feelings: of being both defenseless and connected for the first time.

"As long as I can get a drink," said Lawrence, cupping his hand over his eyes against the sun.

"I'm getting this strange feeling that I may have been wrong about you for about half of my life," said Tuttle. He tapped lightly on the window of the Mercedes, waking the driver from a sound sleep. The steering wheel had left pressure marks against the right side of the driver's face. Tuttle climbed in without mentioning a word about face. The concept had already opened and closed enough accounts for one day.

13

Asanee wore white sneakers, jeans, and a baggy sweatshirt with UCLA on the front in bold blue letters. She floated a half an inch above the ground. An hour before Lawrence's Mercedes and driver arrived, she had received a phone call from Lek, who said she would be coming back to school in two days; she had promised. And she told Asanee about the strange *farang* in his tailored suit and tie who had sat on the edge of her bed, held her hands in his and begun to cry.

"It's the suit, man," said Snow, when Asanee broke the good news to him. "A pin-striped tie around your neck and a Thai girl will eat out of your hand."

"Maybe it was what Khun Lawrence said; not what he wore," said Asanee.

"You're dreaming in technicolor."

"Isn't that better than black-and-white!"

"Get outta here," smiled Snow. "You're getting too smart in English. I can't handle it, man."

ONE success led Tuttle to believe that Lawrence might have other uses. He thought about Fawn. If Lawrence had inspired Lek, then he could reach Fawn as well. He walked in silence alongside Lawrence. He thought about the night before and felt a surge of shame. He had used his own daughter and he found it difficult to look at Asanee the next morning. Though she believed—and he let her

A Killing Smile

have that illusion—she had manipulated him into arranging the meeting. But Tuttle knew the truth and he had a pang of guilt. The unspoken bargain between Tuttle and Lawrence was the working off the moral paralysis of that moment when the truth came home and there was no place left to hide.

During the trip back to Lawrence's hotel, Tuttle explained that for the past year, Asanee had tried to recruit her for the school—not as a student, but to sign on as a teacher. Fawn was a *look krueng*; her father, Howard Stone, came from a middle-class Jewish family in New York City. He was thirty-three years old when he came to Bangkok; the assignment was a promotion, and Howard was being groomed for rapid advancement in the marketing division of an international finance company. Fawn's mother had worked in an exclusive private members' club—and whoring had a caste system like every other occupation—which put her at the peak, where only the most beautiful, fluent, and sensual girls were selected to work.

The wealthy and powerful international clientele included Japanese, Taiwanese, Koreans, and *farangs*. The Parrot Club was the equivalent of reaching K2; while HQ was somewhere below Death Valley elevation. Membership was by invitation only. The waiting list was reputed to be five years long. Howard gained entrance as a guest of the general manager of the Bangkok branch of his corporation. He immediately felt like he belonged; no one paid any attention to the fact that he was a Jew. He was lumped in with all the other *farangs*; one indistinguishable mass who were interchangeable. There was no apparent restriction of his coming and going. At once, Howard felt freer than he had ever felt in New York where the clubs either allowed or restricted Jews.

Military and police generals, minor nobility, and important politicians sipped cool drinks, sitting back in rattan chairs on a long veranda, as they watched the long-tailed boats and ferries navigate the *Chao Phraya River*. The Parrot Club was a place where business and finance were discussed; where deals were made, and a generous member was known to have offered a business associate the services of beautiful identical twins as a gesture of goodwill.

Fawn's mother and father met under a ceiling festooned with crystal chandeliers. She had descended a circular staircase wearing an ankle-length navy blue silk evening dress. The manager, a

178

Swiss man, who affected an English accent, had worn a monocle in his right eye. Gunter noticed Howard's moonstruck expression as Siri reached the foot of the stairs; he immediately brought her over and introduced her to his "good friend" Howard Stone who was from the Big Apple. Gunter neglected to explain to Stone some essential background information: Siri had been a *mee-uh noi*—a minor wife—to an influential Chinese merchant.

Perhaps Howard wouldn't have understood the implicit warning of those three words: influential, Chinese, and merchant, strung together to create the impression of a successful businessman. If he had asked what a Thai meant by using those three English words, he would have learned three more words: Watch your back. Cross an influential Chinese merchant and you had better watch your back. In less than four months, Howard had proposed to Siri, and she had accepted. When she became pregnant in the fifth month, they were both overjoyed.

Then Howard received a phone message from a stranger, "Maybe you leave Thailand soon. Go home alone. Think it good for you to go to airport."

"I'm an American, asshole. Fuck off," he had replied, banging down the receiver.

Still he didn't understand the rules. There was no such thing as a former *mee-uh noi* of an influential person in Thailand. It came down to a question of loss of face. Howard announced one night at the club, having bought a round of drinks at several tables, that he intended to marry Siri, and make an honest woman out of her. He didn't detect from the hard mouths and narrowed eyes among certain tables that this was beyond foolish talk.

He didn't watch his back. Two weeks later a motorcycle rider wearing a red helmet pulled up alongside his car one morning, pulled a 9-mm handgun from inside his windbreaker and shot Howard in the face four times. Fawn's *farang* father had been dead four months on the day of her birth. All she knew of him were the newspaper clippings her mother had saved; blurred, finger-smudged photographs of a man sprawled out in the gutter like a puppet whose strings had been cut. A couple of uniformed Thai policemen stood smoking cigarettes beside the body. They smiled nervously into the camera.

Howard's parents refused to accept Fawn as their granddaughter. According to Jewish tradition, since her mother wasn't Jewish, neither was Fawn; according to Thai tradition, since her father was *farang* she wasn't Thai; and since her parents never married, she wasn't an American. Like most *look kreung*, she learned, at every turn, and in every face, to expect rejection; and she had been rarely disappointed. Though, in Fawn's case, she had collected the full hat trick of abandonment. No one wanted her. She started on the outside rim and never managed to find a way in.

After a year of hammering away, Asanee was frustrated; the chip on Fawn's shoulder was as big as ever. Working in a rough go-go bar, going back with low-class *farang* acted as some kind of personal revenge on herself. It was as if Fawn needed to punish herself over and over again; her mother had never helped matters, always hinting that her father had been killed because of Fawn.

THEY ate dinner in a Chinese restaurant opposite the school where no wall or window sheltered them from the traffic fumes, dust, yapping soi dogs, and motorcycles opened at full throttle. Lawrence squatted with his knees thrusting to his chest on the low stool dressed in a fresh suit with a blue pin-striped tie. Asanee smiled to herself, thinking of Snow's remark that afternoon about Lek being taken in by the tie. Lawrence's white collar was stained with sweat. He caught Asanee looking at him. But only a brief glance. What he felt the night before returned as a kind of energy field.

"Fawn's been in fourth-year law for two years now," said Tuttle, as a large steamed fish arrived.

"She keeps failing two subjects," Asanee said, serving her father a slice of fish.

"I have a theory about those two subjects," added Tuttle, watching his daughter carefully place a piece of fish onto Lawrence's plate. "If she passes, then she's finished school and has to make some decision about her future. If she fails, well, she says she's always failed, and at least the money she makes working the bar is good."

"Then she's bright?" asked Lawrence, finding Asanee's eye lingering with his a moment too long.

"She's a very smart girl," answered Asanee, flipping the fish over and helping herself.

"We could use her at the school. No offense, Larry, but there are enough lawyers in the world." Tuttle used the small spoon to sprinkle the spices over his fish. "She has a loose arrangement at Mister K's Bar. She dances when she feels like it, and does not ask Riche, the guy who runs the bar, to pay her. She wants only the money that comes from turning a trick. An example of a peasant's mind with a legal education; like all lawyers she calculates every act as some fraction of a billable hour."

Asanee said something in Thai to Tuttle.

"I'm at a slight disadvantage. I don't speak Thai," said Lawrence after a moment.

"Maybe not all lawyers are *satang jai*—money heart," said Asanee, looking down at the table.

"My daughter reminded me of our meeting with Lek. And she's right. It's hard changing your way of thinking about something in one afternoon. Asanee's disciplined me; put me gently in my place." Tuttle broke into a grin.

Lawrence felt the devil of passion at his elbow; he avoided Asanee's eyes, as he looked out at the broken piles of concrete where the sidewalk had been ripped out. He had been married to Sarah longer than Asanee had been alive. She was a child; Tuttle's child, and he hated himself for the feeling that surged through him as they sat across from each other at the table. Tuttle was so damn trusting, he thought to himself. The side of his face where Tuttle hit him throbbed in the heat of the night. Had it never occurred to Tuttle that Lawrence still might be attracted to his daughter, attracted to the point of distraction? And that it would take much more than one punch in the mouth to change that?

Asanee brought Lawrence back to earth by invoking the name of his wife. "Sarah told me that a woman should prefer a man who admires her brain, her thoughts and ideas, and not just her body."

"Sarah never stepped foot in Bangkok," said Tuttle, emptying the last of his Kloster into the glass.

"If she had, I think she would still have told you the same thing," said Lawrence. "I know she would have."

"I talk to Fawn but she closes her mind," Asanee said.

Lawrence's thoughts drifted back to his Los Angeles law firm. His office, his partners, clients, and Kelly Swan expertly handling a meeting in the conference room. And he wondered what offer Asanee would accept to leave Bangkok. He sensed that she was bound in ways he could only guess; that was the truth about her; the same truth that Sarah must have embraced in this girl with the Thai name meaning lightning, a quality of her father, this deep, burning obligation to decency.

WHEN Fawn strolled into HQ it appeared that she had come alone. Lawrence had felt the rest of the world drop away; her very presence was enough to rock him back on his stool. She *waied* to Tuttle, and turned toward Lawrence. Fawn knew the distinct expression. The furtive glances the nervous laugh, the mobile eyes, unblinking, as they moved like a military squad down her thighs. She was tall, with slender frame, wasp waist, and long, tapered legs with calves that appeared to have been turned on a lathe operated by the gods. Fawn walked up to their table wearing a G-string, six-inch high heels, and a black bikini top. She spoke perfect English—she had gone to Convent School in Bangkok. A *farang* customer grabbed her arm on the way across the room. And in fluent French, she told him to go home to his wife. She was a woman, who on the outside appeared in complete control.

"At least she's not with that asshole, Riche. He loves bringing her here," said Tuttle above the roar of music, as he leaned toward Lawrence. "He can't speak a word of Thai after three years in Bangkok. Riche is someone she can run circles around. She's twice as smart as well. And she likes that sense of power."

When Fawn spotted Asanee, who had squatted down, playing a hide-and-seek game, she rose to her feet and broke into a run. Fawn chased after Asanee across the bar, and finally caught her from behind, picking up Asanee, swirling her around, and all the time, Asanee kicked her feet and, laughed, making no serious attempt to break away.

"I sometimes worry that Fawn might end up recruiting Asanee back to the bars," said Tuttle, his eyes following his Asanee as she wrapped an arm around Fawn's waist. They sat, giggling, at a booth near the bar. "She's like a wild animal. This was the kind of place where I found her. There is always a pull for her to return."

From the corner of his eye, Tuttle saw Riche coming out of the toilet, checking his zipper. A cigarette with a long ash was in one corner of his mouth.

"That's Riche," Tuttle said to Lawrence.

"Looks like he came after all," said Lawrence.

"How you doin', old buddy?" Riche said, shaking Tuttle's hand, and then Lawrence's. "If you're a friend of Tuttle's then you must be in deep shit. Don't mind me. I've got a Midwestern sense of humor. I tell people I'm the true middle American. You look at a map of the 48 states and draw a line east and west or north and south, and you'll find a hair-trigger right over Topeka, Kansas. I've been here nearly three fucking years." He took a long drink from his whiskey and soda. His cheeks billowed out and he shuddered, gesturing for the bartender to bring him another double.

"You see those tight little buns on Fawn?" said Riche, as the new drink arrived. It was ten o'clock and he was already drunk. "Man, I don't care how old she is. I'd love to test out those buns. But I can't. I got a Thai girlfriend. I'd like to test out a lot of these girls. But my girl worked a bar. She knows I work a bar. You think that makes any fucking difference? I try to fuck one of these girls and it gets back to her."

"Did I tell you that I had a new toilet put in for all the customers?" asked Riche, as, taking the last cigarette, he crumpled the empty pack into a ball and threw it at the stage, hitting one of the girls on the leg. The girl cursed at him in Thai and stuck out her tongue.

"What's the problem, Riche?" asked Tuttle, winking at Lawrence.

"I had a separate toilet for the women. But the goddamn Thai girls wipe their ass and throw the tissue in the fucking wastebasket. And that little whore who stuck out her tongue is the biggest offender. These girls are so goddamn clean. You take them home for a screw and what is the first thing that they do? Take a shower.

You screw them, and what is the first thing they do afterwards? Take another goddamn shower. Then they take a shit, and the first thing they do? Throw the goddamn shitwipe in the wastebasket. You figure that.

"And what does Fawn say when I tell her the story? She says upcountry the plumbing can't take the tissue. So they're taught to throw their ass-wipe in the wastebasket. But this ain't goddamn *Korat* or *Surin*, I said to her. It's fucking Bangkok. Fawn was born with a silver spoon in her mouth or up her ass; she knows ass-wipe goes in the toilet. My plumbing takes their shit and tissue.

"I have a meeting at six o'clock at night. Before I've taken a single drink; before any girl had turned a trick or shot up. I stand them up shoulder to shoulder. I get Fawn to translate every last goddamn word I'm saying. I'm holding the fuckin' wastebasket in my hand, Tuttle. This is a speech with visual aids. There can be no confusion. Fawn tells 'em that. You think they can fuckin' change? Not on your life. Ten o'clock I check the toilet and what do I find in the wastebasket? A wad of shit-covered tissue.

"I was raised on a farm. I know something about country life. No one in my fucking family ever wiped their asshole with tissue and left it in a wastebasket. How do I get through to these people? And they have this idea in their head—even Fawn—and she speaks English—they think there's a ghost in the toilet. Jerry's ghost. So I tell Fawn, 'Tell them that Jerry's ghost is gonna pull out their guts if he finds any ass-wipe in the wastebasket. *farang* ghost will go straight up their asshole if he sees a tiny brown stain on any tissue in that basket.'

"And it goddamn worked. Well, for the last week, it's worked.

"It's a question of their attitude. Take my two most popular dancers. Every night they get bought out by customers. That's good for the bar; and good for them. One is a goddamn lady-boy. In seven months, no one's ever come back complaining they got themselves a gender-bender. Probably too damn embarrassed or they simply didn't know. Ignorance is the problem, Tuttle. Ignorance is throwing shitloaded tissue in a wastebasket. Ignorance is screwing a lady-boy and thinking you're humping a Thai girl with a tight pussy.

"So she had the big operation on the other side of the river. She paid twenty thousand baht to have her dick cut off. My girlfriend threatens to do it for free. Makes no fucking sense. Now this ladyboy's got an attitude. Thinks she's hot shit.

"That bitch, she don't dance.

"I said to my partner, 'Bobby, it don't dance. And if it don't dance, I don't give a fuck if it gets taken out. That's fine. Good for the bar. But if it don't dance, then I cut her.'

"She says, 'Honey, I get bought out every night, why you cut me.'

"And I say, 'You get your ass bought out, that's real good. But you ain't no better than the rest. You get your ass dancing, or I cut your pay again.'

"She just stands leaning against the pole. And I just cut her. Fuck that bitch. She ain't gettin' special treatment from Riche. She ain't no bigshot. Even if she does get her ass bought out every fuckin' night of the week. You getting the idea of what I mean by the Thai attitude? You can't fuckin' change them. Not on your life."

Lawrence reached inside his jacket and removed his wallet. The wall of plastic credit cards inside caught Riche's eye. "How much does it cost to buy out Fawn?" he asked.

Riche raised an eyebrow, and shook the ice in the bottom of his glass. "Seeing you're a friend of Tuttle's, it's two hundred baht."

"It's two hundred baht if you're not a friend of mine, too," said Tuttle, spinning around on the stool.

Lawrence handed Riche a purple Thai note—five hundred baht. "Keep the change," Lawrence said.

Riche's eyes lit up like a slot machine when three watermelons come up in a row. He turned and addressed Tuttle. "You should tell your friend to be careful flashing around large amounts of money."

"Use the money to make a sign in Thai and put it beside the toilet," offered Lawrence, leaning back against the bar, making a sideways glance over at Fawn.

"Now there's a goddamn good idea. Only one problem, half of them can't fuckin' read."

Only Lawrence wasn't listening. He was thinking that for the first time in his life he had bought another human being in a cold, hard cash transaction. All those years as a pension lawyer in the merging and acquisition business, he had structured deals that had bought and sold the lives of hundreds, and sometimes thousands of employees and their families; it had been like high-level bombing raids in a bomber at thirty thousand feet. He had never witnessed the smaller, street-level game, where the object of acquisition possessed a face, a pulse, the attributes of a human being like any other, except she hired herself as a mount.

"Is she the first one you bought out?" asked Tuttle.

"Does it show?"

"The convention is you talk to the girl before you buy her out. Tell her she's beautiful, that you like her, and let her size you up with the standard bar girl questions. Where you from? How old are you? Are you married? How long you stay in Bangkok? Where you stay? Lawyer-to-lawyer transactions might be different," Tuttle said, nodding over at Fawn.

Riche had leaned over and whispered in Fawn's ear, pointing his finger in Lawrence's direction. Fawn nodded, covered her mouth in an embarrassed gesture, and then leaned over and whispered something to Asanee, who cupped her mouth as she answered her.

"And what you're seeing is Asanee answering all the questions you were supposed to answer," added Tuttle, smiling at his daughter, and giving her the thumbs-up.

The old mamasan with the bad nose job rose from her stool, a couple of two-baht gold chains dangling around her neck as she walked over to a shiny whiteboard hanging on the wall. The board contained columns of numbers separated by a black dividing line. The kind of display that looked out of place in any Bangkok bar. How was Lawrence to judge, having never entered more than a couple? She looked like a stockbroker or schoolteacher as she took the small eraser from the lip of the board, and erased number 27 from the left-hand side and carefully wrote the number in the right-hand margin. The left side was the dance order of the girls; the right side the number of the girls bought out for the night. Number 27 had been sold like pork bellies. Only this wasn't a future market. This was the present, now, here and forever in the moment market, where the numbers on the right signified the transition from a girl smiling at a customer from the stage of a go-go bar to smiling at him inside his hotel room.

Tuttle pointed at the mamasan writing with the black Magic Marker on the board. "The sale's complete," said Tuttle. "You've bought something you can't put a name to. A girl in Bangkok. Her time for the night. It belongs to you."

"To talk to . . . about the school," protested Lawrence.

"To talk to," said Tuttle, nodding with a wan smile.

FAWN had disappeared to the back and changed into her street clothes. When she reappeared she did not resemble the same girl who had walked across the room in a G-string and high-heel shoes. She had transformed herself back into a respectable twenty-two year-old law student at the open university. She's seen pictures of American women lawyers in magazines, and with some major Thai modifications, altered the professional outfit to her own liking. She came out dressed in white high heels, nylons, a tight white skirt, and blouse with hundreds of sequins. Lawrence had never seen an American lawyer dressed like that. No client would ever remember his legal problem, or care about a solution, in her presence.

Fawn arrived at the table with a black leather handbag slung over one shoulder and an English law book in her right hand. Lawrence read the title on the spine: *Introduction to English Contract Law.* She plunked down beside Lawrence, laid the book on the table, and offered her hand to him as she nodded to Tuttle.

"You always carry a contract book with you?" asked Lawrence, as he picked up the book. "When you go out?"

"Why not? Sometimes a lawyer buys me out. And we talk about law. Asanee never believes me when I tell her I'm going to New York City to practice. My father was a New Yorker."

"Larry knows the story," said Tuttle, looking around for Asanee. She had not returned from the back with Fawn.

"You talk too much about me, I think," said Fawn with a nervous frown. She turned back to Lawrence, pressed her hand on his wrist and playfully pulled at the hair. "I like to touch *farang* hair."

"The school," whispered Tuttle across the table. "Don't let her distract you. She's very good at that."

Lawrence's chin snapped up, he looked wide-eyed and guilty. Slowly he removed his hand from Fawn's grasp. She looked slightly rejected and folded her arms around her chest; a stubborn, heavy expression ruffled her smoothskinned brow with whorls.

"Robert, you are just like my mother," she snapped. "You are always trying to make me feel guilty. Maybe you think I'm a stupid girl because I failed two courses. But I know why you keep coming here. And why you bring your friend? And why did he buy me out?"

"I come because I think you could help. Help other girls just like you who come to the school," said Tuttle, rising from his stool. He strolled off searching for his daughter.

Fawn cupped her hands around the corners of her mouth. "I'm a bar girl. I don't think I'm better than the others," she cried after him. "Not like some people I know."

But she was working up to a larger question that she wanted to ask Lawrence.

"If you were me, would you tell your mother that you worked in a bar?" She was testing him; she had that ability to scatter those around her with unexpected questions and asides. Like an investigative reporter she plunged right into the thick of the controversy. Lawrence understood why both Tuttle and Asanee thought she would make an excellent addition to the teaching staff.

The first question she asked him was about personal honor, or the Thai variation called loss of face. "Did your mother ever tell her mother she worked in a club?" He answered her question with his own. A lawyer's delaying tactic, he knew. But he wanted to see how quick her reaction really was.

"No way," she said swiftly.

"Because your mother would have lost face." Lawrence thought he had hit the marrow, finding the precise answer.

She shook her head, brushing her fingers through her long hair. Her eyes saw his disappointment. Again she grabbed his hand, and he didn't resist. Then she offered him the key to the relative quality of truth in Thailand. "Not that reason. I don't tell my mother because of my own face. Same, same. She don't tell her mother for same reason."

In Thailand a person's own face always came first. Her father had died because he didn't understand that one driving force that pressed people to rewire the control panels of truth in their own lives. Each person's face came first in his or her life. And beyond face was the need to earn merit. Because with each breath, he was travelling toward the next life. Face and merit: the two legs that carried one forward from one life to the next. Everything he did, each act, had consequences. Everywhere one moved, in every word, action, and thought, ripples were spreading out, carrying him higher or driving him lower.

Lawrence listened to Fawn talk, thinking he was listening to a law student, but what he heard was a bar girl talking in code that defined the night. And if she broke that code, she would be sucked under and emerge alone in a void of fear. And it wouldn't stop there. She would continue to tumble, falling from the earth to some alien surface, coming back in some lower form. She was unsure of her rebirth in this cycle. Had she come back as a bar girl or lawyer? Whatever her decision, there was a price in the rebirth from this form and this life to the next.

Inside that bundle of ironies called face, she and her mother had worked as prostitutes, her father had been killed, and as Lawrence turned sharply, hearing Tuttle's voice raised in anger, he saw Asanee wearing Fawn's G-string, high heels, and bikini top. Asanee had met Fawn's challenge: "You think you're better than me, Asanee. That you're better than a dirty bar girl. You try and pretend you never worked the bar. So you think you're better than me. Why should I want to work with a girl who looks down on me?"

The demons had been unleashed, the worst of Tuttle's fears twisting to the music. He was in no condition to be reasoned with. He chased after his daughter, knocking over stools and chairs, jumping over the bar. Riche struggled to pull Tuttle down from behind, but he had drunk too much, and was too slow to duck as Tuttle caught him square on the chin. Riche stumbled back half a step and fell backwards, taking down a bar girl and chair with him. Tuttle leaped onto the stage, swept Asanee, her feet kicking, into his arms, and carried her straight out the door and into the night.

She screamed in Thai. "Let me go, she say," was Fawn's translation. "I not little girl. Leave me make my own life."

Had Asanee gone on stage for his benefit, Lawrence wondered? This strange, exotic, innocent creature who had entered the hotel lobby less than twenty-four hours earlier had transformed herself into a person he couldn't recognize. "I'm sorry for Tuttle," he said softly.

"Robert stay in Thailand long time," said Fawn. "He lose face and he act just like a Thai."

Lawrence remembered how Tuttle had lost face twenty years earlier; how he had tried to rescue Sarah from her parents, from herself; how he had broken into his hotel suite on the same mission. Each time he seemed to fail. Each time he had undertaken the most difficult rescue mission: to rescue a person from themselves.

AT the foot of the Oriental Hotel, Lawrence hired a boat on the *Chao Phraya River.* A high-rise tower of luxury condos occupied the site where the Parrot Club had once stood. Lights shone from the windows facing the river. Fawn pointed at the white concrete tower honeycombed with balconies as the boat passed. She sat opposite Lawrence, her lap covered with orchids Lawrence had bought from a soft-spoken hunchbacked dwarf, who had stopped them just outside the bar.

"Riche didn't tell you about Jerry's ghost?" asked Fawn. "I can't believe him sometimes. He didn't tell you? You want I tell you? Okay, no problem. Mr. K's was run by Jerry and his wife. She's a Thai girl. Jerry's from Scotland. He find his wife fucking around on him. Some girl goes to him and says, 'Your wife she fuck with Thai man.' Jerry ask her about it. She lies and says, 'No fuck around on you.' But he lays a trap and catches her with Thai man fucking her in short-time hotel. He drinks half bottle of Mekhong and locks himself in bar toilet. Takes off his belt and hangs himself. Everyone know that is a bad way to die. Monks come and sprinkled water. Burnt incense. But everyone still talk about Jerry's spirit. Riche and Bobby buy bar. No problem. People start to forget about Jerry.

"Since Jerry killed himself his *pee*—his ghost—is still haunting the bar. He's become the living dead. How do I know? Easy to explain. We start getting strange electrical problems. Every four minutes power stops. The lights go off. It's completely dark. Riche's Thai girlfriend says, 'That's Jerry's ghost. He very unhappy still about fuck-around wife. And something else maybe he want.'

"Then she gets brilliant idea that Jerry wants to smoke. He doesn't have his cigarettes. And Riche says, 'Don't tell me that a goddamn ghost is having a nicotine fit in the spirit world.' She found out Jerry's favorite brand of cigarettes was Benson and Hedges. She buys a pack. Lights a cigarette and takes it back to the toilet on an ashtray. Ten minutes the power goes on. No more problem that night. Every night, one of the girls lights a Benson and Hedges cigarette and take it back to the toilet in an ashtray for Jerry's ghost. Sometime she get so scared inside that she forgets what Riche said about shitpaper in the basket. She does just like home. Wipes ass and gets out before ghost grabs her between the legs."

"Do you believe in ghosts?" asked Lawrence, leaning back and looking at the night sky.

"You think I'm a stupid girl if I say yes?"

Lawrence laughed and shook his head, letting his hand touch the water over the side of the boat. Lawrence wondered if anyone ever died of natural consequences in Thailand; he wondered about Sarah's spirit—was it drifting across time and space, waiting for him at HQ, the school, Mr. K's Bar, on the river, at the hotel? And he remembered how she had written the letter so that he wouldn't lose face. But could her ghost ever rest after this night? He thought of Tuttle tearing out of the bar, cradling his little Asanee like a baby in his arms, the baby he had never caressed or known. Wouldn't Sarah's ghost always be a step away from Asanee watching over her? He liked to think that was so.

"WHY can't girl who studies law absolutely believe in the spirit world? No problem for me," Fawn said, challenging Lawrence later after they had returned to shore and sipped drinks in the Oriental Hotel's restaurant. "I tell you something else, you go north, you look out for black magic or voodoo. I don't like very much. It's dirty. A corruption. Black magic is for dirty people. One girl might get mad at another because she steals her boyfriend. So she makes a black magic against her. She takes a pubic hair and puts it on that girl's head. And the man thinks she's ugly and won't go near her. Not only just him. But all men avoid her. She's no good any more. Of course, I think it's bullshit. Yet, it's very interesting bullshit.

"One girl I know she practiced black magic. She live in the same building as me. One night I wake up. I hear a loud rattling of the main gates, and shrieks in a strange woman's voice. I look out the window, and this girl's shaking the gates, yelling to get in. Not very far away, the security guard sleeps in his chair. Why don't he hear? The sound so loud I wake up. Yet he still sleeps. Why? I think the spirit of the place not let her in. It don't like the dirty things that girl did. So it won't let her key open the door. And it won't let the guard wake up. You know that spirit house in the front yard of houses? This one was right next to the gate. But I don't really believe it was a spirit. This girl does drugs. Shoots heroin. Maybe she's having withdrawal. She's having a fit. And can't use her key because her hands shake too much. But I think the voodoo's not good. It's makes her dirty."

"My wife used heroin, " said Lawrence, sitting back in his chair, and watching Fawn's reaction. She simply shrugged her shoulders, sucking on her plastic straw. "She killed herself. Did Asanee tell you that?"

"No, she just say you a good man. You *jai dee*."

"She said that?"

Fawn nodded; a serious look of concern appeared in her expression. "I think Asanee like you too much. But she afraid to tell her father. Tonight she dance to show him she can choose her own life."

LAWRENCE had been a witness to a part of the Thai mind. Her conversation had been filled with stories of black magic, suicide, ghosts, and drugs. Then doubled back to Asanee's surprise appearance as a go-go dancer; and Fawn implied the dance had two wanted each man to know that she was sending a message to both of them. Either it was telepathy, or Lawrence was beginning to realize the bottom had fallen out of his own life and nothing firm was left from stopping his fall through the void of Bangkok. That he wasn't alone in his grief. Fawn had supplied both an irrational and rational set of causes and effects; explanations that mingled speculation and logic. Both were true at the same time. Reason had cut on and off in her conversation like the faulty electrical system in Mr. K's toilet. She was utterly convinced that ghosts are nonsense and exist; both explanations were correct and not in conflict with one another.

She attended law school during the day, danced in a go-go bar, exchanged sex for money, and dreamed about practicing law in New York City. And she dreamed about working for IBM, of dirty dancing in a disco with the perfect partner—not an American, because they dance like ducks—and wouldn't marry for ten years. But she would have married Lawrence the next day. Her world began and ended with the message that appealed to the heart.

What drew Lawrence to her was a shared sense of how loss installed an undercurrent of emotions that flicked back and forth under the surface of reason. Her experience of life was mixed with her father's ghost. Her life was interconnected with different ways of living and hiding. Healing drew her into one world after another. In each place she sought to heal herself, her face, her dreams.

When Lawrence caught her off guard, staring at the paper lanterns on the wooden river boats, he caught a glimpse of her face undefended. A small portal into what she really was. What she believed in. Things that no one could put a name to. Visions beyond reason; and landscapes faraway and remote from reason. Her vision was so perfectly clear to her. But when Lawrence looked through that lens, what appeared on that other side was a huge stadium packed with people singing and waving Nazi flags. He remembered the Lahu godmen, and he thought maybe, just maybe, he had found a faulty seam where his visions had been badly stitched together. Only the seam had split apart time after time; the center never held for long. And into the void was the place where the Western nightmare of the irrational, the cause of evil, that pulled mankind into conflict waited for another chance. None of these thoughts translated.

So in the Oriental Hotel they reached what he thought was a parting of the ways, never wholly understanding the frequency of their two different ghost worlds were a universe apart. And his efforts to build the perfect receiver to pick up her signals registered with a long burst of static.

"Hello, are you there?" he asked her, leaning across the table.

"What did you say?" She had been watching the lights on the boats passing down the river.

"If working at Robert's school is a matter of money," said Lawrence. Her head tilted to one side in a tentative fashion.

"They have no money."

"And if they did, would you work at the school?"

"And not go to New York City?" She asked, rattling her long red nails against the rim of her empty glass.

"But if the money were right. Say, a thousand a month to start."

"No one can live on a thousand baht a month in Bangkok. Cannot," she said, narrowing her lips and frowning.

"I wasn't talking baht. A thousand US dollars."

She shook her head. "Joking, yes?"

"Not joking."

"And you want me to sleep with you?"

Lawrence removed his chequebook from his jacket and began writing out a cheque. Her eyes dropped down, trying to read as he wrote. "Why you no answer my question? I think maybe you want sleep with Asanee. I can talk to her if you want. No problem for me."

He tore the cheque from the book and slid it across the table. "One month's salary for teaching. Sleeping with the staff is never a good idea," he said. "That includes Asanee."

"Asanee say you want her to go to Los Angeles. Why?"

"Because it's a secret between us."

She looked carefully at the cheque, then glanced up at Lawrence. "I think you be careful. Tuttle know many, many people in Thailand who might not be good for you."

14

L awrence had returned alone and gone straight to his room. It was morning in Los Angeles, and Lawrence had already spoken with his broker, placing a sell order on his shares. Next he phoned his law firm, and with a yellow legal-size note pad, the telephone cradled between his ear and shoulder, he spoke with Greg Walker, one of his law partners. He wrote, as Greg outlined the law governing the formation and structure of a charitable educational trust.

"The client in Bangkok has deposited one million dollars with me, " said Lawrence. "He wants to remain anonymous."

"No problem," said Greg Walker, his partner and former law school classmate. "So who is this angel?"

"No can say," replied Lawrence.

"He's not laundering drug money, is he, Larry?"

The accusation shocked him, caught him off-guard. In an odd way, though, he thought, Sarah's insurance money was drug money. Not money made from buying and selling drugs, but a bundle of cash he had collected when she put an end to her private drug hell, her conflict, and the complex shell game of hiding her habit with a sleight of hand.

"The money is okay."

"He wants to fund a school? In Bangkok? It's gotta be a first. Education isn't exactly what springs to mind when you think of Bangkok." Greg made a point of saying Bangkok in a provocative fashion; "Bang," a short pause and then he uttered the word, "cock." He laughed at his own joke, and waited for Lawrence to join in; an awkward silence followed, and finally Greg changed the subject.

"Kelly Swan made partner two days ago."

"Wonderful," said Lawrence.

"You don't seem all that happy. You were the one pulling for her, Larry. You want me to transfer you over to her?"

He could hear Greg breathing over the line, waiting. "I'll get back to her later. Gotta run. Someone's at the door."

"That's more like it," said Greg. "Engines fired up. Tropical climate. A beautiful woman at the door. Just pace yourself, Larry. And leave the trust documents to me. I'll fax them to the hotel within twenty-four hours."

Crosby, dressed in a rumpled cotton shirt and trousers, was smoking a cigarette as Lawrence opened the door. Tuttle gave him the detail of retrieving Lawrence from his suite at the Bangkok Regent Hotel.

"Your phone was engaged. So I took the liberty of coming directly to your room." Crosby looked over Lawrence's shoulder and into the room. "Very posh," he said. "I suspect you don't have anything to drink." Crosby walked past him into the room and over to a counter lined with bottles of imported liquor. He poured himself half a glass of gin and sat in a chair, stretching his feet out on the carpet. "Very posh, indeed." Crosby possessed that imperil English quality of settling into a situation as if he had been invited; and this making himself-at-home ability was accomplished without the slightest embarrassment, undue explanations, or request for permission.

Sarah's letter lay open on the table next to where Crosby was seated. Lawrence walked over, picked up the letter, and slipped it in his jacket hanging over the back of a chair. "Of course, Fawn lost face—more face than she can recover in one night," said Crosby.

"How did she lose face?" Lawrence was seriously perplexed, as he shoved his yellow legal sized note pad into a drawer.

"A *farang* gives her a cheque for a thousand dollars and doesn't even want to sleep with her," replied Crosby, knocking back a large sip of the gin. He sighed and lowered the glass. "It plays on their minds. Maybe she's not really a sexy girl. You see, the girls like to believe that they earn their money, and that their johns find them totally irresistible. It's a mind game they play among themselves."

The evening had not panned out the way Lawrence had planned. There was something debilitating about trying his best to do the right thing, and falling flat on his face. He felt like a child who needed the constant attention of others to guide him through the most simple situations. Crosby sat in his room, drinking his gin, criticizing his conduct, having appeared out of nowhere.

"Who told you about Fawn?"

"Communication between the girls is measured in nanoseconds," said Crosby, elongating each vowel in nanoseconds. "She phoned Asanee from the Oriental Hotel lobby all weepy, who told her father, and he phoned me. Asked me to come around and have a little chat."

"Why the hell didn't Tuttle come? He tore out of the bar tonight. I had never seen him like that," said Lawrence, sitting down on the edge of the bed.

"Typical family row," said Crosby, refilling his glass and lighting a cigarette. "I wouldn't take it too seriously. Tuttle worries Asanee might return to the bar scene. And from what she's told me—which, mind you, isn't a great deal—your wife had a similar concern about her. Bar girls are a little like junkies. They can kick the stuff for a week or even a year or more, but they always miss it. Sooner or later, most girls end up looking for their fix. Asanee's fix is dancing in a go-go bar."

The phone next to the bed rang. Lawrence slowly picked up the receiver. Crosby had finally established the tie between Sarah and Asanee in Lawrence's mind; that common fear of regression, sloping down the side of a mountain, giving them that rush that made them high on the downward spiral to the bottom. He placed the receiver to his ear.

"I'm more than a little upset, Larry," said Kelly, choking back tears as she spoke from her office in Los Angeles. "I just finished talking with Greg. He said you were too busy to talk. And I've been sitting here crying my eyes out, trying to make some sense of what you were thinking. What you feel about us."

"Congratulations, Kelly," he said in a flat tone. "Ask Greg when he faxes the documents to send the relevant tax code provisions on charitable trusts."

Crosby peered over the top of his racing form. Lawrence stood with his back toward Crosby, who scribbled a note in the margin of the racing form. He rolled up the form and stuffed it in his back pocket.

"Is that all you have to say?" asked Kelly.

"I have someone in my room." He looked straight at Crosby as he spoke. "Yes, a woman. A fourth-year law student. I guess you're right, I have lost my senses. Of course I paid her," he paused, staring blankly at Crosby. "I paid her one thousand dollars."

Crosby heard the muffled sound across the room as Kelly Swan ten thousand miles away slammed down her phone in Lawrence's ear. He raised an eyebrow as Lawrence toyed with the receiver, then rested it back on the cradle. She had never wanted to speak to him again; he was out of her life. Lawrence felt numb as he wiped the beads of sweat away from his upper lip. He was losing the sense of his own personal geography; the distance between one emotional point to the next; the channels from one kind of idea to another. Bangkok had disorientated him, robbed him of his sense of direction and compass.

"Exactly what do you want, Crosby?"

"I've only known you a couple of days. Yet something in the way you affect people interests me. What is even more interesting is the effect they are having on you. As you were handing the cheque to Fawn, I was thinking of how I felt like a fish out of water when I was a kid," said Crosby, as Lawrence paced beside the bed. "When I was in boarding school in England, I carried back a full-blown dose. And I showed up at a country doctor's surgery. I pulled my pants down around my knees, and this Victorian doctor, his hands covered in rubber gloves, sweated for the right diagnosis. He had four or five medical books—the ones with the expensive leather bindings—open on his desk. He ran his finger down one column, then another, turned the page, another page, lit a pipe, sank in his chair, smoking and muttering to himself.

"I knew what I had. I told him. Would he listen to a fifteen-year-old from Bangkok? And when I told him precisely the form, brand, and amount of medication, did that make an impression on him? 'That's a bit of a gory rash you've got. Bangkok, you say. Rub this ointment on twice a day. Once in the morning, and again before you go to bed. Four or five days should do it. There's a good lad. Be on your way now. Give my regards to the headmaster.'

"I did what any intelligent fifteen-year-old whoremonger would do, I took the train into London, walked down Harley Street, found the office of the specialist who had treated me before. We had a half hour discussion on tropical VD. I say discussion, though basically I spoke and he filled a notebook with my medical conclusions. I provided the seminar, and in exchange, he signed the prescription I needed. That afternoon, he asked me if I had time to speak with a few medical students at the hospital where he had privileges. At half-past three in the afternoon, there I was, fifteen years old, my pants around my knees, discussing the symptoms, diagnosis, prognosis, and methods of treatment of what I called "Bangkok nightshade." I was in a small amphitheater with two dozen interns staring down, asking questions, and taking notes.

"Later, I took the train back to Dorset with the prescription I needed. Plus I pocketed a small honorarium from the hospital. Five days later, the dose was gone. I was cured. I went back to the country GP, he had another look.

"'Good, lad. Ointment's done the job. All this nonsense about sexual disease . . . you must put that out of your mind. Filthy thoughts aren't proper for a gentleman. So let's not be spreading tales to the other boys about these poor, wretched girls of Siam.' You're looking for the big cure with your chequebooks. I suspected that might be the case when Tuttle mentioned you might be of some assistance to the school."

Lawrence stopped pacing and turned to Crosby, who smiled, knowing he had gained his full attention. "He said that? Assistance to the school? When, Crosby? When did he say that?"

"About an hour ago," said Crosby, raising his glass of gin.

"You're sure about that? It wasn't earlier? Say, yesterday or a week ago?" Lawrence fired the questions, one after another, not letting Crosby reply.

"Lawyers have this innate ability for aggression," said Crosby, rising from his chair. "Perhaps it's a defect in the genes. But, yes, I'm sure." He paused a moment, looked across the lavish suite, and cleared his throat. "An adjustment in salaries for the rest of us might be advisable. Nothing like the new hire getting special treatment to sow the seeds of discontent."

"How much does Tuttle pay you?"

Crosby smirked. "The princely sum of six thousand baht a month. That is when Tuttle is in funds. He actually owes me two months' back pay; and Snow has carried him three months running."

"That's six times more than the cheque I wrote to Fawn," insisted Lawrence, smiling with self-satisfaction, as if he had captured the high ground.

"Unless I've been misinformed. You paid her a grand."

Lawrence nodded as if that was obvious.

"That works out to almost twenty-six thousand baht, my friend. Or about Tuttle's monthly budget for the school," said Crosby, who had moved to the door. "Don't get the wrong idea. None of us help out Tuttle simply for the money. It's a question of fair treatment, isn't it?"

There was no pulling the cheque out of Fawn's hands. He had acted out of impulse, out of a sense of doing right, out of a desire to accomplish what both Asanee and Tuttle had wanted: Fawn quitting the go-go bar and taking a job teaching at the school. How did he know the sum was excessive? It was less than his law firm paid a file clerk. Crosby had left him with only one honorable way out, he thought.

"I'll see to it you and the others are taken care of," he said.

The gin had flushed Crosby's face, spreading red splotches through his thinning hairline. "You know, it's really much worse for the girls than you suspect. Tuttle's been going soft on you. Perhaps he's afraid you can't take the real *hard-core* stuff. But if you are interested, Snow and I will show you some of the nasty bits."

"Snow's here at the hotel?"

Crosby grinned. "He's down in the lobby waiting for us."

Waiting for the elevator, Crosby rocked back on his heels. He was relaxed, off guard. Lawrence plucked the racing form from Crosby's pocket. "Hold on a minute, " protested Crosby.

"What did you write down while I was on the phone?" asked Lawrence, unfolding the paper.

"The second race tomorrow. I have an eye on a horse named 'Charity.' If you must know," said Crosby. Watching Lawrence flip through the form, his eyes running down the column of horses running in the second race. Lawrence's finger pressed against the name.

"Just curious," said Lawrence, handing back the form as the elevator doors opened.

"You were watching me in the mirror," said Crosby, as the elevator doors closed.

"I didn't know you were a gambler," Lawrence said.

Crosby took great pains to refold the racing form. "Aren't you?"

❖

AS their taxi shot past the Sports Club on Ratchadamri Road, Snow, who sat in front, joked with the driver in Thai. Lawrence sat in the back with Crosby, who lit a cigarette and leaned forward, offering one to the driver. The driver's head pivoted around, and he came within inches of smashing into a tuk-tuk. Everyone but Lawrence laughed as if nothing had happened.

"You wanna gross out Tuttle, talk about the skull bars," said Snow, as they stood on Silom Road, their taxi driver cutting back into the heavy traffic, honking his horn. "Skulls. Not even the fascists in the old man bars in Washington Square like the skull bars, man."

With Snow and Crosby flanking each side, Lawrence entered Patpong. A swirling sea of street-hardened touts, sun-burned tourists, old drunks with leathery faces, half-naked teenage bar girls draped around *farangs* who edged down the street with a half-witted grin on their faces. The middle of Patpong—an ordinary soi of wall-to-wall empty bars, discos, and night-clubs by day—was, by dark, transformed into a sexual Disneyland, complete with rides, shows, games, junk food, and hundreds of makeshift street stalls selling watches, cassette tapes, videos, T-shirts, belts, socks, and handbags. Snow and Crosby expertly navigated Lawrence through hell's tunnel—the tiny, narrow footpath between the vendors and bar touts. A teddy bear vendor, with a misshapen nose and a cast in one eye, grabbed at Lawrence, and Snow stopped him dead in his tracks with his rapid-fire Thai; then a bar tout, his throat and arms covered with tattoos, reached for Lawrence on Crosby's side.

In Thai, Crosby explained that Lawrence had VD; and he backed off. Street vendors and touts could smell a tourist. They had a look, a way of looking, walking, glancing at the bars and street wares. While the resident *farang* had learned to become invisible with a combination of language, dress, and the straight-ahead, expressionless, half-dazed look that signalled their *hard-core* status. Several of the touts, hawkers, flower sellers appeared to know either Snow or Crosby. Lawrence sensed they knew the inside workings of this self-contained world, the back room deals, discussions, decisions.

Patpong was the ultimate sexual consumer's paradise: toys, sex, drugs, alcohol, and sports—if one counted tricks with Ping-Pong balls, cigarettes, and Coke bottles inserted between a girl's legs as a sport. It was the ultimate duty-free shop. Halfway down the street, they turned into a neon-lit bar called Jasmine. Lawrence followed Snow and Crosby to the bar; on the surface, the bar was no different from a bar anywhere else in the world. There were no go-go dancers; no blaring music; no whiteboard with the numbers of girls. After a couple of minutes, Lawrence caught something strange out of the corner of his eye; he looked again, this time in the mirror over the bar.

Gruesome was an insufficient description. Opposite the bar was a series of four couches and a variety of chairs, including a barber's chair. A dozen and a half seventeen, eighteen-year-old girls were on their knees giving blowjobs to bloated, cigar-smoking *farangs*. Old men with sagging jowls, liver-spotted hands, and white, flabby legs; they sat deep in their chair with their eyes glazed over. They looked as if they were passengers on some adults-only Disneyland ride. Minnie Mouse, her eyes closed kneeling on the floor, her head bent forward, not in a prayer, not even in sex, waiting until the customer had finished. The *farang* paid for the fare, and bounced up and down on a leather seat, holding a whisky in one hand.

Snow leaned over and whispered to Lawrence. "The true skullers don't even put out their fucking cigars. The cigar hangs out of the corner of their mouth. The goddamn gray ash drops off onto a kneeling girl."

The young girls worked in commando units of three on each customer. Two blockers in G-strings and bikini tops stood on either side of the skuller. The worker bee dropped down on her knees, closed her eyes, and prayed that the skuller's ashes falling from above missed her face. A skuller tapped her on the shoulder, gestured for her to rise, pointed at one of the blockers, who rotated to the kneeling position. Then the third girl would be given the tap.

Round after round the girls went until the skuller's breathing became irregular, his legs stiffened and he began the wheezing noise of an iron lung; his pale hips pumping, rocking the belt buckle on his trousers, creating the echo of a wind chime against the metal chair. Lawrence looked away from the mirror.

Crosby leaned over and spoke softly to Lawrence. "The girls are called 'skulls.' Not a pretty sight, seeing one of them go down on a slime bag. Work in the rice field or become a skull. Twelve hour days with the sun on her back, standing in water up to her ankles planting and weeding in the rice paddies. Or twelve hours in a skull bar. Forty baht a day in a rice paddy or four hundred baht serving skullers."

Three girls approached Lawrence at the bar. One swung him around on the stool, and in a single action, another girl on her right knelt down, driving her head into his crotch. Out of the shadows, a dark-skinned Thai with a dozen long black spikes of hair on his chin, and a gold chain on his right wrist, stepped forward, squinted through the viewfinder of a Canon 35 mm camera. Lawrence, distracted by the girls, was caught by surprise. Eyebrows arched, he lurched forward from the bar stool.

"Get out of here with that camera," shouted Lawrence.

The flash snapped three times in rapid succession.

"Hey, man, beat it," said Snow, turning toward the photographer. "Get out of my face."

"Not to worry," said Crosby. "These buggers are into the hard-sell." Crosby looked at the skinny Thai and barked three or four Thai phrases that Lawrence didn't understand.

Lawrence struggled to free himself; he tried pushing the girl away from his lap. She clung on for dear life. The entire team, all three girls, held him tightly; each grabbed an arm or leg, as the

Thai with the camera grinned widely, showing a crooked row of tobacco-stained teeth; then he ran out the door.

"That man's a nuisance. He's always sneaking up on customers," said Crosby, seeking to comfort Lawrence. "He's got himself a bit of a reputation on 'The Strip.'"

For the residents, the street between Silom Road and Suriwong Road known as Patpong was known as The Strip. And Lawrence had witnessed firsthand what it was like to run scared, chasing a tout with a camera and incriminating photographs through the narrow lane between the stalls selling tapes, watches, clothes, lacquer on The Strip. The man vanished into thin air. Crosby and Snow, out of breath, caught up with Lawrence in front of the Golden Girls Bar.

"Come inside, handsome man," said a young girl dressed in a superman's suit, pulling on Lawrence's arm. "Many pretty girls for you. Dancing. Come inside, now."

"Forget it, man," said Snow, panting and trying to catch his breath. "He's gone. You'll never find him."

IT was Snow's idea to stop in the bookstore in the middle of Patpong Road; the one cool, quiet sanctuary from the loud voices, the heat, the heavy action. He went straight to the rack carrying American magazines. Crosby had wandered over to the Thai travel guide section of the bookstore. A young *farang* couple in shorts and hiking boots, their backpacks on the floor, leaning against a bookcase, sat on the floor studying a guide. Lawrence, still shaken from the skull bar experience, stared at the street outside the window.

"You won't see him," said Crosby, stopping beside Lawrence. "They become invisible. It's rather frightening."

"Why did you take me to that bar?" asked Lawrence. A bar girl stood outside, looking at Lawrence in the window. She smiled and gestured for him to come out. She blew him a kiss and stuck out her tongue. She opened her nylon robe and flashed him. But his expression didn't change; because he was lost, looking at a distant spot somewhere above and beyond where she stood jumping up and down and clapping.

Given the nightly scams, fights, and other disturbance inside the rim defining Patpong, the incident with the photographer hardly ranked as even minor league. Crowds of hungry young Thai men roamed in wolf packs, aggressively pushing for a confrontation with lone tourists; raking the customers with machine-gun bursts of fighting words and provocative glances. They dived like falcons at their prey. The *farangs* appeared so white, slow, bovine, confused as the Thai touts and vendors encircled them, going in for the kill. The pure chaos of Patpong spun a mixture of fear, grudges, and nocturnal violence. Outlaws, whores, and merchants were competing for the attention of the crowd, selling to market their products and services. Somewhere during the long night, private enterprise found the pathways beyond the ordinary boundaries of disgrace and shame. There was no such thing as moral excess so long as profits flowed.

Crosby in his unconventional fashion blended on The Strip in a way Lawrence had only begun to see; and so did Snow, and he suspected, Tuttle surpassed them both. He glanced over at Crosby.

"I suspect you're wondering why are the *farangs* the skullers?" Crosby asked, reaching for a cigarette. "Why not the Thais?"

"What's the answer?" asked Lawrence.

From across the bookstore, Snow groaned loudly. "Man, listen to this. Fifty reasons why American men are disgusting in bed. Another ball-breaking feature article." He had shouted across the room. Several heads jerked up from a book or magazine and a number of eyes stared at Snow, who gave no indication of caring that a number of *farangs* glared with disapproval. He repeated the title, this time in Thai. This brought a series of giggles, whispers, and grins from the shop girls. Two of whom knew Snow by name and shouted back, again in Thai, that the article must have been written about him.

Lawrence turned to Crosby, who had lost his train of thought; he had that far-off one million miles into the outer universe look. "Why are only the *farangs* in the skull bars?"

"You are interested," said Crosby with emphasis, his attention snapping back to the moment. "Opinions differ. Over the years I formed my own theory."

Crosby paused, waiting for Lawrence to request an excursion into this zone; into a region where outrage was practiced. Lawrence decided to play along. "Let's hear your theory, Crosby." Crosby carried a racing form and circled the name of a horse that had corresponded to a chance remark overheard on the telephone.

"All the skuller wants is the skull as a receptacle.

"I asked an old skuller once. He said, 'I'm going to hell any fucking way. So what's the big deal? The girls get into it. They get paid.'"

"Not much of a theory," said Lawrence, opening a book called *Thai Style* and flipping through the pages of traditional teak houses in the north.

"It's not the theory. But his answer aims one in the right direction," Crosby continued, lighting his cigarette." In the West people believe the soul survives death. There is a God who either pushes the up or down button in the elevator containing your soul. You go up or down. Once the doors close, you are sealed inside. You got a one-way ride. There is no second chance. You go out of the gate once; the race ends. Bets are turned in; winners and losers get their rewards and punishments. So any punter who knows his horse has already lost packs up and leaves. If you believe you've already lost in the next world, and there isn't ever going to be another race, then nothing can ever scare or intimidate you in this life; no shame, no bad, no horror can touch you. And you're reborn in this life as a skuller.

"Not the *kohn Thai*—a person of Thailand. In Buddhism, you will have a rebirth to this world. You keep coming back, life after life. So a Buddhist has an entirely different perspective of cosmic payback. It's not a one shot judgement and you either go to heaven or to hell. We have all been here before. Now we are back. In this life there are the top acts with the minor billings, the small-time acts, the back alley shows, the stuff you can only see under a powerful microscope. When you die, you find a rebirth slot, and it is showtime all over again. Top billing is birth as an upper-class Thai male. From there, it is a rapid fall down the mountain slope. At the base of the mountain are the women. No one wants to come back a woman in Thailand; not even the women want rebirth as a woman.

"It's a question of merit—and you get merit by becoming a monk for two weeks, feeding the monks for a few years, setting turtles or birds free. Gain merit and the next life is better than the current one. But you do something really bad, like deface a statue of Buddha, you've bought yourself five hundred consecutive lives as a woman. If you major league fucked up in this life, then you come out of the starting gates for the next fifty races on a skull-bar turf. Sucking off an old fat *farang's* dick, that scares the Thais. You rarely see a Thai male in a skull bar. They don't want to witness how far the descent is from one life to the next."

TUTTLE occupied his usual corner booth at HQ. It was a heavy traffic night, new faces and old circling the jukebox; waiters pushing through with plates of noodles, rice, hamburgers, and drinks. He saw in the booth mirror Lawrence trailing half a step behind Snow and Crosby as they emerged from the back entrance. Over the years he had become an expert using the mirrors to explore the interiors of the booths, the narrow walk lanes between the booths and tables, and those off-guard moments when a girl, thinking she was alone and unobserved, displayed her true face.

"Sorry about running out earlier," said Tuttle as Lawrence slid across the seat.

Lawrence shrugged off the apology. It had seemed like light-years since he had first laid eyes on Fawn and listened to her boss Riche talk about toilet paper in the wastepaper basket. "We made a minor detour through a skull bar," said Lawrence.

"You're picking up the language fast," replied Tuttle, looking over at Crosby who sat smoking a cigarette and vacantly staring out at the floor and then at Snow, who flipped through a copy of *Vogue* magazine.

"Unfamiliar territory. The whole experience was weird. Public orgasm. Several girls hitting on me. And a guy starts taking pictures of me."

Tuttle smiled, he knew the interior map of the skull bars. "How much did he want?"

"Who?" asked Lawrence.

"The photographer."

Lawrence's forehead wrinkled with worry lines. "He took off. He didn't ask for money."

Crosby shook his head. "It's a bad lot on 'The Strip' these days. Crazies on pills, sniffing paint thinner. You can't predict what they will do. It's all a gamble."

Tuttle caught sight of the former bar girl who had come back alone on holiday from her husband and kids in Rhode Island. An old, familiar face. She and her American husband worked in a cannery. She had increased her knowledge of English substantially from the old days, Tuttle remembered. She knows all about the future, and she has arrived looking like her old self; she is dressed to kill, scouting the prospects among the *farangs*, looking to make a score, flashing a flamboyant smile, enjoying the moment, but most of all, like Crosby and Snow, thought Tuttle, she thinks that she is smart enough to have discovered a foolproof formula, one so tightly organized that no mark could ever escape.

Tuttle had talked to the girls at three-thirty in the morning. He had listened to their point of view on the HQ world; one not that different from Snow or Crosby. The girls had a love hate relationship with HQ as Snow and Crosby had with the school. He had known both men for nearly ten years; he knew how they thought. A freelance working girl, like working as a freelance English teacher, wasn't anyone's dream career. They had fallen into it along the way to someplace else, and stayed with it so long they had forgotten where originally they had been headed.

They had wanted, just like the girls, for someone to love them. Take care of them. Someone who has a horizon longer than one night or one lecture. And together formed an alliance, keeping a common vigil at HQ, waiting for that one person, who will walk into their lives and rescue them from themselves. He had been just as guilty as Snow and Crosby, thought Tuttle. Hadn't he looked at Lawrence in exactly the same light? Lawrence Baring, the golden opportunity offered on a plate; the last person a couple of months earlier who would have sprung to mind as someone to save the school.

You heard the same arguments from Snow, Crosby, and the girls. They lacked choice; they lost the ability to hold a regular job. And even if they could, well, there were expenses. Horse races and women for Crosby. Drugs and women for Snow. The girls had a menu of expenses longer than a Chinese restaurant's. The father who was dead or sick. The brother who was in school and had no money for fees due the following morning. The son or daughter who needed an operation tomorrow or would die. The rent that was two months behind. The friend who had borrowed five thousand baht and disappeared. The boyfriend who had stolen her jewelry to pay a gambling debt. The husband who had beaten her. The husband who had been killed in an accident.

And what was on Tuttle's personal menu? He reflected for a moment, looking across the room. A daughter who had a chance to become respectable, he thought. A daughter to whom he had made himself accountable. A daughter who had given him a gift he could never repay. A school that tried to be that father to other girls like Asanee, girls whose own father would never find them, girls who needed to know they were not alone, that they had a chance.

The girls told Tuttle about smiling on the outside and crying, breaking up on the inside. He looked across the room and watched a pretty girl sitting next to an overweight *farang*, whose thick brown moustache was wet with beer foam, wore a shirt stretched like a sheet of canvas over his bloated gut, and dirty, wrinkled shorts and shabby sandals. His right hand worked down the girl's blouse, squeezing her nipples; he laughed and talked to his friends. He was not looking at her. Tuttle watched her face. The expression was neither pleasure nor even boredom, but sorrow cracking like a whip across the span of her mind. Inside something was breaking apart. Her eyes turned liquid but she's trained herself not to spill the tears: never to permit the *farang* to see them run down her cheek. She sat biting her lip, and trying to smile. Because he might have the magical purple for her later. She couldn't take a chance someone else would come along later that same night and offer to take her. Tuttle had seen her go home alone many nights; too many nights of going home alone had a way of stealing away the last fragment of self-esteem. A chance, any chance was better than walking out of HQ in front of all her friends alone. She buried her face in her hands. He didn't have to say he loved her. He didn't have to say anything.

The school had seemed dead. Snow and Crosby had made a deal with the photographer; the entire skull bar incident had the fingerprints of their planning; they had set up Lawrence in Patpong because they were afraid. Just like the girls, afraid of walking out alone, without a prospect. As Tuttle looked back at Lawrence, who was sipping his beer, looking cheerful, happy, settled, even relaxed, he said to himself—Lawrence had walked into HQ like any other mark. He came on his own, looking for something, and hadn't Tuttle and Asanee supplied whatever that thing was?

He thought suddenly of Sarah, and that morning he had waited at the bus station, looking at his watch, not knowing whether to pull his bags off and go after her, or climb on the bus. She had done what he had believed in his heart of hearts she had been incapable of doing—betraying him; she had set him up, never intending to meet him at the bus station. She had been seeing Lawrence behind his back two, three months before. He had found out; but he didn't confront her. He asked her to go away with him. Her decision would be the only answer that mattered—and the answer came in that quiet last moment at the bus depot, when he stood on the first step of the bus, and looked out one last time at a sea of strange faces.

One betrayal followed another, thought Tuttle. It spread a disease. Snow and Crosby had struck fast. The question Tuttle had was what he could do about Lawrence—what he was able to do, prepared to do, and, above all, with Asanee's eyes on her father as the one man who had committed himself to her, what was the right thing.

SNOW had returned to the booth after smoking an entire joint. He came in waving the *Vogue* magazine he bought in Patpong, and a small group of girls fell in step, following him through the crowd.

"It's time for extreme measures. Entire peu-un pods are dozing in the corner booth," said Snow. He pointed around the room with a crooked finger. "And over there! At that table! A sleeping Tommy. It's not fucking professional. Some wando can slip up and rob them blind. Sleeping on the job. It's bad for business. So I've come equipped tonight."

He opened the *Vogue* on the table. He glanced up at Crosby and giggled. "This is better than drugs, man. The one item that gives them a real buzz. Has them jumping up and down, laughing, sitting on my knee, eyes bright. Never fails as a wake-up call." Girls swarmed around the booth, sliding onto everyone's lap. Snow had a girl bouncing on each knee. Crosby had another two ignoring them, as they stretched forward to look at the magazine. Three more climbed over Tuttle and Lawrence; and half a dozen others stood at the front of the table inside the booth.

Snow casually flipped the pages, their eyes grew large and bright and intense; a dozen small fingers touched the photographs, sliding down the images of high-fashion dresses, furs, shoes, bags, and jewelry. Snow had transported them to another world.

"No, you can't take the magazine, sweetheart," said Snow. "You sit here on Uncle Snow's lap like a good girl. And your friends over there on Uncle Tuttle, and Uncle Crosby and . . . Uncle Lawrence is going to give you a quiz, so study hard."

Lawrence registered an expression somewhere between disgust and amusement. "This is as deep as the girls ever get," said Crosby. "Selling their sweet ass for a lovely mink stole. Just the garment you need in Bangkok."

"*Soo-ay*, yes, beautiful," said Snow, shifting the weight of one of the girls. "Everything in Vogue is *soo-ay.*"

The girls had reverted to a two-word Thai vocabulary.

"*Soo-ay*-beautiful. And *chawp*!-like."

Snow had opened the book of dreams; of happiness; of what they should desire so much that they would be willing to sell themselves to acquire those objects. They worked to buy, and Snow arrived, like a Lahu Godman, with his bag filled with illusions.

"Open that beautiful Rolex foldout this way," said Snow helping the girls to peel back the flaps. "Now we're awake, aren't we, sweetheart? Uncle Snow's got you day-dreaming in color. Or is it night dreaming? Or does it matter, the dream is the same day and night. Now you're into it, turn the page. What do we have here? A cocktail dress for that special gathering at Trump Tower. *Soo-ay.* *Chawp*! Forget about these guys. Uncle Snow is your dream maker. I understand what you ache for, daydream about, gossip about, worry over. What's in your head when Gunter slips it between your legs? A world of beautiful things to cover your sweet little ass. The *farang* model? *Soo-ay.* You love that white skin. Those blue eyes and blonde hair. You'd give the Klu Klux Klan a run for their money. *Soo-ay.* You would change lives with the model in the picture if you could. Now there is a dream to ride out the night. You want to live inside the parlor of her country house, ride her horses, sit in her chair. Uncle Tuttle talks about rebirth, man. But this is what you want to come back as. *Soo-ay.* As a rich bitch in a Greenwich house. We're not talking real deep, Larry. But then, look at their role models in these pictures. They haven't been given the tap for what's in their minds.

"So what flashes through their sleepy brains when they see us at HQ? A ticket to ride, man. And you saw it with your own eyes. I pulled out the dream book, and their brains kicked into overdrive, thinking, here, at last, is a *farang* who understands what is important in life. What's fucking soo-ay. If you can't point to the soo-ay in life, then what fucking good are you? You offer your sweet little body—or if you're feeling real good a body from your *peu-un pod*—so you can get your share of what's on these pages. You sweet baby, you really don't want Uncle Snow to fuck you. But he has that five-hundred baht note somewhere on his person. And that purple's gonna get you closer to what's on that page. You can get your little piece of that soo-ay.

"You're not saving your purples for season tickets to the Met or a leather-bound edition of William Shakespeare. Man, that's not *soo-ay* is it, darling? If you can't wear it, smell it, taste it or feel it or eat it, you've wasted your purple. Right, sweetheart? That one on the page. Pearls. *Soo-ay.* That strand will set you on your backside for about 250,000 baht. Yes, Uncle Snow knows that is a very big number.

"Let's break it down in terms of the HQ formula. The pearl necklace is five-hundred purples. Five hundred nights getting your ticket punched at HQ. Hordes of horny Gunters crammed in a couple of 747s. Loads of Huns singing beer hall songs. As Uncle Tuttle says, when you've got that long horizon filled with thousands of lifetimes ahead, what's five hundred screws? And that car is called a Rolls Royce. *Soo-ay.* You will have to fuck yourself into the next lifetime, darling, to get enough purples. You better scale down. Here's two baht for the jukebox. Play something nice like '*Women in Love.*' I like sincere music this time of morning. A *soo-ay* little tune. Crosby raised his glass; Snow followed his lead, reaching through the tangle of arms and hands around him. They clinked glasses, saluting each other, before turning to Lawrence.

"To the school," said Crosby.

"And pay-day," murmured Snow.

"And a back pay-day."

Snow laughed. "The cheque is in the mail. Maybe."

Tuttle, at last, felt he had found the answer to Lawrence Baring, Esquire. He touched Snow's glass, then Crosby's with his green bottle of Kloster beer. "To the school," he said.

15

Three days later, Khun Kob invited Tuttle to join him as his guest for dinner. He expressed his desire for a private meeting between two colleagues and friends, who had the best interests of the school at heart. And Khun Kob reminded him that in one month any person running as a Member of Parliament had to place a deposit, showing their goodwill and bona fide intentions.

Khun Kob selected a small, back soi Thai restaurant, where he knew the owner and had slept with one of the waitresses. The location provided him with a home base feeling, and the owner, owl-eyed behind gold-rimmed glasses, and waitresses with broad cheekbones and round faces from *Si Sa Ket*—a town in *Isan*—calling him *ajahn*—teacher in the hushed tones filled with respect. Tuttle relaxed; he anticipated that once dinner had finished, Khun Kob would announce his resignation as headmaster and his decision to run for public office. Three years earlier Khun Kob had used the same restaurant to announce his candidacy for public office; he had twenty supporters present, made a speech, and shook everyone's hand twice.

As the last plate was taken away, Khun Kob removed his sunglasses, wiped the lens with the edge of the tablecloth. He squinted at Tuttle and smiled, masking a nervous half laugh. Tuttle sensed Khun Kob was about to take the final lap of the evening.

"I have made a decision about becoming a politician," Khun Kob said, laying his sunglasses on the table. He folded his hands, rotated his head from one shoulder to the other. Putting his thin neck in the noose again, thought Tuttle, returning Khun Kob's smile. "I have decided to form my own party."

"Good idea," said Tuttle. "We will miss you at the school. "

Khun Kob' s nervous laugh whipped around the room. He shook his head in a solemn manner, and slowly put his sunglasses on. "I couldn't leave the school without a headmaster. That would be bad for my image as a politician."

"Then you will stay on?" asked Tuttle, deciding he needed another drink. He gestured at a waitress hovering nearby and ordered a double whisky on ice.

"With, of course, a salary adjustment. A headmaster in Thailand is paid two hundred percent more than a regular teacher. This is true," said Khun Kob, as Tuttle's drink arrived.

Tuttle took a long sip, not taking his eyes off Khun Kob, who lapsed into silence. Lawrence's money was becoming a tropical sickness. First Fawn, then Snow and Crosby, and now Khun Kob were planning a new future fuelled by feverish speculations. Playing "what if" scenarios in bed, the classroom, the shower, on the toilet. In Khun Kob's mind, thought Tuttle, he would have sufficient funds to buy a seat in the next election.

"Khun Lawrence made a mistake. Fawn's cheque was a joke. Think of it as a *farang* joking with a bar-girl."

"Lawyer's don't make mistakes or jokes," said Khun Kob, tapping the tips of his fingers together and smiling behind his sunglasses. He glanced at his watch and then over at the door.

Tuttle wasn't going to deprive Khun Kob of his share; of his dream, and let the *farang* laugh at him behind his back. The owner brought over the bill, and Khun Kob held it out to the light, reading the column of figures with his sunglasses on. He removed a five-hundred-baht note from his wallet and laid it on the silver tray. Once again, his head moved toward the entrance, as if he were waiting for someone. Slowly, clearing his throat, he removed his sunglasses again and stared straight at Tuttle.

"You stay in Thailand a long time," he said. "The bad thing happen to the *farang* who cheat a Thai. But I don't think we talk about that. Your friend has a very good heart. He will help the school very much. We will have better conditions. Better teachers and books.

Our students have better performance in English. That is good. A headmaster is like a commander. He must guide well. The one who guides must have the good reward. I think you understand me."

Not more than a moment after Khun Kob had finished, he rose in his chair and gestured to a Thai-Chinese, dressed in a business suit, who stood inside the entrance, looking across the restaurant. "This is my close friend, Colonel Chao," said Khun Kob. "And I have very good news. He has consented to become our partner."

The Colonel nodded. He was in his mid-fifties, nearly bald with bushy, black eyebrows and a round, hard mouth. An orchid was pinned to the lapel of his jacket; the fastened middle button gave him a formal board of director's meeting called to order appearance. The orchid adding the look of a shareholder's campaign in progress. He had stepped away from a wedding celebration at the Dusit Thani on Rama IV. A tribute to his status as an influential person who headed an important police district. The Colonel had been the guest of honor; he had a reputation for his social connections and political aspirations. His beat included some prize concessions: brothels, massage parlors, and a string of bars.

On his smooth, hairless left wrist, the crescent of a gold Rolex watch emerged like the face of a half-moon from a double-stitched silk cuff. Tuttle threw back the last of his double whiskey, stood and shook the officer's hand. He noticed, as Colonel Chao held out his name card, that his hands, square-knuckled fingers, manicured nails, and smooth, long palm appeared tailor-made for gripping a high-power sniper's rifle.

Tuttle took the card with engraved letters in both English and Thai, glanced at it with the minimum amount of decorum he judged was sufficient to leave the Colonel with his face undamaged, his own expression not changing, and put it down on the table.

"And to what do I owe this honor, Colonel Chao?"

Khun Kob sucked in his chest, as he rocked back on his heels, beaming with pride. The calm, neutral expression on Tuttle's face amused Colonel Chao, who could see that the *farang* had taught himself how not to give away his emotions. "Perhaps the *ajahn* has neglected to explain our project?"

Tuttle looked at Khun Kob, who refused to meet his glance. "Our project? No, I can't say I've heard," said Tuttle.

The Colonel shot Khun Kob a chilling glance; the kind a cat uses to freeze a mouse in its tracks. Khun Kob smiled as if the larger, more visible grin on his lips, the greater his capacity to rise above the immediate problem.

The Colonel shook his head, shrugged his shoulders at Tuttle, as if to say, the trouble with schoolmasters is they smile when they suffer, and whipped a gold-plated ball-point pen and papers from his dinner jacket. He put on a pair of gold wire-framed glasses with half-moon lenses. "This is our project, Khun Robert," said Colonel Chao. "Come, now, sit. Relax. Order another drink. We will look at the documents together. Partners must understand the technical aspects of their business. Don't you agree?"

In the sticky air of the restaurant, the owner saw that Khun Kob's table had moved up the social ladder quickly. He brought a bottle of champagne and glasses. "Compliments of the house," he said, bowing to the Colonel. This one of the perks of having the "power."

A member of Colonel Chao's district office staff, who was related by marriage to the manager of the business service bureau at Lawrence's hotel had commented on a twenty-five page fax from Los Angeles. It had cost the hotel guest over a thousand baht just to receive the fax! The manager, a university graduate, possessed a normal curiosity; he read the fax, and made a copy, for security reasons, of course. The fax might be lost and the hotel would be greatly embarrassed if the guest could not be given a duplicate.

Not long after the fax had been received, a copy of contents had been delivered to Colonel Chao's office. Several officers were immediately assigned to study, evaluate, and report upon the document. The name of Tuttle English School appeared a number of times in the document. Upon examination, the Colonel's staff informed him that three trustees were to be appointed with the advice and consent of Robert Tuttle.

Colonel Chao spread his copy of the document out in front of Tuttle. Appropriate passages had been underlined in red ink. On the second page a sum of money was in boldface type: ONE MILLION US DOLLARS. A red ink box had been drawn around those words. Tuttle sighed, flipped to the end of the document, and turned it over, face down on the table. This time, no one had to tell Tuttle to watch his back. He looked at the Colonel who leaned forward, extending his hand.

"Whenever you need funds, just phone me," the colonel said smiling for the first time. He spotted his namecard on the table, reached over with a pen, and wrote on the front. He looked up. "My personal home phone number. A sign of my good faith. If you should need to reach me about anything."

"We are honored to have Colonel Chao administer the funds," said Khun Kob. "Property and assets must be in the right hands, or otherwise we may have some danger. And I can personally speak of my support for his willingness to be of assistance."

Colonel Chao glanced at Tuttle's untouched glass of champagne. "You don't drink champagne?"

"I never developed an appetite," said Tuttle.

Colonel Chao raised his glass, holding it out towards Tuttle. "Here's a toast, then, to a change of appetites?"

The Colonel waited until Tuttle raised his glass before drinking. Tuttle left his glass suspended motionless in midair until Colonel Chao pulled back his chair.

"We must find me to play a round of golf," said the Colonel.

"Your club or mine?"

The Colonel stared for a moment without blinking, as if taking in the total of Robert Tuttle. "You have quite a sense of humor, Khun Tuttle. Sometimes that make a problem."

The Colonel did not wait for a reply and vanished as quickly as he had arrived. Tuttle dropped the glass on the floor. The owner and waitresses scurried around with towels, broom, mops, barking at one another as if they had been responsible. Khun Kob chased Tuttle out into the street. "You forgot this," he said.

Tuttle looked down at Colonel Chao's name card, shoved it in his shirt pocket, and wondered what had ever possessed him to give Khun Kob the courtesy title of headmaster. He cut down the sub-soi. A scrappy dog with swollen teats barked in a hoarse, tentative fashion, then turned and ran through an opening in a fence as Tuttle walked past. Large bamboo trees arching overheard rustled in a light wind, rustling the leaves above the narrow paved soi. In the far distance, the roar of jet engines penetrated the night. Children's voices, cranky and tired, travelled from a fenced compound. Someone clapped hands and shouted in Thai. The dull, worn, aching cry of a baby echoed from an open window. The smell of rice soup drifted from a kitchen. A hundred fibers of sounds and smells knitted a blanket thrown over the night; and any one strand alone was sufficient to exhaust the capacity for human compassion.

But as hard as Tuttle tried to blot out Khun Kob and Colonel Chao, Lawrence's million-dollar document, with the distractions of the night, his mind couldn't shake free of the number of hands reaching for the pie. How could he blame them, he thought. Hadn't he been the first to think of Lawrence as a potential asset for the school? Someone who might turn around his fortunes with a pledge of funds? He was all but certain that Lawrence would use money to bring Fawn around to accepting a teaching position at the school. Did he actually think that he could contain the information? Perhaps not, but what he hadn't done was identify the complex framework of new wage demands, political intrigue, and an alliance with a Thai police colonel, who had pulled away in a new baby-blue Mercedes, leaving Khun Kob on the pavement bowing from the waist.

SNOW'S hands made loops in the air, slicing through the smoke from Crosby's cigarettes. It looked as if he were trying to rope the smoke; pull it to the floor; tame it and make it harmless. Lawrence, sitting opposite in a shirt open at the throat and market-stall trousers, was laughing as Tuttle came to the table carrying a large bottle of Kloster.

"So Kob's out," said Snow in a voice that could have been either a question or declaration.

"Kob's in," said Tuttle, sinking into the booth.

"Giving up his politics?" asked Crosby.

"He sees no problem in doing both," said Tuttle, putting the beer bottle to his lips. Old Bill emerged smiling from a group of girls; he slowed down, reaching the table, and waited until Tuttle pulled the bottle away from his lips and set it on the table.

"That Lotus in the parking lot," said Old Bill, standing perfectly erect, his white hair slicked back. "I ask myself, who are these people? Where do they get this kind of money in Thailand. I look around the room, but I never see them. Where are they, Robert? It's a mystery."

"Business dealings, Bill," said Tuttle, using his thumbnail to tear at the edge of the label on the green bottle of Kloster. "Cement?"

"The same stuff used to construct your lighthouse in Cornwall."

"I can't figure it." And Old Bill turned, taking his fountain pen from his safari shirt pocket, unscrewing the cap, and admiring the nib, walked away, muttering softly to himself like a child who no longer expected a meaningful answer from an adult.

"It doesn't surprise me about old Kob. I figured him for someone you couldn't trust," said Crosby, blowing out a cloud of smoke.

"Everyone gets used, man," said Snow. "The girls think they are the only ones who get used. Yesterday, I woke up at nine, there is Lek perched on the end of the bed in the floor squat position stark naked. She's eating a banana and staring at me. She's waiting for me to unlock the bank vault. Draw her purple and flee the scene. The banana peel covered her little fist and she chewed away. Lek didn't blink. Her tiny cheeks were bloated with contraband banana. And what was going through her head at that moment?"

Lawrence helped himself to one of Crosby's cigarettes. "Well, what was going through her mind?" he asked Snow.

Crosby cut off Snow with a quick reply. "I can tell you what's in her head. 'This is my life,' she's thinking. 'This is what I do for a living. What I do serves no purpose. I serve no purpose. So I squat and eat and stare.' Not wholly different, I suspect, than what goes through Khun Kob's mind."

"Wrong, man, his mind's more complex. 'I squat and eat and stare and plan to run for public office,'" said Snow, pursing his thin lips and nodding his head back and forth like a nodding toy dog in the rear window of a teenager's car.

"You sound a little bitter, Snow," said Lawrence.

"Me bitter?" asked Snow, snapping his head back, and fanning away at Crosby's smoke. "Tuttle, remember when the Pope came through Bangkok in '82. The Bureau in Hong Kong asked me to cover his stay. I'm thinking here's my chance to score a by-line. You remember those stories I wrote, Tut. I showed them to you. Some of my best writing ever. I had an entire series of great articles about the Pope, man. Lots of local color, impressions of the Thais, the role of the Catholic community. Every night I phoned the Bureau Chief, in Hong Kong. Susan, I'd say, you're gonna love what I've got for you. And I'd start reading the copy out over the phone. Slowly so she could take it down. A paragraph into the story, I could tell from the tone in her voice that she was bored out of her fucking mind. Susan wasn't writing down a goddamn word.

"I'm a chump, I just keep reading out the stories. I phoned in every day. 'Good job, Snow.' Man, that's all the fuck she said four days in a row. And I say to her, 'Susan, you're not telling me something. You're holding back on something I ought to know. Can't you give me a hint?' And there would be this long, fucking silence. 'You're doing a good job. Snow, you are giving us exactly what we want,' she finally said.

"Two years later in Singapore, I ran into Susan. We both got drunk. Susan tells me the truth. I had been a local hire for the wire in the event the Pope was shot. They hired me for the deathwatch patrol. And decided not to tell me. They thought I might be demoralized. The job was one rung below local scum. No one in their right mind would touch the job. Absent a direct hit on the Pope, they didn't want to hear from me. Or take my calls. All that brilliant background color in my stories. Stories they knew from day one they'd never use. I was in Bangkok to cover their ass. If someone killed the Pope, and they didn't have some local scum covering the hit on the scene—well, it was their ass on the line.

"You know what she said at three in the morning? She's naked next to me in bed. She's about to pass out. We had gone through a bottle of gin. But she has to tell me something. Man, she's deep into private confessions. She says, 'Snow, in Hong Kong, we thought of you as our foreign guide. Our man on the scene. I couldn't tell you, though. You had too much fucking pride. You would've told us to kiss our ass. We needed a foreign guide on the scene.'

"I roll over on my side and raise up on my elbow, and I say, 'Susan, lay off the girls for calling themselves foreign guides. You can call me a whore. '

"And. . . ? She's puking out her guts. I pulled a banana out of the fruit bowl and sat in bed beside her eating it. I was thinking. 'This is my life. It serves no useful purpose.'"

Snow's face sagged; he seemed embarrassed with what to do with his hands. He clowned with a girl in a yellow T-shirt—her name embroidered in Thai at the back of the neck by a worried mother; she leaned forward, talking to a friend, her hips arched against the table edge. She had been disappointed he arrived without the *Vogue* magazine. Snow poked her hip with his forefinger. "Now that serves a useful purpose," he said.

Lawrence recognized an aspect of himself in Snow's sorrow. He understood the full force of that remote private vision that had struck hard, without warning, a force that knocked Snow down from behind. His imagined his own face must have had the same startled expression, one that never quite emptied from the face of the person whose legs had been cut out with a few sharp words, lines jotted on a piece of paper. It was his own face that he saw; the face he noticed one morning shaving, the morning after he had found Sarah's diaries inside her university office filing cabinet.

"SARAH collected your short stories," said Lawrence. His tone was serious, confiding, as if the information had been classified.

A long silence followed. Lawrence waited for Tuttle to say something. But he was lost in his preoccupations with Colonel Chao and Khun Kob.

"Why did you stop?" asked Lawrence, drumming his fingers to the music from the jukebox. A middle-aged woman with heavy makeup, chewing gum, caught Lawrence's eye, smiled, snapping her fingers to the music. He quickly looked away. "You stopped writing. Why Bobby?"

Tuttle looked over at him. "I had an epiphany in a massage parlor."

Across the booth, Snow was babbling. "Drugstore touts will hit the strip next. Grab your arm and show you a card with fifty kinds of pills. Pills to make you fly. Pills to make you high. Pills to trim your sails. Pills to make you hard. Pills to make you laugh. I can hear them calling out these slogans at five in the morning outside of Foodland."

"In a massage parlor?" repeated Lawrence, with a forced laugh. The forces of logic suggested this couldn't be true. He tried to imagine a young Thai woman kneading Tuttle's muscular shoulders; Tuttle's serene face sheathed in the warm light slanting from a small lamp.

"I was in the room with the girl. I can't remember her name or badge number," Tuttle said, watching Snow come apart at the seams. His Hawaiian shirt was open at the neck, and a ridge of sweat pooled and dripped from the hollow of his throat; Snow had smoked too much in the alley, something he always did when he was trying to put something out of his mind.

"She had a trolley cart beside the bed," Tuttle resumed, worrying about Snow. "Q-tips, hot towels, cold towels, nail clippers, and scissors all laid out like an operating room procedure was about to take place.

"She kept a box of condoms in a small hilltribe silver box. The box had been cast from melted-down nineteenth century French franc coins. There were dragons and trees and people and mountains on the sides and top. She undressed, hung up her white uniform on a door hook, and began peeling back the white foil, exposing the pink condom. She put the lid back on the box. She had me wrapped with that expert, one flick of the wrist motion; she was smooth. For her, it was like sticking the key in the ignition and switching on the engine. After we finished, she climbed off—no, it wasn't a climb, it was like the show-pleasing flip of a gymnast dismounting the parallel bars. Sweat clung bubbling, smeared from her neck to her pubic hairs. She floated over to her trolley, towelling herself. Underneath the trolley was a magazine rack. She leaned over, still naked, pulled off the first magazine, opened it, tore out a page, and leaned over the bed.

"The formula is, she does the wrap but once it's been used, she won't touch it. Once the rubber has been contaminated so the duty is on the guy to dispose of it quickly. Put it out of sight. *Farang* fill container, *farang* empty container. She tells me in Thai to take it off and shoves the magazine page in my face. She doesn't want to know what's happening below my chin.

"I reached down and slipped off the rubber. I examine the pinkish nose cone of this thing. It looks like a parachute that didn't open. I shift over onto my right side, and she spreads a fresh towel around my neck. She has the glossy magazine page two inches from my face. She has this bored, distracted look of a checkout counter girl when you spend too much time finding your money. I glance at the page. I did a doubletake. She is holding the first page of '*The Boy Who Loved Marilyn Monroe*'—one of my short stories. There is my name in fourteen-point type. Story by Robert Tuttle. I recognized the artwork; the photo insert of Monroe with the drawing of a *farang* kid suspended midair between the diving board into a swimming pool. She's waiting for me to get on with it.

"But I am looking at the story which she's holding like Christmas wrapping paper, wanting me to deliver the gift, the used rubber. I start to laugh. She ripped the Durex II out of my hand and made a classy one handed dunk shot smack into the center of the page hitting the tip of the diving board and Marilyn Monroe's chin. Then she stepped back from the bed; she had mistaken my laugh as aimed at her; the laugh had cost her a great deal of face, and she wadded up the page. She flexed the muscles in her jaw, grinding her teeth and making a dreadful face. She pulled back her arm and threw the balled-up page with the rubber wrapped inside straight at me; a great shot, straight through the hoop; she caught me square on my right eye. Then she turned, walked stark naked out of the room, carrying her dress, and slammed the door. She had felt betrayed, laughed at, put down, left to feel like a fool, however you want to phrase it.

"As far as I knew, no story of mine on the printed page had ever had such an impact. I lay alone in that small room, and carefully unwrapped the page; a wet stain had spread across my name and the story title. So much for craft, the petty actions of others, throwing people together on the page, inventing ways for them to scramble, to deceive, lie, overthrow one another. To what point or end or reason? What happened to '*The Boy Who Loved Marilyn Monroe*' at the end of the day? In the words of Snow, to what purpose had I devoted so much concentrated energy? If the writing had surpassed John Updike, or F. Scott Fitzgerald, so what? In the end, it was a whorehouse wrapper.

"I had knocked out the middleman; I had become my own ultimate consumer. And my consumption had absolutely nothing to do with the story; good, bad, sad, funny, entertaining, it didn't matter in the end. All that mattered was the paper; a disposable wrapper to package whorehouse debris. I had found myself at the end of the chain, where an honest, practical, basic use of fiction had been shoved in my face. What was the point of writing to be read? There were millions of pages that would do as a receptacle for a used Durex. Why not camp at that end of the chain? Rather than filling the page with words, drop a used condom from the height of about a foot; stare down at the pattern of your own sperm on the page. There was the clue that had eluded me. Form and substance had almost nothing to do with what I had written on the page.

"A couple hundred thousand of my sperm were swimming around in the condom and spilling over, reversing position, blocking, dying; exerting themselves for specific purpose—to become, no, to create the shape of a personal story for which anyone knew at a glance was totally futile; but that wouldn't stop them from struggling to sustain life for one more second smack in the middle of the *Marilyn Monroe* story. There was no level of the story—all about holding a magnifying glass to the word rescue—that could match the level of drama happening on that page. I had backed myself into a corner. I felt bad. I tried to write a couple more stories but everything I put down seemed like foreground, unimportant.

"I returned to the massage parlor, picked the same girl. She had remembered me, shooting one of those tired, worn shrugs as she carried a fresh set of towels and walked ahead of me. I had discovered a new game in which sex was no longer the ultimate goal. Get me to the magazine rack. I got her to rip out pages of books, and I stood on the bed, the used condom elevated over my head and let it drop. Hitting a bull's eye on some bad review, some bitching and moaning tirade written by a backroom goon squad of hacks bonded by their ignorance, their hatred for the truth, none of what I wrote mattered. I watched the newsprint bleed into an inky patch without any meaning, without any intelligence, and saw that before and after were really the same. That was eighteen months ago."

Crosby rolled his eyes and nudged his elbow into Snow's ribs. "Every time you tell that story, I get very depressed. I would much prefer to talk about horse racing or girls or shopping. While a bit of money remains in the old pocket, my thought is to buy a girl. Maybe I'll spring for a three, four-month contract."

"Like Dtoke," said Snow. Conversations concerning women brought him back to life. He had a better memory for their names than any other *hard-core* at HQ. His memory extended to the names of women that Crosby and Tuttle had slept with years before and forgotten. Dtoke's name registered a smile on Crosby's lips.

"Yes, that's it," Crosby said, the memory pleasing him. "Someone memorable."

"He bought Dtoke from a brothel," Tuttle said, seeing the bewildered expression on Lawrence's face.

"I bought her contract out of a knock-shop on my 21st," explained Crosby, crossing his legs, his shoulder sloped forward as if throwing off a sudden chill. "Daddy had given me quite a lot of money. I got the brothel owner down to ten thousand baht. A fair price, I thought. Of course, he made a profit. Since Dtoke didn't have that many miles on her, I paid a bit of a premium. I made her a present to myself. It was all perfectly legal. I bloody well owned her. Then a thought crossed my mind, I could make a grand gesture. Like a good Buddhist, I could let her fly away. Like opening a caged bird in front of *Wat Arun*—The Temple to the Dawn. That would gain me merit. Probably a great deal of merit.

"I had never really bought a girl for more than a night. That doesn't feel like ownership. It's just simply good whoring. You see, I owned all of Dtoke's time. The long haul. Her frequency was tuned in to my station only. I was only twenty-one, but even I saw it as the major turning point of my life. If I wanted to advance the next step in Bangkok, I had the normal intelligence to understand what I was expected to do next. What maturity meant world-wide was different here than any place else. You showed you were an adult by setting up a household. I rented an apartment, bought furniture, a car, and Dtoke." Crosby paused, like he had done in Patpong at the skull bar. He lit a cigarette. It gave Lawrence an edgy feeling as if another photographer would jump onto the table and snap pictures of him in a half-drunk stage.

Tuttle sensed Lawrence's discomfort; he also had known Crosby long enough to know he often employed this little piece of harmless manipulation to gauge the attention span of his audience. Unlike

Lawrence, he was in the mood to wait Crosby out, let him scratch his neck with his cupped hand and watch a blue cloud of smoke rise from his own nose.

"Come on, man. Tell them what happened to Dtoke," said Snow after a few moments of silence. "Lawrence here is simply dying to know if you sliced her up and deep-fat-fried her."

"Dtoke? She wasn't edible, I'm afraid. Two years after I bought her, I concluded my experiment had failed. I had been too clever by half. I thought I bought her, but in reality she ended up own-ing me. Not something I bloody well had counted on happening. I celebrated my twenty-third by buying her a beauty shop, and setting her free. I asked a monk if this might gain me merit. He decided probably not. He said, if anything she had gained merit. Since by taking the shop, she had set me free. A fancy piece of logic. The fact remained, she had what all the girls want, her own life. She still turns the occasional trick—even though she doesn't need the money. For a couple of years she was a minor wife to a bank manager. That fell through.

"But she's better off than if I'd left her sweating it out on her back in the knock-shop. She was turning six, seven tricks a day. She only was getting fifteen baht a trick from the owner. She was on a pay scale not all that different from our school. But times have changed; we have come into a period of good fortune."

"That's pretty much what Khun Kob said tonight," added Tuttle.

CROSBY and Tuttle exchanged glances. Their lives had been threaded together for years. Crosby had stuck by him. For the first time in years, he had a chance to reclaim the promise of his twenty-first birthday; when he was still on speaking and financial terms with his family. Was it so bad that Crosby wanted a decent salary for a change? thought Tuttle. Or Snow, who had left newspaper reporting, and came to the school when Tuttle had been desperate and could find no one willing to work for next to nothing. He owed them both a great deal. Even cutting in Colonel Chao and Khun Kob would leave enough to pay both of them, he thought. What had Lawrence Baring ever done to deserve the money? It was a windfall, an insurance break, because his wife had killed herself.

"You're living in the past," snapped Snow, puffing up his cheeks and blowing out the surface smoke. "You're in a time warp, Crosby. Getting off in knock-shops. All the girls lined up against the wall like slave girls. You walk up and down the line like landed gentry eyeing the breeding stock herd. You're living in a time before flush toilets and Handy-wipes. Horseshit-in-the-street times. And you're living so far back in time you get future shock every time you light a match."

Number 33, '*Shot in the Dark*,' played on the jukebox. Snow stood up from the booth, stuck his hands in his pockets, tapped his sandal buckle against the table leg. "Time to split," he said. "Anyone for going to The Strip?"

Crosby gave him a knowing nod that wasn't lost on Tuttle. They were going back for the photographs of Lawrence in the skull bar; Tuttle would have laid money on it.

"Never figured you guys for skullers," said Tuttle.

Snow's face flushed. Crosby looked at the floor, pretending to rub his eyes. "Skullers are slime, man," said Snow.

"You won't get any disagreement on that," said Tuttle, breaking the spell that Snow's guilt had created for a moment.

"One thing, Crosby. Before we hit Foodland, no sneaking off to eat dried cuttlefish. Like some Stone Age freak. There's a new regulation, man. No cuttlefish street vendor within a hundred yards of go-go bars, whorehouses, Foodlands, or massage parlors. No one wants the smell of cuttlefish and the smell of sex getting confused. Then you'd really be lost in the back streets of Bangkok.

"Crying out, with cuttlefish on your breath, 'Any slave ships arrive from the Northeast? Say you, my good man, have you seen where are they unloading the new breeding stock from *Roi Et*? Yes, you might say I'm an expert, of sorts. That I've been to more than my fair share of slave auctions'."

After they left, Tuttle saw Lawrence staring at him in an odd fashion. Those lawyer's eyes penetrating deep into his own mind might see the architecture of a master web built surrounded on all sides by an invading host of other spiders; and if Lawrence could peer into his heart, he would surely see beyond the thin protective shield straight into his fear of losing the school, his anxiety over Asanee, and his gloom over the prospect of every possibility slipping out of his hands. No one occasion, condition, or place could be hoarded as personal property like clothing or tools. Lawrence's arrival in Bangkok was the occasion, his wealth a condition, and the place—Tuttle had chosen that carefully—had been a reunion of the past.

"I figured out the expression from Sarah's letter," said Lawrence, reaching into his jacket, he pulled the letter out.

Tuttle, holding his breath, white knuckles circling his beer bottle, watched Lawrence carefully open the letter. A narrow channel of hope opened. Lawrence pushed the letter across the table. Tuttle looked down as Lawrence withdrew his fingers. He had so much wanted to know what had been inside; but, that was before Lawrence had walked back into his life, and there it was, unsolicited at his fingers tips. He opened the envelope, and, without looking up at Lawrence, immediately recognized Sarah's tight, perfect handwriting; the rows of words and sentences, tumbling off the page like objects hurled from the past.

"*Dtam Jai, koon*—follow your heart," said Lawrence.

The dim, smoky light played games with eyes and mouths; spinning flexible expressions that were neutral. Tuttle's face, with a grizzled, listless, down-turned mouth peered across the table. He felt his throat swell and knew he dare not try and speak. Deep inside an airship had taken flight and exploded; the bumping noise of his own heart pounded in his neck, telegraphing the image of the accident, the loss of life, the pure, tragic hopelessness of exploring the wreckage.

"It's not been an easy exercise," said Lawrence, his voice breaking. Tuttle folded the letter and handed it back. "When we were rooming, I looked up to you. I don't think I ever told you that before. I envied that you had the strength to care deeply about other people. Maybe I never quite believed it was real. And, I was jealous that you had Sarah. I pretended to be your friend, Bobby. Two months before you left, I was sleeping with Sarah. And I never had the guts to tell you that. I convinced her to cheat behind your back. Some friend. The worst part is I never really got over the shame.

"You know how many times I'd wake up in the middle of the night, and I would look at Sarah sleeping and I would feel this huge sadness. We never spoke about it. But it was always in the background. You know how the mind works, you justify things to yourself. I told myself she had a much better life with me. I played that game. She had everything any woman could dream of possessing. House, car, profession, recognition, and devoted husband. But it had never been enough. And I understand why now. If only you hadn't come back for Asanee that night. Then I could have been right. God, I wanted to be right about you. Why do you think I came half-way around the world? But you couldn't do it. No matter how much you hated my guts for taking Sarah, you didn't have the stomach to use Asanee. It would have worked. I can tell you right now, Bobby, it was a brilliant plan. And I could have been destroyed by her. Just like you thought. Just as you closed in, your streak of decency stopped you. Robbed you of what you had waited for all these years. I am no Robert Tuttle. I wouldn't have come back for her."

Tuttle slid across the bench, he tried to break away from the table, Lawrence, Sarah's letter, and his own past that had come crashing through the back entrance of HQ. Lawrence grabbed his wrist and pulled him back. He felt the firm, resolute strength in Tuttle's hand dwindling like someone fighting against being pulled over the side of the boat into a kind of uneasy trust and acceptance.

For more than twenty years, Tuttle had seen fights, shoving matches, threats inside the laboratory of human emotions that ran from one end of HQ to another. But he had never seen a *farang* cry once during that entire period of time. Not a single tear, as far as he had ever known, had fallen from the eye of a *farang* inside HQ. A half-dozen girls sandwiched around the booth in a circular band whispered and nodded at Lawrence. Was it a mistake, a hallucination, some abnormal condition of cigarette smoke and whiskey? Or was it a truly revolutionary idea for the girls: that a *farang* with human emotions would arrive in their midst with a message beyond the collective agreement? A *farang* who was looking for some kind of rescue, just like them? The hand-to-hand combat expressions and battle-ready eyes evaporated on the faces of the girls around the table. Tears balanced on the lower lid, then spilled from a girl trying to blink them away. Soon three or four girls sniffled, heads leaning against one another.

"Bobby, I'd like to ask if you'd forgive me."

Tuttle forced himself to look directly at Lawrence. "It was all a very long time ago, Larry."

"You didn't answer my question. Can you forgive me? I know I have made some mistakes here. The cheque to Fawn was stupid. I was trying to buy what can't be bought. The classic mistake of my life. And I was doing the same thing in Bangkok. I understand it's probably hard for you. But I'm asking for a pardon."

Lawrence let go of Tuttle's wrist and extended his hand. Several girls assembled half a step away, watching as Tuttle, his bottom teeth sunk deep into his upper lip, grasped Lawrence's hand.

"If you have time tomorrow, I have a document I want to go over with you," said Lawrence, his hand locked around Tuttle's. "It's for the school, Bobby. It's what Sarah wanted in the letter."

The red ink box filled with the boldfaced words: ONE MILLION U.S. DOLLARS was an image that appeared in Tuttle's mind. This was not wrapping paper for a used product of lust. This was the one chance for Asanee, and the sixty-four other girls like her; the orphans of misfortune. That piece of paper meant something to their lives.

"Tomorrow afternoon. Make it four."

After Tuttle had gone, three girls walked Lawrence out to the street. Two held his hand like schoolchildren. One offered to lend him money for a taxi—she assumed he was not only sad, but broke as well. They told him in Thai not to give up; Lawrence seemed to understand this wasn't a negotiation session. They ushered him into the back of a taxi, gave the driver Tuttle's address and paid his fare. All the while, one girl kept saying over and over in broken English, "No trouble, no trouble. Khun Tut good man, he help you."

He hadn't been invited to Tuttle's house once since his arrival in Bangkok. As the cab pulled away from Soi 11, made a sharp U-turn against heavy traffic onto Sukhumvit, he thought about going back to his hotel. The driver looked at him in the rearview mirror. Why not play it out, he thought. And as he leaned back in the seat, he remembered Tuttle's story. 'The Boy Who Loved Marilyn Monroe' had been open on Sarah's office desk the day he had entered; not one thing in her office had been touched or altered.

16

THE BOY WHO LOVED MARILYN MONROE

A SHORT STORY
by
Robert Tuttle

"Can I wear my new shirt on the plane? The one with deadly spiders? It's brilliant," said Andrew, aged eleven, as he climbed out of the swimming pool, took a couple of steps before flopping into a deck chair beside his mother who was reading the newspaper. From beneath a beach towel wrapped around his head, he belched.

"Andrew!"

"Sorry. Well, can I?"

"Better wear the blue shirt. Customs people dislike deadly spiders."

It was Andrew's last day in Bangkok before returning to boarding school in Boston. On this last Monday of August, Andrew packed, said good-bye to friends, bicycled on the back lanes called sois, and worried. He worried about being fat. He worried about bagging a corner bed at school next to his best friend. Jeremy, his father, appeared in shorts and sandals on the pool deck with two tall drinks and a Coke on a bamboo tray.

"Why do you swim wearing a T-shirt?" Andrew's father asked.

Andrew turned, walked two steps, and dived into the pool.

"Jeremy, you've hurt his feelings."

"His feelings?"

"Andrew feels fat. He wears the T-shirt because he doesn't want to draw attention to himself."

❖

THEY ate their last family dinner in an Italian restaurant on Soi 18 that had been depressingly empty. Andrew ordered a pasta with cheese and ham and a bowl of chocolate and strawberry ice-cream. Susan ate a salad and pasta; and Jeremy polished off a lobster. Andrew pushed aside his ice cream dish and looked around at the rows of unused tables with fresh linen tablecloths and the half-dozen waiters and waitresses hovering in the background.

"Why don't we stop in *Soi Cowboy?*" Andrew suggested. "We can go to the airport from there."

"Excellent idea," said Jeremy. He turned to his wife. "Our Way Bar, okay, love?"

"Why not," said Susan with a half-smile.

The old Our Way Bar had been a hole in the wall, one-shop bar. A nonsense go-go bar much like any one of thirty odd other dives that lined both sides of a small lane called *Soi Cowboy*. Most of the girls wore a standard bar uniform: G-strings and bikini tops. Many were peasant teenagers with dark skin, four years of education, and large families who lived in the dirt poor village found in the Northeast. These teenage girls rented their bodies to a *farang*—foreigner. The rental fee for the night was twenty dollars.

A week earlier Our Way Bar—which had expanded into the adjacent shophouse—had reopened; the architectural plastic surgeon's knife carved out the features that matched the glossy face of a Patpong styled bar.

Andrew slid across the upholstered bench to his mother's side; as Jeremy—a regular customer, a punter, as they are called—ordered Klosters; and Andrew got a Coke. Lek, one of the bar girls, was Jeremy's "special friend." In the traditional display of respect, Lek folded her hands, with the tips of her thumbs pressed together, slowly bowed, raising her hands in a wai to Jeremy and then to Susan. The two women locked eyes for a moment seeking a common channel, some shared frequency where a message could be sent or received.

Susan, who was thirty-seven, imagined Lek was about eighteen; maybe nineteen, with the sweet face of a girl buried beneath the painted mask of a harder, older, more experienced woman. Just as Susan felt a connection of sorts, Lek looked away as a tray of cold towels arrived. It was time to go to work.

She unwrapped a towel from the plastic bag and carefully wiped Jeremy's face, starting with his forehead and working down his cheeks to his neck. Another girl massaged his hand, gently cracking his knuckles. When Lek finished, Jeremy wrapped the cold towel underneath the collar of his shirt and stared forward at the dancers swinging and twisting among the jungle gym of silver poles on the elevated stage. Lek's girlfriends, who wore hot pink Our Way nylon robes like prize-fighters before going into the ring, encircled Andrew's end of the table. Their job was convincing customers to buy them Colas. Having spotted Andrew in his baggy shorts, dirty tennis shoes with laces that glowed in the dimly lit corner, and a T-shirt with deadly spiders, they became distracted from their normal duties.

A gang of three giggling girls enveloped Andrew, tickling him. Six hands on his chest, belly, and legs. Andrew scooted out from his corner and streaked down the side of the bar, with two of the girls giving chase. He ducked into the gents' bathroom. A moment later he reappeared, flushed and out of breath.

"You can see the women's bathroom inside the men's," he said, trying to catch his breath. "There's no door or anything. Girls can see you pee."

"Two hundred baht," Lek said to Jeremy. Half jokingly, she had offered to buy Andrew for the night. She glanced over at his baby-fat face and sparkling, bright, terrified blue eyes; a shank of his light brown hair reflected in gold highlights in the rotating overhead lights.

"He's just a boy. Only eleven years old. He's not for sale."

"You buy me, " she whispered in his ear. "Why not I buy him?"

"Cannot," said Jeremy.

"Can," teased Lek.

Jeremy looked over at Andrew. His son was overexcited, vulnerable, and confused. The restaurant had been so empty and boring;

and the bar overfilled with girls focused solely on him. Andrew had a similar look one day earlier in the summer when he had taken his son fishing off Pattaya and Andrew felt heavy pressure from his bowels. They were nearly a kilometer offshore. Jeremy ordered his son to strip off his clothes. Andrew thought about it for a couple of minutes and then ripped off his clothes. He remembered lowering his son over the side of the boat and into the sea.

"I can't shit in the water," moaned Andrew.

"Take your crap."

"But I'll pollute the sea, dad!"

"Where do you think whales shit? In their hotel rooms?"

Andrew had submerged himself for the bowel movement and then crawled back into the boat, with the same anxious, worried expression of helplessness as the three bar girls lowered him into the corner and tousled his hair and stared at his blue eyes. Andrew tried to avoid capture by darting, diving, running in the down-field pattern of a rugby player.

"One day all this will seem perfectly natural to him," Jeremy said to Susan. "He won't have our hang-ups. That bodies are shameful. That sex is bad."

"Most eleven-year-old boys don't like girls." Susan raised her glass to Lek.

Andrew came up for air and slid in between his mother and father.

"I forgot to tell you," he said, panting. "I ran out of money on Sukhumvit today. So I went into Asia bookstore and read all afternoon. Did you know that Marilyn Monroe died on August 4, 1962."

"The date of my first erection in midtown," Jeremy whispered to his wife.

Susan pretended to ignore this remark. Where on earth did you find that?" She asked Andrew.

"In a book. She died on August 4th. My birthday is August 4th. Isn't that weird?"

"You were born much later than 1962."

"I know, I know. But Marilyn Monroe was brilliant. When she was eleven she was fat. When she grew up she was beautiful. Everyone loved her. I love that she was fat as a kid." He ducked as one of the girls reached for his hair. "Why are they always trying to get at me?"

"They're not trying to get at you. They want to play," said Jeremy.

"You won't forget to give the letter to your grandfather?" said Susan, wrapping an arm around her son.

"Won't forget."

"And the tape . . ." Susan began to remind Andrew.

"Recorder," said Andrew, finishing her thought. "I won't forget to give the tape deck to aunt Liz. God, you never believe anything I say, Mom."

"I always believe you. But, like your father, you sometimes forget," said Susan. She glanced over at Lek, wondering what kind of half completed sentence they might finish for each other.

"Doesn't seem right this should be the end of summer," sighed Jeremy. "Marilyn Monroe! Where does he come up with this jazz."

"I saw sixty videos this summer," said Andrew.

"And read . . ." began Jeremy, pausing to let Andrew fill in the blank.

"Twenty-three books, not counting the one on Marilyn Monroe, which makes twenty-four."

"What do I forget?" Jeremy asked. Susan did not reply.

Lek sat, arms folded, smoking a cigarette. She stared off into the middle distance. A flower vendor, a dwarf with a large tattoo of a skull on his bare right arm hobbled up to the table and stuck a fist of roses into Susan's face. Andrew dug deep into his trouser pocket, removed a crinkled ten-baht note, and bought half a dozen roses. Smiling, he handed them to his mother.

"That was a sweet thing to do," said Susan. She glanced over at Jeremy, his eyelids half closed, as he stroked Lek's leg under the table. "Don't you think that was sweet of Andrew?"

"Of course he never forgets."

Susan divided the roses in half. She caught Lek's eye again and extended three roses to her. Their hands brushed together for a second. This time Susan sensed a connection; as their eyes explored each other through the roses, a halo of understanding and feeling registered in that region beyond words.

❖

THEY hated the end of summer and were trying to be very brave. Summer's end was the start of another long period of separation. Jeremy hated these comings and goings because they made him aware of the tick-tock sound of his own mortality. He wanted to stop time and the world inside the Our Way Bar. But he didn't know how except by ordering a third round of drinks.

"We'll miss the plane," said Susan.

"We have plenty of time," said Jeremy. "Just one more drink, love. It is the end of summer. Indulge me."

Susan smiled. "Yes, why not?"

"Sixty movies," sighed Jeremy.

"Yeah, and back at school the headmaster always lets me pick the video. Because I've seen them all. You see, it makes perfect sense. And if I'm really lucky I'll bag a really great bed next to Eric this year."

"True," said Susan.

"And when I get older I want to sell Apple computers in New York, and London, and Paris, and Disneyland."

Jeremy frowned as he thought about the cities on his son's list.

"You'll want to return to Bangkok. You can sell computers here, can't you?"

"Maybe. It's not too bad. But the girls don't leave you alone. I don't like them pulling at my hair and trying to tickle me. It's rude."

"When you're older your software and hardware might change your mind."

"No way."

That was true innocence. The ability to perceive the world without hormones driving the engines of passion and desire, fuelling every glance, touch, and word with the texture of a rumpled sheet. The bar girls flocked to Andrew for that very reason. Innocence in a Soi Cowboy bar was as rare as honesty in politics. Andrew reminded the girls of something lost deep inside themselves. Not that many years earlier they had waited on that same runway edge between childhood and adolescence; they couldn't wait to take flight, to be airborne into the world of grownups.

Only no one had told them Our Way Bar would be their landing field. Just to touch Andrew was to reunite with that forgotten world they had left behind. Lek and her friends were not flying off to an exclusive American boarding school that evening—not any evening; they were off to board for a couple of hours, or the entire night, with a middle-aged *farang*. Next year, they would still be dancing and caging drinks. And the year after. Sooner or later the summer would arrive when Andrew would see them through his father's eyes. But for the moment, they were lost in the magic of a boy who didn't understand the place of girls in the sea of grownups. A beautiful, fair-skinned boy who watched videos, read books, rode his bicycle and knew when Marilyn Monroe had died.

"WHY did Marilyn Monroe kill herself?" asked Andrew looking at his father.

"Because she didn't like growing old."

"She was very sad," said Susan.

"But she was a brilliant movie star!" insisted Andrew.

"Sometimes people do strange things. Think strange thoughts. They try to hold onto things they should let go of." Susan glanced over at Jeremy and found he was staring at her. "Another beer?" There was a glint in his eye. As if to say, please stop the time; please stop my boy from going away and adding another year to his life; please save me from the tick-tock of my own life winding down.

"We can't. We'll miss the plane."

"And who the hell would care?"

"But, Dad, I'd miss rugby practice on Wednesday," said Andrew with a sense of alarm.

"It would screw up his first term, Jeremy," said Susan firmly.

"Eric's dad said that there is only one rule for living: avoid changing airplanes," said Andrew, noisily sipping his Coke through a plastic straw.

"Eric's dad is an asshole who managed to say one clever thing in his whole life," said Jeremy, taking the bar chits from the plastic cup. He tallied the bill, wrapped them together with a five-hundred-baht note, and then pressed them into Lek's hand. A few feet away, with disco music blaring, lights spinning and flashing across the room, the go-go dancers were churning, twisting, kicking, and laughing all the way to the bank.

238

"I know why Marilyn Monroe killed herself," said Jeremy, counting his change after Lek returned.

"Really! Tell me!" said Andrew, sitting erect and leaning forward in an attentive attitude.

Jeremy looked over his son and at his wife. "Because she felt under pressure never to forget who she was."

"I don't get it," said Andrew. "I think Eric's dad explains things better."

Susan, with her long, slender fingers, brushed the hair out of Andrew" eyes. "Your father's not Eric's father, is he?"

"Let me try and be profound like Eric's dad, then," said Jeremy. "Why did Marilyn Monroe kill herself? You really want to know?"

Andrew nodded.

"Okay, the truth. She wanted to forget all the stuff that had happened to her. Everything she had done . . . or had been done to her. The faces, the places, the names. But no one would let her forget. Maybe she was ashamed of her past. Maybe a little frightened, too. My theory is someone pushed her, maybe forced her to relive those old memories. She couldn't take it and went for the big sleep."

Andrew looked puzzled but said nothing. There was something strangely sad in his father's expression. He looked straight past his son and at his wife, as if he wanted to tell her a secret but couldn't find the words or the courage to convey the words he had found.

This time Susan found Lek's eyes watching her. Lek fingered the rose petals; a feathery bed of red petals covered one end of the table.

"I think she was disillusioned," said Andrew. "You know, kind of sad?"

"Marilyn Monroe was world-famous, " said Susan, looking at Lek as she spoke. "A beauty, a goddess, and she thought men truly wanted her. Only she discovered a very hard lesson. There was no one there. No one for her. No one really cared. In July when your father took you fishing and put you over the side of the boat. You knew he'd pull you back in."

"Right," said Andrew.

"In Marilyn Monroe's life, the men just rowed away. Left her out there all alone."

And Jeremy looked over at Lek, and for the first time saw that she had Marilyn Monroe eyes. The rose stems had been picked naked; all the petals had been stripped away. Susan, with the tips of her fingers, touched the side of Lek's cheek. Marilyn Monroe's terror had been in Lek's eyes the entire evening; a billboard message written in neon tears.

As Susan looked around the room she saw the same billboard message in the eye of every one of the girls. "Rescue me. Save me. Pull me back to safety." The same, urgent message flashing through the hot tropical night. Each time they looked at Andrew, they wore their girlhood expression of innocence, play, and hope. At the end of his eleventh summer, Andrew had begun to teach parents about life.

Only when Andrew was much older would Susan buy him a Kloster and reminisce about the end of a summer in Bangkok when he was very young. About a final evening in Soi Cowboy when he had asked his father a question, about Marilyn Monroe's suicide. And how his mother had found the answer in a teenage bar girl's eyes.

17

At three in the morning, along The Strip, the varsity team of thieves, smugglers, drug dealers, gamblers, hitmen drifted onto the empty field, as if Patpong's sex-exotic attractions had been a pre-game warm-up. As Tuttle wandered along down the street littered with cartons, broken bottles, old newspapers, empty boxes, the carnival atmosphere was gone; like a circus that had pulled up stakes and left in a hurry. On the side lanes shadowy figures glided past a lone beggar with a shiny scar where an arm once had been attached. A drunk puking in the gutter; a guard whacking a stray dog with the end of his flashlight; a group of men wearing turbans and beards examining a long-bladed knife for sale by a man who straddled a black Honda motorcycle.

Tuttle had little difficulty tracking Crosby down to an upstairs redneck bar off the main strip; a bar tucked away in a labyrinth of cubby-hole bars, massage parlors, barbershops, and restaurants nestled next to a gray concrete multistory parking lot. Inside the bar, he looked through a bamboo partition. A fat man of indeterminate age, with hair dyed a raven black, coifed in a 1950s biker gang style, turned red behind a wooden table. He coughed and hacked into his enormous fist, a screaming cough deep from blacktarred lungs. The clasped fist cast a quivering shadow that danced against the bamboo like a great python struggling to swallow a small pig whole.

"Where is that bitch in the little green shoes," he roared. "Tell her to get her ass over here. I need a drink." His guttural southern voice sounded as if it poured forth from a small speaker inserted in the ham hock rolls of fat rippling beneath his chin and operated by remote control from Mississippi. Seated around the table were five other middle-aged players—Vietnam war vets. Tuttle watched the card dealer who had short-cropped silvery gray hair and forearm tattoos of the American flag and a bald eagle. They had nearly finished a third bottle of Mekhong; the thin, sickly sweet smell of the cheap whiskey perfumed the fat man's cigar smoke. The blades of an overhead ceiling fan rotated on slow speed, mixing smoke, whiskey fumes, and lies.

Red, blue, and black plastic chips lay in the center of the table. A stuffed water buffalo head, with lifeless eyes stared down at the fat man's hand. The panelled walls were covered with photographs of famous racehorses, formula A racing cars, greyhound dogs with numbers on their side. A coyote skin had been stretched out and nailed across the opposite wall, and at the tail-end of the coyote was a confederate flag.

"I got a son forty-three years old," said the fat man. "So I've lived long enough to know a few things, asshole." As Tuttle stepped towards the table, it was clear, the fat man was talking to Crosby who sat with his cards face up on the table. "You wanna get killed? Then just try and pay with a fucking third-party cheque. Do I look like a goddamn banker?" he thundered, hitting the edge of the table with the palm of his hand, rattling the chips and glasses.

"The cheque is good," said Tuttle, standing behind Crosby and looking down at Lawrence's cheque for two-thousand dollars.

"And who the fuck are you? And who in the hell let this asshole in?" The fat man glared at two young bar girls in jeans and sandals who scurried through swinging doors and into the kitchen.

Everyone looked away. "You look like a goddamn draft dodger to me. So get the fuck out of here. We have some business to settle with your friend."

"Let's go, Crosby."

"I don't think you heard me, asshole," said the fat man. "He ain't going anywhere until he pays me five hundred dollars. That's cash. Shit, this fucking turkey wants change! I ain't giving him change for any goddamn bad cheque."

"Who runs this broken down whorehouse," said Tuttle leaning over the table, his face inches from the fat man.

"You just bought yourself a whole truckload of trouble, friend," said the fat man, nodding across the table at two of the men. One moved away from the table, and took a branding iron off the wall. The other man's hands disappeared under the table, and reappeared holding a bowie knife.

"You got it the wrong way. You see, my partner, Colonel Chao gets real upset when some fat-assed *farang* calls me an asshole. That's real trouble. Maybe you never heard of him. Ask the first cop you see. Just mention his name."

"That's the oldest bluff in the book," said the fat man, knowing who Colonel Chao was and his reputation for having a complete absence of opponents inside or outside the police force. That flicker of doubt in the fat man's face betrayed his fear Tuttle might be on the level; the two men with knives and branding iron waited like an attack dog for its master's order.

Tuttle pulled out Colonel Chao's card, containing his rank and the district police office address, and dropped it on the table. "Here's his card. He's an old golf buddy of mine. Why don't you call my bluff. There's his personal home number. Dial it. Tell him you just called Robert Tuttle an asshole and you want permission to have your redneck friends stick a knife in me. You be in Thailand a long time, "Tuttle said breaking into *Thai-ling*, that patched together language which was part English, part Thai. "Maybe you no hear expression, 'Watch your back'? Because you don't let my friend go, you got a very big back to watch. And the Colonel is not someone to fuck around with."

The fat man looked down at the Colonel's card, lifted it up in his stubby fingers, lit his cigar. He held it to the light as if he were checking out a hundred-dollar bill. "Golf buddy, my ass. Get the fuck out of here. Both of you. I can't stand your fucking sight. You make me want to puke blood."

Crosby was still shaking by the time they had walked back to Silom Road. He hadn't said two words to Tuttle. Every time he had tried to speak, the narrow passage in his throat constricted as if he felt the fat man's hands strangling him. The entire time, he had been staring at the white skull of a water buffalo that had been nailed to the wall; the empty, dark sockets sucking away the light. All he could think at the moment before Tuttle had arrived was,

"This is where I'm going to die. In front of this stupid creature. The only witness will be a dead skull."

"That card was a brilliant scam," said Crosby, having taken in a deep breath. "He was bloody well going to have my balls."

"Couldn't you even wait to cash the cheque?"

Crosby lit a cigarette. "Sorry, Father."

"Forget the irony. I have a little problem of my own, I need the pictures," he said, as they walked across Silom Road.

"And what pictures might we be talking about?"

"The ones Snow and you arranged of Lawrence and the girls."

Crosby stopped at the corner of Convent Road, and leaned against the show window of Philips electronics. "What kind of problem are we talking about?"

"He's having second thoughts about the funding. I want to persuade him otherwise," said Tuttle, watching Crosby stare at the new television inside the window.

"Why do you think we have the photographs?"

"Because I caught up with little Lek at Jason's and for three hundred baht he told me." Tuttle shifted anxiously from one leg to the other.

"The sod. The problem in the world is there's no loyalty. And no honor."

"I need the photographs."

Crosby rolled his eyes, bared his lower teeth, sinking them softly into his upper lip, he bounced his teeth up and down off his lip, looking at his reflection in the window. "You did save me some difficulty back there." He paused and turned, facing Tuttle. "And it is for the good of the school? And what is good for the school, I presume, is good for the rest of us?"

Tuttle nodded, sensing Crosby's resistance weakening by the moment.

"Snow has them in his room."

As Tuttle stopped a cab, turning off Silom Road onto Convent Road, Crosby leaned into the window. "Don't forget, that's our pension plan you're dealing with."

❖

CONVENT Road ended at Sathorn Road, and on the opposite side, nestled between the Australian Embassy on one side and a brothel the size of Bloomingdale's on the other, was the Highland Hotel. Snow's room was on the third floor. As Tuttle walked down the corridor the hash smells drifted across his path. Snow had lived in the Highland Hotel for almost five years, and Tuttle had never once been invited inside. He guessed why. The interior had all the charm of a Thai slum; all that was missing were snotty-nosed, naked kids running around and basins of muddy water filled with clothes and dishes. The corridor had the cramped, shut-in feeling of a place where desperation was hatched; an anchorage where cheap pleasure floated on the edge of the night.

Snow took a long time coming to the door. Tuttle could hear whispers inside the room. Someone's sweaty barefeet made a sucking noise on the lino floor. "It's Bob," said Tuttle, knocking on the door again.

Finally the door opened a crack, and Snow stuck his head out, looking at Tuttle, then up and down the corridor. "Jesus, man, you know what time it is? Four in the morning." He spoke in chopped sentences. The hashish smoke rolled out of the door.

"I won't stay long."

"All right," said Snow, seeing Tuttle was determined. "Only a couple of minutes."

The large eyes of a young Thai girl, sitting erect in bed, with a sheet pulled to her neck followed Tuttle as he stepped over the threshold into Snow's world. Three candles flickered on saucers near the bed, the warm slanting light danced against her face, reworking her expression like wax, from terror and fear to the fine etchings of worry. *"Peu-un—friend,"* said Snow to the girl..

"You had Ning sucking wind, man. She thought you were a ghost. A little dope makes her paranoid."

Tuttle stared at Snow's gaunt face. It had been the first time he had ever seen him without glasses. His eye sockets looked like blurred slots; the eyeholes that look like the ones in the steer skull nailed to the gambling den wall. On the door was a six-foot poster of a shaman priest. Snow looked over at Ning, who had squeezed a thick red cushion against her breasts, watching every move Tuttle made. At the foot of the double bed, two tables had been pushed together. Beakers, cubes, scarfs, cones, ropes, chain, sheets, and a black top hat were scattered on the tables, chairs, end of the bed, and the floor. Draped over the edge of one table was a black cape with red lining. It looked like a child's room, disorder and toys that suggested a spirit of impatience in a child and drugs in an adult. Snow reached over and picked up a deck of cards.

The Lahu Godman joke had not been totally a joke; Snow had plowed that ground a hundred times, and Tuttle would have bet his last ten baht note that Snow had never taken the idea beyond HQ talk. A potential scam on some greenhorn who had stumbled over to the booth. Snow shuffled the deck.

"Pick a card," said Snow.

Tuttle took the eight of clubs, looked at it.

"Put it back in the deck."

Tuttle shoved it back into the deck, and Snow grinned, glancing back at Ning, as he reshuffled the deck. "Ning loves this trick, don't you, baby?" A moment later he pulled the eight of clubs off the top of the deck. "Is this your card?" Then, as Tuttle nodded, Snow reached out, touched Tuttle's right ear, and showed him a large one-baht coin.

"I need the photographs, George," said Tuttle, catching the coin that Snow had flipped into the air.

"My act is about ready for a cross-country tour."

"Crosby told me you had them."

"Crosby's fucking insane. Everyone knows that, man."

"Baring's not going through with the deal," said Tuttle. "I plan to lay the photos on him. It's between me and him, George. Don't get in the way."

Snow who stood in a pair of blue bikini underpants, turned and slipped the cape over his shoulders. He produced one, then two, then three colored balls between his fingers and tossed them one by one onto the bed, bouncing them off Ning's knees. "Those photos are our future, man."

"That's why I need them," said Tuttle.

"How do I know you won't fuck us around?"

"You got to trust someone, sometime, someplace. Besides, what's good for the school is good for you. Just in case you change your mind about going on the road with your act."

"Hey, man. That's like saying what's good for General Motors is good for America. And looked what happened to America."

"It's going to be unpleasant business. Of course, if you want to handle it with Lawrence Baring, be my guest." Tuttle made a move toward the door.

Snow looked distressed, and blocked Tuttle's path.

"I thought this guy was your friend?"

"Since when does money have anything to do with friendship?"

Snow smiled, danced over to the table, swept his hand from one end to the other, picked up his black cane and tapped the brim of the top hat. He reached in and pulled out a brown envelope. He tossed the envelope to Tuttle. "Crosby and I are counting on you, man."

In the photographs the girls had assumed a skull bar pose; mouths open, tongues extended, eyes wide open, the pupils turned up to find the camera. Lawrence held a hand pressed forward in one. He needed a shave, the knot in his tie was unfastened, his legs spread apart. A small childlike hand, fingers splayed, covered his crotch. His lips were parted, as if he were about to deliver an closing argument before a jury who needed a lot of convincing. In one photograph, one eyelid was half closed, giving Lawrence the expression of a bad drunk. There had been only three shots. Each revealing a different profile of torment, not anger or hostility as Tuttle had expected, but the anguished expression of someone trapped, his mask of control stripped clean off his face. Tuttle thought about the passage in Sarah's letter, playing up to Lawrence's need to be in control. Had she ever seen this face? If she had, would she have killed herself? It might have given her hope that, he, too, was vulnerable, frightened, scared as anyone else.

HALFWAY down Soi 27, Tuttle's house was one among half a dozen located behind a large, gray metal gate. The cab driver knew which of the two buzzers beside the mailbox to press. Lawrence stood on his tiptoes and peered over the barbed-wire crisscrossing the top of the gate. Finally, he saw a light go on in a window at the end of a narrow path. Asanee, sleep lines on her face, appeared wearing a T-shirt, jeans, and sandals.

"I want to see your father," said Lawrence.

She rubbed her eyes, stretched out her arms, shaking her head. She yawned. "He's not home."

"I'd like to wait for him."

Asanee looked at the driver, then Lawrence. She spoke to the driver in Thai, and he, nodding, got back into the taxi, backed into the drive of a modern high-rise apartment block, and disappeared into the night, leaving Lawrence standing on the pavement.

She threw her arms around him, and on tiptoes kissed him long and hard on the mouth. "You better come inside," she said.

"Your father?"

"He not here." She squeezed his hand. "I think you not like me."

"We need to have a talk."

He followed her down the paved pathway, past the rows of small houses. Palm and coconut trees with thick trunks shrouded the doorways and windows in dark shadows. He realized it was late; and he had a sudden feeling that for the first time in his life he had no reason or explanation for being in a place. He had arrived because three HQ girls had sent him; he didn't seriously question their judgement. He had gone. For what purpose or object, he didn't have the slightest idea. The last thing in the back of his mind was discovering Asanee alone. All he knew was that for some unexplained reason, it seemed right that he should see Tuttle's house; at least once before he left for Los Angeles the following evening.

The entire compound slumbered within another world of shrubs, flowers, lawns, and Lawrence felt like an intruder. His hands were clammy in the heat. Tuttle's white-framed house, near the end of the path, had screened windows and a flat, corrugated roof; a small passageway linked the main house to a small, enclosed room where the door was ajar. Several pairs of shoes were lined up outside the door to the small room; another row of shoes beside the entrance to the main house. Lawrence stopped and peered inside as Asanee stood with the screen door open to the house.

"Father's study," said Asanee, gesturing to the little room on her right. "He's usually working in there now."

"I had no idea his work at the school kept him out late," said Lawrence.

She laughed, standing inside the screen door of the house. "Not school. He writes stories. Tries to sell them. And when he makes a sale, the money goes to the school."

"I thought he stopped writing," said Lawrence.

Asanee frowned, sniffling from a tropical head cold. "That was the party line. The money wasn't coming in. Every day Snow or Crosby would ask him. 'Make a sale yet, man?' Or 'Say, old boy, why don't you write something on horse racing. That always sells' So he told everyone he quit. I can't see how it matters now. We don't have to worry about money for the school. That's what everyone is saying. It is true?"

Lawrence walked through the door and entered the small shed. "Mind if I have a look?"

"Up to you," said Asanee, closing the screen door and walking over to the converted maid's quarters. She reached inside and turned on the light. She had a disappointed look.

"He sleeps in here?"

Asanee nodded. "Only one bedroom upstairs. I tell him Father, no good you sleep here, and I stay upstairs. He say, Asanee, *mai pen rai*—never mind."

Tuttle's study was inside what should have been the maid's quarters. The cramped room was just large enough for a desk, chair, and a single bed. It struck Lawrence that the room was less a place to work and sleep than a place to do penance. A kind of shrine built to house his personal sorrow. Books lined a makeshift bookcase on one wall. The desk, jumbled with manuscripts, letters, old books, and an ancient Remington typewriter. A sheet of paper was in the typewriter. Several lines were x'd out; several sentences appeared midway down the page, "I was about to drop the used condom on the torn page from the magazine. Something made me read the page. There was something familiar about it. Then I had recognized that it contained my own story '*The Boy Who Loved Marilyn Monroe.*' I stared at my by-line, then let the condom drop, pretending I was in a bomber at high altitude and had found my name on the target 35,000 feet below."

There was a row of framed photographs. A photograph of Tuttle and Sarah from their college days. Another of Asanee and Tuttle in front of a wat. Another of Tuttle with Karen rebels, another of Tuttle next to a tank parked beside a road sign pointing to Saigon. A stack of rejection letters were secured in place by a five-hundred-gram bronze elephant, an opium weight bought in *Mae Sai*, Asanee informed Lawrence. He picked up the picture of Sarah and Tuttle smiling in the camera. He recognized the interior of the Angel Lady Bar in LA and the jukebox in the background. He remembered '*Hey Jude*.' Tuttle's arm was around her waist, his face turned, looking at her; he was smiling, a relaxed, idle smile of someone revealing adoration. He remembered that '*Hey Jude*' was the only sound that had come from Sarah's MG. For the first time since her death, Lawrence saw himself looking in the mirror of Sarah's last few moments.

"Sarah," whispered Lawrence, setting the framed photograph back on the desk. His eyes closed, he still saw their mental image. He heard Sarah singing along to the lyrics of the song like another person in another time, before confusion had entangled her, and swept her downstream. Slowly he looked up at Asanee.

"That's the way Sarah looked long before you knew her. When she was about your age. When she was in love with your father."

Asanee sat in the chair, leaned forward on her elbows, and stared at the photograph in silence for nearly a minute.

"She was very good to me. I loved her very much."

"I'm going to ask you a very big favor," said Lawrence, turning her around on the chair.

"Can," she said, moving her face close to his.

"You don't know what I'm going to ask."

She relaxed, touching his face with the back of her hand; he looked a little scared, she wondered if he was worried about Tuttle coming back.

"I can lock my room. My father never come inside. Ever," she said, running her fingers through his hair. "Sarah talk about you. I think you good for her."

If Sarah's diaries had revealed anything, they were one long document of how he hadn't been good for her, Lawrence thought.

"What did Sarah say?" he asked

"That you take good care of her."

"And you think I could do the same for you?"

"You want I make love with you?" she asked, her English deteriorating by the word.

It would have been so easy to destroy Tuttle. All he had to do was carry her upstairs to her bedroom. He had offered her on a silver platter before. Taking Asanee to bed would have allowed Lawrence to win. What was inside his mind was Sarah sitting behind her desk, talking to Asanee. She hadn't said that she loved him, or that he loved her, only that he had taken care of her.

"Promise me you won't tell Bobby I was inside here," he said.

"Why? He not care. *Jing! Jing!*—Honest."

"Just promise me."

"Not tell Fawn, or anyone else this time," she said, dropping her head.

She looked ashamed. Asanee had lost face with just about everyone over the Fawn affair. She felt that she had dishonored her father; humiliated herself; disgraced the school; and carelessly abused Sarah's memory.

"Promise me." He slowly pulled up her chin.

"I promise," she said. Asanee ran crying out of Tuttle's room, slamming the screen door behind her, into the house. He heard her feet on the stairs, the distant slam of her bedroom door.

THE feeble croak of a rooster broke through the early morning sky as Tuttle walked into the main house, finding Asanee and Lawrence at the kitchen table, drinking coffee.

"Any coffee left?" asked Tuttle, as he walked across the wooden floors in his socks.

Lawrence watched him go into the kitchen and pull a mug from a cupboard. "Aren't you just a little surprised that I'm here?"

Tuttle shuffled back to the table and sat down. "Bangkok is full of surprises; you get motion sickness if you rock on your heels every time someone surprises you here." He added milk to the coffee, and Asanee stirred in her chair.

"I go to bed now," she said, leaning over to kiss her father on the forehead. "You look very bad. You not take good care of yourself. Why?"

"An old girlfriend." Tuttle winked at Asanee, and nodded for her to climb the stairs to her bedroom. It was an excuse that she would both accept and like. She had a romantic notion that a man without a woman was an electric system without any current. "Ning. You remember Ning?"

"Too tired to think. Cannot remember."

After his second cup of coffee, Tuttle ran his open hand through his hair and pulled out the envelope of photographs. He tossed them to Lawrence. "The skull bar photos. Don't ask how, where, who, or why. It doesn't matter."

Lawrence watched as Tuttle rose from the table, walked across the main room. It had begun raining. He opened the screens one by one, and closed the windows. The boom of thunder rolled in the distance; stopping, the rain splashing outside off the flat roof, a flash of lightning, followed by another rumble, this time closer. They listened to the rain and thunder, saying nothing, as Lawrence, his face grim, his hands shaking, looked through the photographs.

"Elegant, aren't they?" said Tuttle.

"I don't mean to he ungenerous, but I'm about to turn over one million dollars. Why are you showing me these?"

"The school can't accept the money, Larry."

"You're turning it down?"

Thunder splintered the brief silence after Lawrence's question. It was followed by another intense clap that shook the windows. Lawrence felt the vibration running up his arms from the table.

"More than half my life, I've been exiled, between lives, countries, relationships, jobs; but I found a kind of contentment, even happiness, Larry. Not because I ever succeeded at anything. I have mostly failed. But failure buys you something that success never does—your freedom; you get ignored, the greatest luxury of all time—you are left alone. The moment someone smells your success, it is the same as the smell of the blood of another man's fresh kill. Your head rises above the crowd, and there is always a Colonel Chao, waiting in the wings to become your partner, to cut himself into your life. To cut your life apart if you say no."

"I know how to go through all the legal hoops," said Lawrence. "Plug any loophole. That's my job."

"How do I explain this," said Tuttle, waiting for a roll of thunder to end. "There is no rule of law here. Not in the sense you use it. There are loose arrangements. Accommodations that people must make to stay in business and alive. A million dollars is a sponge that attracts a large pool of people; it sucks them up in a thousand tiny holes. Sarah's money will be divided up like spoils of war. Easy loot. You can't fix it with all the legal documents ever written in America. This is not home territory, Larry. Forget the law of contract. Small-arms fire pierces any contract. About Asanee's back, about the rest of the kids. It won't work. The money has already made an armored carload of new friends I don't need or want."

Lawrence eased back in the chair, crossed his legs. For a long time, he listened to the driving rain.

"Did you?" asked Tuttle.

"Did I do what?"

"Take her to bed."

Lawrence sighed and wetted his lips. "She wouldn't give me the time of day. Not that I didn't try. You think I could do that to my father, she asked me. She was right, Bobby. She couldn't. Whatever has gone on between you two has nothing to do with me. You might have thought you couldn't trust her. After Sarah, I could understand that. But this girl loves you, Bobby. No stranger is going to come between you. Not me. Not anyone."

"Tomorrow we have to fix things."

"I know," said Lawrence, stretching his arms and rising from his chair. He left before Tuttle could thank him. Thank him for what, he wasn't exactly sure.

18

Fawn and Asanee giggled as they crossed the small waiting room area. As far as anyone could remember no one had ever seen either Snow or Crosby in a necktie. Tuttle had sent them over to Silom Road to price computer equipment for the school, and gave them the rest of the day off—a holiday—and with an order—stay out of the bars. He wanted them both out of the way.

Since lunch everyone had been stealing glances at their watches. Snow and Crosby waited for Lawrence's arrival, edgy, gangling their legs over different ends of the same desk. Over several Singha beers, they had pieced together their separate encounters with Tuttle the night before, leaving out those aspects that made them appear small, and simple-minded, and taking credit for independently arriving at the same conclusion that the matter of Lawrence's change of heart was best left to Tuttle.

Yet there was an unspoken tension. If things, for any reason, fell through, the other was already listing reasons why it was not his fault but rested squarely on the shoulders of the other.

"The trouble with you, Crosby, is you're fucking doomed, man. You probably had that nanny sucking on your wick when you were six. You gotta be bent. Twisted, man. Tuttle wormed the information out of you just like that." He snapped his fingers.

"He got me out of a rather tight spot," said Crosby. "A combat squad of bloody Yanks had their bowie knives at my throat. One knife and a branding iron to be exact."

"Gambling with rednecks, man. You've got your head up your ass. And what does a goddamn limey know about Americans?

254

Fuck-all. What is England anyway? A land of cave-dwellers who go out and suffocate each other at soccer games. Grim. A fucked-up place definitely on the skids. You patrol the town like Chinese body-snatchers. Except you're not benevolent or an association.

"But you and the Chinese body-snatchers live for the old body grab. They're sitting in a van over on Soi Asoke right now. Those little reedy-voiced assholes with radios that allow them to tap into the police and emergency bands. They make merit by arriving at the scene of a fatal accident and picking up the bodies. Crash victims mangled and broken; head bashed in, arms and legs cut off. They scoop them up in plastic bags. Oh, shit, there's a finger over on the curb I've missed. Damn, wait a sec, man. It's got a fucking big gold ring on the knuckle. That's gotta be worth some big bucks. They haul ass back to their temple, take a couple of Polaroid photographs of the body and tape them in the window. That's lunchtime entertainment for the office workers. They go up to the window drinking their Cokes and point at the latest man, woman, or child with the smashed-in heads. And you know what their reaction is? You'll like this, Crosby. They're fucking laughing their heads off. Man, there ain't a grim face among them. They're joking and laughing. You'd think they were looking at a high school yearbook. That's the high point of their day.

"And everyone of them is saying the same thing, 'That fucker's dead as shit. Man, that could've been me. But I'm looking at this dead fucker, I'm alive. I've got a good destiny. Ain't life wonderful.'

"They really get their rocks off if there's a picture of a dead *farang* in the window. They laugh themselves sick. This is a special treat. A white face that's been splattered all over the streets of Bangkok. They can't wait to get back to the office and tell their friends. Phone their relatives.

"Guess what I saw in the temple window today? Mangled *farang*. Man, his face looked worse than a temple dog. He's gonna come back to Bangkok as a snake or a pig or a monkey. And that will be a step up. *Farang* to monkey. That is progression. Advancement."

Crosby swung his feet off the desk. He walked over to the window and looked out at the soi. There was no sign of Lawrence's chauffeur-driven Mercedes. Crosby checked his watch; out of reflex,

Snow checked his. Snow drummed his fingers on the desk, beating out a tune and humming.

"They could have been Aussies," said Crosby.

"Who?"

"Last night at the poker table."

It had become something of a tradition for them to rally around the neutral ground of bashing Australians whenever the conversation became too personal, or they needed relief from the boredom of waiting.

"No way, man."

"Why not the fucking Aussies?" Crosby sounded slightly hurt as if Snow wasn't playing the game properly.

"They're the Appalachians of the Orient. Those wandos could never learn how to play poker. If you could teach one, he wouldn't have any money. Besides, who's going to play cards with an Aussie? You look across the table, and whammo, there's this guy with a thick jawline. Heavy brows. Caveman head. He's grunting for dead meat. I keep telling Tuttle, flood Australia. Turn it into rice paddies for the people on Java. Think about it. Fifteen million albino cavemen on that huge island. It's a stone's throw away from Java, man. You know how many Javanese are crowded on their tiny shithole island? One hundred million. And they're starving their asses off. On a clear night the Aussies can hear all hundred million of them chanting.

"Rice, man. Need rice.

"Only the Aussies can't understand them. Man, they only understand caveman lingo. Sooner or later someone's gonna tell the Javanese to build ships. Put their people inside and invade Aussieland. Train the Aussies to plant rice. But that may be beyond the Aussie ability level. Planting rice takes a certain state of civilization. You gotta be able to use your thumb and index finger together. So how the fuck are they gonna play cards?"

Crosby looked away from the window, grinning. "That's Lawrence Baring's car."

Khun Kob came out of the headmaster's office, wearing an orchid in his lapel and sunglasses, and walked to the window, standing shoulder to shoulder with Crosby. His personal comfort violated, Crosby stepped back, lit a cigarette, raising his eyebrows behind the headmaster's back. Tuttle sat deep in the padded chair inside the office, leaned far behind so his head touched the wall, reading the *Bangkok Post*. An influential person, whose company traded on the stock exchange, had been machine-gunned on his way to the golf course the day before. There was a photograph of the bullet holes in the car door and the shattered windshield.

Lawrence, in a gray business suit, walked straight past Crosby, Snow, and Khun Kob, without exchanging a glance or word.

"Let's hope the photography works," Crosby whispered to Snow.

They gathered outside the office, ears pressed against the closed door.

"So what's the problem, Larry?"

"You know what the goddamn problem is. I won't play any more games. I want my own people in this school. You call Snow, Crosby, and that . . . that buffoon running around with a cataract in a jar, teachers? And this joke you call Old Bill? He's pure dead wood. You're carrying a pack of losers."

"You're talking about my friends."

Lawrence's shrill groan echoed through the door. "The money goes through the American Embassy. They will supply the teaching staff. Let those clowns interview for a job. One more thing. No more bar girls teaching, or as students. I want a clean-cut all-American image. The Embassy has agreed to supply American flags for each student. You get the picture?"

Tuttle cleared his throat and in a clear, controlled voice said: "I don't think so, Larry. Have a look at these. You're looking at the picture. Maybe the American Embassy would like to know who is putting up the cash and for what? Lawrence Baring, Esquire, skull-fucking little Patpong bar girls. That doesn't set well with the American flag and loyalty oaths, does it? And what will your law firm think about that little girl—what is she, Larry, twelve, thirteen years old, going down on you at a bar?"

"You sonofabitch."

Tuttle nodded and mouthed the words, "Do it."

Lawrence's punch broke his nose. The force knocked him back into the padded leather chair. He staggered to his feet, surprised that Lawrence had packed so much into the blow; he nodded for a second punch. This one put him down. He looked up at Lawrence in a half blurry, spinning room. Then the door opened, and Lawrence stood framed in the doorway. "Any one sees those pictures, and I personally will make a phone call. One of my clients is a Teamsters' local. I keep their pension funds straight. They owe me. And they know people who know people. People from Los Angeles who are world class with guns, bombs, and other toys; people you, and your Khun Kob, Snow, and Crosby might wish they had never met. And they will kill you so slowly you will want to help them with the process."

Lawrence was given a wide berth leaving the school; his feet fell heavily on the wooden staircase. Crosby, Snow, and Khun Kob stood at the window, not saying a word, and after the Mercedes left, they found Tuttle, bloodied, his face swollen; his left eye puffy and nearly closed.

"You need a doctor. You'll take a couple of stitches to close that cut above your eye," said Crosby, kneeling down with a handkerchief, and wiping the blood away from Tuttle's face.

"The guy was an asshole, man."

"His demand to fire us was totally unreasonable," said Khun Kob. "He cannot!"

"Lay off," said Crosby. "The man's been beaten because he wouldn't let that lunatic fire us. Think how much face you would have lost. And with an election in the wind."

"Forget about politics, man," said Snow. "Shit, remember Jimmy Hoffa. The Teamsters. The guy does pension plans for hitmen."

Khun Kob hooked his thumbs into his belt hoops. He knelt down beside Tuttle, who was shaking his head. Tuttle moved his jaw back and forth, moaning. "I won't forget your good ethics," said Khun Kob. "We defeated this enemy together. Now we will make a better school. Colonel Chao has expressed an interest in our school. I will make an appointment and explain to him the drawback."

"Just tell the Colonel we did our best," said Tuttle, looking up at Snow and Crosby. "Friendship above money."

"You may be the only *farang* in Thailand who put friendship and money in that order," said Crosby.

"Being beat up in Thailand by a fucking American mob lawyer," said Snow. "That's why America's doomed."

It had gone so smoothly, thought Tuttle. But nothing in Thailand ever was quite as it appeared. A small, missing fragment of doubt lodged in Tuttle's mind; he thought of the room where the Colonel would cross-examine Khun Kob, twisting each detail, and ask him to account for any inconsistency in the story. Khun Kob was a civilian; the Colonel, a police official, who had heard every conceivable account of how money had gone missing in action.

❖

PATIENCE is the ability to withhold action over a long period of time; and wisdom is judging the right moment in which patience has paid off and the time for acting has arrived. The Colonel was both a patient and wise man. Genius was the rare ability to generate impatience in another because, in the state of rushing, mistakes are invariably made. The Colonel had a reputation as such a genius.

Two men waited for Tuttle outside the school in an air-conditioned yellow BMW. In the three months since Lawrence's departure, he had often seen the same car parked in the alley with the motor running, windows rolled up, and the occupants hidden behind aviator sunglasses. Tuttle stepped outside the school, carrying his briefcase; a small gust of hot wind and bus fumes made his eyes water. The Bangkok heat recoiled off the pavement and building like angry gunfire. He blinked several times, then closed his eyes tight, shivered, and when he opened them the two men from the BMW were on either side of him.

"Kinda hot," said Tuttle.

"We give you a ride," said the taller of the two men.

"I doubt we're going the same way," said Tuttle, clutching his briefcase playing out the options in his mind. He was one hundred meters from the street. No one else was around. Both men were armed; it was difficult to conceal a handgun in Bangkok, the sweatsoaked clothes moulded against the gunstock. The two men had been out of the air-conditioned car no more than three minutes and they were sweating.

"We go your way."

Tuttle shrugged and walked away with the two Thais on either side. He sat, briefcase on his lap, in the back with the shorter man,

259

whom the other called Lek. He felt like a complete fool, he felt angry, but above all he felt the helplessness. The feeling went with the territory of expat existence, where the security of tenure might be no longer than a one-night stand.

The BMW drove the back sois, getting stuck in a snarl of *tuk-tuks*, trucks, buses, and cars on *Soi Asoke*. For over an hour nothing moved. Lek and his nameless companion smoked smuggled American cigarettes. The nameless one, a mobile phone attached to his ear, spoke with his minor wife about weekend arrangements; glancing throughout the conversation at Tuttle through his sunglasses in the rearview mirror, he never forgot his assignment in the backseat.

ASANEE stayed home from school with a head cold. Before lunch she had gone downstairs and placed a courier pack on Tuttle's desk. She leaned it against the photograph of the two of them. It had arrived around ten that morning while she was still in bed; it was from New York City. After she had gone back to bed, a houseboy who worked for a neighbor in the compound entered Tuttle's office, removed the pack, and delivered it to a man waiting on a motorcycle outside the main gate.

The motorcycle driver, who had been kept waiting nearly an hour in the heat, was in a foul mood. He kicked one of the soi dogs, the dog sprawled against the outside wall and howled with pain. He grabbed the packet, executed a sharp turn, and without a word, accelerated down the soi. The houseboy watched him turn onto Sukhumvit Road and disappear into traffic.

The howling dog woke Asanee. She went downstairs and straight into the kitchen, opened a Coke, stood at the counter, tipped the Coke back and took a long drink. Some instinct whispered something was wrong. She returned to Tuttle's room, taking the bottle with her. She sat heavily in his chair, wiped the moustache of sweat off her upper lip with the back of her hand. She saw the courier pack was gone. A feeling of violation, panic, confusion hit her hard, doubled her over with fear. She dropped the bottle and she ran back into the house, shot upstairs and picked up the telephone. The line was dead. She heard someone else breathing in the room.

"You stay upstairs. Wait for your father. He'll come home soon," said a man, who stood inside the bathroom.

"How did you get in?" she asked, doubling up her fists. "Get out of our house." She threw the telephone at him.

"Sit down and shut up. Or you get hurt bad," said the young Thai, dressed in a white cotton shirt and jeans.

"You dog-mouthed sonofabitch," she shouted.

He moved toward her, his jaw cemented with anger and fear.

Asanee yelled, screaming her lungs out, but he grabbed her, knocking her down and covering her mouth with his hand. His eyes were several inches from Asanee's. He pulled a hunting knife. The six-inch blade reflected the sunlight from the window as he held it an inch from her face.

"You scream again, I kill you," he said, between clenched teeth, smelling of garlic.

Her eyes terrified, she nodded her head and slowly, he removed his hand. She gasped for air, heart pounding in her neck and throat, she slumped on the bed. Her captor nervously shifted the knife from one hand to the another, glancing at his watch. He appeared as scared as she was. Asanee buried her head in a pillow. She had an overwhelming feeling that her father was in danger, and her assault was the start of something ugly, brutal, and cruel, something she did not fully understand had entered their lives, something barbarous had curved into their path. It was the distress of someone who had been hunted and captured.

THE letter inside the courier pack read:

PEGASUS HOUSE PRESS
25 East 36th Street
New York, New York 10026

Dear Mr. Tuttle,

Our fiction editor has been following your work for some time. Your short stories offer an unique vision of Southeast Asia at a time when Americans are asking about the people culture and customs of countries like Thailand. It would be our honor to make fifteen of your stories available in a collected work. We would like to offer you a contract for the enclosed list. We are pleased to offer you an advance of two hundred thousand dollars, against a ceiling of one million dollars.

We look forward to a long, mutually enjoyable relationship extending over many books and many years. With your permission, we would like to market your book under the title: '*The Boy Who Loved Marilyn Monroe*'. We understand that you have lived in Asia for many years.

Perhaps you might supply us with a suitable dust jacket cover photograph: one perhaps taken while you were a foreign correspondent covering the Vietnam war. The photograph should have something to make it identify for the reader such as a street sign pointing to Saigon.

Our lawyers in Los Angeles will he in touch with you early next week.

Sincerely,

Jerry Harris, Acquisitions Editor

THE BMW swung off Sukhumvit Road, passing rows of street vendors on both sides of the soi. Dust from the construction sites hung heavily in the air. Heavy trucks lined the road in long queues. One driver raised a small brown bottle of Singha beer to his lips and drank, his Adam's apple bobbing in the heat. Long-necked boom cranes penetrated the skyline. Tuttle watched the sweaty faces of the workmen shoveling cement. Bangkok had become a maze of construction sites. A place of invisible, powerful connections, with overlapping personalities from business, politics, police, and society; complex links and associations near the altar of the commerce god. Elements anchored with money split off in random directions, turned back on themselves, poked up in a newspaper here, a TV interview there, in the back of a Mercedes, behind a conference table, and no one could ever be sure how these elements fit together. The uncertainty of connections within connections made everyone edgy, looking for their cut, expecting to win, and isolating the risks. It fed the paranoia of the front line, constantly shifting, stranding someone, benefiting others; and as with every front line, there were masses of porters, some troops, and an elite group of officers.

A few moments later, the BMW turned into the Sukhumvit Golf Driving Range, and hard-braked into a parking slot in a gravel lot. Tuttle leaned forward, looking at what was a kind of privileged officers' outpost in the midst of all the construction. A golf ball driving range. Mesh-net draped over a superstructure of poles rose ten stories on three sides. A vast open, green space littered with thousands of golf balls. Expensive, new imported cars were parked behind the main pavilion. Beyond the cars, dozens of green-shirted young women slept, gossiped, ate rice and chicken in an old wooden shed.

The teenaged caddies, like bar girls, wore numbers. They squatted on a small wooden block, knees locked together, staring down at the feet of a golfer. Tuttle watched one of the girls tee-up a golf ball on the narrow wedge of green artificial turf, her eyes cast down at the ground, waiting patiently, without a sound, for the loud thwack. Tuttle was uncertain if it was the crack of the ball or the position of the club that made him jump. With the club passing within inches of her face, she pulled out another ball, and without looking up for instructions, automatically set it on the tee. The gunshot sound of golf balls being struck pierced the air. Lek swung open the back door first and then motioned for Tuttle to get out.

In Bay 27, Colonel Chao stood in profile, wearing gray slacks, white golf shoes, and a white short-sleeve shirt; his knees slightly bent, his arms forward, he concentrated on the golf ball; the muscles in his forearms twitching, his face immobile as if he were mediating on the patch of green artificial turf at his feet. Effortlessly the Colonel, expertly and gracefully, raised the head of a number-two wood, and in a clean, single motion, struck the ball. His body in a half turn, his weight shifted to his left leg, his number-two wood frozen skyward like a smoking gun, the Colonel watched the trajectory of the ball. Tuttle watched the ball land near the two hundred-yard marker, bounce against another golf ball, and roll in front of the Singha Gold ad sign at the back of the range. He was a careful, methodical golfer, thought Tuttle. No rush in his shot; the patience of waiting for the moment of perfect concentration, and then following through.

Without turning around, the Colonel lowered his club. "Mr. Tuttle, how good of you to join me."

"It was an unexpected invitation," said Tuttle, sitting down on the bench behind the playing area.

"Do you play golf?"

Tuttle shook his head.

The Colonel raised his eyebrows, concentrated over the ball, and sent it sailing toward the one-fifty yard green on the left hand side of the range.

"Now that is a surprise. My sources in Patpong told me about a rumor going around. You were in an upstairs gambling parlor and you were telling the owner I was your golf buddy."

Tuttle sighed, thinking of Crosby sitting at a gambling table and over his head in trouble. Bangkok was the smallest town of ten million people in the world. His bluff to save Crosby had come back to haunt him.

The Colonel smiled with satisfaction as the ball bounced onto the green and rolled towards the flag. "I learned to play at Korat. During the Vietnam war, I was stationed at the air force base at Korat. You Americans installed a first-rate golf course and driving range." He paused, changed to a five-iron, and hit another ball.

"And?" asked Tuttle, breaking the silence.

"I wonder if your friend Lawrence is a golfer?"

A waitress arrived with a coke for Tuttle. He refused to take it, tried to wave her off, and, taking her direction from the Colonel, she set the bottle and glass on the table beside Tuttle's bench. She disappeared as quickly and quietly as she had arrived. "I never asked him," said Tuttle, finally.

The Colonel smiled, then changed clubs, this time pulling a driver from his golf bag. His first drive bounced off the Singha Gold advertisement sign at the end of the range. "It's been two or three months since he went back to America," said the Colonel, leaning forward into another shot.

"Three months," said Tuttle, waiting for the Colonel to gradually tip his hand.

The Colonel reacted with a shrug of the shoulders.

"One of my men caught a thief. He had stolen an air courier packet addressed to you. This criminal opened it looking for valuables," explained the Colonel. "Instead, all he found was a letter from New York City. It has some very good news. Since we are friends, I wanted to bring the letter to your attention, personally." He nodded to the driver of the BMW who handed Tuttle the letter.

The Colonel turned his concentration back to hitting golf balls as Tuttle read the letter. He reread the letter again. On the driving range, the loud whack of balls resounded. Tuttle was confused, angry, but above all he was scared. The Colonel waited until Tuttle raised his eyes from the letter, then he slowly took off his golf gloves.

"You are about to become a very wealthy man ," said the Colonel. "So you should take up golf."

The indirect, circular way of going around the main point left the burden on Tuttle. It was a grinding-down process. Guerrilla warfare tactics in fighting toward a goal; the Colonel was waiting for Tuttle to become angry, to make a mistake, to explode and lose control. Instead, Tuttle pulled back from the deep edge of anger he circled, and smiled.

"I played a few times in California," he said, walking into the bay, and removing the Colonel's three-iron from the bag. The caddie set a ball on the turf. Tuttle leaned forward, swung and missed the ball.

"You may want some lessons to brush up," said the Colonel.

Tuttle felt his cheeks flush and burn red. He swung the iron again, this time slicing the ball into the netting off the right. The young girl squatting on her haunches showed no expression as she mechanically placed another ball on the turf.

"As a Vietnam war correspondent, you will appreciate how important help is in battle," said the Colonel, pouring the Coke into the glass and taking a sip. "During the war, a crew would fly out of *Korat* in the morning for a bomb run, and in the afternoon, they were back playing a round of golf. Sometimes, a foursome didn't return. Then all the Americans left. They turned the air base over to us. The golf course is still there. We are still playing golf.

We have gone nowhere, Mr. Tuttle. This is our home ground. We always play the full eighteen holes; we never leave, say after nine. And like every world-class golf club, there are membership fees to consider. No one can play for free. That's an important rule. If you're not a member, then you must join."

"And you want to be my sponsor?" asked Tuttle, looking down at the golf ball. This time he sent the ball sailing high and straight toward the one-fifty yard marker.

"You see, you have potential," he said, taking a drink from the glass. "I have a theory about the Vietnam war. Since you covered the war, maybe you will agree with it. The Americans built the golf course at *Korat*. So they think it would always belong to them. That was a mistake. Victory takes a commitment to play every day. With your friends and your family. A desire to win. An American mind builds a very good golf course; but an Asian mind masters the game."

The Colonel took a practice swing, nodded for his caddie to set up another ball. He steadied his feet, concentrated, holding his breath, and slowly raised his club. The ball sailed toward the 150-yard marker, hit the ground six feet from the red flag and bounced. He did not take his eyes away from the shot until the ball had rolled to a complete stop.

"You might say the Vietnam war improved my game," said the Colonel, reaching into his bag to change clubs.

"Yeah, well, I was a draft dodger," said Tuttle, looking for some shock value.

The Colonel registered a smile. "Who went to Vietnam?"

"I wasn't looking to play golf. I was planning on finding something else."

"So was I. And maybe we found what we were looking for. Today, I think to myself, maybe there is some lesson in all of this for Mr. Tuttle. I want to talk with you. I want to discuss these matters, and of course, to report that we have your stolen letter."

Tuttle leaned forward on the iron, staring down at the ball. "Exactly what did we find, Colonel?"

"It's up to you," said the Colonel. "But with letters stolen in the post, I might worry about bank accounts. Some people are bad, dishonest, like in your country. They can be powerful. But if you

266

should decide to deposit the money into a certain account, it might be a good idea. You have my personal guarantee no one will touch you. I think no problem for you."

The mobile phone hooked on the side of the golf bag rang. The Colonel reached over and answered in Thai. He frowned, looking at the ground; barked several orders. He laid the phone down on the table and stared straight through Tuttle. "You have many problems in Thailand. Your daughter, she have a problem, too."

"Asanee," said Tuttle in disbelief. Her name hung in the air thick with the clean thwacking sound of golf balls sailing skyward. The sides of his rib cage heaving, Tuttle took a step forward. The two men from the BMW grabbed his arms; but he shook one loose, bringing the end of the iron into his gut. The driver, his sunglasses knocked off, collapsed in a heap across the bench. Lek, an ex-kick boxer, aimed several rapid kick shots at Tuttle. On the down swing of the last kick, Tuttle waited with the iron. He caught Lek's ankle with the iron head, rolling him head over heels into the parking lot.

"If anything has happened to her," said Tuttle, turning the iron over in his hand.

"She's okay. She had problem with a thief," said the Colonel, the chilling smile on this face. "He was drunk. He broke into your house. She's not hurt. No problem."

The Colonel extended the mobile phone to Tuttle, who hesitated; the Colonel's two goons struggled to their feet. This was the kind of trouble he had preached for years to avoid. Never cause a Thai to lose face; never show anger, and never, never raise a fist. Because they will always win, and they will kill you. Tuttle had gone over the top of what was sensible and prudent, and he knew from the expressions on their faces they wanted to kill him. The driver, a smear of blood over his mouth, reached for his gun, but the Colonel waved him off with a nod.

The Colonel, his golf shoes clicking on the concrete, turned back to Tuttle. "I underestimated your skill with a golf club, Khun Tuttle." He paused and swallowed hard. "You have assaulted two Thai police officers. That is very serious. Remember, finesse wins the game."

Tuttle had not only lost his temper. Through his use of force, he allowed the Colonel a victory; a moral hole-in-one with a golf club owned by the Colonel. Tuttle was angry with himself. He watched the driver and Lek return to the BMW, slamming the car doors. The car reversed out of the parking lot at high speed, raising a cloud of dust. Tuttle watched the BMW disappear. He should have foreseen the set-up, he thought. Watching the Colonel, Tuttle slowly brought the phone to his ear.

Asanee sobbed, choking on her words. "Daddy, he had a knife. They shot him. Daddy, I am scared. He's dead in downstairs." Her voice sounded tiny, remote.

"Where are you now?"

"Home," she whispered.

"I'm on the way. Stay calm, I'm on Soi 18 with Colonel Chao. Everything is okay, sweetheart. It's over. We'll be okay. Promise," said Tuttle, passing the phone back to the Colonel. A sense of relief flooded over him. He looked out over the driving range. The sun split through the advertisement signs, slanting the light at right angles across the vast expanse of grass and the thousands of golf balls like shiny white unexploded bombs scattered across a vast expanse of lawn.

"You knew the man your men killed at my house?" It was the kind of question Tuttle felt he already knew the answer to. He wanted to make the Colonel blow just one shot.

"He was a petty criminal," said the Colonel. "A thug. Someone no one will miss." He hit a perfect nine iron shot.

"Executed." Tuttle pronounced each syllable slowly as the photo of the famous cold-blooded Saigon street execution flashed through his mind. The Saigon police chief, a routine expression of this-is-just-another-job, squeezing a round off into the head of a civilian in the street. The Vietnamese war photo hung above the piano at the Foreign Correspondents' Club. This image of death reminded every journalist that the war had never been about ideology, but over who selected the people who held the gun and pulled the trigger. This image from the street execution played back in Tuttle's mind as he visualized one of the colonel's men killing the guy who had been sent in to terrorize his daughter. That was how power was exercised in Southeast Asia. The executioners knew no fear. Why should they? Who could protect him or Asanee? The American government? That was a joke, thought Tuttle. The

Saigon police chief had gone on to run a string of liquor stores in Southern California.

"My guess is your men executed him," said Tuttle.

"He was shot resisting arrest. My men execute orders, not people."

Tuttle nodded, looking at the Colonel for a long ten count. "Resisting is dangerous," said Tuttle.

"Sometimes fatal."

Tuttle, his mind shifting to Asanee, dropped the bent iron on the concrete walkway. "Let me know the name of the bank and the number of the account," he said. The colonel's caddie caught the dropped iron on the first bounce.

The colonel was right about one thing, thought Tuttle. He had found something in the Vietnam war. Peace or war, Indochina was constructed on influence, money, family; a canvas of private spheres of power, an elite imprinted into the fabric of history. Men like the Colonel were both immune and dispensable. They served a larger purpose and as long as they created benefits, they remained immune; as soon as they caused detriment, they were dispensable. The Colonel, at the moment, and that was the only frame of time that counted, lived beyond the law. Such men were capable of crossing any boundary, sanctioning any crime, could confiscate any property and then withdraw deep into the secret underground bunker of their class and culture.

SARAH had once written in her dairy about Tuttle's smile on her wedding day. If only she had lived to witness the Colonel smiling against the backdrop of the driving range, thought Tuttle. If only she could have seen the fluid way he swung a golf club, sending a golf ball skyward, his spiked shoes dancing on the smooth, gray concrete surface. If only she had known in Los Angeles, before she decided to die, the way money circulated in Indochina; not in the direction of idealism—or not for long, because the world was a far more deadly place for the living than the dead. Tuttle thought back to the day of her wedding to Lawrence. He saw himself in the back of the church. He saw in that image something he had missed before; the reflection of his own smile on the Colonel's face; that kind of knowing smile worn like a garment, and cut from the same cloth in every language—a smile announcing its authority and issuing a demand for an unconditional surrender.

"It's up to you," said the Colonel.

Tuttle walked out of the bay. "Yeah, it's up to me," he said. He started to walk away, then, stopped himself. He turned and faced the Colonel. "You know what we found in the war?" asked Tuttle.

"What, Khun Tuttle?"

"Never keep your money in a country when you can hide it in a Swiss bank. Never keep score unless you intend to win. Never call a colonel your golf buddy unless you're prepared to play his game. And never promise a girl on the game or drug addict what you can't deliver," said Tuttle.

"What can't you deliver, Khun Tuttle?"

"That I could save her. That I could protect her against herself." Such promises were fraught with difficulties. He swallowed hard, thinking of Sarah, of Asanee, and of all the faces from HQ he could never remember.

He walked through the gravel parking lot, passed the shed housing the caddies waiting to be chosen. Everywhere on the horizon were construction cranes like artillery batteries targeting an empty sky. He thought about those who were builders and those who made the rules of the game. It was their world, their private country club, and like every other porter on the soi, Tuttle was simply grateful he had made it through the minefields with his daughter and survived another day.

Breinigsville, PA USA
21 December 2009
229629BV00001B/119/P